SHEER FOLLY

Murder in the grotto...

March 1926: Daisy Dalrymple, at work on her book of architectural follies, heads for Appsworth Hall, famous for its fine example of a grotto. Daisy's plans are blown off course, alas, when the grotto explodes, taking with it houseguest Lord Rydal. Faced with an array of suspects, all with good reason to want the abominable, tactless and womanising Lord Rydal dead, it is sheer folly for Daisy even to attempt to find the killer...

SHEER FOLLY

SHEER FOLLY

by

Carola Dunn

Magna Large Print Books
Long Preston, North Yorkshire,
BD23 4ND, England.

British Library Cataloguing in Publication Data.

Dunn, Carola
    Sheer folly.

    A catalogue record of this book is
    available from the British Library

    ISBN   978-0-7505-3302-7

First published in Great Britain in 2009 by Robinson,
an imprint of Constable & Robinson Ltd.

Copyright © 2009 Carola Dunn

Cover illustration by arrangement with
Constable & Robinson Ltd.

The right of Carola Dunn to be identified as the author of this work
has been asserted by her in accordance with the Copyright, Designs
and Patents Act, 1988

Published in Large Print 2010 by arrangement with
Constable & Robinson Ltd.

Magna Large Print is an imprint of Library Magna Books Ltd.

Printed and bound in Great Britain by
T.J. (International) Ltd., Cornwall, PL28 8RW

When lovely woman stoops to folly
And finds too late that men betray,
What charm can soothe her melancholy?
What art can wash her guilt away?

The only art her guilt to cover,
To hide her shame from every eye,
To give repentance to her lover,
And wring his bosom is – to die.

– Oliver Goldsmith,
'When Lovely Woman Stoops to Folly'

CHAPTER 1

'Daisy, do you really need to stay away over the weekend?' Alec asked plaintively, folding the *News Chronicle* and pushing back his chair from the table. 'There's just a chance I may actually get a couple of days off. You've got egg on your chin.'

'No! How careless.' Daisy dabbed with a napkin. 'As far as my work is concerned, I could easily manage the writing part for the book in a couple of days, though I do hope I might get an article out of it as well. Lucy's photographs are the trouble. She has to hope the weather will cooperate, and one can't exactly count on it in March. Three or four days gives her a better chance of getting decent conditions.'

'Surely you don't have to stay to hold her hand!'

'But you see, darling, in this case I rather do.'

'Are we talking about the same Lucy? Lady Gerald?'

'Yes, of course.'

'I don't believe Lucy ever needed her hand held in her life!'

'The trouble is,' Daisy explained with a sigh, 'she doesn't care for the man who presently owns Appsworth Hall and its folly.'

'What's wrong with him? I don't know that I want to let you go and stay with–'

'Darling, you've gone all medieval again. Victorian, at least. This is 1926! You don't *let* me do things, remember? Anyway, there's nothing wrong with the poor man except that he's a manufacturer of bathroom fixtures.'

Alec burst out laughing. 'I can't see how you persuaded her to visit him in the first place! Not that she has any justification for such an attitude. Didn't you tell me her great-grandfather was a manufacturer of umbrella silk?'

'Great-great, I think. I suspect that's why she's so touchy,' said Daisy, the origin of whose family's title was lost in the mists of time.

Lucy, granddaughter of an earl and Daisy's closest friend, had been very difficult when Daisy first started going about with a middle-class policeman, albeit a Detective Chief Inspector from Scotland Yard. In fact she had disapproved quite as strongly as had Daisy's mother, the Dowager Lady Dalrymple. Unlike the viscountess, she had revised her opinion and given a qualified approval when he promised to support Daisy's writing career even after they married. Lucy, too, was a career-woman, continuing her photography studio since marrying the easy-going Lord Gerald Bincombe.

But writing, photography, and even detecting were one thing. Manufacturing bathroom fixtures was another, quite beyond the pale.

'It wasn't easy to get her to agree,' Daisy admitted.

'Haven't you collected enough follies for your book to skip this one?'

'We have towers, temples, cloisters, pillars, and

fake medieval ruins aplenty, even a campanile, but not a single grotto. Appsworth has the best grotto in the country. There are a couple of others, but they've rather been let go to rack and ruin. Mr. Pritchard–'

'Of Pritchard's Plumbing Products?' Alec laughed again. 'The man behind the blue PPP insignia in half the wash-basins and lavatories in the country? Instigator of a million vulgar jokes?'

'Lucy seems to think it makes it worse that it's one of the biggest concerns in the country. Our Mr. Pritchard is semi-retired and Chairman of the Board – or something of the kind – I believe. But if he weren't so successful, he wouldn't be rich enough to have bought Appsworth Hall and done a marvellous job of restoring the grotto. Or so we've heard.'

'All modern plumbing?'

His teasing grin made Daisy's lips twitch, but she said, 'It wouldn't surprise me in the least. There's a stream running through it, and it's chalk and limestone country, the Marlborough Downs, where streams tend to appear and disappear whenever they feel like it.'

'Do you have to go this week?'

'March isn't the best time of year for outdoor photography, but our publisher is baying at our heels. Besides, we're invited for this week, for the long weekend, and having accepted, one can't simply say, "Oh, sorry, it's rather inconvenient, may we come next week?" That's another reason it wouldn't be at all the thing to duck out and come home for the weekend.'

'I could ring up, when I know whether I'm

11

really getting time off, and claim a family emergency.'

'Darling, I'm shocked!' she told him severely. 'A policeman inventing an alibi? Well, not an alibi, exactly, but I call it disgraceful. What is the world coming to? I'll tell you what, though: When I get down there, I'll see if I can cadge an invitation for you to join us.'

'All I wanted,' he said mournfully, 'is a quiet day at home with you and the babies.'

'Oh dear, I can't very well expect the poor man to invite the twins and Nurse Gilpin, too.'

'No, that would be a bit much. How on earth did you manage to wangle an invitation from Pritchard's Plumbing in the first place?'

'It's a long story, involving a cousin of Gerald's in the Ministry of Health, an old school friend, Mr. Pritchard's fondness for titles, and... But you're going to be late, darling. In spite of her reluctance, it's Lucy's doing. I'm not sure I've got it all straight, and you wouldn't believe it anyway.'

Alec came round the table and kissed her. 'I wouldn't believe it from anyone but you, love. You're leaving this afternoon?'

'Yes, Lucy's coming to lunch, then we're driving down.'

'Lucy's driving?' At her nod, he groaned.

'You may need our car.'

'True. Ring up this evening to tell me you got there safely, will you? Leave a message if I'm not home yet.'

'Right-oh, darling.' Daisy stood up and gave him a hug. 'I'll probably see you Sunday evening. We can stretch the weekend till Monday if necessary, but Lucy's not likely to want to, as long as we have decent weather for her shots. Unless you'll come to join us?'

'I'll leave it to you to assess the situation. It's up to you to decide whether I want to meet the Bathroom King, work permitting, and whether he wants to meet me.'

Alec went off to catch criminals, and Daisy went up to the nursery.

Mrs. Gilpin ruled the nursery, but she had long since been induced to concede that Daisy and Alec might visit Miranda and Oliver whenever they chose. They were even allowed to take their own children out for a walk without Nurse tagging along, though the nurserymaid, Bertha, usually acted as her deputy. Nonetheless, Nurse Gilpin was always cock-a-hoop when Daisy went out of town for a few days, as her work sometimes required, leaving the twins in their nanny's sole charge.

This led Daisy to put off informing her of an impending absence till the last minute. Of course she always gave the housekeeper, Mrs. Dobson, plenty of warning. From Mrs. Dobson to the parlourmaid, Elsie, was no distance; from Elsie to Bertha, little further; and whatever Bertha knew, Nurse Gilpin knew.

As Daisy opened the nursery door, five pairs of eyes turned her way. Three small bodies launched themselves towards her. Naturally the dog, Nana, arrived first, her cold wet nose bumping Daisy's knee in greeting. The twins toddled in her wake; Oliver in such a hurry that he sat down unexpectedly and completed the course crawling, still

13

a faster means of locomotion as far as he was concerned. Single-minded, he beat Miranda, who put much of her effort into shouting, 'Ma-ma-ma-ma!' as she came. Daisy, as usual, ended up sitting on the floor so as to accommodate everyone in her arms.

'You'll spoil them, Mummy,' said Mrs. Gilpin disapprovingly.

Bertha bobbed a curtsy and went on ironing nappies. The twins used positive mountains of nappies. How on earth, Daisy wondered, did mothers manage who couldn't afford to pay nannies and nurserymaids and laundrymen? Presumably their babies survived without beautifully pressed, crease-free nappies. Ironing them seemed an unnecessary expenditure of time and energy, but Mrs. Gilpin certainly wouldn't tolerate such a suggestion. Daisy decided to save her energies for the battles that were sure to arise as Oliver and Miranda grew older.

'I'm going to be away for a few days, Mrs. Gilpin,' she said. 'I'll leave a telephone number, of course, in case you need to reach me.'

'Oh, I'm sure that won't be necessary,' said Nurse with a smug smile.

And there – as Hamlet would no doubt have said had he taken any interest in child-care – was the rub. It was nice to know the babies would be very well taken care of while she was out of town, but depressing in a way that they didn't really need her.

'Will you miss me?' she whispered in Miranda's little pink ear, half hidden by her froth of dark curls.

Miranda giggled. Oliver stuck his tongue out and blew a raspberry, an act so screamingly funny that he roared with laughter and then repeated it.

'All right, Master Oliver,' Mrs. Gilpin commanded, 'that's quite enough of that!'

But Daisy couldn't help giggling, too, especially when Miranda tried to copy her brother, with indifferent success.

Perhaps it was just as well that Nurse Gilpin ruled the nursery, Daisy thought as she stood up half an hour later. Otherwise the children might grow up to be horrid undisciplined brats. Or perhaps, like Daisy herself, they had the best of both worlds: Nurse to make them mind their p's and q's, and Mummy to indulge and laugh with them. All one could do was love them and hope for the best.

'I'll only be gone a few days,' she assured Oliver, and stooped to tickle his tummy one more time. 'I'm going to stay with a plumber,' she said to Miranda, who regarded her solemnly. 'It should be interesting, as long as your godmother controls the bees in her bonnet and isn't rude to the poor man.'

CHAPTER 2

Lucy braked her Lea-Francis two-seater in a
swirl of gravel, having exceeded the speed limit
practically every inch of the drive from town.

'Gates welcomingly closed,' she said sarcastically, glaring at the ornate ironwork two inches
beyond the bonnet. On either side, a stone pillar
topped with a Triton guarded the gate. She leant
on the horn.

'There are deer in the park,' Daisy pointed out
as soon as she could hear herself think. 'Look,
over there. Darling, I do hope you're not going to
spend the next four days finding fault. The sun is
shining, the lambs are gambolling on the hillside'
– she waved at the surrounding chalk hills, their
short-cropped grass scattered with sheep busily
cropping – 'and it's really too kind of Mr. Pritchard to invite complete strangers to stay and to
photograph his grotto.'

Lucy was determined to take a gloomy view.
'He'll probably expect me to let him use the
photos to advertise his beastly bathroom stuff.'

'Keep your hair on till he asks you, which he
may very well not. Here comes the gatekeeper.'

A boy of ten or eleven, wearing grey-flannel
shorts and a school jersey, came out of the neat
stone lodge. 'Sorry, miss,' he called, swinging the
gates open without difficulty. Well-oiled, Daisy
noted. 'I were eating me tea.'

'Miss' rather than 'ma'am' worked its wonders: Lucy gave him a gracious nod and sixpence. To Daisy's relief, she didn't then shower the lad with gravel but proceeded in a stately manner – as stately as a sports car could attain – up the curving avenue of chestnuts. On the trees, brilliant green leaves were just beginning to unfold from the sticky brown buds. They moved slowly enough to see clumps of primroses and violets blooming on the verge. Fallow deer, including antlered males and a few spotted fawns, lifted their heads to watch the intruders.

They rounded a beech copse, and Appsworth Hall rose before them, spread across the hillside. Built of the local limestone, the northwest front took on a rosy cast in the slanting light of the sinking sun. Though large, in size it was more comparable to Daisy's childhood home, Fairacres, than to Lucy's family's vast nineteenth-century mock-Gothic mansion, Haverhill.

With any luck, Daisy hoped, the comparative modesty of Appsworth Hall would avert another outburst from her friend. In that respect, at least, Mr. Pritchard could not compete with the Earl of Haverhill.

Daisy had a chance to admire the house because Lucy was sufficiently struck by the sight to stop the car. In fact, she jumped out to get her tripod and camera from the dicky. In style, Appsworth Hall was similar to neither Haverhill's fantastic elaboration nor Fairacres, which had grown haphazardly over centuries rather than being planned. The Hall was pure neo-Classical, with symmetrical wings on either side of a central block marked by a portico with a pair of Doric columns on each side. The pediment was adorned with a simple laurel wreath.

In the quiet with the motor turned off, Daisy heard the first cuckoo of spring. The first she had heard, anyway.

'Blast,' said Lucy, 'I'll have to walk across the grass to get a good shot. Look at the way those shadows make every feature stand out! The light's perfect but it's going to change in just a moment. Bring the plates, would you, darling? That satchel there.'

'I'm wearing new shoes, and it rained yesterday!'

Intent on finding exactly the right spot, Lucy ignored Daisy's protest. Somehow she managed to look stylish even while tramping heavily laden across the park.

It had been a beautiful day, though it was chilly now, threatening a frost tonight. Fortunately for Daisy's shoes, the chalky soil had dried quickly. The shoes survived unscathed, a matter of some importance as Lucy's equipment had left little space in the dicky for luggage. True, anticipating this situation, they had each sent ahead a suitcase to the nearest station, Ogbourne St. George. However, one could never be certain that the Great Western Railway would regard the matter with quite one's own degree of urgency.

Daisy was wondering whether their host would mind sending for the bags or if they'd have to go and fetch them themselves, when a large open touring car sped round the spinney. With a blare of the horn, it stopped behind the Lea-Francis, abandoned by Lucy in the middle of the drive. It dwarfed the sports car.

'Darling, be an angel and move it for me?' Lucy begged. 'Just a couple more shots.'

'All right, but you can jolly well carry the plates back yourself. They're heavy.'

Daisy waved to let the newcomer know his plea had been noted. He climbed from the Bentley as she approached, and took out a cigarette case that glinted gold in the last of the sun. Fitting a cigarette into an ebony holder, he lit it with a gold pocket lighter.

He looked vaguely familiar. His admirably cut suit of country tweeds could not disguise the bulky figure and heavy shoulders. When he raised his hat to her, she saw that his neck was as thick as his head was wide. He had small eyes set close together on either side of a pedigree nose perfected over centuries by his noble family.

He was unmistakable. She had met him a couple of times, and remembered hearing about him from her brother, Gervaise, who had attended the same public school. His distinctive appearance had led an unkind schoolfellow to nickname him 'Rhino.'

It would have been easier to sympathise had Rhino not been an exceedingly rich earl.

'Hello, Lord Rydal,' she called. 'Sorry to be in your way. Half a tick and I'll move it.'

'Please do so ... er...' His voice had a singularly irritating timbre, rather like a well-bred crow.

Or like a rhinoceros, perhaps, Daisy thought, suppressing a giggle. But she had no idea what sort of sound a rhino was likely to produce.

19

'Mrs. Fletcher,' she prompted him. 'Daisy Fletcher. We met quite a long time ago, I can't recall where or when.'

'Fletcher? I haven't the slightest recollection–'

'You were at school with my brother, Gervaise Dalrymple.'

'Oh, Dalrymple, yes, how do you do.' He didn't offer her a cigarette, not that she wanted one. He continued, complaining, 'Miss Beaufort seemed to think I was the only person who could be spared to fetch your bags from the station, yours and Lady Gerald's.'

Daisy decided not to enquire as to why, with such reluctance, he should have done Julia Beaufort's bidding. 'Did you get them? Splendid. How kind of you. You see, Lucy's – Lady Gerald's – car is too small to carry all our luggage.'

'Just large enough to block the drive.'

'I'll move it!'

'Hold on, darling!' Lucy had approached unseen and unheard across the grass, carrying her camera and bag of plates. 'Let me get my stuff in first. Hello, Rhino.'

'Good afternoon, Lady Gerald.'

'What on earth are you doing here?'

'Running other people's errands, it seems. I just picked up your luggage at Ogbourne St. George.'

'How kind. While you're at it, I left my tripod back there. Would you mind frightfully...?'

'I suppose not,' he said grumpily, 'as I can't get past till you go on.' He loped off across the grass, the cigarette holder gripped between his teeth.

'The perfect gentleman,' said Lucy sarcastically.

'I'd forgotten.'

'Forgotten what?'

'Gervaise said it wasn't just his looks and money that earned him the nickname. The rhinoceros is also noted for its thick skin.'

Lucy laughed. 'He has that all right. But we ought to make allowances for his being disappointed in love.'

'What do you mean?'

'Didn't you know? He's crazy for Julia.'

'Oh, so that's why he so demeaned himself as to fetch our bags! She persuaded him to.'

'Probably just trying to get rid of him for a while. Of course Lady Beaufort wants Julia to marry him, but Julia doesn't want anything to do with him. One can't really blame her, however rich and noble he may be. I expect he drove them down here – they haven't a car – and talked the plumber into letting him stay on.'

'I do think you might have warned me, darling. One needs some mental preparation before being plunged into the throes of someone else's unrequited love affair. And you *must* stop calling Pritchard "the plumber." You'll slip up and call him that to his face.'

'No fear. However ghastly he is, now I'm here I'm not leaving till I've got some decent shots of the grotto. I just hope it's all it's cracked up to be.'

'You're not telling me Lady Beaufort has the slightest interest in the grotto. If she's so determined to catch a rich earl for Julia, what do you suppose has brought them to Appsworth Hall?'

'That's easy: a rich plumber's rich nephew.'

21

'The plot thickens,' Daisy remarked with a sigh. 'Intended to make Lord Rydal jealous?'

'Unnecessary. He's absolutely potty–'

'Hush! Here he comes.'

Without missing a beat, Lucy continued in her penetrating soprano: '–about cars. Aren't you, Rhino?'

'Aren't I what?' He bunged the tripod into the Lea-Francis's dicky on top of the camera and satchel, with a carelessness that made Lucy wince.

'Mad about cars,' she said through gritted teeth. 'Daisy was admiring your Bentley.'

'Cars?' he said incredulously, lighting another cigarette. 'What is there to be mad about? As long as it's comfortable and clean and runs properly. My man sees to all that. I'd have sent him to fetch your stuff, but he had to get a grease spot off the sleeve of my dinner jacket. Should have been done last night, of course, but he claims he couldn't see it till he looked in daylight. Lazy as a lapdog. But aren't they all? It's impossible to get decent servants these days.'

Daisy had been working for a couple of years, in a desultory manner, on an article about various aspects of what middle-class matrons called 'the Servant Problem.' She was aware of the complexities of the issue and was quite ready to discuss them, but Lucy muttered in her ear, 'Don't waste your breath.'

'Well, what are we waiting for? Are you going to move your car out of my way or not?'

Lucy's withering look, a masterpiece of its kind, had absolutely no effect upon the thick-skinned

Earl of Rydal. Her stony silence as she got into the Lea-Francis and pressed the self-starter was equally lost on him, Daisy was sure, although she didn't deign to look back. However, their glacial pace as they proceeded up the middle of the avenue irritated him to the point of honking his horn again.

'Rather childish, don't you think?' said Daisy. 'You, I mean. It doesn't need saying where he's concerned.'

'I'm admiring the view. It's a splendid building, isn't it?' Lucy slowed still more, and the Lea-Francis stalled.

She got out, folded up one side of the bonnet and peered inside.

Rydal stormed out of his Bentley. 'What the deuce is the matter?'

'I'm not sure. How lucky you're on the spot. Perhaps it would start if you crank it for us.'

'Why don't you crank it yourself?'

Lucy sighed. 'Gallantry is dead. Never mind, we'll just sit here until your man has cleaned that grease spot, then no doubt he'll be able to repair whatever's wrong, since he takes care of yours.'

'Good lord, he doesn't do the mechanical stuff himself. He takes it to a garage. In town.'

Lucy turned a glittering smile on him. 'What a pity. I'll tell you what, why don't you push us up to the house?'

His mouth dropped open. 'Push you? *Me?*'

'It's a small car. I don't expect it will be too heavy for a big, strong chap like you. Daisy, you don't mind walking, do you, to lighten the load, while I steer?'

23

'Not at all. But I have a better idea. Why don't I drive the Bentley, then Lord Rydal won't have to come back for it after pushing you up the hill.'

'What a good idea,' Lucy said approvingly. 'You drive almost as well as I do. You probably won't do it too much harm.'

'I'll do my best, and he did say he didn't much care about it. If you'd just show me which pedal is the brake, Lord Rydal, then–'

'No! No, no, no! I won't have you driving my car. I didn't say I don't care about it. I just said I'm not crazy about cars. In general. But I won't let you drive my Bentley. I'll tell you what, I'll drive it and push yours bumper to bumper, Lady Gerald.'

'Not on your life! You'd probably step on the accelerator too hard and run right over me. I'll give it another go.'

The Lea-Francis started at the first try.

'Miraculous,' Daisy commented, as they rolled onwards. 'How did you stall it?'

'Simple. I just shifted up to top gear and took my foot off the clutch. Don't tell me you didn't stall a few times while you were learning to drive.'

'Of course, but I'm not sure I ever really worked out what I did wrong, just learnt to do it right. Well, honours even, I should say, but definitely childish.'

'At least I pierced that insufferable shell of complacency, however briefly. Besides, you did your bit. That was a neat touch, asking him which was the brake.'

'Yes, that's all very well, but I do hope you're not going to spend our time here sniping at him.'

'Hardly, darling. We have work to do. It was a perfect demonstration, though, of why we mustn't let Julia weaken. Lady Beaufort's the sort who still believes parents can tell their daughters whom to marry.' Lucy stopped the car in front of the portico. 'Here we are.'

They got out. As the Bentley swept past them and disappeared round the side of the house, Lucy retrieved the tripod from the dickey and handed it to Daisy. She shouldered her precious camera herself and heaved out the satchel of plates.

'Do you suppose the plumber will provide someone to garage the car for me, and bring in the rest of our stuff?' she added plaintively.

'If not, I'll do it,' said Daisy resignedly. She had been worried about her friend's attitude to Mr. Pritchard. Apparently she was going to have to protect Lord Rydal and Lady Beaufort from Lucy's scheming, too. She rather hoped Alec would be able to come down for the weekend to lend a hand.

CHAPTER 3

A very proper butler admitted Daisy and Lucy to the hall.

'Mr. Pritchard's chauffeur will convey your ladyship's motor to the garage, my lady,' he assured Lucy.

The grand staircase, black-and-white chequered

marble floor, and pillared niches in the walls were just what one would expect to find behind the classical façade. However, Mr. Pritchard was clearly not bound by tradition. Illuminated by electric wall-sconces, the cold stone of the floor was half hidden by a broadloom Axminster in green and gold chequers, and, instead of marble gods and goddesses, the niches held a selection of ewers. These ranged from white china decorated with forget-me-nots and rosebuds to elaborate gilt-rimmed porcelain with scenes from classical mythology. Gods and goddesses in fact, Daisy thought, amused – as well as reminders of the days before modern plumbing.

'At least, no chamber-pots!' Lucy hissed in her ear. A modern career-woman she might be, but like Queen Victoria, she was not amused. She instructed the butler in the proper handling of her camera equipment.

A short, spare, grey-haired man in a navy pin-striped suit came bustling through a door on the right side of the hall. He greeted them with a cheerful smile.

'You must be Lady Gerald and Mrs. Fletcher.' He spoke the King's English with a slight Welsh intonation. 'I'm Brin Pritchard. Very pleased to meet you, I'm sure. And I'm delighted my grotto's going to be in your book.'

Lucy muttered, 'How do you do?' without offering her hand.

'We're looking forward to seeing it, Mr. Pritchard,' Daisy assured him, shaking his hand. 'It's very kind of you to invite us.'

'Not at all, not at all. I had a marvellous time

26

restoring it to its old condition, or maybe even just a bit better, and I like to show it off. I wish you'd been able to arrive in time to see it in daylight this afternoon. Barker,' he said to the butler, 'bring a fresh pot of tea. Or perhaps you young ladies would prefer a cocktail at this hour?'

Regarding her host with a somewhat more kindly eye, Lucy declared that a cocktail would exactly fill the bill, while Daisy opted for tea.

'I expect you'd like to powder your noses before you join us,' Pritchard suggested, adding with an air of gallantry, 'not that I mean to suggest your noses need powdering. The cloakroom's just through there, first door on the left.'

As they followed his directions, Lucy said, 'Thank heaven he didn't offer to demonstrate the plumbing!'

'I wish you'd stop expecting him to drop a brick. I think he's rather a nice little man.'

When they returned to the hall, the butler, Barker, was waiting to usher them into the drawing room. It was a large room, furnished with an eye to comfort and cheerfulness. The only sign of plumbing was several radiators, augmenting with their welcome warmth the fire crackling in the Adam fireplace. The delicate plasterwork of the mantel was complemented by the ceiling's wreathes, rosettes, and ribbons. If Mr. Pritchard had been tempted to embellish these with depictions of urns, fountains, or other evidence of his trade, he had resisted the temptation. The walls hinted of watery influences, however, being papered in willow-green with a slight sheen, narrowly striped in pale blue.

Pin-striped, in fact, Daisy thought, as their equally pin-striped host bounced up from a easy-chair and came towards them. He must be in his mid- or late-fifties, she thought, but he was as spry as a man half his age, and his hair, though grey verging on white, was still thick.

'Come in, come in do, come to the fire and get warm. Let's see, now, you know Lady Beaufort, don't you, and Miss Beaufort? A reunion of old friends. What could be better?'

Sir Frederick Beaufort's widow, a large stately woman in forest green, seated at the fireside, gave a small stately bow, but her smile was friendly. 'Lady Gerald, Mrs. Fletcher, how pleasant to see you again. Julia has been looking forward to your arrival.'

'I have indeed,' Julia said warmly. 'Hello, Lucy. Daisy, it's ages since I saw you.'

'Years,' said Daisy. Seven years, since her father's funeral in 1919. What with the death toll of the War and the influenza pandemic, which had killed Lord Dalrymple, his funeral had not been well attended, but Julia had been there.

They had not been particularly close friends at school, in spite of both being fonder of books than sports. Julia had been shy, at that age a crippling affliction, one that Daisy never suffered from. Julia had been cursed with spots, while Daisy's Nemesis was freckles, much easier to live with. And though Daisy had never attained slimness, and now likely never would, Julia in her teen years had been positively pudgy.

But Julia, in her late twenties, had emerged from her chrysalis and was absolutely stunning.

28

Her hair could have been described as spun gold without too much of the usual gross exaggeration. Worn in a long bob, it framed a spotless peaches-and-cream complexion with no need of powder or rouge. Without being rail-thin, she was slender enough to look marvellous in a silk tea-dress in the still-current straight up-and-down fashion, with hip-level waist, which Daisy had hoped would die a natural death long since.

Daisy looked at her with admiration and envy. The envy faded as she reminded herself that despite her own unmodish figure and merely light brown hair, worn shingled, she had Alec, whereas Julia apparently faced a choice between a rhinoceros and a plumber's nephew.

Not that Daisy had anything against plumbers.

Mr. Plumber ... Mr. Pritchard, rather, next introduced a short, tubby woman, sixtyish, her coils of white hair sternly confined in a net, her plumpness sternly confined in a black frock embroidered with jet beads. 'My sister-in-law, my late wife's sister, Mrs. Howell, who keeps house for me.'

'Acts as your hostess, Brin!' Mrs. Howell hissed crossly. Any hint of Welsh in her voice had been carefully obliterated. 'You'll be making the ladies think I'm the housekeeper. I've been acting as Brin's hostess since my poor sister went to her reward, Lady Gerald. How do you do? My husband was Brin's partner, you see.'

'Partner?' Lucy enquired languidly, as though she had never heard the word before, though Daisy was pretty certain Gerald was a partner in a City firm, something to do with stocks and shares, as well as sitting on numerous boards.

'Business partner,' Mrs. Howell elucidated.

'Sleeping partner,' Pritchard corrected her mischievously.

'Owen's your Managing Director!' she snapped.

'My dear Winifred, you were talking about Daffyd.'

Short of an actual yawn, Lucy could hardly have shown her lack of interest more clearly.

To compensate, Daisy said, 'I've always wondered what a sleeping partner is exactly. Presumably not one who comes into the office, puts his feet up on the desk, and slumbers away the day?'

Pritchard laughed. 'Indeed, he doesn't usually turn up at the office at all, Mrs. Fletcher. It's what we call someone who invests in a private business without taking part in the running of it. Daffyd Howell was—'

'Really, Brin, I'm sure the ladies don't want to hear about the business.'

'Daisy's a writer,' said Lucy. 'Writers are interested in the most unexpected subjects.'

'Later, perhaps,' Daisy suggested. Not that she was particularly interested in the financial arrangements of Pritchard's Plumbing Products, but she didn't like the way Mrs. Howell had snubbed her brother-in-law.

'Just say the word.' He gave her a cheerful wink. 'Your tea will be here any minute, Mrs. Fletcher. Now, what can I get for you, Lady Gerald?'

'Gin and It, please.' Lucy followed him over to a huge oak Welsh dresser, beautifully carved. It had been converted into a drinks cabinet. The shelves were crowded with bottles, decanters, and glasses. One side of the top of the base section lifted to reveal a small sink – with running water, of course, given their host's business – and the cupboard below concealed an ice chest.

It was very neatly done, without spoiling a splendid piece of furniture. Daisy considered it vastly preferable to the current fad for glass and chromed stainless steel bars.

'Anyone else for a cocktail?' Pritchard invited, pouring Lucy's drink.

'I wouldn't mind a pink gin,' said Julia, going to join them.

Mrs. Howell muttered something disapproving about it being much too early for drinks.

Lady Beaufort said soothingly, 'Young people today are very different from the days of our youth, aren't they?'

Though Daisy thought it was very kind of Lady Beaufort, who surely could have given the other a good decade, Mrs. Howell didn't appear to be mollified. 'Not so young, neither,' she snapped.

'Old enough to decide for ourselves what we want to drink,' Daisy commented, 'though the three of us are too young to vote for a couple of years yet.'

'Why women want to vote I simply can't see,' Mrs. Howell declared. 'One thing I'll say for Brin, he's stuck by Mr. Lloyd George through thick and thin. So what need have I for a vote?'

Daisy refrained from pointing out the fallacy in this argument. 'Ah, here comes my tea,' she said with relief.

31

Lord Rydal came in just behind the butler. He made a beeline for the drinks – or was it for Julia?

'I fetched your friends' bags from the station, Miss Beaufort,' he told her irritably, jabbing with his cigarette holder towards Lucy. 'But I still don't see why one of the servants couldn't have gone. Slackers!' he said to Mr. Pritchard. 'You should give them all notice.'

'But...' Pritchard caught Julia's alarmed eye and continued with a look of enlightenment, 'but the only one who can drive is my chauffeur, and it's his afternoon off, I'm afraid. Sorry, Lady Gerald, I ought to 've changed his day.'

'That's all right,' Lucy said dryly. 'I'm sure Rhino was delighted to make himself useful.'

Rydal snorted.

Daisy didn't hear any more. Mrs. Howell, having dismissed the butler with a brusque 'That will be all, Barker,' asked her if she took milk and sugar in her tea. 'The scones are all gone. I hope you didn't want any, because they're busy with dinner in the kitchen.'

'They're better hot from the oven anyway,' Lady Beaufort pointed out.

'There's plenty of Welsh-cakes,' Mrs. Howell went on. 'Brin insists on Welsh-cakes. I myself consider sponge cake far superior.'

Daisy politely disclaimed any interest in scones. She accepted a Welsh-cake.

Without any reason that Daisy was aware of, Mrs. Howell seemed to have taken against her, not even having greeted her properly. Her curiosity was piqued. It didn't make sense. For one thing, if the woman disapproved of cocktails at half past five, she should have approved of Daisy's choice of tea. She could at least have apologised for the dearth of scones, or better, not mentioned it at all rather than aggressively announcing the lack thereof.

Lady Beaufort cast a mildly malicious glance at Mrs. Howell and enquired, 'Well, Daisy, how is Lady Dalrymple? The Dowager Viscountess, I should say. She seemed very well when we met her in town at Christmas.'

'Oh yes, Mother's flourishing, thank you.' Even though the lady in question bitterly resented living at the Dower House and still refused to admit that the present Lord and Lady Dalrymple had any right to Fairacres – but Daisy's mother wouldn't have been happy with nothing to complain about. 'Did you see my sister, Violet, and Lord John? They didn't bring the children up on their last visit, alas. I don't see enough of my nephews and niece.'

'Lady John was there, but her husband had already gone back to Kent. I understand you have little ones of your own to keep you busy.'

'Twins, a girl and boy. They're just over a year. And my stepdaughter, of course. Belinda is nearly thirteen already and away at school.'

'I wish Julia would hurry up and give me grandchildren.'

During this conversation, the most extraordinary change had come over Mrs. Howell. Scarlet in the face and pop-eyed with indignation, she had jumped up and rung the bell (an electric button rather than a tasselled rope, as befitted Pritchard's discreet modernisation).

When the butler came in, she berated him.

'Barker, why didn't you bring scones for Mrs. Fletcher?'

Surprised, Daisy was about to assure her she was perfectly happy without, when Lady Beaufort gave her a slight shake of the head. While the butler apologised with proper impassiveness and went off to repair the deficiency, Daisy finished off her Welsh-cake.

The reason for Mrs. Howell's change of heart was all too obvious. Until Lady Beaufort enquired after the Dowager Viscountess, their hostess hadn't realised that Daisy was a sprig of the nobility. The daughter of a viscount must not be denied scones just because the kitchen staff were busy preparing dinner.

On the whole, Daisy preferred Mrs. Howell's discourtesy to her sycophancy. However, she felt obliged to eat a buttered scone, though she really didn't want it after the delicious but rich and sugary cake.

Bolstered by Lucy's admonitory gaze – Lucy was sure she could slim if she tried – Daisy adamantly refused a second scone. She returned the admonitory gaze, however, when it looked as if Lucy was about to accept a second cocktail. It really was a bit early for drinks.

'Hadn't we better go up to our rooms, Lucy?' Daisy suggested. 'You wanted to get your frock ironed before changing for dinner, didn't you?'

Mrs. Howell looked horrified. She prised herself from her chair, saying, 'Oh dear, Mrs. Fletcher, I'm afraid your room may not be ready. I must go and have a word with the housekeeper.'

'Why don't I take you both up to Lucy's room?' Julia gracefully extracted her arm from Rydal's grasp. 'It's next to mine. Willett can iron Lucy's frock for her, can't she, Mother? They came in Lucy's sports car and didn't have room for her maid.'

'Of course,' said Lady Beaufort with a gracious nod.

Mrs. Howell scuttled out ahead of the three young ladies. She was disappearing into the nether regions as Julia led the others into the hall and up the grand staircase.

'What was all that about, Daisy?' Lucy demanded as they ascended. 'When that woman said your room wasn't ready, you looked as if you were about to burst, trying not to laugh. It's disgraceful. They've known we were coming for ages!'

Daisy let a giggle escape. 'It was so funny! Mrs. Howell apparently hadn't realised my august antecedents, until Lady Beaufort asked after Mother. She's probably put me up in the garrets with the servants. It suddenly dawned on her, when I said we'd go up, that it wouldn't do.'

Julia smiled, but Lucy was inclined to take umbrage on Daisy's behalf.

'Calm down, darling. The garret room is pure fantasy.' Daisy wished she'd kept it to herself. 'Besides, if you want to stay long enough to photograph the grotto, you can't go accusing Mrs. Howell of insulting me. She can't help being a snob.'

'She is one, though,' said Julia, turning left on the landing. 'You wouldn't believe the treatment

35

she puts up with from Rhino, without a murmur. He acts as if she's the housekeeper she's so anxious not to be taken for.'

Daisy slipped her arm through Julia's. 'I hope you're going to tell us all about Rhino and everything. I'm dying to hear what's up.'

'Nothing's "up,"' Julia said grimly, as she opened a door off the passage, 'and won't be if I can help it. Here's Lucy's room. I'll just pop into mine and ring for Willett. Back in half a tick, then we can catch up on each other's news.'

Lucy went ahead into her bedroom. 'The Beauforts know you married a policeman,' she said. '*I* didn't tell them, but Lady Beaufort kept up with the English papers while they were living in France.'

'Darling, half the world knows I married a policeman.'

'What they *don't* know is that you keep getting mixed up in his cases.'

'You're the only person who knows about more than one or two of those. Except Scotland Yard, of course, and they do their best to hush it up.'

'Thank heaven!'

'Don't you think it's really very unfair that I never get any credit for all the help I give them?'

'No! You're not going to tell Julia, are you?'

'Why not? I'm sure she's not the gossipy kind.'

'Daisy!'

'Just teasing, darling.' With a mournful sigh, Daisy continued, 'I'm quite used to hiding my light under a bushel. I don't suppose anyone at Appsworth Hall will ever have a chance to find out what a brilliant sleuth I am.'

CHAPTER 4

Lucy's bedroom was a typical Edwardian country-house guest room. Daisy guessed the Pritchards must have taken over the furnishings along with the house from the previous owners. Things had been refurbished, but fundamentally everything was much as the unfortunate Appsworths had left it, with none of Pritchard's – or the late Mrs. Pritchard's – individuality. Rather, Mr. Pritchard's stamp was purely practical, a modern radiator under the window and hot and cold running water in the wash-basin. Lucy could hardly object to these evidences of their host's trade, adding as they would to her comfort.

Spotting her camera case on the dressing-table, Lucy visibly relaxed. She went over to check the contents thoroughly before she conceded, 'It seems to be all right.'

'I'd be very surprised if it weren't.'

'Surprised?' Lucy prowled to the wardrobe and found her frocks hanging neatly. She took out the one she wanted ironed for this evening and laid it on the bed. Daisy wondered whether her own clothes were being hurriedly repacked, or whether they hadn't been unpacked for her in the first place. 'Why surprised?' Lucy asked.

'Because Mr. Pritchard must be a pretty efficient manufacturer to make enough money to buy this place, and efficient people usually won't stand for inefficient servants. Come and sit down, do. You were talking to him. Prejudice aside, what's he like?'

'Not too bad. No kowtowing, at least.'

'Mrs. Howell seems to be the kowtower of the family. You should have seen her attitude change when she heard that Mother's a viscountess.'

'Mrs. Howell?' Julia came in. 'The poor woman's in quite a quandary.'

Daisy was intrigued. 'A quandary?'

'How many courses to serve her august company for dinner,' Lucy guessed languidly.

'Rhino put her straight on that question the first night we were here, when the soup was followed directly by a leg of lamb. "What, no fish?"' Julia produced a very creditable imitation of Lord Rydal's caw. 'Mr. Pritchard said he didn't like fish, and didn't like the smell of fish. Rhino insisted that liking had nothing to do with it, a proper dinner must have a fish course.'

'What did Mr. Pritchard say to that?' Daisy wondered.

'I was hoping he'd tell Rhino to pack his bags, but his manners are much better than Rhino's. He let the subject drop. Mother murmured something soothing about the odour of fish tending to penetrate and linger. And I said the lamb smelt simply delicious, which it did, and as it was Welsh lamb, Mr. Pritchard was delighted. He's rather a dear. If only Mother...' Julia sighed.

'Don't tell me you'd rather marry the plumber than the Earl of Rydal!' Lucy exclaimed. 'Apart from anything else, he must be sixty if he's a day.'

38

'Fifty-five,' Daisy amended.

'Good heavens, there's no question of my marrying Brin Pritchard. Mother's worried, not demented.'

'Why don't you start at the beginning,' Daisy said.

'The beginning? I suppose it all goes back to the War, really.'

Lucy groaned.

'Careful, darling,' Daisy warned her. 'You'll turn into another rhinoceros.'

'Don't worry,' Julia said with a smile, 'I shan't rewrite *À la recherche du temps perdu*.'

Lucy looked more puzzled than reassured. Neither of the others bothered to explain.

'Your father was a general, wasn't he?' Daisy asked.

'Yes, but the widow's pension of even a general doesn't go far these days. Mother decided she'd rather be poor in France than in England.'

'Hence the Christmas cards from Dinard, these past few years,' said Lucy.

'Yes. We moved there in '21. I didn't mind at all. I was able to get English books, and then my French improved enough so that I could read it just as easily.'

'Julia, don't tell me you read the whole of *À la recherche du temps perdu* in French?' Daisy asked, awed. 'I've never got through it even in English.'

'I had plenty of time. There wasn't much else to do. That's really why Mother hated it. What got her down was not so much having only one servant and only three courses at dinner, usually fish because it was cheap–'

39

Daisy and Lucy looked at each other and laughed.

'What's so funny?' Julia asked. Daisy couldn't blame her for looking a trifle resentful.

'Sorry!' she gasped. 'It's just that when Lucy and I shared digs, we didn't have a live-in servant at all, just a daily, and we practically lived on eggs and mousetrap cheese and sardines. To this day I simply can't face sardines. Of course, it's different for someone like Lady Beaufort.'

'But, as I was saying, pinching and scraping wasn't the trouble. It was not having enough to do. Army wives are used to being busy. Writing letters and playing an occasional game of cards with the few other English residents just wasn't enough. She had too much time to worry about me.'

'I suppose an army pension doesn't go on forever,' said Daisy. Lucy's attention was elsewhere by now. The Beauforts' maid had come in and had to be advised about ironing the evening frock, a dazzler in crimson charmeuse with a fringed, scalloped hem designed to play hide-and-seek with the knees.

'It's meant for the widow, not grown-up children,' Julia explained, confusing Daisy until she realised that 'it' was the pension, not the frock. 'Mother used to have nightmares – I told you she's not much of a reader; well, all the books she did pick up seemed to feature impoverished young ladies working in hat-shops and starving in garrets.'

'Why hat-shops, I wonder?'

'I can't swear some of them weren't dress-shops. I don't know where she found them! I told her to stop worrying because if the blasted things were so popular, I could probably write them as well as anyone and make my fortune.'

'So have you written one?'

'As a matter of fact, I'm about halfway through. But it isn't exactly– I found I simply can't manage the right tone. It's more like *Northanger Abbey* in relation to *Udolpho* or *The Castle of Otranto*.'

'What fun! I can't wait to read it.'

'I was hoping you might take a look and tell me if it's worth the effort of going on with it. Not right now. I left it in town.'

Lucy rejoined them. 'You've been living the high life in town for a couple of months now,' she commented, her tone questioning.

'Mother came into an unexpected inheritance and decided to blow it all to give me a last chance to find a husband. So we came to London, hired a lady's maid, refreshed our wardrobes, and looked up old friends. The trouble is, the few men I've met whom I could bear to marry have either not been interested in a penniless bride past her first youth or failed to meet my mother's criteria.'

'One of which, I assume,' Lucy drawled, 'is money.'

'Well, of course,' said Daisy. 'Lady Beaufort wouldn't want you to have to live on sardines for the rest of your life. And you wouldn't want to, either, unless you were absolutely nutty about him. But surely she can't want you to marry someone just because he can keep you in seven-course dinners for the rest of your life.'

'Hence the unlovely Rhino,' said Lucy, 'but this doesn't explain the intrusion of plumbers into your high life, nor Mrs. Howell's quandary.'

Julia laughed. 'We met her son, Mr. Howell, at a perfectly respectable dinner party in Richmond. Apparently Pritchard's Plumbing is trying to get some huge government contract or other. Mr. Howell, as Managing Director, went up to talk to Sir Desmond Wandersley, the man in charge of plumbing at the Ministry of Health – not bathtubs for bureaucrats, it's something to do with slum clearance, I gather. Sir Desmond invited him to dine, much to Lady Ottaline's fury.'

'Lady Ottaline Wandersley?' Lucy asked. 'Yes, she wouldn't be happy to find a plumber at her table.'

'Especially as it was a last-minute invitation and ruined her numbers. What's more, he's a quiet chap and didn't pay for his dinner with sparkling conversation.'

'One could almost feel sorry for her.'

'Who's Lady Ottaline Wandersley?' Daisy enquired.

'Darling, you are so out of the swim! She was a Barrington, the Marquis of Edgehill's daughter.' Trust Lucy to know the pedigree of any member of the aristocracy. 'She was rather a vamp in her day, they say. The trouble is, she's rather desperately trying to go on vamping.'

'When was her day?'

'Before the War. A siren, they'd have called her, I expect, or a *femme fatale*. She must be in her forties, don't you think, Julia?'

'Early forties, perhaps.'

42

'"She may very well pass for forty-three, in the dusk, with a light behind her"?' Daisy quoted.

'Oh no, she can't be more than forty-five, and she's kept her looks and figure.'

'With a lot of help,' Lucy said cattily. 'Though I must admit she positively bristles with nervous energy. She can still dance all night. But the Wandersleys are beside the point. I suppose the junior plumber fell instantly in love with you, Julia, and begged you on bended knee to visit his unancestral home, but why on earth did Lady Beaufort accept the invitation? She can't possibly want you to marry a plumber.'

Julia sighed. 'He's well-off. And presumably will be richer when Mr. Pritchard dies, as there are no young Pritchards. But I don't think Mother really regards him as a desirable son-in-law. She expects the contrast with the noble Lord Rydal to illuminate hidden virtues in the latter.'

'And has it?' Daisy asked.

'Good heavens, no! If anything, Mr. Howell has better manners, but like Lady Ottaline, he's over forty. And I'm not half as convinced as Mother is that he's interested in marriage. If you ask me, the firm is his only love. His father made plenty from his investment in the business without dirtying his hands, but our Owen chose to get involved.'

'So if he's not mad about you, darling, how is it you're here?'

'The invitation didn't drop into our laps; Mother had to prise it out of him. In any case, I don't intend to marry either of them, even if it means living on sardines for the rest of my life.'

'Well, that settles that, but I'd stick with the mousetrap cheese, if I were you.'

'Which leaves the question of Mrs. Howell's quandary,' Lucy pointed out.

'She can't make up her mind– Oh, here's Willett with your dress, Lucy.'

'I hope it's satisfactory, madam.' The middle-aged maid held up the frock by its exiguous straps for inspection.

Lucy approved the result and tipped her.

'Thank you, madam. Miss Beaufort, her ladyship said to remind you it's time you were changing for dinner.'

'All right, Willett, I'll be along in a minute. Daisy, we'd better go and find out where they've put you.'

'I can show madam, miss. It's just along the passage.'

Julia went with them. 'Do you need a frock ironed?' she asked Daisy.

'Probably, but I haven't anything half as elaborate as Lucy's. A chambermaid should be able to cope.'

'Certainly, madam. They keep a very good class of servants here, no matter what some people may say. Here you are, madam, this is yours. There's a bathroom next door, with a connecting door, and another down the passage a bit on the other side. Mr. Pritchard's put modern gas geysers in every bathroom, so there's always plenty of hot water, and no fear of them blowing up like the old kind, and that's a blessing I can tell you. I'll tell her ladyship you'll be along in a minute, miss,' the maid said to Julia and as she bustled off.

'No matter what "some people" say?' Daisy asked as Julia followed her into the room.

'Rhino.'

'Of course. He told me all servants are lazy good-for-nothings within three minutes of our meeting this afternoon. Whereas you have yet to reveal whatever is bothering Mrs. Howell.'

'She's afraid that if Owen marries she'll lose her position as chatelaine of Appsworth Hall to her daughter-in-law. On the other hand, she'd love to be able to talk about her son's mother-in-law, *Lady* Beaufort. But against that, she strongly disapproves of Mother, as a widow, not wearing black. She simply can't decide whether to encourage Owen's suit or scotch it. Such is my impression, at least. Naturally she hasn't confided in me.'

'Wouldn't it be simplest just to tell her – or him – that you're not interested?'

'Certainly, if he were in hot pursuit!'

'But as he hasn't actually displayed any serious interest... Hmm, yes, I see the difficulty. One can only hope she'll decide lording it over Appsworth Hall is more important to her than your mother's title.'

'Isn't it lucky Mother's merely the widow of a knight, not the wife of a marquis?'

'Except that marchionesses never – hardly ever – have to survive and provide for their daughters on a widow's army pension, so you wouldn't be in this fix to start with.'

Julia sighed. 'You know, Daisy, I haven't really got anything against Owen Howell except his mother. He is a managing director after all. It's

45

Mother who thinks I have to marry into society. You didn't.'

'And I'm very happy with my policeman,' Daisy said firmly. 'But I'd appreciate your not mentioning his profession unnecessarily. You wouldn't believe how presumably law-abiding people suddenly start twitching when they find out my husband's a detective.'

Julia laughed. 'Not really!'

'Really. And now we'd better think about getting changed or we'll be in hot water with your mother, Mr. Howell's mother, your maid, and the butler when we're late to dinner.'

'Not to mention the cook. I'm on my way.'

It was all very well, Daisy thought, to compare a managing director of a plumbing factory with a detective chief inspector of Scotland Yard, but she had married Alec because she was madly in love with him. Without that, she could never have coped with the hostility of his mother and her own, let alone the move from the upper class, however impoverished, to the middle class, however comfortably off.

Because, however modern and egalitarian one was, there *were* differences. Different expectations, different ways of doing things, a different group of people around one, not necessarily better or worse but indubitably different. Alec's love had pulled her through the complex adjustment.

Unless Julia unexpectedly fell in love with Owen Howell, she ought not to marry him. Daisy looked forward with interest to meeting him.

CHAPTER 5

Daisy and Lucy went down together. Lucy looked spectacular in the crimson frock, rather too spectacular for an evening in the country, in Daisy's opinion. It was designed to be shown off in a West End nightclub, or at least for dining and dancing at the Ritz. Lucy was usually frightfully particular about the right clothes for the right occasion. Perhaps her intent was to show off to the plumber. Perhaps, Daisy thought more charitably, she simply wanted to keep her end up vis à vis Julia, who would probably look lovely in rags. Or, most charitably, perhaps she hoped to distract Rhino from his persecution of poor Julia.

Three men in dinner jackets stood by the drinks dresser, Mr. Pritchard, Lord Rydal, and an unknown man, somewhere between the other two in age, with slicked-down black hair. Taller by a head, Rhino outweighed his companions combined. He was talking in his abrasive voice, punctuating his words with stabs of his cigarette holder.

As Daisy and Lucy entered the drawing room, Mr. Pritchard stepped forwards in what Daisy was coming to regard as his usual welcoming way.

'Lady Gerald! Mrs. Fletcher! What a pleasure to entertain so many lovely ladies here at Appsworth, eh, Owen?' He frowned at Rhino's disparaging snort. 'This is my nephew, Owen Howell, ladies.'

47

'My pleasure,' said Howell, politely but without any great interest. 'You've come to see my uncle's grotto, I hear? What can I get you to drink?'

Lucy stuck to gin and It. Daisy opted for Cinzano and soda. As Howell picked up the syphon, Daisy said, just for something to say, 'It's an ingenious device, isn't it, the soda syphon?

'The invention of the soda syphon to add carbonation to drinks is not more than a century old,' he told her with unexpected enthusiasm, 'but the principle of syphoning has been understood since ancient times. It's of great importance in modern plumbing.'

'Really?' she murmured.

He continued to expound upon the subject. Daisy listened with half an ear, the rest of her attention on Lucy, Pritchard, and Rhino. She was relieved to hear that Lucy, far from being rude to the plumber, was sparring with the earl. He was disparaging what he called her mania for her 'hobby' of photography and she was mounting a spirited defence. Mr. Pritchard appeared to be enjoying the battle. He even put in few words supporting the right of women to have careers. After that, Lucy looked on him with a much kindlier eye.

In the meantime, Mr. Howell had moved on to the latest safety improvements in gas geyser water heaters. True to Lucy's joking remark about writers being interested in everything, Daisy found herself pondering an article on new inventions and their effect on modern life.

'I can't really follow the technical stuff without seeing it,' she told him. 'Would you mind demonstrating for me sometime?'

'Not a bit!' He pulled out a gold pocket-watch and consulted it. 'We've just time enough before– Oh, here are the Beauforts. I'd better get them drinks. But I'll give you a proper demonstration before you leave, that's a promise!'

'What are you going to demonstrate, Mr. Howell?' Julia asked gaily, coming up to them. 'I hope you don't mean to exclude the rest of us from the show.'

'I hardly think you'd be interested, Miss Beaufort,' he said candidly.

'How can I tell until I know what it's all about?'

'Plumbing, no doubt,' put in Rhino with a sneer.

'Can you imagine what life was like before plumbing?' Julia demanded.

Lucy gave a delicate shudder. 'It doesn't bear thinking about.'

Daisy stared at her. Rhino must have really offended her to make her take up the cudgels in defence of plumbing.

'In the course of my life with the Army,' said Lady Beaufort, 'I lived in a number of places without plumbing of any sort. I can assure you, it was extremely disagreeable. Yes, thank you, sherry if you please,' she added to Mr. Pritchard who was waving a decanter at her.

'Leave it to me, Uncle,' Howell offered. 'What can I get you, Miss Beaufort?'

'Sherry, thanks.' Julia waited until her mother had moved away, following Owen Howell, then she said in a low voice to Daisy and Lucy, 'Mother thinks drinking cocktails is fast. That's the trouble with being out of the country for so long. She doesn't realise how times have changed.'

'Fast!' Lucy said indignantly. 'I don't know anyone who doesn't–'

'Calm down, darling, Mother's not saying you're fast. Or rather, she believes a certain degree of rapidity is acceptable in daughters of the aristocracy, particularly married ones, but not in the spinster daughter of a mere knight, even if he was a general.'

Lucy blinked. 'Rapidity?'

'Well, fastness doesn't seem quite the word I want.'

'I wish we had a well-fortified fastness to retreat to,' said Daisy. 'Here comes Rhino, and he's already on his second cocktail.'

'Your sherry, Miss Beaufort.' Handing Julia the glass, he ignored Daisy and Lucy. 'This place is too boring for words. Can't you persuade Lady Beaufort to go back to town before Monday?'

'I'm sorry you find us boring,' Julia said sweetly. 'You really mustn't feel obliged to stay. Mr. Pritchard or Mr. Howell will certainly drive us into Swindon to the mainline station when we leave.'

'You're not boring, it's all these others.' He made a sweeping gesture that encompassed everyone in the room, and nearly sent Daisy's glass flying.

She didn't bother to protest.

'How has he survived all these years with no one throttling him?' Lucy marvelled. She made no attempt to lower her voice, but Lord Rydal gave no sign of hearing her.

'If it was summer,' he continued to Julia, 'we could go for a stroll, but at this time of year there's no chance to be alone together.'

'Thank heaven,' she murmured.

'Your mother won't let you go out in the car with me. Doesn't she realise you're much too old to need a chaperone?'

'Rhino, how crass!' Lucy said in disgust, and stalked off to speak to Lady Beaufort.

Daisy exchanged a glance with Julia, who appeared to share her feelings. They combined a pressing desire to giggle, alarm at what Lucy might say to her ladyship, and amazement at Rhino's apparent belief that he could win his beloved by insulting her.

'"A mad-brain rudesby,"' said Julia.

'"Full of spleen,"' Daisy finished off the quotation. *'Taming of the Shrew?'*

'Yes. Kate, speaking of Petruchio, of course.'

'If you ask me, you need to be a bit of shrew to cope with a rhinoceros.'

For once Lord Rydal seemed to realise he had offended. At least he made a feeble attempt to explain himself: 'I don't care for schoolgirls.' Or perhaps he was simply objecting to their display of erudition. With a sulky look, he tapped out his cigarette butt in the nearest ashtray and his lighter flashed as he lit another.

In a way it was just as well that he was so obviously appalling. Surely after a week at close quarters, Lady Beaufort would be forced to abandon her plans to see her daughter a countess.

Daisy had just reached this comforting con-

51

clusion when Mrs. Howell burst into the drawing room.

'Brin,' she cried, her face tragic, 'Cook says the soles have gone bad!'

'Good job you invited the vicar,' Pritchard quipped.

'Really, Brin, you mustn't joke about such things.'

'Sorry, I thought you were talking about fish, not religion,' he said. He sounded penitent, but he looked pleased with himself, and Daisy had seen his eyes slide sideways towards Lady Beaufort, who hadn't quite been able to hide a discreet little snort of laughter.

'I *was* talking about fish,' Mrs. Howell snapped. 'In any case, the vicar couldn't come, so I invited Dr. Tenby instead. But the fish has gone off and there's none for dinner.'

'Where's it gone off to?' Having got into a facetious vein, he continued to mine it.

'Don't be ridiculous. You know perfectly well what I mean. It's high.'

'Flying fish? I don't believe I've ever seen them at the fishmonger.'

'Brin!'

'Well, what do you want me to do about your flipping fish? Take a rod out to the grotto pool? No, a net would be best, I don't think there's anything bigger than minnows in it.'

His sister-in-law shot him a glance of pure loathing.

'With such splendid dinners as you give us, Mrs. Howell,' said Lady Beaufort, 'I'm sure we shan't feel the want of fish.'

Owen Howell brought his mother a glass of sherry, and he and Lady Beaufort set themselves to smooth her ruffled feathers.

Daisy looked at Rhino to see how he was taking the prospect of no fish course. He was staring after Julia, who had drifted quietly away to speak to a young man who must have entered the room in the wake of Mrs. Howell. The stranger was nothing out of the ordinary – sandy-haired, slightly snub-nosed, no more than a couple of inches taller than Julia – his evening clothes respectable, but clearly not from Savile Row. He was puffing at a pipe. His chief attraction appeared to be that he was not Rhino.

The earl might have been glowering at them, but his usual expression was so like a scowl that Daisy wouldn't have sworn to it.

His attention was distracted by the entrance of another couple, followed by a sleek, blond young man. Owen Howell instantly abandoned his mother and hurried to greet them.

'Lady Ottaline, Sir Desmond, welcome to Appsworth Hall.'

Sir Desmond apologised for the lateness of their arrival. '–unavoidably detained by my wife's loss of a glove just as we were leaving.' His words were sarcastic, but his tone was indifferent.

Lady Ottaline, Sir Desmond. Where had Daisy heard those names recently? Ah, the Wandersleys, at whose house the Beauforts had made the acquaintance of the Managing Director of Pritchard's Plumbing Products. Wandersley was a civil servant, she recalled, and the two had business together.

Sir Desmond Wandersley looked like a senior civil servant, suave – not to say bland – impeccably turned out, his impressive girth evidence of decades of good living, but he had the height and the tailoring to carry it off. A well-barbered mane of white hair and gold-rimmed eyeglasses added to his distinguished air.

Daisy was more interested in his wife. Lucy and Julia agreed that she was an aging vamp, and her appearance did nothing to contradict their description.

Lady Ottaline wore a slinky grasshopper-green frock, with a long, gauzy, spangled scarf draped over her pointed elbows. Her angular arms emerged with insect-like effect. Her collarbones and face were all sharp angles, pointed chin, pointed nose, even pointed lobes to her ears, exaggerated by long, dangling, glittering earrings, faceted like an insect's eyes. Her face was powdered white, with a touch of rouge on high, sharp cheekbones, loads of eyeblack, and blood-red lipstick to match her fingernails.

A cross between a mosquito and a praying mantis, Daisy thought fancifully. She was quite surprised when Lady Ottaline's voice turned out to be not a high, thin whine, but low and husky.

Howell introduced his mother and his uncle to the Wandersleys and their follower. Sir Desmond turned out to be a Principal Deputy Secretary at the Ministry of Health, and the sleek young man was Carlin, his Private Secretary.

As Owen Howell provided the newcomers with drinks, Daisy, still standing next to Rhino, was aware of his lordship's tension. And when Lady

Ottaline glanced round the room and caught sight of him, Daisy was perfectly placed to see that she was unsurprised – and pleased. Her crimson mouth curved in a small, smug smile, but she made no other move to acknowledge him.

He turned away to fuss with lighting yet another cigarette.

'Are you acquainted with the Wandersleys, Lord Rydal?' Daisy asked.

He didn't respond. Though it could have been just another example of his rudeness, Daisy was convinced there was more to it. He and Lady Ottaline knew each other, but he didn't want to admit it. Rhino, being who he was, had probably irredeemably offended her. Judging by her smile on seeing him, she had either revenged the insult or had immediate plans to do so. Of course, Rhino, being who he was, probably didn't realise he had offended, or didn't care, and he might well not recognise the revenge for what it was.

Dying to expound her theory to Lucy, Daisy decided she had complied with the requirements of civility where Rhino was concerned and deserted him. Before she had a chance to talk to Lucy, the doctor and his wife arrived, and a few minutes later they all went in to dinner.

CHAPTER 6

Daisy found herself seated between Sir Desmond and the doctor. The latter, a tall, gaunt, melancholy man, and a silent one, proved more interested in his food than his neighbours. When Daisy asked him politely whether he was a native of Wiltshire, his answer was an unpromising, 'No.'

'I don't know it well, but it seems to be a beautiful county.' This, phrased as a comment rather than a question, received no response whatsoever. Daisy made one more attempt. 'Do you enjoy living here?'

'Not particularly,' he said in a low, despondent voice.

Daisy gave up. Fortunately, Sir Desmond was less inclined to taciturnity than the medical man, or just more socially adept.

'I gather you're not a local resident, Mrs. Fletcher? What brings you to Appsworth Hall?' Implicit in the question was an inference that she did not belong in the world of plumbers. Hearing her speak a few words to somebody else had been enough to make him place her on his side of the fence.

'I'm a writer,' she told him.

A fleeting spasm of distaste crossed his face, quickly hidden. 'Ah, one of these modern clever young women.'

'I don't claim to be clever,' Daisy said coldly. 'I'm a journalist; I don't write literary novels, or blank verse, or anything like that. Mostly just articles for magazines, about places and history, but Lucy – Lady Gerald – and I are doing a book about follies.'

'"When lovely women stoop to follies..."' he misquoted.

'Stoop! Most of them are on hills and we have to climb. But obviously you're ignorant of the existence of the Appsworth grotto. "Where ignorance lends wit, 'tis folly to be wise."'

'Wise after the event, I'm afraid! You and Lady Gerald are writing a book about the follies of eighteenth-century landowners, not of mankind in general, or lovely women in particular.'

'Strictly speaking, I'm doing the writing. Lucy is a photographer.'

'Tell me about the Appsworth grotto.'

'We haven't seen it yet. We arrived too late this afternoon. According to what we've heard, though, it's the best in the country. There never were very many, and most are in a shocking state of dilapidation, but when Mr. Pritchard bought Appsworth Hall, he repaired this one. Practically rebuilt it, in fact. They say he did an excellent job of it.'

'I expect he did, as far as the physical fabric is concerned, at least. The firm is noted for good, solid workmanship. Aesthetically–'

Daisy laughed. 'Aesthetically, grottoes are noted for a mishmash of Romantic sentimentality, Gothic grotesquerie, and Classical pretensions.'

'Indeed! I shall have to make sure to visit the place while I'm here.'

'I understand you're at Appsworth to do business with the firm.'

'Not on my own account,' Sir Desmond said quickly, as if Daisy had accused him of robbing a bank.

'Of course not.'

'You're laughing at me, Mrs. Fletcher. Your generation may find it quaint, but I assure you, it's not so long since being personally involved with a manufacturing business could get one blackballed.'

'How fortunate that you're involved only on behalf of the government – or so I hear? And in the building business, rather than manufacturing.'

His eyes narrowed, though on the surface his manner remained urbane. 'You seem to know a great deal about my business. You're a journalist – but this isn't the place or the time. I'd like a word with you after dinner, if you please.'

'I'm not a reporter. And even if I were in the habit of regaling the scandal sheets with tidbits, which I'm not, I rather doubt they'd be interested in this particular snippet of news. But if you need further reassurance, I'll be happy to give it to you later.'

He gave an abrupt nod, and turned away to respond to Mrs. Howell's anxious twitterings on the subject of the lack of fish.

While sparring with him, Daisy had overheard Rhino, seated on Mrs. Howell's other side, ragging her about the bad soles. Lucy now distracted him with a question about some mutual acquaintance on the London social scene. She had been chatting quite happily with her other neighbour, the sandy young man, who had a Canadian accent. His name was apparently Armitage, but Daisy hadn't been able to hear enough of their conversation to work out what his place was in the scheme of things. His attention, in turn, was captured by the doctor's wife, as loquacious as her husband was taciturn. Perhaps, Daisy thought, her loquacity accounted for his taciturnity.

At least his silence left her free to study the rest of the diners. Armitage, though attending to the doctor's wife sufficiently to make the proper noises in the proper places, was gazing diagonally across the table at Julia, with a besotted expression on his face.

Oh dear, Daisy thought, another victim, and by the look of him one who was not likely to win Lady Beaufort's approval even if he earned Julia's.

Julia was on friendly terms with Owen Howell, as far as Daisy could tell, though they were on her side of the table, beyond the doctor, so she couldn't see them properly. A pleasant chat at the dinner-table was hardly significant, but what a turn-up if Julia were to fall for the plumber! It seemed at least as likely as that she should accept the abominable Rhino.

At the far end of the table, the unlikely quartet of Mr. Pritchard, Lady Ottaline, Lady Beaufort, and the young bureaucrat were getting on like a house on fire. Daisy decided Pritchard must be a brilliant diplomat, wasted on the world of plumbing.

A couple of maids removed the soup dishes. Sir Desmond turned to Daisy and said in a low voice, 'Why all this fishy business?'

'Much ado about nothing. I'll tell you later if you really want to know.'

The maids reappeared. An astonished silence fell as they placed in front of each diner a small plate with a couple of sardines, decorated with croutons and parsley.

Daisy looked at Lucy. Lucy looked at Julia. All three burst into fits of laughter. The infectious sound made most of the others smile, but Mrs. Howell looked ready to weep. Rhino didn't help by saying disdainfully, 'Fish! This might just possibly be adequate as a savoury.'

'I told Cook to do the best she could.'

'Very ingenious of her,' said Daisy. 'I'm sorry, Mrs. Howell. We were just laughing at a private joke. Nothing to do with your cook, or your excellent dinner.'

'Are you going to share it with us?' Pritchard enquired with a grin.

'Certainly not,' said Lucy, simultaneously with Julia's, 'Oh, we couldn't possibly, I'm afraid.'

'Just a bit of juvenile schoolgirlish nonsense,' Daisy explained. 'Not at all funny to anyone else.'

'Well, Lord Rydal, at least your obsession has given us all a bit of a laugh. If this isn't enough fish for you, you're welcome to mine, too. Winifred, you know I don't like fish.' Ignoring her resentful look, he beckoned to his butler. 'Barker, present this to Lord Rydal, with my compliments.'

60

Rhino looked askance at such a brazen departure from ordinary etiquette, but to insult his host at his own table would be an even worse breach of decorum. He was apparently conversant with the rules of good manners, even if the guiding principles escaped him. Daisy noticed that he ate all four sardines.

Dinner continued without further untoward events. Mrs. Howell managed to eat with her lips pursed. Daisy wondered whether she was contemplating revenge, perhaps in the form of offering her brother-in-law nothing but kippers and kedgeree for breakfast. Silent, she made no demands on Sir Desmond's attention. He apparently forgave Daisy for being a journalist and entertained her with a smooth flow of small talk. He had an endless fund of anecdotes, no doubt very useful to a civil servant, and some of them were even quite amusing.

At the end of the meal, Mrs. Howell was still lost in a brown study. She made no move to lead the ladies from the dining room. Daisy disliked the practice except insofar as it allowed her to escape cigar smoke – it was bad enough that Rhino had lighted a fresh cigarette after each course. She wondered whether the plumber's household had abandoned the custom of the ladies' withdrawal, or had never followed it. Then she realised that Lady Beaufort was staring at her with a slightly desperate fixed look. When her ladyship saw that she had Daisy's attention, she nodded towards their hostess.

Daisy leant forwards and said gently, 'Mrs. Howell, shall we leave the gentlemen to their port and cigars?'

She came to with a start and a shudder. 'Cigars? Horrible things.' She stood up. 'He *will* smoke them, though he knows I hate the smell.'

Daisy didn't believe it was the thought of cigars that had made her shudder.

The host went to the door and politely held it as the ladies departed. Daisy hung back so she was last to reach him. 'Would you mind awfully if I used your telephone, Mr. Pritchard?' she asked. 'It's a trunk call, I'm afraid, but of course I'll reverse the charges.'

'Of course you won't, my dear. Make as many calls as you want.'

'Thanks, one will do! I promised my husband I'd ring to let him know I arrived safely.'

'That's the ticket. But don't hang about waiting for the connection. Barker can fetch you to the telephone when the call goes through. I'll tell you what, how's this for a notion? Why don't you ask Mr. Fletcher to join us at the weekend? I don't know why I didn't think of it before. He'd be very welcome.'

Daisy beamed at him. 'That's frightfully kind of you. I'm not sure whether he's going to be free, but I'll pass on the invitation.'

'And ... I don't suppose... Do you think Lord Gerald might like to come down as well?'

'I've no idea what his plans are, but I'll tell Alec to ring him up and ask.'

'Better check with Lady Gerald first.'

'She won't mind. If he comes, either she'll be glad to see him, or she'll be too busy taking photos to notice. We're both so much looking

62

forward to exploring the grotto tomorrow.'

'No need to wait if you'd like to take a look later this evening. I had gaslights put in, you know.'

'Did you really? I'd like to see it.'

'I think you'll find the effect quite ... interesting.' Pritchard's tone had suddenly become mysterious, even creepy. 'I'll have it prepared.'

'Thank you.' Daisy went after the rest of the ladies.

How odd, she thought. Could anything be more prosaic than plumbing? Or manufacturing? A creepy manufacturer of plumbing supplies seemed like a contradiction in terms. All the same, she was jolly well going to drag Lucy out into the frosty night to accompany her to the grotto, like it or not.

CHAPTER 7

Daisy's call came through quite quickly. Barker summoned her before the men rejoined the ladies in the drawing room. He led the way across the front hall.

'The master said to use the apparatus in his den, madam,' he said, opening a door.

'Thank you, Barker.' Pritchard's den, at a glance, resembled any country gentleman's private retreat. Somewhat to her disappointment, she saw no obvious reminders of plumbing, historical or modern, just a large leather-topped desk, leather-covered chairs by the fireplace, several bookcases. She promised herself a quick look at the books after her call. It wasn't nosiness, she assured herself, just her usual inability to resist satisfying her curiosity about people. Reading a few titles wasn't snooping.

She sat down at the desk.

'If madam would be so kind as to hang up the receiver when the call is finished...'

'Of course,' said Daisy, surprised.

'I beg madam's pardon for mentioning the matter, but the fact is, one of our present guests never does so.'

'Lord Rydal? It would be just like him!'

'Far be it from me to contradict madam. Will that be all, madam?'

'Yes, thank you, Barker.' Daisy picked up the phone. 'Alec? Darling, we arrived safely.'

'So I gather.'

'You do sound grumpy. Bad day at work?'

'So-so. I got home early enough to play with the twins, for once. It would have been nice if you'd been there, too. Mrs. Gilpin was at her most difficult.'

'She always is when I'm away.'

'What's more, I'm going to have the weekend free, barring trouble, and you're off in the wilds of Wiltshire.'

'Do come down, darling. Mr. Pritchard's invited you, without my saying a word on the subject. He's rather a nice little man.' Daisy remembered the creepy feeling and added, 'I think.'

'You think? What does that mean?'

'I don't know exactly. I can't explain, not on the phone. It's nothing really.'

'I'm coming down, as soon as I can get away.'

64

Alec's tone said, *I'm a policeman, don't argue with me.*

'Oh, good!'

'Ring me every evening till I arrive. Not before Saturday afternoon, I'm afraid. And if I find you're making a mystery just to get me to come–'

'Darling, I wouldn't! Oh, by the way, the invitation is for Gerald as well. Could you ring him, and if he can manage it, you could drive down together.'

'I can't see squeezing him into the Austin.'

'Why not? If you can fit Tom Tring in, you can fit Gerald.'

'I was thinking more of his dignity than his size.'

'Gerald's not that fussy! But let him drive.'

'Then the Bincombes would have two cars there, and we'd have none.'

'That's all right. I'll go back to town in luxury in Gerald's Daimler, and you can have the grand adventure of being driven by Lucy.'

'Not on your life! I'm too fond of mine. I'll ring him and we'll work it out one way or–'

'Caller, your three minutes are up. Do you want another three minutes?'

'No, thanks,' Alec said. 'Don't forget to ring tomorrow, love.'

'I won't. 'Night, darling. Give the babies a kiss from Mama.'

She wasn't sure how much of that he'd heard before they were cut off, but the babies were young enough not to notice if they didn't get a proxy kiss from Mama. In fact, they'd long since

65

be in bed and asleep anyway. She missed them already.

Hanging up, she took extra care to make sure the receiver was securely in its hook. She didn't want the butler thinking she was as careless as Rhino of other people's convenience.

Beside the desk was a deep cabinet that appeared to hold wide but shallow drawers. Blueprints, Daisy guessed vaguely. She wasn't absolutely sure what a blueprint was, but something to do with technical designs, she thought. Resisting the temptation to peek, which really would be prying, she turned to the nearest bookcase.

The titles left her not much the wiser. There were books on hydraulics, hydrology, metallurgy, geology, and a couple more 'ologies she'd never heard of. Her school had not considered it necessary, or indeed advisable, for young ladies to study the sciences. Ceramics wasn't much more comprehensible, and how could anyone find enough to say about coal-gas to write a whole book on the subject? But others included pottery, porcelain, earthenware, and tile-making. Bathtubs and lavatories and wash-basins, sewer pipes and drainage tiles, Daisy assumed. As a landowner's daughter she had at least heard of these last. At Fairacres, the watermeadows by the Severn had flooded every winter and the drain tiles were constantly in need of upkeep.

Plumbing was a much more technical and scientific occupation than she had realised. And then there was the financial side of creating and running a large and successful business, successful enough to enable Mr. Pritchard to buy the estate from the impoverished Appsworth family. He must be a much cleverer man than he appeared on first acquaintance.

Daisy returned to the drawing room. During her absence, the men had gone in, but as she entered, the doctor said to his wife, 'Time to go, Maud.'

'Yes, dear.' She went on talking to Lady Beaufort.

'Maud!'

'Coming, coming. So you see, Lady Beaufort, I had absolutely no choice. I told her there was no question...'

Giving his babbling wife a look more likely to kill than cure, the doctor sat down in a corner and brooded.

Mr. Pritchard saw Daisy come in and came over to her. 'Call go through all right?' he asked.

'Yes, thank you. Alec will be happy to come down on Saturday if he can get away – he can never be absolutely sure till the last moment, I'm afraid. And he's going to ring Lord Gerald to see if he's free.'

'Excellent, excellent. And the children, how are they getting along without you? Lady Beaufort mentioned that you have twins.'

Daisy warmed to him again. No one who enquired after her babies could really be creepy. 'They have a very good and trustworthy nanny, or I wouldn't leave them.'

'Glenys and I always wanted children,' he said regretfully, 'but it was not to be. Her nephew Owen is like a son to me. He'll have everything when I go, the house as well as the firm. But let's not think of such gloomy things. Have a liqueur to warm you and then I'll take you to the grotto. I recommend a Drambuie. Those Scots know a thing or two about keeping out the cold.'

Having accepted his offer, glass in hand, she looked for Sir Desmond, intending to reassure him about her lack of interest in writing about council house bathrooms. She wondered why he was so anxious about it. Was there some sort of shenanigans going on? Bribery and corruption, she thought vaguely, but she didn't know enough about any aspect of the subject to have a clue whether he was in a position to sign a contract in favour of Pritchard's, or anything of the kind. Perhaps Alec would be able to enlighten her, though she wasn't at all sure she really wanted to be enlightened.

The Principal Deputy Secretary was talking to Julia and Rhino, so Daisy joined Lucy, who was chatting vivaciously with the Principal Deputy Secretary's Private Secretary.

'Daisy, did you meet Mr. Carlin?'

'Not properly. How do you do?'

'How do you do, Mrs. Fletcher.' Carlin was very young, scarcely down from Oxford, at a guess. His family must have influence for him to be a Private Secretary rather than a common or garden secretary or a mere clerk; not sufficient influence to get him into the more prestigious Foreign Office, however.

'I've told him Alec is a civil servant, too,' said Lucy, her eyes sparkling with mischief. She knew that was Daisy's usual evasive description. Most people equated bureaucrats with dullness so it generally served to head off further enquiries.

But to young Carlin, not yet jaded, the civil service that had recently swallowed his life without a hiccup was still a subject of absorbing interest. 'Which office is Mr. Fletcher in?' he asked eagerly. 'What's his line?'

'Oh, this and that.' Daisy gave a vague wave intended to signify that she'd never bothered to find out what Alec did every day. 'Lucy, Mr. Pritchard has offered to show us the grotto tonight. You will come along with us, won't you, Mr. Carlin?'

'I say, of course! Only too delighted.'

'Darling, you can't be serious,' Lucy protested. 'At this time of night? It's freezing cold outside, and I wouldn't be able to take any photos. You can write about the grotto by night if you want, but I'm not wasting plates and flash-powder when I can't even see what I'm photographing.'

'Mr. Pritchard has put in lighting. He says the effect is worth seeing so you're jolly well going to come and see it, photos or no. You won't be cold if you wear your motoring coat.'

Between them, Daisy and Mr. Pritchard rounded up most of the party for the expedition. Lady Ottaline wasn't keen, but when she realised it was the older ladies – Lady Beaufort, Mrs. Howell, and the doctor's wife – who were staying behind, she obviously didn't want to be counted among them.

Daisy noticed that it wasn't till Lady Ottaline committed herself that her husband agreed to go. However, as they all set out across the gardens behind the house, Sir Desmond offered the support of his arm not to his wife, but to Daisy.

The only person unaccounted for was the mysterious Mr. Armitage. He hadn't joined the others in the drawing room. Daisy resolved to interrogate Lucy about him. After sitting next to him at dinner, she surely must have learnt something about him.

The gravel path was well-lit by wrought-iron gas lampposts of an old-fashioned appearance though no doubt the workings had been refurbished to modern standards. The light was bright enough to be helpful without being garish. On either side of the path, the ghosts of trees, bushes, and hedges loomed ahead, to vanish behind as they passed.

'One might almost suppose oneself in Hyde Park,' said Sir Desmond derisively.

'It may not be according to Repton or Capability Brown,' Daisy retorted, 'but the lights seem to me extremely sensible if one has an attraction in the gardens that is worth seeing at night and one doesn't want one's guests to break their necks.'

'I hope it actually is worth seeing at night.'

'You should have waited to hear from the rest of us before going to see it.'

He glanced back at those of the party following them – in front were Julia, young Carlin, and Pritchard. Daisy thought Sir Desmond frowned, but they were halfway between lamps and the light wasn't bright enough to be sure. All he said was, 'I'd rather see for myself.'

She, too, looked back, turning slightly and using the movement as an excuse to let go his arm. She didn't need his assistance on the smooth path, and she was not altogether comfortable with him. Lucy was a little way behind them. Like Daisy, she had changed into walking shoes. She was with Owen Howell and was being polite, as far as Daisy could tell.

At the rear came Lady Ottaline and Lord Rydal. She was clinging to his arm, tottering along on her high heels, which were most unsuitable for a night-time excursion in the garden, or any time, come to that. Daisy heard a giggle that certainly didn't come from Lucy. Odd, she thought, considering the looks they had exchanged on meeting earlier. And why hadn't Rhino stuck to Julia's side as usual?

Looking away from the lights, Daisy saw a glint of hoarfrost on the grass. The air was crisp. Above, the floor of heaven was 'thick inlaid with patines of bright gold,' as Lorenzo put it with the aid of the Bard, millions of stars seldom seen in England's cloudy climate and never in the smoky skies of the metropolis. Ahead, against the backdrop of the Milky Way and its attendant swarms, swirls, and clusters, loomed a black hill, smoothly rounded, with a spinney at the summit looking ridiculously like a poodle's topknot.

The path started to ascend, with short flights of steps every now and then.

'Aren't you glad now to have the lamplight?' Daisy asked teasingly.

'One might certainly come quite a cropper without,' Sir Desmond admitted. 'Especially on the way down.'

They crossed a wooden bridge over a gurgling

brook. Daisy leant for a moment against the stout wooden rail, looking down at the ripples.

'I doubt that it's very deep,' said Sir Desmond, 'but there, I concede, you have another good reason for the lights. I wouldn't want to take a dip in this weather. I'll have to give you best, Mrs. Fletcher.'

'Give it to Mr. Pritchard,' Daisy suggested.

'Yes, I can see Pritchard is above all a practical man.'

'I wouldn't go so far. Rebuilding a ruined grotto is hardly a practical act. If you ask me, it shows he has a distinctly romantic streak.'

'A romantic plumber! Dreadful thought.'

'It does rather boggle the mind.' Daisy agreed, laughing. 'But there's really no reason even the most practical person shouldn't have his romantic moments.'

CHAPTER 8

Beyond the bridge the path followed the stream's meanders, rising higher and higher above the water. Ahead of Daisy and Sir Desmond, Pritchard, Julia, and Carlin passed a lamppost and disappeared round a limestone bluff.

'Oh!' Julia's exclamation rang out above a low, sonorous hum almost like the buzzing of a swarm of bees. 'How marvellous!'

'I say, sir, splendid!'

'Do let's go in.'

'If you don't mind, Miss Beaufort, let's wait for the others,' Pritchard suggested.

'I can't think why you haven't showed it off to Mother and me before. We've been here nearly a week.'

'I was saving it till Mrs. Fletcher and Lady Gerald arrived.'

Daisy hurried forward to see the cause of all the enthusiasm. Her foot landed on something large, hard, and unstable, and her ankle gave way. Luckily Sir Desmond had kept pace with her. Her desperate clutch found his arm. 'Ouch!'

'Steady! What happened?'

'I twisted my ankle. I think I've just ricked it. Yes, it's better already. Thank you for catching me. I stepped on something...' She glanced back at the path. 'Yes, look, a big stone. It must have fallen from the cliff.'

'I'd better chuck it in the stream before someone else trips and lands in the water.' He suited action to the words and fastidiously dusted his gloved hands together. 'There, one hazard the less. Gas lamps or no gas lamps, you'd better slow down, Mrs. Fletcher.'

They proceeded round the bend at a more decorous pace, joining the first arrivals on a sort of paved landing.

'Oh!' Daisy echoed Julia in the only possible reaction to the spectacle before her.

A waterfall plunged twenty feet or so into a dark pool. The cascade itself was anything but dark, because the ingenious plumber had somehow placed lamps in niches behind it. The sheet of falling water glowed, flinging out droplets that flashed and glinted as they caught the light.

'Isn't it wonderful, Daisy?'

'It is. How very clever, Mr. Pritchard. I wish Lucy could take a photo of it.'

'Of what?' Lucy came round the bluff with Owen Howell. 'Mr. Howell refuses to tell me–' She fell silent, contemplating the luminous cascade. 'That's quite a sight, Mr. Pritchard,' she said with a sigh.

'I could go back to the house and fetch your camera, Lady Gerald,' Howell offered.

'Believe me, if I thought I could do it, I'd fetch the camera myself. But I'm afraid a photograph simply wouldn't do it justice.'

'Why not?'

Lucy started to explain about long exposure times and moving subjects. Meanwhile Daisy, who had heard it all before, looked up at the source of the waterfall. Issuing from a dimly lit cavern, the stream was split in two by a plinth on which posed a marble female in Greek draperies, rather like the statue in the fountain at home. Instead of water streaming from her urn, however, she poured forth a marble river. She had small wings on her head and the lower part of her gown was decorated with a relief of bulrushes. Daisy racked her brain.

'Tethys!' she said triumphantly, and scribbled a few descriptive words in the notebook she had, of course, brought with her. Her version of Pitman's shorthand was at the best of times rather hit and miss. She hoped she'd remember what she'd written.

'You know your Greek mythology,' said Pritchard. 'Most people ask me why not Poseidon.'

'Tethys?' Sir Desmond mused aloud. 'Wasn't she a goddess of the sea? So why not Poseidon?'

'She was the mother of rivers, sir,' Carlin said eagerly. 'A minor figure. I'm not surprised you don't remember her.'

'Hmph.' His superior was not pleased to be reminded of the gulf of years separating him from his education. 'You've studied the classics, Mrs. Fletcher?'

'We read the myths at school, in English. I expect you concentrated on the gods, but I, at least, was always more interested in the goddesses.'

Julia giggled. 'Wasn't Tethys the one who had an incredible number of children? As well as the rivers, I mean.'

'Circe among them,' Carlin chortled, 'if I'm not mistaken.'

'Miss Harrison passed rather rapidly over Circe, d'you remember, Julia? I expect we missed a lot, reading the expurgated translations.'

'I wonder where my wife's got to?' Sir Desmond said abruptly. 'I hope she didn't turn her ankle, like Mrs. Fletcher. In those ridiculous shoes of hers, she'd certainly sprain if not break it. Perhaps I'd better go back and see. Don't wait for us.' He turned on his heel and was gone.

'Dear me,' said Pritchard, 'did you wrench your ankle, Mrs. Fletcher? I'm so sorry. The gardeners rake the path regularly, but I'm afraid bits and pieces keep rolling down the slopes.'

'No harm done. I can't even feel it any longer. Do say we can go up to the grotto now.'

'Perhaps I ought to make sure Lady Ottaline is

all right...'

'Sir Desmond and Lord Rydal can take care of Lady Ottaline between them,' Lucy said impatiently, 'if in fact she's come to any harm.'

'Which I haven't.' The lady in question came into view, swathed in furs, leaning heavily on her husband's arm. 'You didn't tell me it was such a long way,' she said reproachfully to Pritchard.

'It's not really very far, Lady Ottaline. I'm afraid I didn't notice your footwear.'

'You didn't?' Pouting, she held out one slender – not to say bony – ankle and green glacé shoe with a diamanté clasp and very high, narrow heels. She turned it this way and that. 'They're intended to be noticed.'

'Charming,' said Sir Desmond dryly, 'but not intended for a walk through a garden at night.'

Rhino had arrived close behind them, the smoke from his inevitable cigarette curling up into the still air. He made straight for Julia's side. He murmured in her ear while Lady Ottaline was complaining, then said to Pritchard, 'Well, are we going into your dashed grotto or not?'

'There are steps. I don't know if Lady Ottaline will be able to–'

'I'm freezing, standing here. I'm going up.' Lucy started the climb.

The steps, cut into the limestone cliff surrounding the mouth of the grotto, ascended steeply for about ten feet. Daisy was glad to see a stout-looking iron railing. She set off after Lucy, whose fashionably tubular frock didn't appear to impede her much, one of the advantages of a knee-length hemline.

Each step was worn, the centre lower than the sides. Daisy deduced that the flight had been cut by the original creators of the grotto and trodden since by generation after generation.

Lucy, plodding upwards ahead of her, glanced back. 'Darling, this had jolly well be worth the effort.'

'You must admit it looks intriguing from below.'

'I wouldn't be up here else. I hope Pritchard's going to lend me a gardener to carry my stuff tomorrow.'

'Has he given you any reason to suppose he might not?'

'No,' Lucy admitted grudgingly. 'He seems quite a decent little man.'

Dismayed, Daisy looked behind her to make sure the 'decent little man' was not close at her heels. He was not, but his nephew was a few steps below her. The roar of the waterfall had covered the sound of his footsteps, and she hoped it had also covered the sound of Lucy's condescending words. Unlike Lady Ottaline's husky contralto, Lucy possessed a penetrating soprano.

Owen Howell showed no sign of having heard, or perhaps he didn't care a hoot about Lucy's opinion of his uncle. Looking up at Daisy, he said something she couldn't make out.

'Sorry?'

He raised his voice. 'My uncle would like you to wait till he gets there to explore.'

'Of course.' Why? Because he wanted to see their initial reactions at firsthand? Because parts were dangerous – falling ceilings, perhaps? Daisy wondered, glancing up a trifle nervously as she followed Lucy from the steps onto the floor of the grotto. Surely not! Pritchard would never permit such inefficiency, and if the hazard was a recent occurrence, Howell was there to keep them away from it. Or was the request to wait related to their host's mysterious and somewhat sinister eagerness to show them the grotto at night?

'Hold on,' she called to Lucy, who was heading for the rear of the cave. 'Mr. Pritchard doesn't want us wandering about before he comes up.'

'Why not? I can't see that he'd be much help if one of us fell into the Styx.'

'Lucy!'

'I just want to... Oh, all right! I probably can't tell in the dark, anyway.'

Though murky, it wasn't really dark in the grotto. Just above head-height on the walls gas lamps burnt, the mantles shielded by translucent shells that diffused the light. Among the thousands of shells encrusting the rugged walls, here and there mother-of-pearl gleamed and crystals glittered. The floor was polished limestone, five or six yards in breadth, ending at a low stone parapet beyond which the stream flowed swift and smooth, satiny black, to its drop into the pool beneath.

One couldn't walk into the stream unaware, Daisy thought, but it wouldn't be difficult to fall over the low wall.

'At least it's warmer in here,' said Lucy with a shiver.

'That's partly the gas lights,' Howell told her, 'and partly the insulating effect of the tons of rock around us.'

'Don't remind me!' With another shiver, Lucy looked up.

The upper part of the walls sloped inwards and gradually converged on either side. Their meeting point was beyond the reach of the lights.

'Are there stalactites?' Daisy asked. 'And stalagmites? I can never remember which is which, but this is the right kind of rock for them, isn't it?'

'Yes, the same stuff that furs pipes and kettles. There are some knobs and protuberances up there that may grow into stalactites in a few centuries. My uncle considered bringing some in from elsewhere or having some manufactured, but he decided against it.'

'Are the shells real?' Lucy sounded suspicious.

'Oh yes. Most of them were already here when Uncle Brin bought Appsworth, though many had fallen off the walls. He brought in more to fill the gaps. In fact, some are where nature put them. Limestone and chalk are made up of ancient shells, you know. There are fossils, too.'

'I'd like to see those.' Julia joined them.

'I'll be happy to show you tomorrow, Miss Beaufort, if I get home in time. I'm afraid the light's not good enough now to see them properly.'

'It's not good enough to see anything much,' grumbled Rhino, lighting a cigarette as he appeared on the heels of his beloved. 'What a waste of time!'

Daisy had to suppress an urge to shove him backwards down the steps. Someone else was probably behind him.

'Rhino, darling,' came Lady Ottaline's plaintive

79

voice, 'do get a move on. I can't balance on this step forever.'

'I'm right here, my dear,' said Sir Desmond soothingly. 'You can't possibly fall.'

Rhino lumbered forwards. The Wandersleys entered the grotto, then Carlin, and bringing up the rear, Mr. Pritchard.

'Well, here we all are,' said their host, with a sigh of relief at having safely shepherded his unruly flock to their destination. 'It's as close to the way it used to look as I could make it, but the old pictures and descriptions aren't too clear.'

'Don't tell me the Appsworths had gas lighting put in,' Rhino said aggressively.

'No, it would have cost much too much if I wasn't in the business. Don't worry, you can't see them in daylight.'

'No good for photography,' Lucy grumbled.

'It's wonderful, but a bit spooky, isn't it?' said Julia.

'Don't!' Lady Ottaline's shudder combined the delicate with the theatrical.

'Grottoes were originally intended to be eerie.' Daisy had done her preliminary homework. 'That is, *originally* originally they were caves where hermits lived, the religious kind. But in English parks and gardens, they were supposed to be both picturesque and grotesque, and in general frightfully Gothic and romantic. The owners—'

'It's haunted!' shrieked Lady Ottaline, pointing towards the rear of the cave.

Everyone swung round. A cowled figure lurked in the dim depths. On silent feet, it glided to one side, started to withdraw, then suddenly vanished.

80

CHAPTER 9

'By Jove, an intruder!' exclaimed Carlin. 'Tally-ho! Don't worry, I'll nab him! Hey, you, stop!' He sprang after the monkish shape.

'Yoicks, tally-ho!' Rhino, too, rumbled into motion. Like his namesake, he was slow to get going but once under way would be very hard to stop.

But Daisy, as she turned, had seen Pritchard and Howell exchanging a conspiratorial glance of glee. Remembering Pritchard's mysterious eagerness to show her the grotto by night, she caught Carlin's arm as he passed her.

'Hold on! Something tells me our host is quite well acquainted with this particular ghost.'

'What?' asked the bemused young man. 'Let go, he'll get away!'

Uncle and nephew had managed to grab Rhino before he got up steam.

Pritchard chuckled. 'We are,' he confessed.

'Mr. Armitage,' said Julia.

'Exactly, Miss Beaufort. I should have realised Mrs. Fletcher was too knowledgeable to be fooled.'

'I was just about to say, the owners of grottoes in the eighteenth century often had an aged and infirm retainer in residence playing the hermit to give visitors a thrill.'

'He certainly gave me a thrill,' Lucy admitted

dryly. 'Not that I believe in ghosts, but—'

'I do.' Lady Ottaline played the fragile damsel to the hilt. 'Are you sure that wasn't...?'

'Quite sure,' Howell assured her. 'Come back to his lair and see.' He offered his arm, but she chose Rhino's.

Julia had already set off in pursuit of Armitage. Rhino followed her, Lady Ottaline attached to him at the elbow. The others went after them.

'I wonder if a photo of the hermit in daylight would look silly?' Lucy said to Daisy. She started muttering to herself about exposure and focus and filters.

Sir Desmond was on Daisy's other side. 'Quite a surprise,' he murmured. 'I'd never have credited Pritchard with sufficient imagination.' He sounded slightly amused, but Daisy got the impression that underneath, well hidden by his shell of imperturbability, was a different sentiment. Anger? Surely he couldn't be seriously annoyed by the apparition's having given his wife a shock.

Lady Ottaline was much easier to read than Sir Desmond. She had been startled but not, Daisy was sure, genuinely frightened. Was her husband unable to see through her penchant for melodrama? He hadn't rushed to her side to comfort her. Something else must have provoked him, or Daisy had mistaken his emotions.

The latter was probably the case, she decided. She wasn't well acquainted with him, and she couldn't even see his face clearly. In fact, she was indulging in pure speculation, as Alec would undoubtedly have pointed out to her.

As she pondered, they penetrated deeper into the grotto, passing a number of statues on the way. Most stood in niches in the walls, impossible to identify in the prevailing gloom. Ahead however, a stalwart Neptune barred the way. From the navel down, as a change from the usual scanty drapery about the loins, he was modestly clad in stylised marble waves with the heads of horses in place of whitecaps. From this frozen sea emerged a naked torso, a head adorned with the usual wildly curling hair and beard, and two muscular arms, one wielding a trident.

Lucy stopped to contemplate the water-god. 'I wonder if it's always being wet that makes his hair curl. Rain plays havoc with mine.'

Daisy laughed. 'I bet you're the first person in history who's posed that particular question!'

'What about the original artist who depicted him that way? Back in Rome or Ancient Greece or wherever it was?'

'Neptune or Poseidon. Sir Desmond, which do you–? Oh, he's disappeared.'

'He went round behind the statue. Everyone must have gone that way.'

'Yes, I can hear them. Come on.'

Poseidon stood sentry to one side of a low arch. His wife Amphitrite guarded the other side, crowned with shells and crab-claws, dolphins frolicking about her legs. Beyond the arch was a short tunnel.

'It's much lighter at the end,' Lucy said thankfully. 'I'm getting tired of groping through the dark.'

'Hush a minute. I heard Rhino say something

about a second monk.'

'Here's a stone one,' Lord Rydal cawed as Daisy and Lucy emerged from the tunnel. 'Much to be preferred to the real thing, what?'

'St. Vincent Ferrer,' said Pritchard, 'the patron saint of plumbers.'

'Popish nonsense!'

'What makes you think you have the right to disparage anyone's religion?' Pritchard demanded angrily. He had put up with a lot from the earl, but apparently this was the last straw. 'I happen to be a Methodist, and as you can see, I've put St. Vincent out here with a lot of pagan gods, not in a shrine in the house, but I don't hold with disrespecting other people's beliefs.'

His outburst stunned Rhino. 'Hold on, hold on! No offence meant. I just say what I think.'

'It's about time you started thinking before you say.'

'Gosh,' Lucy whispered in Daisy's ear, 'I thought Pritchard was a bit of a milksop, but Rhino is positively cowering.'

'A milksop wouldn't have risen to be Bathroom King. Though I wouldn't exactly say Rhino is cowering.'

'Perhaps not quite, but I've never seen him even slightly taken aback before. It must have been a severe shock to the system. I bet he's seething.'

'He wouldn't try to...'

'Try to what?'

'Oh, you know, get his own back.'

'Do him in, you mean? Don't be silly, of course not. You've got murder on the brain, my girl.

That's what comes of marrying a detective. I'm going to see what excuse Mr. Armitage has for playing the fool in a monk's robe.'

'You were talking to him at dinner,' Daisy said, trying to keep an eye on Pritchard and Rhino as they went towards the hermit. His cowl thrown back to reveal Armitage's roundish, snub-nosed, sandy-haired, altogether un-ascetic countenance, he was chatting with Carlin and Julia. 'Who is he?'

'Some sort of colonial,' Lucy said vaguely. 'Canadian? Yes, Canadian. Quite amusing. Mr. Armitage, I do think you might have warned me you were planning to scare us all to death.'

'Would you have been scared to death if I'd warned you, eh, Lady Gerald?' he asked with a grin.

'I must say,' Carlin put in, 'you ladies don't look as if you turned a hair.'

'Hairdressers can work wonders these days,' said Daisy.

'Naturally, I wouldn't have risked making your hair stand on end if I hadn't known modern hairdressing methods could put it right in a trice.'

'I, for one,' said Julia grandly, 'am quite capable of brushing my own hair. Lucy, Daisy, Mr. Armitage has been telling us that Mr. Pritchard employs him to play the hermit.'

'Not exactly "employs," eh? He doesn't usually bother with a hermit at this time of year, but I wanted to take a look at some old papers he has in the house, and he offered me access and room-and-board in exchange for playing hermit now and then. He'd already heard from you, Lady Gerald, and Mrs. Fletcher, about putting the

85

grotto in your book. In the summer, when he has constant requests to see it, he hires an actor full-time. He's even built in quite a decent sort of bed-sitting-room through there.' He pointed at another archway.

'Gas and water laid on, I assume,' Lucy drawled.

'But of course. All the same, I'm glad he doesn't expect me to live there at this time of year. In the summer it would be OK.'

Pritchard came over to them. Daisy looked to see if Rhino was pouting in a corner, but he had joined the Wandersleys and Howell. He was lighting a cigarette yet again, and his expression was no more bad-tempered than usual. No doubt Pritchard's rebuke had disconcerted him for only a moment. In fact, if anyone was pouting, it was Lady Ottaline.

Daisy wondered momentarily what irked her. However, what little she had seen of the lady had not inspired any desire to become better acquainted. Curiosity might be her besetting sin, but she simply didn't much care what her ladyship's troubles were.

'Mr. Pritchard,' Julia greeted him gaily, 'how could you play such a trick on us? If my mother had come, she'd have been startled out of her wits.'

'No she wouldn't. I consulted Lady Beaufort first. I wanted to be sure she had no objection. Besides, she has too many wits ever to be startled out of them.' He patted Armitage's shoulder. 'How do you like my hermit?'

'He's quite the best hermit I've ever seen,' said Daisy.

'The only one, I expect,' he said, laughing.

'Unless you count hermit crabs. They'd have a wonderful time in here with all the shells.' She glanced about. In his shell-walled sanctuary, St. Vincent dwelt among Oceanids, Nereids, and Naiads, all scantily draped.

'Do tell,' said Lucy, 'is the hermit's lair decorated in the same style? Mr. Armitage says you've provided living quarters here in the grotto.'

'No, creosote to keep the place dry, and plain white distemper. You can have too much of a good thing. Would you like to see it?'

Lucy started to deny any desire to do so, but Daisy forestalled her. 'Yes, please. I doubt I'll use it for the follies book, but I've been meaning to ask if you'd mind if I wrote a magazine article about Appsworth...?'

'As well? Delighted. I'm sure Armitage'll be able to help you with family history, the way he's been poring over all those fusty old papers the Appsworths left behind.'

Armitage muttered something, looking as if he could think of approximately fifty-thousand ways he'd rather spend his time. He dug his pipe-and-tobacco pouch out of the depths of his robe and started stuffing the fragrant shreds into the bowl.

'Did you light the gas in the back room?' Pritchard asked him.

'Yes, sir. Both the lights and the fire.'

'Good, good. This way, anyone who'd like to come.'

As Julia took Pritchard's arm and moved towards the next arch, Daisy hung back and said to the Canadian, 'I don't want to bother you if

87

you'd rather not.'

'That's all right. Mr. Pritchard's been very accommodating. I guess if he wants me to give you a hand...' He struck a match and started that desperate puffing that eventually results in a lit pipe. Sometimes. Pausing in mid-puff, he asked, 'What sort of information are you looking for? What sort of articles do you write?' He sounded annoyed and a trifle defensive.

Why defensive? Not that she was after scandal, but in any case, if the Appsworths had wasted their last pennies in riotous living, it was no skin off his nose, nor Pritchard's. What exactly was his interest in the Appsworths' history?

The only explanation she could think of was that he'd found a really good story and wanted to keep it for a scoop of his own. But what had brought him to Appsworth Hall in the first place? All the way from Canada!

Curiouser and curiouser.

Armitage struck a fourth match as he and Daisy followed the others into a surprisingly spacious room. At last the tobacco caught and blue smoke wafted up. Alec smoked a pipe and Daisy didn't mind the smell as much as cigarette smoke, or worst of all, cigars.

They were followed in turn by the Wandersleys, Rhino, and Howell. They were all smoking, Rhino waving his cigarette holder as he made some vehement remark Daisy didn't catch. She hoped the hermit's lair was well ventilated.

'Well,' said Armitage, 'what about this article of yours?'

'I'll tell you later. Hush, I want to hear what

Mr. Pritchard has to say.' She moved closer, notebook in hand. Armitage went over to a small wardrobe – brought in in pieces, presumably, given the hazards of the path – and shrugged out of his habit. Emerging in his dinner jacket, he hung up the robe and headed towards Julia like a moth to a woolly jumper.

Pritchard, meanwhile, said with pride, 'You wouldn't guess it started as another natural cave, would you? The workmen broke through into it by accident when we were dolling up the second cave.'

He turned out to be a good storyteller. He made finding the cave and exploring it sound almost like a Rider Haggard adventure. Even Rhino listened. Daisy took a few notes, on both the original discovery and the resulting room.

With ten people in it, the room felt crowded, but for its intended solitary inhabitant it was more than adequate. Apart from the lack of a window, it could have been anywhere. Though there was no natural light, the plain white walls made it bright, and rush matting gave it an air of comfort. Against one wall was a divan bed covered with a counterpane in a jazzy blue-and-green pattern. Two Windsor chairs flanked a deal table. A gas fire dispelled the subterranean chill.

'As you see,' Pritchard continued, 'we've laid on gas. There's good natural ventilation, luckily.' With the flourish of a conjuror, he drew aside a curtain to reveal a wash-basin and a copper geyser. 'And hot and cold running water. This is one of the same new-style safety geysers as we have in the house. Unless the water supply is turned on, the gas won't turn on, so it's not likely to blow up from steam pressure and practically impossible for it to get hot enough to melt down.'

His nephew started to explain the technical details. Daisy's mind wandered.

A row of paperback books on a shelf nearby made her squint to read the titles. Thrillers and detective stories! It was all very well Lucy saying she was obsessed with murder. Not only was it untrue, she wasn't the only one by a long chalk.

Carlin asked about the ventilation. He seemed to be the only person still concentrating on what Pritchard and Howell had to say. Julia, Lucy, and the hermit were chatting in low voices. Armitage's pipe appeared to be giving him trouble; he was striking march after match, and puffing away without apparent effect. Daisy decided one reason she didn't mind pipe smoke was that pipe-smokers so rarely actually managed to keep their tobacco alight for long.

Lady Ottaline had sat down on one of the chairs. She had her husband and Lord Rydal in attendance. As Daisy glanced that way, Rhino was staring hungrily at Julia. He started towards her, only to be called back by Lady Ottaline.

'Rhino, darling, you'll take me back to the house, won't you? I'm getting frightfully cold. I do believe my toes are frost-bitten.'

With obvious reluctance, Rhino turned.

'Those shoes!' Sir Desmond said testily. 'You'll be colder outside. Just wait till everyone's ready to leave.'

Pritchard couldn't help but have heard Lady Ottaline's complaint. Fortunately, he seemed to be amused, rather than justifiably affronted. 'Owen, we've got carried away by our hobby-horses again. Time we were heading back to the house.'

Howell took out a gold pocket-watch. 'Good lord, yes, Uncle. Mother will be worrying about when to serve coffee. I'll show you the rest later,' he added to Carlin. 'We've the same machine in the house, and I already promised to demonstrate it to Mrs. Fletcher.'

'Thank you, sir,' the young civil servant said with every appearance of delight. He should rise high in his chosen profession.

Daisy, however, had decided against an article on modern inventions.

'Coffee!' exclaimed Lady Ottaline. 'Bliss! Anything hot. I'd even drink cocoa. Rhino!' She grabbed his arm as he once again drifted towards Julia, who was on the way out with Armitage, heads together. 'I'll need your support on those dreadful steps.'

'You can take my arm, Ottaline,' said Sir Desmond. 'It sufficed on the way up.'

'But darling, these ridiculous shoes! I shan't feel safe without a *strong* arm.'

The three of them followed Julia and Armitage, who had retrieved a lamplighter's pole from the niche behind one of the naiads. Lucy, Daisy, Carlin, and Pritchard went next, with Howell bringing up the rear, making sure all the gas fixtures were safely turned off.

Carlin went first down the steps. 'I'll catch you if you slip,' he told Lucy and Daisy.

Pritchard was close behind Daisy. One hand on the railing, she looked back to say to him, speaking loudly, over the sound of falling water, 'Such a good idea to illuminate the cascade. I'm glad you persuaded us to come out in the dark.'

'So am I,' he said with a grin, 'even though you spoilt my little surprise.'

'I shan't spoil the surprise when I write about your ghostly hermit,' she promised. 'Unless you'd rather I gave away the secret so that you don't get too many people coming to see the ghost for themselves?'

'I enjoy visitors. Make it as mysterious as you like.' As they reached the bottom of the steps, Pritchard stopped and said, 'Put your fingers in your ears, Mrs. Fletcher. I have to signal to Owen that we're all down and he can turn off the waterfall lights.'

'Oh, of course, you won't want them burning all night.'

Even with her fingers in her ears, Daisy heard his piercing whistle. One by one the lights went out. The tumbling water still caught some light from the cave mouth above, then that too was extinguished. The only light was from the lamp where the path curved round the bluff.

Daisy's eyes took a moment to adjust to the lower level of light. In that moment, cutting through the waterfall's hypnotic roar, someone screamed.

Daisy had a confused impression of flailing arms and legs tumbling off the path towards the stream below.

CHAPTER 10

Just ahead of Daisy and Pritchard, Carlin started to run forwards, shrugging out of his overcoat and ripping off his dinner jacket as he went. He stooped to lever off his shoes, at the same time peering over the edge, then straightened, pinched his nose between finger and thumb, and jumped.

'Good job he didn't dive,' Howell commented, coming down the last steps. 'There's only three or four feet of water there. Who went in?'

'Lady Ottaline,' Daisy told him.

'Those ridiculous shoes!'

'Owen,' his uncle said sharply, 'get back to the house, quickly, and tell Barker what's happened. They'll need hot drinks, hot water bottles, dry clothes – he'll know what to do.'

Howell departed at a trot.

In the meantime, Armitage had dashed back round the bend, stripping as he ran, and followed Carlin over the edge.

Julia appeared with her arms full of Armitage's discarded coat and jacket. 'He said there's an electric torch in the pocket of his coat. Hold on.' She dropped the jacket and delved into the coat-pocket. 'Here.' She switched it on and directed the beam down at the stream, but it was too weak to show anything but a reflective gleam from black waters.

Pritchard call down through cupped hands,

'Anyone hurt?'

Armitage's voice echoed back: 'No. But we're bloody freezing.'

'You'll have to go downstream. You can't climb out here. We'll meet you.'

'Right-oh!'

'Rhino!' Julia said in a surprised voice, 'I thought you'd have been the first in. But I suppose you *are* a bit elderly to go rushing to the rescue.'

Rhino stood a prudent foot back from the brink, peering into the darkness below. He had got as far as unbuttoning his coat, and no further. Sir Desmond, at his side, hadn't even gone that far, though it was his wife who'd fallen in. Still, he did have the excuse of being a couple of decades older.

Sir Desmond didn't appear to hear Julia's words, but Rhino said indignantly, 'Elderly!' With obvious reluctance he shrugged out of his coat and next moment he was on his way downwards.

'He was pushed!' Lucy hissed in Daisy's car.

Daisy had no chance to question this extraordinary assertion, as Pritchard herded his remaining flock down the path. 'We'll have to give them a hand down by the bridge,' he explained, anxious and apologetic. 'The water's not deep but the bank is a couple of feet up. They shouldn't come to much harm. I can't think how it happened. It's never happened before!'

'Those ridiculous shoes,' Daisy, Lucy, and Julia chorused.

'I certainly don't hold you to blame, Pritchard,' Sir Desmond agreed. He sounded more amused than anything. 'My wife will always put fashion above common sense. It's entirely her own fault.'

By the time they reached the stretch of low bank just before the bridge, a sodden trio had appeared round the bend. Carlin and Armitage, knee-deep, supported Lady Ottaline between them. She had lost or abandoned her coat and hat, and her hair hung in rats' tails round a face blotched and striped like an Indian brave on the warpath.

'*Escob annwyl!* Her face!'

'No need to go all Welsh,' said Lucy. 'Her make-up's run, that's all.'

'Oh, well done!' Julia cried encouragingly. 'Just a little farther.'

Sir Desmond and Mr. Pritchard hauled Lady Ottaline out, streaming with water and shivering convulsively. Between chattering teeth, she spat out, 'My m-mink! They m-made me leave it!'

'Too heavy,' said Armitage, taking the hand Julia held out to steady him as he climbed onto the bank.

'We couldn't have got Lady Ottaline out of there in her coat, sir,' Carlin agreed. Daisy and Lucy lugged him out. 'It weighed a ton, wet.'

'So do you,' said Lucy.

'No matter,' said Sir Desmond. 'I must thank you, gentlemen, for retrieving my wife. Her coat can wait until tomorrow.'

'It'll be ruined,' Lady Ottaline wailed.

'I daresay. I told you it was unsuitable for a country weekend. Here, wrap yourself in mine.'

'I can't walk back to the house with no shoes!'

'You couldn't walk *with* shoes. Come along, you

95

don't think you could manage in mine, do you? And I'm not carrying you.'

'Rhino will!'

Everyone turned back to the stream. Unnoticed, Lord Rydal had arrived and stood glowering. 'I most certainly will not. Get me out of here!'

Pritchard stepped forwards, but Carlin and Armitage were ahead of him. Each grabbed one of Rhino's outstretched hands.

'On your marks...' said Sir Desmond, 'get set ... heave!'

For a moment it looked as if Carlin and Armitage were going to join Rhino in the water. Then they did. They landed face down and Rhino went over backwards with a tremendous splash that showered those on the bank.

Though Daisy's coat protected most of her, the water that hit her legs and face was icy enough to make her gasp. She realised how cold Lady Ottaline must be, even with her husband's coat over her wet things.

'Mr. Pritchard,' she said, 'Lady Ottaline needs to get dry and warm, and she shouldn't walk back to the house alone.'

'I can't walk,' Lady Ottaline moaned.

'Bosh,' said Lucy, 'it'll warm you up.'

'My shoes are squelching,' Daisy put in hurriedly, if not quite accurately. 'I'll take them off and walk on the grass with you. It won't be as uncomfortable as the gravel.'

'All you young ladies had better go,' said Pritchard cheerfully. 'Sir Desmond, that leaves you and me to help the others out.'

'I ought to go with my wife.'

Julia scotched his escape. 'Don't worry, Sir Desmond, we'll take good care of her.'

'We'll send out a search party,' Lucy promised satirically, 'if you don't catch us up by the time we reach the house.'

Lady Ottaline complained constantly as she and Daisy crunched across the frosty grass. Daisy didn't want to sound equally whiny, so she held her tongue though she was sure her toes must be getting frost-bitten. Lucy and Julia crunched along the gravel path beside them, Julia making encouraging remarks.

Halfway to the house, they met Howell returning with three menservants to the rescue. A practical man, he had brought several pairs of wellingtons.

'Rubber boots!' exclaimed Lady Ottaline. 'I've never worn rubber boots in my life. I wouldn't be seen dead wearing those hideous things.'

'I would,' said Daisy. 'Thanks, Mr. Howell, just what I need.' She hung on to Lucy's arm and thrust her feet into the smallest pair. 'They're better than nothing, Lady Ottaline, honestly.'

'Don't be asinine, Lady Ottaline,' Lucy said sharply, adding with more truth than tact, 'No one's going to see you whose opinion you care a fig about. Do you want to catch pneumonia?'

'The others will need your help, I'm sure, Mr. Howell,' Julia suggested.

As soon as Howell and the servants went on, Lady Ottaline gave in. She might not care a fig for his opinion, but he was male – and she couldn't see the figure she already cut in a man's overcoat that could have gone round her three times, with her hair dripping in lank rats' tails and her face streaked in clownish red, white, and black.

Clomping along with numb feet in boots two sizes too large, Daisy tottered. Lucy propped her up and supported her the rest of the way. Just behind them came Julia and Lady Ottaline, the latter complaining constantly.

'All I want,' Daisy said when they reached the terrace behind the house, 'is a hot bath.'

'You won't be the only one. I wouldn't mind it myself.'

'At least we won't run out of hot water, thanks to Pritchard's Plumbing.'

'I never said plumbers aren't a good thing in their place. Oh lord, the old biddies are waiting to hear all about it.'

Mrs. Howell and Lady Beaufort were peering out of the French windows of the drawing room.

'This is where my t-t-t-teeth start chat-t-tering uncontrollably,' said Daisy. 'Can you get us past them without stopping to chat?'

'Of course, darling. In any case, we can't go in that way dripping, in gumboots.'

'Well, find a way in quickly, or my teeth really will start chattering uncontrollably.'

'Serves you right for that nonsense about your shoes squelching!'

'I had to do something, or we'd still be standing there trying to persuade her to budge.'

'*I* wouldn't.'

'No, I don't suppose you would, darling.' Daisy sighed. 'You always were much more strong-minded than I am.'

Julia caught up with them and was pointing out a side door when it opened and the butler appeared. Barker showed his mettle. Not turning a hair at the sight of four aristocratic ladies in varying states of disarray, he quickly ushered them in. Relieving them of wet shoes, rubber boots, and other impedimenta, he assured them that maids had been alerted, baths were being drawn, and hot drinks prepared. He would take it upon himself to make their excuses to Mrs. Howell and Lady Beaufort.

A few minutes later, Daisy was wallowing in hot water, murmuring to herself, 'A butler is a lovesome thing, God wot,' and beginning to believe she might thaw out someday. Twice she turned on the hot tap with her toes, without any diminution in the blissful warmth.

'A plumber is a lovesome thing, too, God wot,' she told herself as she reluctantly heaved herself out of the water and wrapped herself in a vast towel, warm from the heated towel rail.

Beside her bed, she found a thermos flask of cocoa and a plate of Marie biscuits. Clearly she was not expected to put in an appearance downstairs if she chose not to. She chose not to, but she did want to talk to Lucy. She reached for the bell to summon a maid, intending to ask whether Lady Gerald was up and about. Just before she rang, she heard a tap on the door.

'Come in?' To her relief, Lucy appeared, elegant as ever in a silk kimono of her favourite peacock blue. 'Oh, it's you, darling. Come in and sit down. I was afraid it might be Mrs. Howell come to fuss.'

'It might have been, but I persuaded her if you didn't come down you'd rather be left in peace.'

'Thanks!'

'She sent all sorts of anxious messages, which I can't remember. Actually, I think she's too busy fussing over Lady Ottaline to be frightfully concerned about lesser beings.'

'Is Lady Ottaline all right? She bore the brunt of the whole thing.'

'Sir Desmond insists she's healthy as a horse. I doubt she'd be pleased to hear it.'

'She does rather cultivate the fragile look, though it's very much the brittle kind of fragility. Lucy, what on earth made you say Rhino was pushed? Did you see someone give him a shove?'

'Heavens no! Nothing Alec would call evidence. It was too dark to see much, anyway, but that's what made it seem so opportune. You can't say he was exactly keen to jump in and help the other fellows rescue Lady O.'

'Rather the reverse.'

'So there he stood balking on the edge with someone on each side who had good reason to wish him ill. And in he went.'

Daisy thought back to the scene. 'Julia and Sir Desmond. He'd been pestering Julia to death, but I can't see her resorting to such drastic means, especially as all she has to do is keep saying no. As for Sir Desmond, his wife was flirting with Rhino – strange tastes some people have! – but if anything, Rhino was trying to deter her. At least that's what it looked like to me.'

'What you don't know, darling, because you

retired from the world, is that they've been having a torrid affair for months.'

'Are you serious? There really is no accounting for tastes! But that's hearsay, of course.'

'If you mean did I see them come out of a hotel bedroom together at dawn and draw my own conclusions, no, I didn't. But it's not gossip I went digging for. I'm not turning into a second Great-Aunt Eva. It's been common knowledge among people one meets everywhere.'

'Does Julia know?'

'I think not. As a matter of fact, I've been wondering whether I ought to put her in the picture.'

'She must have seen that there's something between them. This evening, I mean. I should let sleeping dogs lie, if I were you. It's not as if she's fallen madly in love with him and you have to prevent her making a terrible mistake.'

'That's a good point. My lips are sealed. Actually, it'd be more to the point to tell Lady Beaufort.'

'Why don't you?'

'Catch me!' said Lucy, in a rare descent into vulgarity. 'You do it.'

'Not likely! What about Sir Desmond, did he know?'

'Oh, Daisy, what does it matter? No one was hurt, and in any case, I told you, I was joking when I said Rhino was pushed. Though I must say, if I'd been close enough, I'd have been awfully tempted.'

CHAPTER 11

Bright sun streamed through the window of Daisy's bedroom when Lucy flung back the curtains next morning.

'Get up. It's a glorious day.'

'What time is it?' Daisy mumbled, screwing her eyes tight shut.

'Breakfast-time. Come on, darling, we daren't miss a moment of this sunshine. It could be snowing by midday.'

'I can write perfectly well in snow.'

'But I can't take photos, as you know very well. Besides, you wouldn't want to walk along that path in snow, would you?'

'Nor in rain, come to that, which is much more likely.'

'In any case, even if it's shining the sun will be all wrong later.'

'Right-oh, I'm on my way.'

'Fifteen minutes, or I'll be back to fetch you,' Lucy threatened.

'Have a heart! Twenty. Now buzz off and let me get dressed in peace.'

When Daisy went down, she encountered Barker crossing the entrance hall with a silver coffee-pot on a tray.

'The breakfast parlour is that way, madam, second door on the left. May I venture to enquire as to whether madam has suffered any ill-effects from last night's – ah – adventures?'

'Not at all, thank you, Barker. The hot bath and cocoa were just what was required. Do you know how Lady Ottaline is faring? She had the worst of it.'

'I understand her ladyship desires to remain abed this morning, madam, but Sir Desmond does not consider it necessary to send for a medical attendant.'

'Thank you, Barker.'

'Does madam prefer anything in particular for breakfast? Tea or coffee?'

'Tea, please. Indian. For the rest, I'll take what's going.'

'Very good, madam.'

In the breakfast parlour, Daisy found Lucy with Pritchard, Howell, and Armitage. None of the other ladies had yet put in an appearance. Pritchard bustled about seating her, helping her from the buffet.

'Will you try a little Welsh ham, Mrs. Fletcher? You've likely not eaten it before. We cure a leg of mutton instead of pork, you know, Wales having the most flavoursome mutton in the world. I believe you'll find it tasty.'

'Thank you, do give me a slice.' Daisy glanced at Lucy to see if she was indulging in Welsh ham, but she was sticking to her usual coffee and toast. 'You're very patriotic, Mr. Pritchard. I'm surprised you ever left Wales to come and live in England.'

'That was my father's doing. He started the firm in Wales, just when people were beginning to want indoor plumbing. As it grew, he found most of his sales were in England and it was more practical to have the factory here. That's when Owen's father, my wife's brother-in-law, invested in the company, which made the move to Swindon possible. My da made the right choice. We've continued to prosper. Then Appsworth Hall came on the market just when I was thinking of leaving the day-to-day business to Owen. Glenys wanted to move out of the town, so here we are – or rather,' he said sadly, 'here I am.'

'I hope your wife had a chance to enjoy living here.'

'We had a couple of good years before I lost her, thank you kindly.'

Daisy was itching to find out what had become of the Appsworth family. However, she didn't think it proper to ask the man who had profited, however legitimately, from their misfortunes.

Absently consuming the Welsh ham, she turned her gaze on Armitage. He was said to be 'taking a look at' old papers left at the Hall by the Appsworths. What his work involved and for whose benefit he was doing it had not been mentioned. He was the obvious person to ask, all the same.

Lucy was telling him about the photos she had taken of the front of the house in the evening light the day before.

'Would you be willing to sell me a print?' he asked. 'I've taken a few snaps with my Kodak, but I'd like to have a good professional picture of the old place.'

'By all means, if they come out well after the way Rhino was chucking my stuff about.'

'Chucking your stuff about?' Howell demanded

in outrage, temporarily forsaking his methodical attack on his breakfast. 'Your photographic apparatus, you mean? Chucking it about? Why was he chucking it about? Did he damage anything?' Clearly the thought of machinery being abused was anathema to him.

'I don't think so,' said Lucy, 'but I can't be sure till I develop the plates.'

'He fetched Lucy's tripod for her,' Daisy explained, 'then dropped it on top of the camera and bag of plates.'

'How on earth did he come to do anything so halfway helpful?' Armitage exclaimed.

Lucy exchanged a glance with Daisy and they both laughed.

'My car was in the middle of the drive and he couldn't get past,' Lucy said dryly.

'Of course, *force majeure*. The only possible explanation.'

Pritchard said a trifle fretfully, 'I don't see why an earl can't be as polite as the next man. If it was up to me, he'd be long gone, but Winifred won't hear of me asking him to leave.'

'You don't need Mother's permission to kick him out, Uncle Brin.'

'Ah well, my boy, it's her home, too, now, and it doesn't do to cross a woman in her own home. It just makes everyone uncomfortable. Be thankful Lord Rydal is a late riser and won't be here forever.'

'I am, Uncle, I am.'

Presumably Rhino would stay until the Beauforts departed, so Owen Howell's heartfelt retort suggested that his heart was not preoccupied with passionate love for Julia. On the other hand, he was not a demonstrative man. Could his outward calm hide a passionate heart? Daisy wondered.

He had returned to his pigs-in-blankets, unconcerned or oblivious of Daisy's scrutiny. She was still watching him when Julia came in. He looked up from the bacon-wrapped sausages to say good-morning, and his expression was definitely admiring. Still, Julia in a tweed skirt, silk blouse, and cardigan was just as ravishing as Julia in an evening frock. No man under eighty could possibly look at her without admiration. Only in this mercenary age could she have failed to find a suitor acceptable to both her mother and herself.

Though to be fair, Daisy thought with an internal sigh, one had to make allowances for the fact that so very many altogether eligible young men had died in the War.

Pritchard bustled about again to get Julia settled with her breakfast. Sir Desmond and Carlin came in and helped themselves to hearty platefuls. Howell took out his watch and checked the time with a frown. But the civil service could not be expected to keep business hours. Daisy had more than once heard Alec animadvert upon the slothful habits of bureaucrats.

Lucy, on the contrary, was all business this morning. 'As soon as you're ready, Daisy,' she said crisply. 'I left my equipment in the hall.'

Daisy swallowed a last gulp of tea. 'I'm right with you.'

'Would you mind if I came with you?' Armitage asked. 'I'd like to see how you work, and I can be your packhorse, eh. And being well acquainted

106

with the grotto, from a hermit's point of view, of course, I may have helpful information.'

Lucy looked dubious, but Daisy said firmly, 'We could definitely do with a packhorse. Those photographic plates weigh a ton.'

He grinned. 'I'm wholly at your disposal.' As he stood up, he exchanged a glance with Julia and she smiled.

'I may drop by later,' she said, 'if it won't disturb you, Lucy.'

'Why not? I might as well invite the whole world.'

'Don't be snappish, darling,' Daisy admonished her. 'I'll herd them out of your way if they encroach.'

'A packhorse and a sheepdog,' said Pritchard with a chuckle. 'That's the ticket.'

The walk to the grotto was very different on that bright morning. Urns on the terrace spilled cascades of aubretia with a few purple flowers already opening here and there. The gardens were sheltered to the north by the house and to the east by a high beech hedge still thick with last year's leaves. Daffodils, narcissus, and crocuses already bloomed in great sheets of colour, mostly yellow, as if reflecting and intensifying the sunlight.

'The Victorian gas lamp standards add a delightful touch of whimsy to the landscape,' Daisy remarked, and pleased with the phrase she whipped out her notebook to write it down.

'You may want to save the word *whimsy* for the grotto,' Armitage suggested. The heavy satchel of plates didn't appear to discommode him in the slightest. He carried it over one shoulder and the tripod over the other.

'Since follies are whimsical by their very nature,' said Lucy, 'Daisy's trying to avoid overuse of the word.'

'This is for my article about the house, darling, not the grotto book. I can be as whimsical as I like.'

'You still intend to write that, eh?'

'Definitely. I'm sure my American editor will be interested, even if *Town and Country* isn't. I don't want to bother you with my questions, though. I expect I can get enough information at the British Museum library. Victorian vicars were forever writing dim little volumes about the history of local notables.'

'I've read a few, but I haven't been able to trace any from this parish. No, I said I'd help you, and I will. But you never told me what sort of articles you write.'

'Oh, I just describe interesting country houses, with little tidbits of the history of the family thrown in. I don't write about the present residents – well, just a bit about "gracious permission" and so on – nor any of the skeletons in cupboards if they don't want me to. Most don't mind as long as none of those concerned are still living.'

'You may write about dead skeletons, but not living ones, eh? That sounds reasonable. All right, you can ask, though I can't promise to answer.'

'Fair enough. The best stories usually come from members of the family, who've grown up hearing them. What–'

'Not now, Daisy,' Lucy interrupted. 'Wait till we've finished what we're doing. Let's concentrate on the grotto for the moment.'

They came to the first set of three shallow steps. The path was now leading them up the lower slopes of the downs. The lawns on either side gave way to rough tussocks. Ahead, sheep-cropped grass rose steeply to the rounded summit, crowned with a spinney. More steps, then they reached the bridge over the stream.

Here Armitage paused. 'You may not want to mention this,' he said, 'as it somewhat detracts from the picturesqueness, but the channel is lined with some sort of tile. Otherwise, I'm told, the creek would often dry up in the summer.'

'It tends to happen in chalk and limestone country,' Daisy said.

'You grew up in this sort of country?'

'No, quite different. The valley of the Severn, in Worcestershire. It's just one of those useless bits of general knowledge one remembers from school.'

'Knowledge is seldom useless, especially for a writer, though its usefulness isn't always immediately apparent.'

'That must be why Daisy's such a successful writer,' said Lucy, impatiently moving onward. 'She has a vast fund of apparently useless information.'

'Whereas you, Lady Gerald, have a vast fund of specific technical information.'

'I wouldn't say *vast*,' Lucy demurred, but she looked pleased.

Amused, Daisy realised he was buttering them

up, in a rather roundabout and subtle fashion. Doubtless he wanted them on his side if Julia asked what they thought of him. She was sure by now that they were attracted to one another, though to what degree the attraction was acknowledged she couldn't guess.

The stream was below them now, though the gorge was by no means the fearsome chasm it had seemed last night. On the far side, here and there, small plants clung to the whitish cliff. They turned the corner of the bluff. The sun, still quite low in the southeast, shone directly into the mouth of the grotto. Sparkling, the waterfall flung itself down into a pretty pool fringed with reeds and watermint. It was a delightful scene, but Daisy was glad she had seen its dramatic aspect the previous evening.

Lucy called a halt. Armitage put down his burdens and started setting up the tripod at her direction.

'I'm going up,' Daisy said. 'I'll make a list of things I want to write about, and then you can decide which will make good photos.'

'Right-oh. Stop at the top, though, while I get a couple of shots. A human figure gives an idea of the scale,' Lucy explained to Armitage.

Gazing back the way they had come, he made some indistinct reply. Daisy grinned. Lucy shrugged, shook her head, and rolled her eyes.

Daisy went up the steps, much less steep and narrow by daylight. At the top, she went over to the stream. As it approached the lip of the cave, the low wall confining it to its bed sloped down from eighteen inches high to no more than six, so that it wasn't noticeable from below.

She moved forwards, stopping a prudent couple of feet from the edge, and waved to Lucy, who was peering through her viewfinder. Lucy motioned her to come closer. Daisy shook her head.

Lucy turned to Armitage, who by now had returned at least part of his attention to what she was doing. (Another part was on filling his pipe.) Pointing up at Daisy, she said something. As he replied, he glanced back down the path again. Lucy looked at her wristwatch, tapped it, and shook her head vigorously. Daisy guessed what she was saying: 'Julia won't be here for ages. She was just starting breakfast and she may seem ethereal but she has a healthy appetite.'

Armitage blushed, cast one last longing look backwards, then headed for the steps, his unlit pipe clenched in his teeth. Lucy generally got her way when she was being forceful.

'Besides,' said Daisy as the lovelorn swain arrived in the grotto, 'she won't want people to think she's chasing after you.'

'How did you know...? What people?'

'Pritchard, Howell, Sir Desmond, Carlin, for a start. Anyone else who goes down to breakfast. Barker – he was just coming in with fresh coffee when she said she'd join us. Then there's her mother, who'd be bound to wonder where she was if she got up and found her missing. She'll probably go up to her and tell her we – Lucy and I, that is – are working in the grotto and she's going to pop along to see how we're doing.'

'You don't think she'll mention me to Lady

111

Beaufort?' Armitage asked wistfully.

'I wouldn't. But then, my mother is much more daunting than Lady Beaufort. Come on, Lucy's getting impatient, and she can be almost as daunting as Mother when she tries.'

Armitage moved into position to be the requisite figure in Lucy's composition, leaving Daisy to explore.

She found herself making reams of notes on everything from the fossils visible in the polished marble of the floor to the curious formations dependent from the roof, which she thought might be incipient stalactites. Armitage would know. She turned towards the cave mouth to ask him.

He wasn't there.

Appalled, Daisy dropped her notebook and rushed to the edge. With one hand on the statue of Tethys, how far over dared she lean–?

'Daisy,' Lucy cried behind her, 'for pity's sake take care!'

Startled, she lost her balance and tottered...

CHAPTER 12

A tug on Daisy's coat made her fall backwards, instead of forwards and down. She staggered back. About to sit down, hard, she found herself clasped in Armitage's arms.

'My plates!' Lucy yelped.

In hindsight – or rather hind-hearing if there was such a word – Daisy realised she had heard a crash just before she felt the jerk on her coat that had saved her. Lucy was on her knees, feverishly unbuckling the straps of her satchel.

'Sorry, Lady Gerald, but better your plates than Mrs. Fletcher.'

'Of course, but– Daisy what on earth were you doing?'

'Charles!' Julia had appeared at the top of the steps. She looked at Armitage with heartbreak in her eyes. 'I mean, Mr. Armitage!'

He whipped one arm away from Daisy's person. 'Can you stand alone?'

'Yes, thank you. He saved me from a wetting, or worse, Julia. I thought *he'd* fallen in–'

'Oh, Charles!'

'Thank heaven, nothing seems to be broken. Darling, why on earth should you think *he'd* fallen?'

'One minute he was there, posing for your pictures. The next minute I turned round and he was gone.'

'It's ten or fifteen minutes since he came down to help me carry the stuff up. It's sheer luck that the plates are all right. Of all the idiotic–!'

'I was being careful. If you hadn't shouted in my ear–!'

'Lucy. Daisy!' With obvious reluctance Julia disentangled herself from Armitage's arms. 'You're only shouting at each other because Daisy had a shock and Lucy's relieved–'

'*I* wasn't shouting,' said Lucy at her most dignified.

Armitage grinned. 'That's what it sounded like to me.' He'd moved several paces from Julia and

113

was smoothing his hair, though it was cut too short to be ruffled by any amount of exertion. Extracting a box of matches from his waistcoat pocket, he set about trying to light his pipe.

'I was,' Daisy admitted. 'I really thought I was in for a ducking.'

'I ought to have told you I was going down,' Armitage said, 'but you were so busy taking notes I didn't like to interrupt.'

'Oh, where's my notebook?'

'I hope you didn't drop it over the edge,' said Armitage, making for said edge.

Lucy, Daisy, and Julia spread out and moved towards the back of the cave, searching.

'Darling,' Lucy said to Julia in a low voice, 'you've only known the man three days. Should you be throwing yourself into his arms?'

'Actually, we first met in town several weeks ago. Mother thinks it was her idea to get us invited here, but I inveigled her into it. You won't give me away, will you?'

'Of course not,' said Daisy.

'Having Rhino drive us down was entirely her own idea however.'

'And a rotten one!' Lucy exclaimed. 'Look, here's your notebook, Daisy. Heavens, you've got masses of notes. No wonder you didn't notice when Mr. Armitage–'

'Guess who's on his way here,' Armitage said in tones of doom, retreating rapidly from the mouth of the cave. 'His ruddy lordship.'

'Rhino? Oh no!' Julia was equally dismayed.

'Let's go into the second cave,' Daisy proposed. 'With any luck he'll think we've left and go away.'

114

'I think he saw me, but we can try it. I'll go first, shall I? It's darkish in the tunnel even on such a bright day. Perhaps I'd better light the lamps in the inner grotto. There's a little natural light, from a rift in the roof, but not enough for Mrs. Fletcher's serious studies.'

He took a small electric lantern from the niche behind a naiad and led the way between Neptune and Amphitrite. After lighting the first shell-shaded gas lamp, he continued striking match after match and applying them alternately to his pipe and the rest of the lamps.

Daisy studied the statue of St. Vincent Ferrer. He was interesting if only because he was an anomaly among the Classical figures and natural adornments of the grotto. He was dressed in a monkish robe and cowl, like Armitage playing the hermit, and like Armitage now he carried a flame in one hand. Patron saint of plumbers, Pritchard had said. The statue was definitely noteworthy, but she couldn't decide whether she should write about it or not.

She turned to consult Lucy. Lucy wasn't there.

'I do wish people wouldn't keep disappearing! Where's Lucy got to now?'

'Isn't she here?' Julia looked round vaguely. 'She must have stayed behind. I'll go and see, shall I?'

'That's all right, I'll go. You two enjoy a moment's privacy – it's liable to be brief enough. But behave yourselves.'

Lucy was feverishly setting up her tripod and camera before Neptune. 'Oh, there you are, Daisy! Come and lend a hand. The sun will have moved too far round in a few minutes and flash photos never come out as well. Get out the exposure meter, would you?'

Daisy had helped Lucy with her photography in the days before she started to make money with her writing, so she knew what she was looking for and where to look. She was taking it from the inner pocket of the satchel when an all too familiar grating voice behind her said, 'What are you doing here? They told me Julia – Miss Beaufort – was coming here.'

'Go away, Rhino, we're working.'

'Julia has no particular interest in the grotto, Lord Rydal,' Daisy pointed out.

'What she's interested in is that damn colonial counter-jumper. And he lives here.'

'Not at this time of year.'

'Rhino, come here,' Lucy commanded.

'What? Why?'

'Because I need your help moving this.'

'Why should I?'

'Are you saying you're not strong enough to move a tripod with a camera attached? Sorry, I shouldn't have put you in such an embarrassing position, where you had to admit it.'

'Darling, don't torment the poor man. He can't help it if he's let himself get a bit–' Daisy eyed him up and down– 'flabby.'

'Flabby! Of course I'm strong enough,' Rhino snarled. He strode over to Lucy and reached out to grasp two legs of the tripod.

'Stop! Half a sec.' Lucy made a big fuss about peering through the viewfinder. 'Let's see, I think three inches to the left should do it.'

116

'Three inches? And you can't manage that yourself?'

'Not after carrying my stuff from the house.' Lucy pronounced this taradiddle without a blink, and without any attempt to look limp and exhausted.

'What difference does three inches make anyway?'

'All the difference in the world. I can see you don't know the first thing about photography. Make it four inches to the left.'

'Show me, exactly. I'm not moving it twice.'

'This leg here,' Lucy said patiently in the sort of voice one uses to a two-year-old – a not very bright two-year-old. 'And this leg here. Hold on, just let me check.' She squinted at Neptune through the viewfinder again. 'It's not quite straight. Rotate it just the tiniest bit to the right.'

Rhino looked daggers at her but obeyed. She managed to keep him busy for several minutes, but he was about to go past Neptune in search of Julia when another distraction arrived.

'There you are, Rhino darling,' cooed Lady Ottaline, hurrying to him and clutching his arm, which fortunately was not supporting any vital bit of photographic equipment at that moment. 'Look, I'm wearing sensible shoes today.'

She held out one silk-clad leg. Her 'sensible' shoes were not proper walking shoes, but at least they had comparatively low Cuban heels. Though she seemed not to have suffered any lasting ill effects from her unexpected midnight swim, she was not eager to repeat it for the sake of fashion.

'Look out!' said Lucy. 'If you knock against the

tripod I'll have to start again.'

Still standing on one foot, Lady. Ottaline turned the other this way and that. 'What do you think, darling?'

'Very sensible,' Rhino said woodenly.

Lady Ottaline pouted. 'Oh, I'm going to fall!' With an unconvincing wobble, she flung her arms round his neck.

'If you *must* stand on one foot,' Lucy snapped, 'please go and do it somewhere else. I'm trying to get some work done here.'

'Poor you, having to work still even though you managed to get married at last.'

'Poor you,' Lucy retorted, 'having no interests beyond the pursuit of men after donkey's years of marriage.'

Lady Ottaline shot her a venomous look, but Rhino had escaped from her toils during this exchange and was rapidly heading for the inner cave. She sped after him.

'I hope they didn't wreck that exposure, the silly asses.' Lucy slid a plate out of the camera. 'It's a pity she drove Rhino away, but I couldn't keep him occupied much longer.'

'I'm amazed that you succeeded in keeping him so long. Or in getting him to do anything at all, come to that.'

'It's just a matter of being firm. It's a pity more people don't try it on him.'

'You could say Lady Ottaline's being firm, I suppose. Or perhaps tenacious is the word. He looked positively hunted.'

'Yes,' Lucy said thoughtfully. 'I suppose he really is in love with Julia, as far as he's capable of it, and he's afraid Lady Ottaline will turn her against him if he doesn't surrender to her wiles.'

'I doubt anyone or anything could turn Julia more against him.'

'No, but you can't expect him to realise that. In his own eyes he's as close to perfection as a man can be.'

'I can't see why Lady Ottaline should be so desperate to hang on to him if he doesn't want her. But then, I can't see what she wanted with him in the first place.'

'Darling, that's obvious. She has to have a lover at her beck and call, and she's getting beyond hooking a new one.'

Daisy shook her head. 'The great advantage of never having been beautiful is that one doesn't have to worry about growing older and losing one's looks.'

'Would you mind going after those beautiful people and stopping them coming back till I've finished this shot? I don't want another one ruined. Besides, you may be needed to help prevent Rhino massacring Armitage.'

'I thought you didn't approve of "the colonial counter-jumper" for Julia.'

'I don't. But I approve still less of Rhino. The man's a menace to civilisation.'

'Perhaps Armitage will massacre Rhino.'

'Not likely. He's outweighed two to one. Rhino's both an irresistible force *and* an immovable object. He'll do the massacring.'

'Oh dear! I don't think it counts as a massacre, though, if it's just one person.'

'Then perhaps Rhino will oblige and massacre

Lady Ottaline, too,' Lucy said dryly.

With great reluctance, Daisy went round Neptune and through the short tunnel. Approaching the end, she heard raised voices.

Armitage and Rhino were shouting at each other, Armitage sounding more Canadian than ever and Rhino's caw raised to roc-like proportions. Since they were both shouting at once, Daisy caught only the odd word here and there. Judging by those, it was just as well she missed the rest. Lord Rydal had the vocabulary of a coal-heaver. Armitage seemed to prefer more esoteric imprecations, including a phrase or two that had a Shakespearian ring.

Daisy emerged from the tunnel. Armitage and Rhino faced each other a few feet apart. Both had clenched their fists. Neither pipe nor cigarette holder was in evidence.

Beyond them she saw Julia's aghast face. Lady Ottaline looked excited. Could she so far have misunderstood the situation as to believe the men were fighting over her? Or was it sheer bloodlust?

'Oh, don't!' Julia begged.

Daisy took out her notebook. 'This will make a wonderful story for the scandal sheets! The noble earl of Rydal attacks a man half his size, in the presence of horrified ladies. I can just see the headlines. But hold off a minute, won't you, please? Lucy will want to see this so that she can give an accurate report to Lord Gerald to spread in the clubs. I expect he'll be able to dine out on the story for weeks.'

The would-be combatants looked at her. Armitage appeared both annoyed and amused.

Rhino glared, his face turning from red to purple.

'It'll make an even better story if Rhino has a stroke. For the papers, I mean. Gerald wouldn't care to—'

'Daisy!' Julia objected uncertainly.

'Not that I'd want Rhino to make himself ill, of course. Or worse. People do die from strokes, and you look awfully overwrought, Rhino. If you could see the way your eyes are bulging... Perhaps you ought to sit down.'

'I'll fetch you a glass of water from the back room,' Armitage offered. He hurried off, just in time – Daisy thought – to avoid laughing in his antagonist's face. Julia followed him.

'I expect you ought to cut down on the cigarettes,' Daisy said to Rhino. 'They're frightfully bad for you.'

'I am perfectly well,' he said through gritted teeth. Then he parted them just far enough to stick his cigarette holder between, stuck a cigarette in the holder, and struck a match as he strode back to the outer cave.

Lady Ottaline gave Daisy a look of pure loathing and went after him.

Lucy's anguished wail was audible in the inner cave. 'Rhino, you blithering idiot! You've ruined another shot!'

CHAPTER 13

Under the circumstances, lunch was bound to be an uncomfortable meal. Business having taken the rest of the men to the works in Swindon, Rhino and Armitage were the only two present, and they, of course, were not on speaking terms.

As well as the strained relations between several of those who had visited the grotto that morning, Mrs. Howell was irritated because the soup was already growing cold when Lady Ottaline at last came down after refreshing her make-up. And Lady Beaufort was annoyed with Julia for leaving it to their maid to inform her as to her daughter's whereabouts.

'Mother, I'm twenty-eight!'

'Past old enough to have better manners!' snapped the usually equable lady.

'I thought you were probably still asleep, so I left a message with Willett. It was very early, but when I came down to breakfast, Daisy and Lucy were just about to leave, because Lucy had to catch the best light for her photographs. I wanted to see what they were doing.'

'It's about time I had a look at this grotto everyone is making such a fuss about. I hope you can spare the time to show me this afternoon, Julia?'

'Of course, Mother.'

'I don't know why you want to see it,' Mrs. Howell grumbled. 'Brin's spent an absolute fortune on it, but when all's said and done, it's just a fancy hole in the ground.'

'I suppose Mr. Pritchard may spend his money as he chooses,' Lady Beaufort said sharply.

'He might spare a thought for my Owen trying to make ends meet after he's gone.'

After the strenuous activity of the morning, Daisy was too hungry to pay their sniping much heed at the time. Later, when they went out to the hall after lunch, she said to Lucy, 'Mrs. Howell's certainly changed her tune, hasn't she!'

'Has she?'

'Didn't you notice? Yesterday she was all deference to Lady Beaufort. At lunch she contradicted her practically every time she opened her mouth.'

'I wasn't listening.'

'But don't you think it's odd? Perhaps she's realising that a title isn't all it's cracked up to be. I must say, Lady Beaufort gave as good as she got.'

'I have to go back and take some more flash photos,' said the single-minded Lucy. 'Will you come and lend a hand?'

'I can't, darling. I'm going to be interrogating Armitage for my article.'

'Blast! Then I can't have him to help with the flash.'

'Try Rhino.'

'Not something likely!'

'Mrs. Howell might lend you a servant. But considering the mood she's in, I'd ask Barker instead, if I were you. Or Julia might do it. She has to escort her mother there anyway. There's nothing to carry, remember. You left all your stuff in the hermit's lair.'

'Yes, Armitage swore it would be safe. Everything will have to be carried back here, though.'

'I'm sure you'll work something out. If you're not back by tea-time, I'll send a rescue party. I've got to fetch a new notebook and meet Armitage in the muniments room. Toodle-oo.'

'Pritchard has a muniments room? That's a bit grandiose for a plumber!'

'I suppose title deeds and other legal documents relate to the property itself as well as to the family that used to own it. I'm hoping Armitage will tell me what became of the Appsworths. I must go. Good luck with the photos. At least Lady Beaufort should be easier to keep out of the pictures than Rhino!'

Following the directions of the ever-efficient Barker, Daisy found the muniments room without difficulty, though it was tucked away in an odd corner of the ground floor near the servants' wing. Armitage was already there, standing at the window, gazing out at a small paved courtyard. A pretty housemaid was crossing it, carrying a basket. By the slump of his shoulders, Armitage did not find the sight cheering.

Daisy hesitated on the threshold, then tapped on the door. He swung round.

'Mrs. Fletcher! Sorry, I was a long way away.'

'In Canada?'

'Well, yes.'

'Whereabouts?'

'Toronto. That's where I live.'

'It's quite a big city, isn't it?'

'Part of your vast fund of apparently useless information? Not by London standards, but yes, it's over half a million, and growing fast.' Abruptly he changed the subject. 'What is it you want to know about the house?'

'Anything that might appeal to the average reader of magazines.'

'The average reader?'

'Do I detect a "tone of intellectual snobbery"?'

'What?' he asked, startled.

'Shaw. George Bernard. At least, I'm pretty sure he's responsible.'

He laughed. 'Now who's using a tone of intellectual snobbery! I've no idea of the intellectual capacities of the average reader of magazines.'

'Well, they're literate,' Daisy explained kindly. 'I'm not writing for the *Illustrated London News*. Let's start with basic facts such as when the house was built and who the architect was. I take it you know?'

He was in fact extremely knowledgeable about the building and quite willing to talk about it.

After scribbling down a couple of pages of notes, Daisy stemmed the flow. 'Hold on! This is far more information than any of my readers, however literate, are likely to want to know. Unless they're students of architecture, which seems unlikely. Is that what you are?'

'Pritchard knows far more about it than I do. You should ask him to give you a tour, as he did me.'

'Really? I didn't know he was interested in anything but the plumbing.'

'He bought the Hall because he'd visited it in

125

his professional capacity and fell in love with it. They consulted him, hoping to modernise the plumbing, but they couldn't afford more than minor updates.'

'They?'

'The Appsworths.' His terseness contrasted with his previous loquacity.

'You've been studying the family papers. What's your interest in Appsworth Hall?'

'I hardly think that's relevant to your article, Mrs. Fletcher.'

'Not at all. I'm just curious. Nosy, if you prefer.'

His lips twitched. 'As a matter of fact, I'm a historian.'

'How very respectable. Why make such a mystery of it?'

'I haven't made a mystery of it.'

'Oh yes you have. Why else would Lucy and I be seething with curiosity? Well, actually, Lucy hasn't been thinking about anything much beyond her photography. But I've been seething like billy-oh. It's one of the perils of my profession. Does Julia know?'

'Yes. Not that it's any of your business.'

'But Lady Beaufort doesn't. Why on earth don't you tell her?'

'She wants Julia to marry wealth and a title. Who can blame her? Julia deserves the best of everything.'

'Don't be soppy. Julia deserves a chance to be happy. Titles don't bring happiness.'

'All right! Forget the title. I can't see much in it myself.'

'Being rich isn't much more to the point. I've

126

known dozens of rich people who weren't happy.'

'Dozens?' Armitage asked sceptically.

'Plenty, anyway. As long as she doesn't have to live on sardines... Are you a professional historian, or is it a hobby? Or are you going to write an article about the Appsworths? That would explain why you don't want to tell me about them. You want to scoop me!'

'Bosh! I may write an article, or even a book, but it'll be the scholarly kind with lots of footnotes, no competition for you.'

'Well, talk about intellectual snobbery!'

'Sorry. But you must agree we have different aims and audiences. As a matter of fact, I'm a lecturer in history at the University of Toronto.'

'What are you doing here in the middle of term-time?'

'I took the term off – what they call a "sabbatical" in the States – to come over and do some research into – some historical research.'

Daisy was sure he'd been going to say something else, but it really wasn't her business, she decided regretfully. 'A lecturer... Surely you can afford to support a wife in reasonable comfort? Things can't be so different in Canada. Or – don't tell me they still insist on dons being celibate?'

'Good lord, no! Even Oxford and Cambridge gave that up decades ago. If I were an Oxbridge don I might conceivably be acceptable to Lady Beaufort. Though I doubt it,' he added gloomily. 'Not with that fellow Rydal hanging about.'

'For pity's sake, you don't think Julia would agree to marry Rhino just to please her mother?

127

Talk about a fate worse than death! If all you're worried about is living with a disapproving mother-in-law, I can give you a few tips. Not that Lady Beaufort could possibly hold a candle to Alec's mother in that respect. Nor to my mother, from Alec's point of view. And you'd have the Atlantic between you.'

'What if she wanted to go with us?'

'You do like to borrow trouble, don't you? I shouldn't think it's likely. Isn't Toronto in the Arctic?'

'Not quite! It does get pretty cold in the winter, though. Another reason for Lady Beaufort not to want Julia to marry me.'

'Do stop being such a defeatist! Faint heart never won fair lady. Think of all the English-women who go off to India and Africa with their menfolk to rule the Empire. They put up with much worse than a bit of snow.'

'Undeniable. Toronto is really a very pleasant city, even under several feet of snow. Mrs. Fletcher, have you ever considered setting up as an agony aunt?'

'An agony aunt? You mean one of those columnists who dishes out advice to people who write letters to the popular papers?'

'Yes. I believe you'd be very good at it.'

Daisy gave him a suspicious look. 'I'm sorry if you think I'm being officious, interfering in your affairs.'

'Well, you are, you know. But kindly meant, I know. And you're making awfully good sense. I'm sure you'd be good at it professionally. I promise I shan't dismiss your words of wisdom out of hand. I need time to think.'

'I'll give you time to think when you give me some information about the Appsworths.'

Armitage sighed. 'Tenacious, aren't you? What sort of stuff are you after?'

Once he'd made up his mind to it, Armitage provided Daisy with several stories of a sort she could use in her article. One she particularly liked was about an eighteenth-century daughter of the house who had eloped with a handsome groom. Unlike most of its kind, the tale had a happy ending. The couple had been welcomed back into the bosom of the family because the groom was the only person capable of managing her papa's favourite stallion.

'Perfect! I suppose they wrote reams of letters about it? And someone saved them all? Being a historian is going to get much more difficult, don't you think, now that people send telegrams and ring each other up on the phone. No one saves telegrams.'

'That's an interesting point, Mrs. Fletcher. When it comes to consideration of our times, future historians will have the newspapers, with everything they consider worthy of being printed, and I don't suppose the bureaucracy will ever cease to produce rivers of paper. But social historians won't have so much in the way of personal papers to delve into, I guess.'

'Still, most of those personal papers were always produced by a very small section of the population, weren't they? So history's been biased towards the rich and literate. Now most people are literate but most can't afford phones

129

and cables, so they write letters, so history will be biased towards them. Does that make sense?'

'Very much so.'

'I'm never sure whether my logic is leading me round in circles. I'll tell you what else they'll have to delve into: gossip columns for the rich and famous, and for the others, the columns of agony aunts!'

'With a good deal more truth in the latter than the former, no doubt!' Armitage said, laughing. 'I hope you have all you need for your article, Mrs. Fletcher. You've just about wrung me dry.'

Daisy still wanted to know what had led to the Appsworths losing their family estate. However, she probably wouldn't be able to use it in the article, and she didn't want to try his patience too far. 'Yes, thanks,' she said. 'You've been frightfully helpful. Now I just have to ask Mr. Pritchard to give me a tour of the house. I wonder whether he'll be going into Swindon tomorrow.'

'I can't help you there. It depends on Wandersley, I guess.'

'You don't know exactly what he's here for, do you?'

He shrugged. 'Only that it involves considerable prestige as well as profit for Pritchard's Plumbing Products. I hope the old boy gets it. He's a good chap. My apologies, by the way, for the excessive alliteration. It's difficult to avoid.'

'Perhaps,' Daisy suggested, 'you should take up writing advertising slogans.'

Not until she was in the middle of transcribing her shorthand into something more readable did she realise that, by chance or deliberately, he had never actually explained his interest in the Appsworths' papers. It was all very well saying he was a historian. The Appsworths had been an obscure country family with no claim to fame, a very minor barony who rarely made an appearance in the public life of the country, and never notably. So what was it about them that had drawn the attention of a Canadian academic?

CHAPTER 14

Of the Swindon contingent only Mr. Pritchard returned to Appsworth Hall in time for tea, as befitted his semi-retired status. He came in a little late, fetched himself a cup of tea from Mrs. Howell, and went to sit by Lady Beaufort.

'I hear you visited my grotto,' he said. 'How did you like it?'

'Sheer folly,' said her ladyship, 'but a most amusing folly.'

He laughed. Daisy caught only snatches of their conversation thereafter, because Lucy was intent on describing every photo she had taken that afternoon. She explained which shots she expected to come out best, and wanted Daisy's opinion as to whether she should take any more.

'I was thinking, I might be able to get something worthwhile of the monk. Sort of blurry and atmospheric.'

'Ghostly.'

'Yes. Too silly, do you think? It's just that this is

the first folly we've tackled that deserves more than a couple of illustrations, at most.'

'Nothing venture, nothing gain. We don't have to use it if it doesn't work.'

'I'll have to persuade Armitage to pose for me again.'

'Not on the edge!'

'No, by St. Whatsit, I think.' Lucy fell silent, pondering ways and means.

Pritchard was urging Lady Beaufort, 'You should really see it by night.'

'Julia tells me it's beautifully illuminated. But I don't know... It's quite a walk up that hill. You should put in some sort of seats for us elderly folk.'

'Elderly? Not you, Lady Beaufort! But that's an excellent notion. I can't imagine why I didn't think of it before. This evening – if you'd like to go up this evening? – I could have chairs carried up.'

'Let's try it,' said Lucy, emerging from her abstraction. 'Where's–? Oh, he's talking to Mrs. Howell. Blast.'

'I think it's more a case of Mrs. Howell talking to him, or *at* him. I expect he'd be glad to be rescued. I'll leave you to it. I'm going to ask Mr. Pritchard if he'll give me a tour of the house tomorrow. And then I'd better rescue Julia from Rhino and Lady Ottaline.'

'Right-oh, but for pity's sake don't breathe a word about going back to the grotto. The last thing I need is that blundering jackass ruining any more shots. I should charge him for the wasted plates.'

'Try sending him a bill. You never know.'

Of course, Lucy's hope of returning to the grotto without a flock of companions hadn't a chance. Lady Beaufort expressed a preference for going there after tea rather than waiting until after dinner. Lucy promptly told Armitage that after dinner would suit her best – she had preparations to make, she said vaguely – and he agreed. Then Lady Beaufort said that of course Julia would go with her; she didn't propose to walk that path in the dark without her daughter's support. Armitage promptly changed his mind.

'Lady Beaufort would like to see the hermit, I expect,' he said, while Lucy simmered. 'I'll go ahead and light the lamps, sir, shall I?'

'Certainly, my boy. I'm sure Lord Rydal will help to carry your equipment, Lady Gerald.'

'Me? What the deuce d'you think I am, a pack-horse?'

'A gentleman?' Pritchard hazarded, a glint in his eye.

Rhino had no answer to that.

'Daisy,' Lucy hissed, 'you've got to come, too, and *please* do a better job this time of keeping everyone out of sight.'

In the end everyone went except Mrs. Howell. Daisy was surprised that Lady Ottaline wanted to venture back to the scene of her accident, especially as Rhino was too laden for her to cling to him. He was too laden even to smoke. Somehow Pritchard seemed to have gained the upper hand.

While Lady Beaufort was exclaiming in delight at the illuminated cascade, Lucy chivvied Rhino

133

up the steps. Daisy couldn't decide whether she ought to follow them to keep him out of Lucy's way or stand guard at the bottom to stop Lady Ottaline chasing after him.

Then Lady Beaufort asked Lady Ottaline how she had come to fall. 'The path is perfectly adequate,' she said magisterially, 'whatever shoes you were so ill-advised as to wear.'

As Lady Ottaline replied, Daisy left them and hurried upwards. The moment Rhino reached the grotto he put down his burdens and lit a cigarette. 'Enough is enough,' he snorted. 'I can't see why you don't use a Brownie.'

Lucy was speechless with fury. Ruthlessly sacrificing Julia's comfort for the sake of Lucy's blood-pressure, Daisy shooed Rhino back down. 'Thank you, we'll manage now. Come on, darling, before they all arrive.'

The hermit came from the rear, robed but uncowled. 'Let me give you a hand. You'll have to explain exactly what you want me to do, Lady Gerald.'

'I'm not absolutely certain myself, yet. Do call me Lucy, won't you?'

'Sure. I'm Chuck back home, but Julia doesn't like it, so let's stick to Charles.'

'And I'm Daisy, Charles. Lucy, I think I'd better go back and try to fend off the others.'

From the top step, holding tight to the rail, Daisy saw Rhino go straight to Julia. The noise of the waterfall prevented Daisy's hearing what was said, but it looked to her as if he interrupted whatever Julia was saying to her mother. To Daisy's astonishment, Lady Beaufort turned to him and said something sharp enough to make him take a step backwards.

Fortunately he was facing the stream – not that Daisy would have been averse to seeing him topple in again.

Could it be, she wondered, that a few days in the same house as the rich Lord Rydal had made Lady Beaufort reassess his desirability as a son-in-law? For Julia's sake, she hoped so.

Rhino might conceivably be doing some re-assessment, too. Lady Beaufort, the widow of a mere knight even if he had been a general, was not the first person at Appsworth to fail to kow-tow before his hitherto invincible complacency. Julia persisted in refusing to marry him, yet at her bidding he did such menial tasks as fetching luggage from the station. Lucy ordered him about. Even Pritchard had made him back down.

On the other hand, Rhino was so conceited, he probably managed to convert these incidents in his mind into further proof of his superiority to the rest of mankind.

'Daisy!' Lucy called from the back of the grotto.

Daisy moved away from the waterfall's roar. 'Yes?'

'Didn't you hear me? We're ready to shoot, but I don't want to start if everyone's about to barge in. Are you on guard?'

'Horatio on the bridge was nothing to me, darling,' Daisy said resolutely.

'Well, don't go plunging into the Tiber if they do overwhelm you, but do your best.' She disap-peared behind Neptune.

135

To carry out the parallel to Horatio, Daisy ought to stand at the most defensible point, the bottom of the steps. However, she couldn't see herself barring Lady Beaufort and Pritchard from his grotto. She glanced around. A couple of basket chairs had been brought in and placed to one side, with a good view of Neptune and the spot where the river emerged from the rock through the gaping mouth of a sea serpent. They were reasonable people and, given a place to rest their bones, would certainly comply with a request not to go through to the second cave to disturb Lucy. So would Julia.

Neither Rhino nor Lady Ottaline could by any stretch of the imagination be described as reasonable. But Rhino would stay with Julia and Lady Ottaline would cling to Rhino.

Or so Daisy hoped.

Julia arrived first, looking harried.

'Hold up the monster till I have a chance to hide!' she begged.

'Sorry, no can do. He'd only come looking for you, and Lucy and I are counting on you to keep him out here till she's finished shooting Charles.'

'Shooting–! Oh, shooting. But–'

'A small sacrifice for the sake of Art,' Daisy urged, 'with a capital *A*. Not to mention for *my* sake. Lucy will never forgive me if he ruins another picture, and I was counting on you to act as my barricade.'

'Oh, all right. But if it makes him think I'm softening towards him, *I* may never forgive you.'

Lady Beaufort reached the top of the steps, panting a little. Pritchard was close behind her.

'You see, Lady Beaufort,' he said triumphantly, 'I had chairs brought up, just as I promised. Do come and sit down.'

'How kind!' Her ladyship beamed. 'Julia, my love, you were quite right to insist on my seeing the grotto at night. It's like something out of the *Arabian Nights*. Daisy, I hope you and Lucy will do it justice in your book.'

'We'll do our best, though I doubt that it's possible. People will have to come and see for themselves.'

'The more the merrier,' said Mr. Pritchard.

'Well, I've seen it before.' Lady Ottaline arrived complaining. 'I don't know why you made me come, Rhino.'

'Made you come! I tried to persuade you to stay behind. I don't know why you insisted on tagging along.'

'I thought I ought to face it,' she said bravely. 'Don't they say one should climb straight back on a horse after falling? But now ... I'm afraid it's too much for me...' And she fainted gracefully into Rhino's unwelcoming arms.

He didn't exactly drop her, but he deposited her none too gently on the cold stone floor and stepped away. 'Mrs. Fletcher, could you–'

'I don't know the first thing about nursing,' Daisy said firmly, giving Julia a nudge. As far as she knew, Julia had no more expertise than she did, but while she was succouring Lady Ottaline, Rhino would be stymied.

Julia moved forwards hesitantly.

'I believe it's a hysterical fit,' Lady Beaufort said in robust tones. 'The most efficacious treatment

137

to attempt is a slap on the face.'

Lady Ottaline made a miraculous recovery. She sat up, saying, 'Oh, where am I?'

'There, just as I suspected,' said Lady Beaufort. 'It's an old-fashioned remedy, but it frequently works even before it's applied.'

The light was far from bright, but Daisy thought she saw Pritchard smother a grin. He came over and helped Lady Ottaline up, saying, 'I'm so sorry your accident last night has had such a lasting ill-effect. I can't abandon Lady Beaufort, but I'm sure Lord Rydal will be happy to support you back to the house. Sir Desmond should be back from the works by now. He'll know what to do to make you comfortable.'

Her husband's name brought a sour-lemon look to Lady Ottaline's crimson lips. It was momentary, outweighed by the prospect of getting Rhino to herself.

Rhino had no such counterbalance to his bile. 'I don't see why she can't go and lie down for a bit on the hermit's bed till she's recovered,' he said mutinously.

'No one may go through the inner cave till Lucy's finished!' Daisy declared, taking up a militant position in front of Neptune.

'I can't believe my ears!' said Julia in a shocked voice. 'Rhino, surely you aren't so ungallant as to make a lady in distress walk alone through the night, especially along that dangerous pathway.'

Rhino was neither capable of looking abashed, nor of giving in graciously, but he did give in.

Just as he and Lady Ottaline departed, Lucy came through from the inner grotto. Looking after them, she asked, 'Where are they going?'

'Lord Rydal is escorting Lady Ottaline back to the house,' Pritchard told her.

'Are you finished, darling?' Daisy asked. 'That was quick.'

'No, Julia! You can't go through. He'll move if he sees you and he has to stand absolutely still for another minute and a half. You must be mad to let Rhino take her back alone after she fell in last time. Got to go. If this works, it's going to be ripping!' And she whisked back round Neptune.

Pritchard frowned. 'What does Lady Gerald mean? Surely she's not suggesting Lord Rydal was responsible for Lady Ottaline's fall? I thought they seemed – quite fond of each other.'

'Say rather, on terms of considerable intimacy!' Lady Beaufort said severely.

'In the recent past, perhaps.' Daisy was hesitant, Alec having frequently reminded her not to mistake speculation for fact. 'We've wondered, Lucy and I, whether he hasn't been trying to convince her it's over.'

'Well, I won't have a guest pushed over,' Pritchard declared, 'not into my stream. I'm going to keep an eye on them.'

'I hardly think he'd do anything drastic when we all know he's alone with her,' said Daisy, but Pritchard was already on his way to the front of the grotto.

'Perhaps Lady Ottaline will push Rhino in,' Julia said hopefully, and followed Pritchard.

'Oh dear,' said Lady Beaufort, 'the earl won't do for Julia, will he? I'm quite disillusioned. He's not at all the sort of gentleman I wish her to marry.'

'Gentleman he's not,' said Daisy, 'for all his wealth and rank.'

'Which doesn't mean I shall allow her to marry a penniless colonial nobody! So don't go giving her any ideas, Daisy.'

Daisy was baffled. Why on earth didn't Julia tell her mother that while Armitage was not rich and titled, he was perfectly respectable and able to support her in better style than she had managed to survive these past several years? Surely his ridiculous qualms weren't holding her back. The weather, forsooth!

He must have told her to keep it secret. Could he be afraid Lady Beaufort might write to the University of Toronto and discover he didn't exist – so to speak? Or he did exist, and was peacefully going about his business teaching history to a lot of young Canadians while an impostor paraded under his name in England?

Pure speculation, Daisy reminded herself. All the same, something was rotten in the province of Ontario. She must get Julia alone and ask her what was going on.

'He hasn't done anything terrible.' Pritchard returned from the waterfall lookout looking cheerful. He was talking about Rhino, of course, not Armitage. 'They're round the bend,' he went on. 'It's much shallower there, so she couldn't come to any harm if she did fall in. And I must be round the bend to let Lady Gerald make me think for a moment that the earl would do anything so wicked.'

CHAPTER 15

In spite of Pritchard's half-joking words, Daisy noticed that on the way back to the house he kept casting anxious glances at the stream. Nothing untoward was visible. When they reached the house, Barker informed them that the Swindon party had returned and everyone had gone up to dress for dinner.

'Including Lady Ottaline?' Pritchard asked.

'Certainly, sir. I myself saw Lady Ottaline go upstairs with Sir Desmond.' The butler addressed his employer in indulgent, slightly condescending, almost fatherly tones, although he looked twenty years younger than Pritchard. Daisy realised she'd heard him speak the same way before.

'As though he used to work for an irascible duke,' she said later to Lucy, when she went to her room to see if she was ready to go down. 'And Pritchard is much pleasanter to work for, besides paying much better, but nonetheless the duke was infinitely superior.'

'For heaven's sake, Daisy, of course he was. If he exists outside your imagination. What a lot of rot you talk! What does it matter?'

'I was thinking I might interview Barker for my Servant Problem article.'

'You've been working on that for three years.'

'You never know, I might finish it before servants go the way of the dinosaurs. Are you ready at last? Let's go. That frock is much more suitable than last night's.'

'Well, I can't compete with Julia, whatever I wear, and to try to outshine Lady Ottaline would be pathetic.'

'The poor thing's rather pathetic all round, isn't she?'

'Darling, if I ever get like that, you will stop me, won't you?' Lucy studied her face in the looking glass. 'I'm not too old and too *married* to care about fashion, am I? Like all those frightful fat matrons who buy the latest frock from Paris straight off the mannequin, expecting to look like her?'

'It'll be a few years yet, darling, and no one could call you fat. I'll tell you when the moment comes, but I expect you won't want to hear. Come on. A single dab of powder more would be gilding the lily.'

Everyone except Lady Ottaline was already in the drawing room. Howell gave Daisy a glass of Cinzano and soda and she glanced around.

Sir Desmond, bland and sleek as ever, was talking to Pritchard. Lady Beaufort had captured Armitage and Carlin and was listening to the former with an assessing look in her eye. Rhino shared a sofa with Julia – how could she have been so careless as to sit down on an otherwise unoccupied sofa? – and was holding forth. Julia's expression of polite interest suggested she was enduring excruciating boredom. Mrs. Howell, in a chair on Rhino's other side, received no share of his attention. She looked disgruntled. She ought, in Daisy's opinion, to be grateful.

Howell handed Lucy her gin and It. 'I hear you had a successful photography session in the grotto,' he said.

'I hope so,' Lucy said cautiously. 'One can never be sure till the plates are developed.'

They went on to technical talk. Daisy drifted over to Pritchard and Sir Desmond.

'I hope I'm not interrupting business,' she said.

'All work and no play makes Jack a dull boy,' Pritchard assured her.

'Oh dear, I'm afraid it's work I wanted to talk to you about, but mine, of course, not yours.'

'How is your "work" going?' Sir Desmond's eyebrows put jocular quotation marks round *work*, making an otherwise innocuous question patronising.

Daisy considered giving him one of her mother's grande-dame looks, but she decided he wasn't the sort to be impressed. Or even to notice. 'Very well indeed, thank you. Mr. Pritchard and Mr. Armitage have been extremely helpful. Mr. Pritchard, I wondered whether you'd be so kind as to give me a tour of the house tomorrow, if you don't have to go to Swindon. Mr. Armitage told me you're a wonderful guide.'

'I'd be happy to, my dear. Owen will complete your business, Sir Desmond. I have every faith in his abilities. You won't really need me there. Excuse me, here's Lady Ottaline. I'll just make sure she gets her cocktail as Owen's busy discussing photography with Lady Gerald.'

Watching him go, Sir Desmond swigged down half a tumbler of whisky. 'There goes a happy man.' He sounded more cynical than admiring or

143

envious. 'Wealth, no wife, no children, no worries.'

Daisy ignored most of this and said, 'Have you children, Sir Desmond?'

'I do, Mrs. Fletcher. For my sins, I do. A son who believes he's a poet, and a daughter addicted to good works.'

Daisy wondered just how much whisky he'd put away. To her relief, Barker came in and announced that dinner was served.

In the hall, he discreetly beckoned her aside. 'A telephone message, madam, from the local exchange. Mr. Fletcher wired to say he and Lord Gerald Bincombe will arrive tomorrow afternoon. About four o'clock, he hopes.'

'Spiffing! Have you told Lucy – Lady Gerald? Mr. Pritchard? Mrs. Howell?'

'Since the message was for you, madam, I have not.'

'I hope Mr. Pritchard informed Mrs. Howell that he'd invited them.'

'I believe so, madam. The housekeeper was aware that further guests might arrive.'

'Thank you, Barker.' Daisy was much relieved. She had no faith whatever that Mrs. Howell would welcome unexpected guests, even if one of them came with a title attached. 'Please pass the word to Mrs Howell and the housekeeper that they're definitely coming.'

'Certainly, madam.'

Daisy caught up with Lucy. 'A message from Alec, darling. They're coming.'

'Gerald's coming with Alec?' Lucy's face lit up at Daisy's nod. 'Oh, good.'

Seated on Pritchard's left, opposite Lady Beau-

144

fort, Daisy told him at once about Alec and Gerald's proposed arrival. He was delighted.

So was Lady Beaufort. 'I'm looking forward to meeting your husband, Daisy.'

Blast! Daisy thought. She remembered Lucy saying the Beauforts knew Alec was a copper, and she hadn't asked Julia to suggest to her mother that the fact was best kept quiet. In her experience people, however honest, tended to act oddly if they knew there was a policeman in the house, however off-duty. She took a spoonful of soup, trying to decide how to carry it off.

But Lady Beaufort was a woman of discretion. She said to Pritchard, 'We met Lord Gerald in London. I know you will like him. He plays rugger, and you Welshmen are all devotees of rugger, aren't you?'

'Naturally. We're the best players.'

'Tell that to Gerald,' Daisy said. 'He played for his university, though I can't remember whether he's light or dark blue.'

'I've no doubt he'll agree with me, Mrs. Fletcher. Half the varsity players are Welshmen, if not more.'

Lady Beaufort laughed. 'I'll have to ask Lord Gerald.'

At the far end of the table, Mrs. Howell said belligerently, 'Well, Brin, Barker tells me we are to expect two more guests. I hope they don't expect fish for dinner. I've taken it off the menu. For good.' And she glared at Lord Rydal.

'Thank you, Winifred. I'm much obliged.'

Daisy was careful not to look towards Lucy or Julia lest they all disgrace themselves again. 'Alec

145

won't mind. His hours are so irregular we don't go in for five-course dinners. Our cook is an expert at casseroles and things that won't spoil keeping hot in the oven.' She suddenly realised she had laid herself open to the question of what exactly Alec did, just what she wanted to avoid. 'What about Gerald, Lucy?' she asked hastily.

'The only kind of fish Gerald really enjoys,' Lucy said dryly, 'is the kind that comes in batter, with chipped potatoes, wrapped in newspaper. Frightfully plebeian, but he says nothing's better after a game of Rugby and a few beers.'

'And beer after the game,' said Pritchard, 'is of course an essential part of Rugby football!'

Throughout this exchange, Rhino had stared in disbelief at Mrs. Howell. 'Well! I thought you'd be grateful for a hint or two about how things are done in the best houses. But it's obviously a waste of time trying to raise people above their natural level.'

'I should certainly never attempt it with you, Rhino,' said Lucy.

Mrs. Howell, taking not the slightest notice, continued to drink her soup.

Lady Beaufort said softly, 'My dear Mr. Pritchard, I can't express how sorry I am we ever brought the man down upon you. If the only way to induce him to leave is for us to go, we'll take our departure tomorrow.'

'Nonsense! I won't allow a boor to upset our arrangements. You were to stay till Monday and till Monday you shall stay. But next time I invite you, I shall send my own car to fetch you from London.'

'How kind!' She patted his hand – not the one holding the soup spoon, fortunately, as he was left-handed. 'I should like to see the gardens in summer, I must admit.'

'So you shall.'

Everyone started talking about gardens. Rhino's contribution was a rant against his head gardener, who never seemed able to supply the required vegetables for his kitchens.

'No doubt he expects French beans in February and asparagus in August,' Daisy said, but she spoke in a low voice, not wanting to reignite the embers.

Only Pritchard heard her. He responded, 'Let's hope no one brings up the subject of fishponds.'

The rest of the evening passed reasonably smoothly. In the morning Daisy got up quite early again, although Lucy wasn't hurrying her to catch the sunlight. In fact, the sun was rising behind a haze of high, thin cloud. Rain before nightfall, she thought.

She had forgotten last night to ask Pritchard what time would be convenient for him to show her the house. She didn't want to keep him waiting. Hence the early rising.

This time only Carlin and Armitage were down before her. They were talking about fly-fishing.

'An innocuous subject, one would think,' said Carlin.

'But to be approached with caution in this house at present,' Armitage added.

'Definitely!' Daisy agreed, helping herself to a couple of rashers of bacon and a muffin.

'Before we ventured into such deep waters, we

were wondering if we ought to offer to throw the rhinoceros out. He's big and stubborn, but between the two of us we ought to be able to manage it. What do you think, Mrs. Fletcher?'

'Should we tell our esteemed host that we're not merely willing but anxious to go big game hunting?'

Armitage grinned. 'It'd make a change from angling.'

'No,' said Daisy.

'No?' Carlin was disappointed. 'Expound, pray.'

'If you ask me, Mr. Pritchard is perfectly capable of routing Rhino if he chooses. If he lets him stay till Monday, which is when he's supposed to leave, it's for his own reasons. Better not to interfere.'

'By Jove, wheels within wheels we wot not of!' Carlin exclaimed facetiously.

'Not at all. Just better to let sleeping rhinoceroses lie,' Daisy advised.

'If only he *would* sleep,' Armitage sighed.

'He hasn't come down yet,' Daisy pointed out. 'Enjoy the peace and quiet while you may. Don't let me interrupt the fishing. You must strike while the fish are biting.'

They took her at her word. She was able to add her own mite to the discussion as her brother Gervaise had occasionally condescended to take her fishing with him on the Severn in her youth, in another world. Gervaise, had he survived the trenches, would not have approved of this world where his sister consorted on the friendliest of terms with a plumber, she thought sadly.

Howell came in next. 'Glad to see you're up

and about,' he said to Carlin. 'What do you suppose is the earliest we can expect your lord and master to be ready to go into Swindon?'

'Eleven. At the very earliest. He has to have his after-breakfast stroll alone with his cigar and his thoughts or his digestion goes wonky. You saw him strolling up and down the terrace yesterday, remember.'

'Pity it's not raining,' said Howell, glancing at the window.

'Believe me, you wouldn't want to try to work with him when his digestion's wonky. It's a concession to work at all today. He doesn't usually come in to the office on Saturdays, though I'm junior enough to have to put in a brief appearance. It's a good job there's not much left to be done. I shouldn't think you'll be able to keep him at it for very long, and he'll expect at least an hour's lunch break.'

'I don't want to hold it over till Monday.' Howell frowned. 'I have other business scheduled. If we don't leave till eleven, I doubt we'll be home before five.'

Carlin shrugged. 'Sorry, old chap, nothing I can do about it.'

'"The customer is always right,"' Howell said with a sigh. 'I sometimes think it's a pity Selfridge ever coined the phrase.'

'I'm supposed to be playing golf tomorrow, myself, in Essex. It's a tournament. I was hoping to catch a train back to town tonight.'

'That shouldn't be difficult. Swindon being a junction on the Bristol line, there are plenty of fast trains.'

'Good! I'll pack my bag and take it with me. But first, another sausage or two. May I bring you something, Mrs. Fletcher?'

Daisy was munching a second muffin when Pritchard, Julia, and Lucy came in.

'I'm going to tour the house with you, Daisy,' said Lucy. 'I have two unused plates left, and plenty of magnesium, so I'll take a couple of photos for you if you see anything you'd like for your article.'

'You're all finished with the grotto, are you?' Armitage asked.

'Yes. A good job I caught the sun yesterday. It looks like rain.'

'The grotto's a bit dank in wet weather,' Pritchard conceded, 'though the hermit's lair is cosy with the fire lit.'

'I know Alec will want to see it,' said Daisy. 'How about Gerald, Lucy? Do you think he's interested?'

'I haven't the slightest, but if so he can go with you and Alec. I've had enough of tramping that path. What time did you say they're arriving?'

'Barker told me four o'clock. Good morning, Rhino.'

Rhino produced a morose grunt and waved a sort of greeting with his cigarette holder, already sending up a tendril of smoke. Without further acknowledgement of the company, he headed for the food.

'It'll still be light enough to see the grotto in daylight, then,' Lucy said. 'Or were you going to show Alec the night spectacle?'

'Depends what the weather looks like. I

150

wouldn't want to tackle the path at night in the rain.'

'Just let me know if you want to go after dark,' said Pritchard, 'and I'll have the lamps lit for you.'

'I'll do it,' Armitage volunteered. He smiled at Julia as he spoke. No doubt she would join the tour.

Pritchard got up. 'I've one or two things to see to in my den, Mrs. Fletcher. If you wouldn't mind, you and Lady Gerald, coming there in half an hour or so, I'll give you the grand tour.'

Having eaten all she wanted, if not more, Daisy sat on with another cup of tea, chatting. Eventually Sir Desmond put in an appearance. Howell and Carlin watched in dismay as the Principal Deputy Secretary helped himself to a huge plateful.

Daisy heard Howell mutter to Carlin, 'We'll be lucky to finish our business before dinner! Never mind, lad, there's a good late train.'

Unfortunately, Rhino also overheard. 'Anxious to get away early, are you?' he said with a sneer. 'All you bureaucrats are bone-lazy slackers. Take the taxpayer's money and do as little work as possible.'

Carlin turned scarlet. 'Sir Desmond, Mr. Howell, I'll be in my room when you're ready to leave,' he said with quiet dignity. 'Excuse me, ladies.'

Sir Desmond turned a long, considering look on Rhino, but sat down without saying anything and began his breakfast.

It was left to Julia to utter what everyone was

151

thinking. 'Rhino, you really are irredeemably vulgar.'

Rhino stared at her with blank incomprehension. 'You must be thinking of some other fellow,' he said. 'My shield has more quarterings than nine out of ten peers. Hasn't been a commoner in the family in three centuries.'

CHAPTER 16

Daisy was a bit disappointed with the house. The trouble was that it was such a perfect example of its kind that there wasn't really much to say about it. Houses with quirks and oddities were much easier to write about. With the grotto to describe and Armitage's stories about the Appsworths, however, she reckoned she had enough for an article of reasonable length.

One noticeable difference from the general run of stately homes was the lack of family portraits and knicknacks. Pritchard told Daisy and Lucy that he had bought almost all the Appsworths' furniture, all except the few pieces the last remaining family members chose to take with them.

'But I didn't think it was right to keep portraits that had nothing to do with my own ancestors,' he explained.

Lucy looked a trifle self-conscious. Her own family's rise was recent enough to provide no portraits older than Victorian. The walls of their huge entrance hall were hung with other people's ancestors.

'As for bits and bobs of precious porcelain on every surface,' Pritchard continued, 'I'd be afraid to move for fear of breaking something priceless.'

'Some of the ewers in your entrance hall must be valuable,' said Daisy.

'I daresay, but they're tucked up safe in those niches and Winifred insists on dusting the finest herself for fear the maids might break 'em.' He laughed. 'The girls are allowed to do the common china ones. Winifred keeps trying to persuade me to get rid of those, but they're *my* family's history.'

Daisy and Lucy settled on what photographs Lucy would take. Daisy helped with the flash apparatus, as usual ending up covered in whitish powder. She went to wash, then sought a place to transcribe her notes in peace.

Given the constraints of Lucy's car, she hadn't brought her portable typewriter, but the sooner she copied out her shorthand in longhand, the easier to remember what her erratic symbols were intended to represent. She tried the muniments room, but Julia was there with Charles Armitage. Though they insisted she was welcome to stay, she didn't want to disturb them. The library should be free. This was not a bookish household.

In the library, lined with tier after tier of leatherbound volumes most of which appeared never to have been opened since their purchase a century or two ago, Daisy found – of all people! – Rhino and Lady Ottaline, the latter in canary yellow this morning. They were standing by a window looking out onto the gravel drive at the front. Both gave her hostile glares. She would have preferred to leave them in peace, but she couldn't think of anywhere else to go. Her bedroom had no suitable table, and she really must unscramble her notes while they were fresh in her memory.

'Don't mind me,' she said brightly. 'I have some work to do. I'll be quiet as a mouse.'

'That's all right, Mrs. Fletcher,' said Lady Ottaline with equally spurious brightness. Unlike Rhino she had manners if not morals. 'We were just going. You're working on your magazine article? Sometimes I wish I had something useful to occupy my time.'

Daisy doubted a suggestion that ladies of her generation often took up charitable causes would be appreciated. Especially as, she now remembered Sir Desmond mentioning, their daughter was addicted to good works. She murmured something vague, sat down at a writing table, and opened her notebook.

They passed her on their way to the door, polluting the air with the inevitable cigarette smoke as they went. Daisy wasn't listening, but she couldn't help hearing Lady Ottaline saying to Rhino, 'I told you, nowhere in the house is really private. That's why we–' The closing door cut her off.

Why they what. Daisy wondered. The weather was not conducive to canoodling out of doors. Surely Lady Ottaline hadn't had the bright idea of seeking privacy in the hermit's lair?

Daisy quickly forgot about them, becoming

absorbed in trying to decide whether she had intended one particular scribble to represent *marble* or *marquetry*. Perhaps she ought to take a refresher course in shorthand.

She finished transcribing just in time for lunch. Lady Ottaline arrived late for the meal, causing their hostess to sit throughout in tight-lipped silence, no great loss to the conversation. Afterwards, Mrs. Howell led the way through to the drawing room for coffee. She sat down and started pouring, while Armitage went to her to hand round the demitasse cups.

'There, that's for Lady Ottaline. Black without sugar, isn't that right Lady— Where is Lady Ottaline?'

'I expect she went to powder her nose, Winifred.'

'Well, I do think she might have said a word to me. Some people never spare a thought for other people's convenience. Now her coffee's going to get cold and be wasted.'

'We can't have that,' Pritchard said jovially. 'Give it to me.'

'You like yours half milk.'

'I'll be a martyr.'

'No need for martyrdom,' Lucy drawled. 'I drink it black, no sugar. I'll take it, Charles.'

'Lord Rydal isn't here either,' Mrs. Howell complained. 'Not that I expect better manners of him.'

Just as Lucy took her first sip, Lady Ottaline came in from the hall. Her make-up failed to hide flushed cheeks, and her eyes glittered.

'Ah, coffee! I don't suppose, dear Mr. Pritchard, I could have a drop of brandy in mine?'

'Of course, Lady Ottaline. Anyone else fancy a drop?'

No one else did. Mrs. Howell poured coffee; Armitage took it to the Welsh dresser, where he added brandy. He handed it to Lady Ottaline, who had followed, and she drifted over to the French windows. She stood gazing out, her back to the room.

Conversation, halted by her entrance, resumed. Lady Beaufort asked Daisy about her progress with her article. Daisy was trying to explain the difficulties of writing about a perfect house without it sounding like a lecture on architecture when Barker came in to announce that Lord Gerald Bincombe and Mr. Fletcher had arrived.

Pritchard popped up. 'Excellent, excellent! They've beaten the rain. You'll be able to show them the grotto, Mrs. Fletcher, without having to brave the path when it's wet.'

He hurried out to the hall. Daisy and Lucy went after him.

Daisy hadn't seen Gerald in a few months. He was the big, solid kind of rugger player, not the little wiry kind. Though Alec was tall and broad-shouldered, he looked barely average in size beside Gerald. He also looked considerably slimmer. Sitting in City boardrooms and consuming City lunches had added a few inches round Gerald's waist. By now, the occasional game of Rugby football was probably a ritual more honoured in the breach than the observance.

Alec, on the other hand, though he did more sitting behind desks than he would have preferred,

156

also did a fair amount of foot-slogging when he was on a case. Not infrequently his lunchtimes were a ritual more honoured in the breach than the observance.

Once all the greetings and introductions were out of the way, Daisy said, 'You're much earlier than we expected, darling.'

'We did manage to leave a bit early. But it's mostly because when I estimated the length of the journey, I failed to allow for Gerald's style of driving.'

Gerald grinned. 'Knew I was safe with a copper in the car. Fletcher kept his eyes peeled for peelers all the way. Would have spotted one half a mile off. Plenty of time to slow down.'

'It would have been very embarrassing to be stopped by a bobby who recognised me, even though I wasn't at the wheel.'

Pritchard turned to Alec. 'So you're a policeman, are you, Mr. Fletcher?'

'You let the cat out of the bag, darling,' Lucy said acidly to her husband.

'My own fault,' said Alec. 'Bincombe's usually such a taciturn chap, I didn't think to mention I prefer not to have it known. My apologies, Mr. Pritchard, if you feel I'm here under false pretences.'

'Not at all, not at all, my dear fellow. I daresay the reaction you get is a bit different, but there are times and places when I don't mention I'm a plumber by trade. No need to tell my sister-in-law, though,' he added hastily. He offered them something to eat, but they had stopped at a pub for a bite.

'Good,' said Daisy. 'I want to show you the grotto before it starts raining.'

'Give me time to catch my breath,' Alec begged.

'Coffee for the gentlemen, Barker,' Pritchard ordered.

'Darling, did you see the babies before you left?' Daisy asked on the way to the drawing room. 'How are they?'

'Blooming.'

'I wish they missed me,' she said mournfully.

In the drawing room, Pritchard introduced Alec and Gerald to Mrs. Howell, the Beauforts, and Charles Armitage. Predictably, Mrs. Howell gushed over Gerald and practically ignored Alec. Gerald let her gush. The Beauforts, having met Gerald in town, were more interested in Alec. They both managed not to reveal their knowledge of his profession, so Mrs. Howell and Armitage were the only two present to be left in ignorance. Unless, Daisy thought, Julia had told her beloved, in which case he was equally discreet.

An elderly parlour maid brought in fresh coffee. Daisy went to the window to look at the sky. The high, thin haze had thickened and lowered.

'Do drink up, darling,' she said. 'We'll have to go now to miss the downpour.'

'How badly do I want to see this grotto?'

'You mustn't feel obliged, Mr. Fletcher,' said Pritchard.

'Yes, you must,' said Daisy. 'Come on. Are you coming, Gerald?'

'Right-oh,' said Gerald, always obliging.

Turning away from the window, Daisy caught a

glimpse of someone moving in the garden below the terrace, just disappearing behind a yew hedge. Lady Ottaline? Surely not. But she was missing from the drawing room, Daisy realised. When had she left, before or after Alec and Gerald's arrival?

'Better take your umbrella, love,' said Alec.

'Lucy, coming?'

'Not me. Run along, children.'

'I'll go with you,' said Armitage. 'The more the merrier.'

'Julia, you'll come, won't you?' Daisy asked helpfully.

'Yes, I'd like to get some fresh air before the rain starts. Are you sure you won't come, Lucy?'

Lucy sighed and said, 'Oh, very well. I'll bring my Kodak and take a snap or two if there's enough light.'

Daisy was afraid Lady Beaufort would veto Julia's going with them now that the party looked so like three couples, rather than simply a mixed group. Perhaps her ladyship failed to hear their plans. A smile on her plump face, she was listening to Pritchard, who leant with one hand on the back of her armchair, bending towards her and speaking in a low voice.

'Sheer folly!' snapped Mrs. Howell. 'You'll all be soaked to the skin and my servants will be put to the trouble of drying all your things again.'

'*My* servants, Winifred,' Pritchard reminded her. '*My* guests, going to admire *my* folly. At least, I hope you will admire the grotto, gentlemen, and let's hope the rain will hold off till you return.'

He shepherded them out to the hall, where the omniprovident Barker had enough umbrellas waiting for all.

'Just in case it starts raining before you return,' he said.

'Barker,' said Lucy, 'do you know how to work a Kodak? It's very simple. I can show you in a minute. Would you come out to the terrace and take a snap of all of us in our expedition gear?'

Barker didn't bat an eyelid. 'Certainly, my lady.'

Five minutes later the six were posed on the flagged terrace, with the butler peering gravely at them through the viewfinder. 'Say "cheese,"' he instructed them.

It was so unexpected that they all laughed as he pressed the button.

At that very moment, as if caused by the action, came a huge *boom*. Behind them, windows rattled. All heads swung to stare towards the source of the explosion. The bare, grassy hillside to the southwest erupted in a shower of rocks. Daisy clutched Alec's arm.

And then, before her horrified eyes, a patch of the slope subsided into a sudden sink-hole. But a sink-hole surely wouldn't throw up boulders, nor sound like a bomb?

'What the deuce was that?' Gerald demanded.

'The grotto,' Armitage said grimly. 'It's blown up.'

'How could a cave blow up?' Alec asked in what Daisy called his 'policeman voice'. 'Pritchard surely didn't store munitions there. An un-exploded German bomb?'

'Gas. Coal gas laid on for light and heating.'

'Gas doesn't ignite itself. Someone must be there. Daisy, ring for police and a doctor, and send able-bodied help. Come along, you two.'

The men set off at a run.

CHAPTER 17

Alec let Armitage take the lead. He hadn't yet had a chance to take the measure of the young Canadian, but at least he knew the way to the grotto.

'How far?' Alec asked as the three men crunched along the gravel path like a herd of stampeding buffalo.

Armitage slowed his pace a trifle. 'Half a mile? Thereabouts. Uphill.'

They passed a yew hedge. The path curved to the right. Ahead were three stone steps going up. Armitage took them at a single leap. Mounting more conservatively one at a time, Alec hoped he'd never have to chase the man with intent to arrest him.

The slope grew steeper. Bincombe, less fit, was already falling behind. Alec was glad he'd resisted the temptation to give up exercising when the twins were born.

He summoned enough breath to ask Armitage, 'Any ideas?'

'Lord Rydal. Went off right after lunch. Smokes like a chimney. Doesn't explain, though, sufficient accumulation of gas. That was a big bang.'

'It was indeed.'

No explanation for the accumulation of sufficient gas to cause a huge explosion? A leak was always possible, but in an open cave it should have quickly diluted to comparatively safe proportions. Rydal – or anyone else – ought to have smelt it as he approached. No explanation, either, of why Lord Rydal should have decided to go off, apparently alone, for a quiet postprandial smoke in the grotto, of all places. But perhaps there were perfectly obvious answers. Alec just didn't have enough knowledge of the situation to begin to formulate theories.

They galloped up more steps and thundered onto a wooden bridge. Armitage slowed to stare down at the brook below.

'The water's draining away! The stream must be blocked.' He came to a halt. 'I don't like the look of this.'

Bincombe arrived, panting. 'What's the matter?'

'The stream is drying up.' Alec looked at Armitage. 'What does it mean?'

'Its source is in the grotto.' His face was white, freckles standing out starkly. He took off his hat and wiped cold sweat from his brow. 'The whole roof must have come down.'

'Wasn't that pretty obvious from what we saw from the terrace?' Bincombe asked.

'I hoped... The thing is, anyone who was in there must be dead.'

'No hurry then. May I stop running?'

'No,' said Alec. 'People survive cave-ins. But not for long, if they're injured or trapped in an airless space. Let's go.'

He started running again, taking the lead as the path rose above the dying stream. The footing was solid chalky limestone now instead of gravel – at least, he hoped it was solid. Cautiously he slowed as he rounded a steep bluff.

He was concentrating on the path's surface, here littered with rocks. For a moment the whimpering sound didn't penetrate his consciousness, then he heard it and looked up. Ahead of him, a greyish-white figure slumped in a heap against the cliff wall.

It stirred. Alive!

'Great Scott–'

'That's not Rydal,' observed Bincombe, coming up behind Alec.

Armitage arrived last. 'Lady Ottaline!'

'Lady Ottaline,' said Daisy. 'I'm sure I saw her going after Rhino, down through the garden. I think I ought to go with them.'

'I shall telephone the doctor and the police, madam.' Barker handed the camera to Lucy as he spoke. 'I'll inform Mr. Pritchard of this unfortunate occurrence – though he must certainly have heard the explosion – and send the gardeners and the chauffeur to help.'

'Thanks.' Daisy hesitated. 'I suppose you'd better tell the police Detective Chief Inspector Fletcher of Scotland Yard is on the spot. Though not in his official capacity!'

'Very good, madam.' Not by so much as a flicker of an eyelash did the butler betray whether this was news to him. He went off with his usual stately mien.

'Coming, you two?'

Lucy and Julia looked at each other.

'Daisy, shouldn't you leave it to the men?' Julia suggested.

'It's not as if you have any nursing experience, darling.'

'No, but I know if I were hurt and frightened I'd want a woman with me. I'm going.'

'She may be dead,' said Lucy bluntly.

'She may not. Why don't you go and make sure Mrs. Howell gets everything ready in case she's alive and injured.'

'Right-oh. That I can manage.'

'I'll come with you, Daisy,' said Julia.

The men were long gone by then. Daisy and Julia hurried after them along the familiar path. Daisy was vaguely surprised that the trees and shrubbery and sheets of daffodils looked no different from last time she had passed that way.

'Do you think it's dangerous?' Julia said worriedly. 'I hope Charles will take care. And your husband and Lord Gerald, too, of course.'

'I haven't the foggiest. I suppose it depends just what they find there. It seems to me the roof, or whatever you want to call it, can't have been very thick or it wouldn't have blown bits and pieces up in the air, just collapsed. Don't you think so?'

'I suppose so. Then Rhino may not be buried very deep.'

'You think it must be Rhino, too?'

'Well, he didn't turn up for coffee, which he usually does, and you said Lady Ottaline went after him.'

'I didn't actually see him go, and I couldn't

swear it was her I saw. It was only a glimpse. Alec's always accusing me of speculating wildly.'

'Not really wildly. Everyone else was in the drawing room, except the three who went to Swindon. Daisy, the awful thing is I have a beastly urge to tell them not to try to rescue Rhino.'

'I know what you mean. But you wouldn't dream of actually saying it, and if you did they'd take no notice, so you needn't feel guilty. I–' She cut herself off as a strange figure appeared where the path curved round a large bush. 'Good gracious, what on earth?'

'It's Charles. What's he carrying?'

Armitage had a large, grey burden slung over his shoulder in a fireman's lift.

'Lady Ottaline,' said Daisy, hurrying towards him. 'She can't be dead or he'd have left her and gone on to help the others look for Rhino.'

'Charles, where did you find her?'

'Just outside the grotto.'

'Is the entrance blocked?' Daisy asked.

'Not as far in as we could see.'

'They're going in, then,' she said resignedly. The thought made her feel nauseated, but nothing she could say or do would change matters. *Stiff upper lip,* she exhorted herself.

'Yes. I've got to get Lady Ottaline to the house. Fletcher thinks she may be concussed. Something about her eyes not reacting properly to light.'

'We'll manage her, won't we, Julia? Lay her down and get back to Alec and Gerald.'

Armitage hesitated. Then, with obvious reluctance, he let Julia and Daisy shift Lady Ottaline from his shoulders and lay her on her back on the grass. She was not heavy. Daisy knelt beside her and started to wipe chalk dust from her face.

'We can manage her, Charles,' said Julia, squeezing his hand. 'Take care, won't you?'

He gave her a strained smile. 'Don't you think I should carry her?'

'People will be coming. The gardeners and the chauffeur.'

Still he didn't leave. Daisy was puzzled. She wouldn't have thought him so callous as to abandon even such an unlovely specimen as Rhino when there might be a chance of saving him.

Lady Ottaline moaned, blinked eyelashes clogged with eyeblack and chalk, and made a premonitory sound in her throat that reminded Daisy all too clearly of Nana about to be sick in the car.

'Quick, Julia, help me turn her over.'

While they were coping with ensuing events, Armitage departed. Daisy would have been more than happy to go with him.

Inside the cave, the chalk dust was as thick as a London peasouper. Alec coughed in spite of having tied a handkerchief over his nose and mouth. Peering forwards, he wished he'd taken the time to get hold of a torch, not that it would have helped much in this murk. He didn't dare breathe deeply enough to try to detect gas.

The floor crunched beneath his feet. He didn't know whether he was stepping on debris or irreplaceable artifacts.

166

'Fletcher?'

Bincombe hadn't wanted to stay outside, but he had sense enough to realise, without a long argument, that they mustn't put all their eggs in one basket. If the roof came down...

Better not to think about it, or only to remind himself that a shout might be enough to trigger collapse.

Turning his head – mustn't lose his sense of direction – he called in a low voice, 'All right so far. I can't see much.' He stood absolutely still for a moment, listening. No ominous creaking from the roof, nor clatter of falling rubble. No calls for help, no screams, no groans.

Slowly he moved on, hands held out before him.

'Ouch!' he exclaimed involuntarily as his knuckles met stone.

He wished he could have sent Bincombe back with the woman, and kept Armitage, who knew the place. But it was no use asking the poor chap to come in here. He'd been willing to try, but he'd have been more of a liability than an asset.

While these thoughts passed through Alec's mind, he had been running his hands over the obstacle in front of him. It was not a disordered heap of broken stone but carved marble, smooth except for a few nicks and a groove gouged by some hard object hitting it from above. He glanced up, uselessly. As well as the dust in the air, it was darker here.

The statue was large and surely would have told him where he was if he were familiar with the grotto. Three linked caves, Armitage had said. Was Alec near the end of the first, or had he already passed unknowing into the second, or had he scarcely begun to penetrate the depths?

He felt his way round the statue. Beyond, empty space began again, but he had taken no more than three tentative steps when once again his knuckles hit a solid mass. A rough wall, a more or less right-angled protruding corner – he reached up and felt the curve of an arch. The way through to the second cave, he guessed.

Behind him stone clunked on stone. He stiffened, arms raised to protect his head.

'Fletcher?' Bincombe's voice was nearby, but muffled, as if he, too, had masked mouth and nose with a handkerchief

And his feet must have knocked the loose stones on the floor against one another, Alec hoped.

'I told you to stay outside.'

'I'm not one of your bobbies, old man. Armitage came back. Met Daisy and Miss Beaufort, left Lady Ottaline with them.'

'Daisy!'

'She's not one of your bobbies, either.' He sounded as if he was grinning. Though laconic, he seemed to have lost his customary taciturnity. 'Lady O will keep 'em busy. I told Armitage to stay outside, poor devil.'

'Poor devil – assuming his story's the truth.'

'You don't believe him? He's in a real funk, I'd swear.'

'Has it occurred to you that he may be responsible for this mess? Inadvertently, or on purpose.

He wouldn't want to find Rydal, alive or dead.'

'If Rhino's in here.'

'If he's in here,' Alec agreed. 'I'm afraid we could easily pass him by without noticing. We need more men. But not Armitage. At least he's more likely to obey you than you are to obey me. Right-oh, now you're here, stay here, *please!* I'm going ahead. I wish we had a rope.'

'Hold on a moment.' He sneezed. 'Phew, dust up my nose. Here, Lucy makes me wear one of these new-fangled belts. Catch hold of the buckle and I'll hang on to the end. Dammit, where are you? It's not very long, though, in spite of my adding a pound or two.'

'Got it. Tell Lucy braces would have been much more useful. We could have tied yours and mine together.'

'And both lost our trousers.'

'You won't lose yours, will you? Fat lot of help you'll be if you trip over your turn-ups at every other step.'

'My tailor's lost a customer if I do. Ties!' Bincombe exclaimed, inspired. 'Yours and mine. Tie them together.'

'Good idea.' A bit miffed that he hadn't thought of this expedient first, Alec pulled off his tie and knotted it to Bincombe's. The tight knot wasn't going to do either much good. He was glad he hadn't worn his Royal Flying Corps tie. 'Here, tie your end through the buckle of your belt. That'll make it even longer. Not that it's going to be strong enough to pull me out with if something happens, but at least we'll be able to find each other.'

'Hope so. I'd hate to have to face Daisy if I lost you. Keep one hand on the wall.'

'Here goes.' He took a tentative step under the arch, and a second. The wall here was masonry, hewn stone with mortared joints, not the natural sides of a cave. There seemed to be much less rubble underfoot. On the other hand, it was dark. Not that visibility had been much better in the first cave, but the diffuse daylight had given an illusion of sight, of belonging to the outer world.

Another step, and another. With one hand on the wall and the other clutching the necktie, he wished for a third to feel ahead for obstacles. He took his hand from the wall and reached forward. Nothing. Fingers found the wall again. Another step–

'Damn!'

'Fletcher, what's wrong? Are you all right?'

'Yes. Overconfident. I stepped on something and... But I'm all right. Half a mo–'Alec's next step met an immovable obstacle. 'I'm going to have to let go of my umbilical cord. I'll lay the end right by the wall so I should be able to find it if you don't pull on it.'

'Right-oh. What–'

'Hang on. I think this is the end.'

With care, Alec went down on one knee on the rubble. His best suit must be past praying for by now, he reckoned. Crouched there, feeling blindly, he could find no way round or through the barrier. He stood up. Stretching upwards, he could touch all but the topmost curve of the arch, but the slope of the rock fall made it

170

impossible to reach to find out whether it met the ceiling.

He lowered his handkerchief mask. Either there was less dust in here or it was settling. He sniffed.

No stink of gas.

'Bincombe, can you smell gas?'

A brief silence, then, 'No,' followed by a sneeze. 'But I can't claim my nose is reliable just now.'

Alec put his hands round his mouth like a megaphone and made a hooting noise towards the top of the obstruction. The sound returning to his ears seemed to him to have bounced off a solid wall.

'What the deuce? Was that you, Fletcher?'

'Yes. I'm pretending to be an owl. It's impossible to be sure without light, but I don't think there's any way through. I'm coming back.'

CHAPTER 18

Over Lady Ottaline's limp body, Daisy and Julia exchanged a glance.

Julia giggled. 'I don't know what she'd say if she knew you were using spit to clean her face.'

'Not couth,' Daisy agreed, 'but I had to do something after she was sick. She's a mess. It's a good job she passed out again.'

'I'll go and wet my hanky in the stream.'

'Here, take my scarf, too, and hurry. I'm running out of spit.'

Julia returned in a couple of minutes. 'Daisy,

the stream has practically disappeared! The source must be blocked.' She knelt opposite and started to dab with a dripping handkerchief at the cashmere jacket the victim was wearing in default of her soaked furs. 'Do you think they're all right? Suppose it breaks through while they're up there?'

'Your Charles must have noticed the drop in water level. He'll have warned them and they'll watch out for any changes.'

'But–'

'Julia, stop it! I know you're not used to having a sweetheart to worry about, but if you carry on like that you'll give me the jitters, too.'

'Sorry. After so many years of one day being just like the day before, I don't know how to cope with the unexpected.'

'You'd soon learn if you married a police detective. I don't suppose it's a skill much required of the wife of a university lecturer, though. Oh, blast, it's beginning to rain! She shouldn't lie here in the cold, getting wet again. I wonder whether she does have concussion.' Eyes dilated by drug use didn't react properly to light. Unequal pupils were a symptom of concussion, she vaguely recalled, but she didn't feel like messing about with Lady Ottaline's eyelids to take a look. 'She must be in shock, at least.'Would that, or the drug wearing off, account for the vomiting?

'I wish someone would come.'

'Do you think we can carry her between us?'

'We can but try,' Julia said with determination. She stood up. 'Oh, thank heaven, here comes a man. It's Pritchard's chauffeur.'

The chauffeur, Madison, like his employer, was a small man, but he was wiry. 'You help me get 'er ladyship up on me shoulders, madam, and I'll get 'er to the house all right. Little bit of a thing like 'er. What 'appened to 'er?'

'I don't know exactly,' said Daisy. 'I should think she must have been outside the grotto when the explosion happened and got blown down. But that's pure guesswork.'

As she spoke, she and Julia lifted Lady Ottaline by shoulders and ankles. Madison ducked underneath and they deposited her face down across his shoulders. He grabbed her skinny legs round the knees on one side, and one brittle wrist on the other, and set off back down the path. Very undignified, Daisy thought, thankful again that Lady Ottaline wasn't aware of the pickle she was in.

When they came to steps, Daisy and Julia had to steady Madison in his descent, but he never faltered beneath the weight.

'I suppose there are other advantages than fashion to being slim,' Daisy remarked to Julia with a sigh. 'Carrying me would be another story altogether.'

'The possibility of being blown up is hardly a good reason to go on a Banting diet.'

'Oh, I don't know. After what Howell said about the new safety features of the hot water geyser, if it can blow up, anything might blow up any minute.'

'I don't think that can have been what did it,' Julia said doubtfully. 'He was talking about a steam explosion. That would happen if the gas

173

was lit and the water wasn't running through. It would be dangerous to anyone nearby, and it would cause some damage, but would it be so huge? There could only be a very limited amount of steam, I'd have thought, just from the water left in the machine after the last time it was used.'

'I'm afraid I sort of lost track of his explanation in the middle. These safety thingummies wouldn't prevent a gas explosion, then?'

'Not if I understood correctly.'

'I expect you did. Technical things tend to muddle me. Or at least to make my mind wander. It must have been a leak in a gas pipe, and poor old Rhino wandered into it waving his cigarette about as usual.'

'But what on earth was he doing there? He wasn't any more interested in the grotto than you were in the workings of the geyser.'

That was a question to which Daisy considered the answer obvious, given Lady Ottaline's presence following Rhino. However, she'd much prefer to save the elucidation for Alec. To her relief, the chauffeur had reached the last steps and called to them. They had fallen behind, not wanting him to hear their discussion.

'Madam, miss, I c'd do with a hand 'ere, if you'd oblige. Don't want to drop 'er, do we.'

As they came up with him, a horde of gardeners – at least, a head gardener, an undergardener, and two gardener's boys – appeared on the scene. Each had a spade on his shoulder. In addition, one carried a pickaxe, one a crowbar, and one a coil of rope.

'Good,' grunted Madison. To the younger boy,

small but wiry, he said: ''Ere, Fred, or whatever your name is, you can carry 'er ladyship to the house.'

'I'll thank you not to give orders to my lads, Mr. Madison,' said the head gardener icily.

'You planning to stand there all night argufying while the pore lady freezes to death?'

'That will do,' said Daisy, who was quite capable of putting even more ice into her voice than the head gardener. The 'servant problem' was between servants almost as often as between servant and employer, she reflected. 'Mr. Madison has already carried Lady Ottaline a considerable distance. Fred– Is your name Fred?'

'Billy, miss.' Billy was clearly delighted by the row between his superiors.

'With your permission, Mr...?'

'Simmons, madam,' the head gardener said sulkily. He gestured at the undergardener and the other boy. 'You two lift her ladyship onto Billy's shoulders. Careful there, you oafs!'

Billy's face fell. He obviously wanted to go with the others to the scene of the disaster.

'You can go after them as soon as we get Lady Ottaline to the house,' Daisy consoled him as the others went on up the slope, Simmons and Madison stiff with indignation.

'She'm a real lady? 'Er don't seem like nuthen but a bit o' bone and hair. Fair dicky, ben't en? 'Er ben't dead, be en?'

'No, but she soon will be if you don't take more care.'

'Oi bain't agoing to flump, missus,' the boy said, injured, 'nor yet drop the lady. This yere rain, 'er'll be shrammed for sure ifn Oi don't peg it.'

Daisy gave up. She and Julia hurried to keep up with him.

Rain drifted down, soft, gentle, but persistent, seeping insidiously into every crack and crevice. Daisy hoped it would not hinder the rescue effort and make it more dangerous.

Towards the mouth of the grotto, a Scotch mist drifted in, permeating the air and beginning to clear the dust. Alec and Bincombe took off their handkerchief masks.

'Whew, bliss to breathe!' Bincombe exclaimed, then issued a final sneeze and blew his nose.

'Bliss to see,' Alec retorted. 'Even though you look like a ghost. A pretty substantial ghost.'

'So do you.'

They were both powdered from head to foot with grey dust. The all-pervading dampness was rapidly turning it into splotches of plaster, but there wasn't much they could do about it at present.

Alec approached the open edge of the cave and looked down. To his right water trickled over a lip of inset granite and down a vertical rock wall into a small pool. Mud and stranded reeds round the margin showed that it had very recently been larger. A slight overflow still gave a semblance of life to the stream, shrunken in its bed at the bottom of the steep-sided gorge.

To his left, perhaps a third of the distance down from the grotto to the pool, he saw the platform where he had found Lady Ottaline. Backed by a solid cliff, it faced the grotto and the defunct waterfall. Armitage stood there, looking up.

'What do you think happened to Lady Otta-line?' Bincombe asked.

'I'd guess that, when the inner cave blew up, the blast was funnelled out through that archway, through the grotto, and threw her against the cliff.'

'Hmm.'

'I doubt it would have been strong enough by then to do you or me much damage, but she's a scrawny little thing. I think she was down there. If she'd been up here she'd have had the fall as well as the impact. She'd probably be dead. All the same, she must have been heading up here. Why?'

Under the blotchy coating of damp chalk, Bincombe's face turned red. 'Hmm, well, none of my business, don't you know.'

Gentlemanly reticence added to natural taciturnity was a strong mix. Alec forbore to press him. Time enough for that if he couldn't get the information – or rumours – from Daisy.

'Right-oh. We'll have to try and get to the site of the collapse. I hope Armitage can direct.'

He started down the steps, treading carefully on the rain-slick stone.

'Here come the troops,' said Bincombe.

Four men loaded with digging implements came tramping along the path. Pritchard's servants, Alec assumed. One carried a rope he could have done with a few minutes ago. He considered sending a couple to try to break through the barrier.

No, too dangerous. It would be better to have

everyone working at the site of the hillside's collapse. He had little hope of pulling anyone out alive, but it had to be tried. It was always possible that Lord Rydal had found shelter in some crack or cranny.

Rhino, Bincombe had called him. An odd sort of a nickname, but this was not the time to ask about it. Alec reached the bottom of the steps and faced a barrage of questions from Armitage, while the others waited to be told what to do.

'Nothing doing there,' he said briefly to the former.

Armitage looked relieved. 'Fletcher, this is Simmons, the head gardener, and a couple of his chaps. And Madison, chauffeur. He took over carrying Lady Ottaline from me.' He turned to the men. 'Mr. Fletcher is in charge.' He looked a bit puzzled, as if he hadn't considered the question before and couldn't quite work out why Alec should be so definitely and obviously in charge.

'Thank you for helping Lady Ottaline, Madison.'

'My second lad's carrying her ladyship now, sir,' Simmons said with inexplicable belligerence.

'Only because Mrs. Fletcher—'

'I'm glad to see you've brought spades, Simmons.' Alec cut short their wrangling, wondering how on earth Daisy came into the matter. 'Good thinking. Now we need to make for the spot where the hillside subsided. I hope you can lead us there, quickly.'

CHAPTER 19

As Daisy and Julia and Billy, with his burden, reached the terrace, Pritchard hurried out of the drawing room, hatless in the rain, and Barker swung open the side door. They had obviously been watching out anxiously.

'Lady Ottaline?' said Pritchard, very upset. 'Bring her in! Lay her on the sofa.'

'She'll ruin the sofa!' objected Mrs. Howell, standing at the open French window. 'And look at the boy's boots!'

'It's my sofa, Winifred. What's more, it's my fault the poor lady is in this condition. Though leaks will happen, you know, no matter how careful you are. Come in, come in.'

'I'm no nurse,' said Daisy, 'but I think she ought to be taken straight to her bed. Billy, you'd better go with Barker. Is a doctor on the way?'

'Yes, madam,' Barker assured her. 'Her ladyship's maid and the housekeeper are making preparations upstairs to receive her ladyship. Not that we expected anything quite so...' At a loss for words, he looked with some dismay at Billy's boots, but ushered him in through the side door.

Regardless of the rain, Lady Beaufort came out, stately as a galleon in her brown tweed skirt and white blouse. She laid her hand on Pritchard's arm and said, 'Don't distress yourself. I'll go up and make sure everything that can be done

179

is done properly.'

'Would you? How can I thank you!'

'I expect I'll think of a way,' Lady Beaufort promised. 'Julia, go inside at once, before you catch your death of cold.'

She sailed off in Barker's wake.

Daisy and Julia, conscious of their muddy shoes and knees, were all for going in through the side door, but Pritchard insisted on taking them into the drawing room.

Mrs. Howell glared at their feet.

'Darlings, you *are* a mess,' Lucy greeted them.

'Aren't you glad you didn't come?' said Daisy, gravitating to a radiator.

Lucy shuddered. 'Very. What happened to Lady Ottaline?'

'We don't know,' said Julia. 'We met Charles carrying her and he left her with us, to go back to the others.'

'Then the chauffeur arrived and carried her until we met the gardeners and Billy took over.'

'This is beginning to sound like one of those endless fairy tales,' Lucy complained.

'It did seem endless at the time,' Julia agreed.

Meanwhile, a maid came in to light a fire in the fireplace.

'I didn't order a fire,' Mrs. Howell told her.

'Mr. Barker said to, ma'am.'

'Whose orders do you obey, mine or the butler's?'

The maid looked nonplussed, the butler clearly as great a figure in her eyes as the lady of the house.

'I think we might have a fire, Winifred,' said

Pritchard mildly. 'Mrs. Fletcher and Miss Beaufort are damp and chilled.'

'Oh, well, if Barker is more important–'

'Barker is doing an excellent job under unusual and difficult circumstances.'

Emboldened, the maid said, 'If you please, sir, Mr. Barker said as how he'd 'preciate a word with Mrs. Fletcher.'

'I ought to change, so I'll go and find him.' Daisy reluctantly abandoned the radiator. 'It'll be marvellous to come down to a real fire.'

'I'd better change, too,' said Julia.

'Mrs. Fletcher,' Pritchard begged, 'isn't there something else I can do to help? I'm afraid I'd only be in the way out on the hill.'

Daisy hesitated. There was one thing she felt should be done as soon as possible, which no one else seemed to have thought of yet. The trouble was, she suspected Alec would prefer to do it himself, in person. She reminded herself that gas leaks happened all the time. She had absolutely no reason to suppose the explosion was anything but an accident – nothing, at least, beyond the character of the apparent victim. But she didn't even know that Rhino *was* a victim.

She made up her mind. 'Someone's going to have to tell Sir Desmond that his wife's been hurt. As their host, I'd say you're probably the proper person. Can you telephone him at the factory?'

Pritchard paled. 'How could I have forgotten? Yes, of course, I'll do it right away.' He squared his shoulders and followed Daisy and Julia out to the hall.

181

Lucy was left with Mrs. Howell. Her manners were too good to desert their hostess, though whether she'd bestir herself to make conversation was another matter. Daisy wished she could watch and listen invisibly.

The butler was waiting in the hall.

'You wanted to see me, Barker?'

'Thank you, madam, yes. I merely wished to inform you that I fear I did not follow your instructions to the letter when I telephoned the police. There was not time to advise you, but being acquainted with the constable in the village, I could not feel it desirable to notify him of Mr. Fletcher's profession and rank.'

'Oh?'

'A man easily flustered, madam, by matters outside his usual purview. Very competent, I understand, where poachers, tramps, boys scrumping apples, and Saturday night fights outside the Spotted Dog are concerned, but apt to lose his head in more complex circumstances.'

'Oh dear. Yes, I quite see your point. A Scotland Yard detective added to an explosion might be altogether too much for the poor man. Thank you, Barker.'

'Thank you, madam.'

'Did you tell the doctor? About my husband, I mean.'

'No, madam. As I recall, you suggested telling the police only. I should perhaps also inform you that, after consulting Mr. Pritchard, I telephoned the landlord at the Spotted Dog and asked him to round up a few able-bodied men and bring them to assist in the digging if required.'

'Barker, you're a regular Jeeves,' Daisy said warmly.

'Thank you, madam. Excuse me, madam,' he added as the doorbell rang. 'I expect that's Dr. Tenby.'

'Jeeves?' asked Julia.

'A fictional butler who's a genius at dealing with extraordinary circumstances. Your reading has been altogether too serious.'

'Jeeves sounds like the Admirable Crichton. You can't say that's too serious. Come on, what are we waiting for? I'm dying to get out of these wet clothes.'

'You go on up. I want to have a word with Dr. Tenby. I'll take him up to Lady Ottaline.'

'Surely Barker... Oh, you're going to tell the doctor about Alec?'

'I think I'd better. It was almost certainly only an accident, but as long as there's the least chance of hanky-panky being involved– Well, the doctor will examine Lady Ottaline with a different eye if he might have to testify in court.'

'Daisy, aren't you rather putting the cart before the horse? I mean, just because Alec happens to be on the spot, it doesn't mean a crime's been committed.'

'I know. But just think about it, a man who manages to make himself thoroughly disliked by– Here's Dr. Tenby.'

'I'm off.' Julia disappeared in the direction of the stairs.

Heading in the opposite direction, Daisy heard Barker remind the doctor of her name before bearing away his top-coat.

'Good afternoon, Dr. Tenby.' As he merely bowed silently, she went on, 'I'll take you up to Lady Ottaline.'

He gave her an enquiring look. She realised that Barker had not known, when he rang up, who the patient would be, or indeed whether there would be a patient at all.

'Lady Ottaline is your patient.' She started towards the stairs and he followed, black bag in hand. 'Lady Ottaline Wandersley. You must have met her the other evening.'

He grunted assent.

'Did Barker tell you what happened?'

'An explosion.'

'Yes, we don't know exactly how it happened, but it was probably a gas leak. Out in the grotto. Have you seen the grotto?'

'Yes.'

'It blew up. My husband is leading a rescue party, in case there are other victims.'

'Burns?'

'What? Oh, Lady Ottaline. No, she's not burnt. I don't exactly know, but my husband thinks she may have a concussion. Something about the eyes.'

'Medical man?'

'Alec? No, but he's a police officer and he's had to deal with a lot of injuries. As a matter of fact, he's a detective chief inspector at Scotland Yard. Not that he's here on business, just as a visitor, but I thought you ought to know. In case he finds out it wasn't an accident and you're asked to testify to an inquest, or even in court.'

He gave an abrupt nod.

'When you've finished with Lady Ottaline, he'd like you to go out to the grotto in case they find another victim.' Alec hadn't actually stated as much, but he'd sent for the doctor before he knew anyone at all was injured.

'Someone missing?'

'Lord Rydal.'

Another grunt. No doubt taciturnity had its admirers, but it made conversation very difficult.

They reached the Wandersleys' bedroom and Daisy knocked. A lady's maid opened the door.

'Dr. Tenby,' Daisy introduced him. She went straight off to change, despite her interest in Lady Ottaline's condition. She was quite sure that her chance of learning anything from the doctor was nil.

A quarter of an hour's tramp brought Alec and his troop to their goal. They stood on the short turf on the edge of a pit some ten or twelve feet deep. A certain amount of debris was scattered about the rim, but most of what the explosion had thrown up had landed back in the hole. After hurrying uphill to get here, all except the gardener's remaining boy were silent, catching their breath as they stared down at the jumbled mess.

The boy said, 'Me mum'll take on something turrible if 'er finds out Oi bin down that 'ole.'

'You'll do what you're told,' snapped Madison.

'I'll not order *my* men into yon death-trap,' Simmons snapped back.

'Volunteers only,' said Alec.

'Oi won't tell me mum,' the boy assured him.

'Death-trap,' mused Armitage. 'I hope he isn't

185

really down there.'

'Friend of yours?' Alec asked.

'What? No, on the contrary. But it sort of spoils one's abhorrence if it's diluted with pity. A nasty end. I've been thinking. Assuming this was caused by a gas leak and not some natural occurrence, gas in the middle cave wouldn't collect in great concentration because of the tunnel to the outer grotto. There's – or there was – also a rift in the roof which let in a certain amount of light and plenty of air.'

'Yes?' Alec encouraged him.

'So if Rydal walked in with a lit cigarette, and he practically always had a lit cigarette in his holder, it might singe his eyebrows but I doubt it would create a disaster of this magnitude. The hermit's lair on the other hand–'

'The *what?*'

'Mrs. Fletcher hasn't told you? I suppose she hasn't had the opportunity.' He explained Pritchard's fancy of keeping a tame hermit in his grotto. 'The room had some sort of natural ventilation, but no source of natural light. It also had a door. It seems to me, the most likely thing to have happened is that Rydal opened the door on a room full of gas. In that case, he'd have been blown backwards, I imagine. He'd be somewhere over there.' Armitage gestured to the left. On that side, the hole sloped up to become a depression that could easily have been a natural part of the hillside.

'We should start digging in that dip?'

'I'm a historian, not a geologist or an explosives expert. But my guess is, the confined explosion

186

blew out the roof of the lair, which then collapsed. It also blew Rydal back into the middle
cave, but quite likely didn't do much direct
damage to the cave itself. It would be the ground
tremors from the blast that brought parts of that
one down, leaving some of it undamaged.'

'So he could quite well be alive in there, and it's
going to be devilish difficult to get him out.'

Armitage, who had been pink from exertion,
turned pale as a ghost and looked down at his
feet. 'I c-can't dig in these shoes,' he stammered
unhappily. He was wearing house-shoes, not
having changed after lunch before the im-
promptu expedition to the grotto. 'I have hiking
boots back at the house – been tramping the
downs to take a look at barrows and the ancient
camps, you know–'

'You'd better go and get them.' Alec, like Bincombe, had donned sturdy walking shoes for
their drive into the country. One could never be
certain even a Daimler would not throw a rod in
the middle of nowhere. 'More to the point, someone must explain to Mr. Pritchard what appears
to have happened, and what we're going to try.
Knowing the territory, you have the best grasp of
the situation. You'd better wait till the police and
the doctor arrive and bring them back with you.'

'Right you are, sir.' The colour began to return
to Armitage's cheeks as he turned to leave.

'But first, old man,' Bincombe put in, 'if Pritchard hasn't yet had the gas turned off at the
mains, make sure it's done, pronto.' He reached
out a long arm and twitched away a packet of
Woodbines the undergardener had just pulled

187

out of his pocket.

While Simmons berated his underling for idiocy, Alec, Bincombe, Armitage, and Madison leant over the edge of the crater and sniffed. Alec caught no whiff of gas. Bincombe and Armitage both shook their heads. Madison thought he could smell it, but Alec suspected it was his imagination. As a man who spent much of his life breathing petrol fumes, he was not likely to have a sensitive nose.

In the meantime, the youth had wandered off round the rim of the hole, poking and prying. He now came back, carrying something in a grubby handkerchief, which he showed to Simmons.

The head gardener snorted. 'A bit o' copper pipe's not going to make you rich, me lad!'

'This 'ere's a *clue*, Mr. Simmons. I bet it's got dabs on it. That's what they call fingerprints in the books.'

'I'll give you dabs!'

'And it ben't just a scrap o' pipe. En's got a gas tap–'

'Chuck it away and–'

'Let me see that!' Alec interrupted urgently. He took the trophy from its eager finder, careful to keep the indescribable handkerchief round it. A few inches of twisted pipe protruded from either end of the tap fitting. The tap itself was parallel to the pipe. Turned on.

Frowning at the damning object in Alec's hands, Bincombe shook his head and said, 'I can't believe even Rhino would be such a fool as to turn on the gas while holding a lit cigarette.'

CHAPTER 20

Daisy was brushing her hair when she heard a tap at the door.

'Come in!'

It was a very young housemaid, her eyes bright with excitement and a touch of apprehension. 'Mr. Pritchard says can you come down, madam. He wants to talk to you. Mr. Endicott's here. He's the p'liceman from the village, madam. It's about her ladyship – Lady Ottaline that is – and the 'splosion. He's ever so upset, madam, Mr. Endicott is.' She chattered on.

Daisy wondered if Pritchard considered that being married to a policeman must make her an expert at soothing members of that profession. On the contrary, she recalled numerous episodes tending to confirm the reverse. Not that she intended to tell Pritchard that she was more likely to exacerbate Constable Endicott's annoyance than to calm it.

'Please tell Mr. Pritchard I'll be down in a minute.'

The girl left. Daisy gave her curls a final whisk of the brush and put on lipstick to give herself courage. Her experience of past battles with Superintendent Crane of the Metropolitan Police, some won, some lost, were no help when it came to facing an irate village bobby.

But when she reached the hall, she found PC

Endicott bewildered, not angry. The round-faced young man, helmet in hand, was saying piteously to Pritchard, 'You see, Mr. Pritchard, sir, there ben't nuthen in the handbook about explosions.'

'So you've already told me, Constable.' More than once, to judge by Pritchard's face. 'Ah, Mrs. Fletcher! This is PC Endicott. His sergeant is down with pleurisy, and he can't make up his mind whether he ought to notify his superiors in Swindon or not.'

Daisy tried to decide what Alec would prefer. Bringing in the Swindon brass hats without telling them he was from the Met was out of the question, certain to cause trouble. Honesty, though not always the best policy, was advisable in this case.

On second thoughts, not just yet. 'I should think, Mr. Endicott, your best course would be to go out to the scene of the disaster and find out exactly what happened. Then you can decide whether it should be reported or not.'

The harried look lifted from Endicott's face. 'Aye, thet'll be best. Thank 'ee kindly, ma'am.'

'If you hurry, you can catch up with the lads from the village,' Pritchard suggested.

Barker was miraculously on hand to show the constable to the back door.

'Just what I would have suggested, Mrs. Fletcher,' said Pritchard. 'Masterly inaction.'

'Why didn't you, then?'

'I wanted to be sure you concurred. I didn't want to make trouble for your husband by either giving information unnecessarily or withholding it. Now it's up to him to make the decisions.'

'Usually the best course,' Daisy sighed. 'Don't they say it's a sign of growing old when police-men start to look like schoolboys?'

Pritchard's eyes twinkled. 'I'd always heard the same of doctors.'

'Oh, that's all right then. Dr. Tenby doesn't look at all like a schoolboy to me.'

'More like an undertaker,' he said in a con-spiratorial whisper. 'But hush, here he comes. How is your patient doing, Tenby?'

'Bad bruising. No concussion. Fainted from pain. Still considerable discomfort. I've left some powders.'

'Should I send for a nurse?'

'No, no, quite unnecessary. Lady Beaufort seems competent–'

'Very competent.'

'And her ladyship's maid can do whatever is required. Where's my other patient?'

'We're not certain there is one.'

'But Lord Rydal is still missing,' Daisy put in. 'Possibly blown up with the grotto. Oh, hello, Charles. What's up?'

Armitage squelched in. 'Fletcher sent me to get my hiking boots,' he said, looking down apolo-getically at his sodden, mucky footwear. 'I just met the copper already on his way, but I'm to escort you back, Dr. Tenby–'

'Galoshes, sir,' Barker rematerialised at the doctor's side, proffering the said objects. 'The weather is inclement, I fear.'

Tenby's gloom deepened, but he didn't protest. Perhaps it would have required the utterance of too many words. 'If you wouldn't mind waiting just a moment while I fetch my boots, Doctor.'

'I shall send a maid for them, sir,' Barker told Armitage, departing once more.

'Thanks!' Armitage turned to Pritchard. 'And most important, sir, Fletcher wants to know whether you've had the gas supply to the grotto turned off.'

'Yes, yes, immediately after the explosion. I take it there's no sign of Lord Rydal?'

'No. There's a dangerous blockage between the outer and inner grottoes – trying to move it could cause further collapse – so the job has to be tackled from the other end.' He hesitated. 'Fletcher didn't say – I think I should tell you three, but for pity's sake don't tell anyone else.'

'My lips are sealed,' Pritchard promised. Dr. Tenby's lips were practically always sealed anyway.

Daisy wasn't prepared to promise the same, but Armitage apparently assumed that as Alec's wife she was entitled to know all. Not that she hadn't already guessed what he was about to reveal with so much premonitory palaver.

'We've found what appears to be evidence that the explosion was not an accident.'

'Hmph,' said the doctor, unimpressed or uninterested. 'Pritchard, a stretcher.'

'I'll see what I can arrange and send it after you. Barker,' he said as the butler silently returned, 'can we provide anything in the way of a stretcher for Dr. Tenby?'

'Certainly, sir.'

'Mrs. Fletcher,' said Pritchard, 'ought I to ring up the Swindon police, now that it looks as if–'

192

'Not unless Alec said to.' Daisy turned to Armitage.

'He didn't. He told me to bring Dr. Tenby and the police– Oh, do you suppose he expected the bobby's superiors to be on their way already? Are they?'

Pritchard shook his head. 'PC Endicott didn't report the explosion to them. He wanted my advice as to whether he should.'

'And I said no,' Daisy admitted. 'I think Alec would want to speak to the constable before anyone sends for anyone else. If he wants them to come, he can send you back again, Charles.'

'That's all right, eh, as long as I have my boots.'

'Here they come.'

A maid arrived with the boots and Armitage put them on. He and Dr. Tenby went out into the rain. It was coming down quite heavily now, Daisy saw. She hoped it wouldn't make the excavations more dangerous. At least Alec had plenty of assistants now – the gardeners, the villagers, Pritchard's chauffeur... And while on the subject of chauffeurs– The butler was back, no doubt having instructed his subordinates to construct a stretcher.

'Barker, did Lord Rydal's man go to help?'

'No, madam. I am given to understand that Gregg failed to give satisfaction. His lordship informed him that his services would no longer be required after their return to London, but he chose to leave immediately.'

'And who can blame him!' Pritchard muttered.

'When was this?'

'This morning, madam.'

'And he actually did leave? How?'

'Madam?'

'I mean, did someone take him to the station, or was he seen trudging off down the drive with his bag in his hand and his box on his shoulder?'

For once Barker was at a loss. 'I'm afraid I don't know, madam. Gregg not being one of the household... Madison didn't take him, that's for sure. But he could have cadged a lift with Mr. Howell, or even with Sir Desmond's chauffeur.'

'They both took cars?'

'I believe so, madam.'

'Thank you, Barker.'

'If you'll excuse me, sir, I must ensure that work on the stretcher is proceeding according to plan.'

As Pritchard waved the butler away, Julia came down the stairs.

'Mother's still with Lady Ottaline.'

'Your mother is a saint, Miss Beaufort,' Pritchard said warmly.

Julia looked startled. 'The old dear is being rather a brick,' she conceded.

'My sister-in-law ought to be at Lady Ottaline's bedside,' he acknowledged, 'but I'm afraid she would not be a soothing companion.'

Daisy and Julia exchanged looks, but tactfully held their tongues. His comment reminded Daisy that Lucy had been left alone with Mrs. Howell for far longer than was advisable. But he had appeared puzzled by her questions about the chauffeur, Gregg, and she owed it to him, if not to satisfy his curiosity, at least to hear him out. He might even contribute something useful. Also, she

194

had questions for him.

'Julia, be an angel and tell Lucy I'm on my way,' she said. 'There's a couple of things I must discuss with Mr Pritchard.'

'Right-oh, but first tell me, have you heard anything more about the grotto?'

'Charles came to fetch Dr. Tenby. You just missed him.'

'Bother! He's all right?'

'Yes, perfectly, apart from wet feet. He came for his boots, too. He said they can't get through the grotto itself so they've all gone to dig in the hole in the hill.'

'That'll be fun, in this weather.' Wistfully, Julia added, 'I suppose I'd be in the way.'

'Definitely.'

'You mustn't dream of going out there, Miss Beaufort,' said Pritchard. 'Mr. Fletcher has plenty of men to help him.'

Julia nodded, sighed, and went off to the drawing room to rescue Lucy from Mrs. Howell – or vice versa.

'Will you come into my study, Mrs. Fletcher? I must ring Sir Desmond again, to tell him Lady Ottaline is in no danger, though I expect he's left the works by now.'

'How did he take it?' Daisy asked, preceding Pritchard along the passage.

'I was afraid you were going to ask me that. It's very difficult to say. Do sit down.' With a little sigh, he sank into the chair behind his desk, looking tired. 'He didn't explode with anger – in the circumstances that's a bad way to put it, but you know what I mean. He didn't sound desperately worried, though I told him I didn't know how badly she was injured.'

'I doubt if Sir Desmond ever sounds desperately anything. Either he's naturally detached or he cultivates detachment.' Even, or perhaps especially, with regard to his wife.

'Yes. There was something in his voice... But I may have imagined it. You know what the telephone lines are like.'

'What sort of something?'

'I just suspected he wasn't quite as indifferent as he wanted to sound. I couldn't pin it down to anything specific. But I hate to believe a man could be so unmoved by his wife being injured, so maybe it's wishful thinking.'

'Perhaps. Or a bad connection. He said he'd come straight back, though?'

'Hmm, not exactly. He said the business was nearly finished and he'd be back shortly. But we can't guess what was in his mind from a brief telephone conversation over a bad wire. What was in your mind when you wanted to know how Lord Rydal's chauffeur left the house?'

'Not so much *how* as *whether.*'

'Ah, yes, a different question altogether, now we know the explosion wasn't an accident.'

Daisy hadn't expected him to catch on so quickly. She should have. He impressed her more and more with his astuteness. She hoped Alec wasn't going to be annoyed with her for letting Pritchard see her suspicion of the chauffeur. To distract him, she said, 'You looked relieved when Charles Armitage said it looked like murder.'

Prichard was dismayed. 'Oh dear, was it

obvious? I'm afraid relief was my first reaction. After all, if the explosion had been caused by a gas leak, I'd have been to some degree responsible; whereas, though it may be unpleasant to have a murder on the premises, I can hardly be blamed if some idiot chose my grotto as a suitable place to blow up Lord Rydal.'

CHAPTER 21

Leaving Pritchard to try to reach Sir Desmond on the phone, Daisy went to the drawing room. She was halfway across the hall when Mrs. Howell came out. She was muttering to herself, distracted, and didn't notice Daisy. She hurried away and Daisy went on in.

'Darling!' Lucy greeted her. 'I thought you'd quite abandoned me to that madwoman.'

'Lucy thinks Mrs. Howell's gone completely off her rocker,' said Julia.

'Why?'

'She never was completely normal, if you ask me,' said Lucy. 'All that fuss about fish.'

'No more fuss than Rhino made.'

'Would you call Rhino completely normal?'

'Well, no. But not *crazy*.'

'He seems crazy to me,' said Julia. 'Swearing he adores me and will do anything in the world for me, and then going off for an assignation with Lady Ottaline.'

'That's men for you,' Lucy averred. 'Though

he could at least have waited till you accepted him! But to be fair, it was she who made the running.'

'You knew he had an assignation, Julia?' Daisy asked. 'Lady Ottaline could just have followed him to see where he was going.'

'Why on earth should he go to the grotto,' Lucy demanded, 'if not to meet her? That divan bed is quite comfortable – I sat down on it. And much more private than anywhere in the house.'

'Willett told me.'

'I knew I should have brought my maid,' said Lucy. 'We'd have known all about it, too.'

'Did Willett tell your mother?'

Julia gave a very Gallic shrug. 'I've no idea. Probably. She's on my side, though she's only been with us a few weeks, so she'd pass on anything that might change Mother's mind about him.'

Daisy wondered why Lady Beaufort hadn't already told her daughter she had changed her mind about Lord Rydal. 'If Willett knew, probably all the servants did, too, at least the upper servants. Hmm.'

'Daisy, are you sleuthing?' Lucy said suspiciously.

'As far as we know it was an accident,' Julia reminded her.

'That I could believe of anyone else, but not of Rhino. Besides, I recognise that look of Daisy's.'

'What look! I don't have a special "sleuthing" look.'

'Yes, you do. You know it wasn't an accident, don't you?' Lucy accused.

Lucy wouldn't believe her if she denied it. 'You won't tell Alec I told you, will you,' Daisy begged.

'You didn't tell us, darling. I guessed, all by my little self.'

'Well, don't breathe a word to anyone else, for pity's sake.'

'Our lips are sealed, aren't they, Julia?'

'Of course. Who do you think did it, Daisy?'

'The obvious person is Sir Desmond.'

'But he was in Swindon,' said Julia.

'Lady Ottaline was right on the spot,' Lucy mused. 'Perhaps she was hoist by her own petard? I've always wondered what a "petard" is.'

'Some sort of bomb,' said Daisy.

'It's in Shakespeare,' Julia elaborated. '*Hamlet*, isn't it, Daisy?'

'I wouldn't like to swear to it. Why should Lady Ottaline want to blow up Rhino? He came to heel very nicely, for a rhinoceros.'

The picture this conjured up made them all laugh for a moment. Then Lucy returned doggedly to the subject.

'He came to heel, yes, but unwillingly. You could see that, Daisy, or you wouldn't have used the phrase. I could see it. So it's not likely Lady Ottaline didn't realise, too. She must have been furious to be supplanted by a beautiful younger woman. That's you, Julia.'

'I didn't want him!'

'No, so she had no cause to be angry with you. All her fury – what's that thing about "hell hath no fury"?'

'Hell hath no fury like a woman scorned,' said Daisy.

'"Nor Hell a Fury, like a Woman scorn'd,"' said Julia.

'Whichever, that's Lady Ottaline to a T, isn't it? It's Rhino she had it in for. All the same, Julia, when she's recovered enough to get out of bed, you'd better watch your back.'

'You're assuming she set up the explosion,' Julia protested, 'but she was caught up in it herself.'

'She wanted to see him blown up,' Lucy said as if it were obvious. 'She miscalculated and got too close.'

'It's possible,' Daisy said reluctantly. 'I suppose we'd better keep an eye on you when Lady Ottaline comes down, unless Alec arrests some-one before then.'

'I hope he does, though I can't believe you're serious!'

'Well, it wasn't necessarily Lady Ottaline. Lucy, what were you saying about Mrs. Howell having a screw loose?'

'Religious mania. She told me Rhino was evil and deserved to be blown up, but it was all her brother-in-law's fault for putting pagan statues in the grotto. They're bound to attract evil people – and I'm telling you, the look she gave me was enough to make one believe in the evil eye!'

'You're the ones who were attracted by the grotto,' said Julia, not without satisfaction. 'So while I'm waiting for Lady Ottaline to stab me in the back you two will be waiting for Mrs. Howell to stab *you* in the back. But I still can't see how Lady Ottaline could have forced Rhino to go to meet her in the grotto, if he was really unwilling.'

Daisy looked at Lucy. The gossip about the

unlikely couple's long-standing affair was her story, and it was up to her to decide whether to enlighten Julia.

Lucy didn't hesitate. 'People have been talking about them for months. We wondered whether she threatened to tell you about their affair if he didn't cooperate.'

'Did you know about it before she arrived here at Appsworth?' Daisy asked.

'No. But I gather you did.'

'Not me. Lucy did.'

'I do think you might have told me, Lucy.'

'I would have, if there'd been the slightest sign you might accept him. Or if I'd had the slightest idea she was going to turn up here. When she arrived, I did consult Daisy. She said as I wasn't an eyewitness and the evidence wouldn't hold up in court–'

'I never did!'

'Near as makes no difference. Anyway, the way Lady Ottaline was behaving, you'd have had to be blind not to notice.'

'But Rhino,' said Daisy, 'being completely oblivious to everyone else's feelings, could easily be brought to believe you remained unaware. Even he, though, could hardly hope that he'd still stand a chance with you if she told you he was her lover.'

'Yes, I see. You almost make me feel sorry for him.'

'No!' said Lucy, revolted.

'I said "almost."'

'It's all speculation,' Daisy pointed out. 'Perhaps he had some other deep dark secret she was holding over him. It would have to be very deep and dark for him to deserve to be blown up. You're allowed to feel a bit sorry for him.'

Lucy shook her head. 'Not yet. We don't even know yet if he actually was blown up, or if so, whether he was killed.'

'Stone dead,' said Alec, 'and I use the word *stone* with due deliberation.'

He was in Pritchard's den, sitting in front of the big mahogany leather-topped desk, instead of in his accustomed place of power on the other side. This was not his only disadvantage. The detective inspector from Swindon had arrived just as Alec and his crew returned from the excavation. Alec had judged it best not to linger to take a bath before speaking to the local police. His hair, his nostrils, his fingernails, and his clothes were clogged with grey-white dust that, dampened by rain, took on the consistency of partly set plaster of Paris.

The butler had been swift to provide a dust sheet for him to sit on.

In response to DI Boyle's raised eyebrows, Alec elaborated. 'He was buried in a pile of chunks of limestone and pieces of marble statuary. One hit him on the temple and appears to have despatched him pretty nearly instantaneously. Just as well, perhaps, as he was badly burnt, probably prior to death. The doctor is a GP, not a police surgeon, and unfamiliar with having to make such determinations.'

'You didn't call in a police surgeon? Sir?'

'At the time I was in a position to send for help,

202

I had no reason to suppose a crime had been committed. The explosion could have been caused by a gas leak.'

'But now, you say, you have evidence of intent. Are you telling me,' said Inspector Boyle sceptically, 'you're here on the spot purely by chance?' Boyle had the sort of face that is naturally inexpressive and a flat voice to match. Nonetheless he managed, when he chose, to make his feelings perfectly plain.

'It happens to be the truth,' Alec insisted. 'My wife is down here to write about the grotto–'

'The one that got blown up.'

'It's the only one, to my knowledge. Look here, man, I'm as unhappy about this as you are.'

'Oh, I doubt it, sir. I doubt it very much.'

'All you have to do is treat my wife and me as ordinary witnesses. In fact, you're in luck. She was here for a few days before the incident, so she knows the people concerned, including the victim. I arrived just as it happened, but I went straight to the scene and I was there when the body was discovered, so I can tell you all about it. You could do worse than to... Sorry.'

'You see my difficulty, sir.' There was a glint of what might have been humour in Boyle's small, pale eyes.

'Yes. I beg your pardon. I'm already telling you the best way to start the investigation, and that Daisy and I are your best witnesses.'

'I'm not saying you're wrong, mind,' Boyle conceded.

A muffled snort came from his detective sergeant, a pale, plump young man in a green bow-

203

tie and wire-rimmed glasses. Boyle turned on him a stare worthy of a basilisk. He coughed and fidgeted with his pencil.

'Unfortunately,' said Alec, 'it's already too dark for you to see much out there.'

'It might have been helpful if Constable Endicott had seen fit to notify us somewhat earlier.'

'Endicott's not to blame. He didn't know until he joined us at the site that the explosion was no accident, and then I discouraged him from leaving to telephone before we knew for certain there were victims. He's a good man with a shovel, your PC Endicott.'

'Is he indeed! I'll have to remember that.'

Alec sent a mental apology winging towards Endicott. In defending him, he'd probably let him in for all sorts of unpleasant jobs in the future. 'We needed every man available. Wait till you see the mess. And we couldn't be too aggressive about clearing it for fear of causing further injuries, or further collapse.'

Boyle looked him up and down, sighed, and said, 'Perhaps I should be grateful to have arrived late. You'd better tell me the whole thing from the beginning, if you'd be so kind, sir.'

'My part started when I arrived here. My wife was eager to show me the grotto before it started raining. We had just gone out to the terrace at the rear of the house when the explosion occurred.'

'It was heard this far, then?'

'Believe me,' Alec said dryly, 'it was not only heard, it was seen and felt.'

Concisely, he described finding Lady Ottaline and exploring the outer grotto. He explained his

204

decision that digging in the tunnel was too difficult and too dangerous.

'Just a minute, sir. You haven't mentioned why you considered it necessary to dig. That is, what made you suppose someone might be underneath.'

'In the first place, gas doesn't explode by itself. There has to be a spark to ignite it, which suggested someone was there. Lady Ottaline was nowhere near the scene of the actual explosion. She was obviously caught in the blast, and she must have been outside the grotto or she'd have fallen twenty or thirty feet and probably be dead. So she hadn't provided the spark.'

'So someone else had.'

'Exactly. Never having been near Appsworth Hall before, I didn't know the lay-out of the grotto. Mr. Armitage explained it and sketched a plan.'

'Armitage? Who's he?'

'For that, I'll have to refer you to my wife. Or, of course, any of the residents of the house.'

'Right. Go on. Please, sir.'

'With Armitage's sketch as guide, we started digging in what seemed the most likely spot. I can explain my reasoning, but I'd prefer to postpone it until I've had a bath.'

Another muffled snort came from the sergeant.

'It can wait,' Boyle agreed.

'We were trying to get into the central cave of the grotto, which was only partly collapsed. We hadn't been at it long when one of the men heard a tapping noise. That made us both more determined and more cautious.'

The inspector nodded his understanding.

'To cut a long and painstaking story short, we found Lord Rydal's chauffeur, Gregg, bruised but essentially unhurt. The roof was more or less intact where he happened to be, over by one wall. A toppled statue pinned him down but also protected him from flying debris. He was able to point out to us more or less where he had last seen his employer. Lord Rydal was less fortunate. From the look of it, he was blown backwards against another statue and knocked it down, and then that part of the roof collapsed, killing him.'

'Lord Rydal's chauffeur,' said DI Boyle. 'What the devil was he doing there?'

'I decided I'd better not ask,' Alec told him. 'After all, officially, it's none of my business.'

CHAPTER 22

'So he wants me to help him unofficially,' Alec said grumpily, sitting on his dust-sheet on the bed. 'The worst of all possible worlds.'

'No, it's not, darling.' Daisy, in the adjacent bathroom, raised her voice to be heard over the rush of tap-water. 'You'd hate to be treated like an ordinary witness. This way, you can poke your nose in without being actually responsible for finding out who did it.'

'Poke my nose in!'

'What about me?'

'I'm quite sure he doesn't want you poking

your nose in. Isn't that bath full yet? I hope the hot water isn't going to run out.'

'The house belongs to a plumber, remember. No stingy boiler; Mr. Pritchard put modern gas geysers in every bathroom. Endless hot water, regulated by thermostat.'

'Gas. You did light the thing, didn't you?'

'Of course. I'd be dead from the fumes by now if I hadn't. Can't you see steam billowing?' She turned off the tap. 'There you are. Be careful, it's really hot. I hope the stuff you wash off doesn't solidify to cement in the pipes.'

'It's plaster, not cement.' Alec picked his way across the carpet, trying to keep the sheet wrapped round him so as to deposit as little debris as possible on the floor.

'Same difference. They both go solid.'

'My coat of plaster is as solid as it's going to get. This house belongs to a plumber. I'm sure he can deal with blocked pipes.'

'Do you want me to stay and scrub your back?'

'No, that's all right, if that's a loofah I see through the steam. I'm certain you're dying to go and poke your nose in.'

'I'll take that as permission,' Daisy retorted, and left before he could deny it.

She was halfway down the stairs when a maid caught up with her. 'Madam!' It was the same young girl who had summoned her to speak to Pritchard earlier, still – or again – both excited and anxious. 'The inspector wants to see you. In the den, madam, right away, he said.'

'Thank you. It's Rita, isn't it? Who else has the inspector talked to so far, Rita?'

'Just Mr. Fletcher and Mr. Pritchard, madam.'

'Really! Are you sure?'

'Yes, 'm. 'Lessn you count Len Endicott, our bobby from the village.'

Clearly Rita did not count PC Endicott.

'Is Constable Endicott still with the inspector?'

'No, 'm. He was sent out to guard the 'splosion.' This was said with such satisfaction that Daisy gathered Endicott was not merely of no account, but had somehow offended Rita. 'There's just 'Tective Inspector Boyle and 'Tective Sergeant Thomkin. Sir Desmond wanted to see them, madam, but Mr. Boyle said he'd have to wait his turn.'

'Odd! I wonder why he wants to see me first.' Daisy didn't expect an answer, far less the one she got.

'It was Mr. Pritchard, madam. He told the inspector he ought to talk to you before anyone else.'

Daisy didn't know whether to be flattered, affronted, or dismayed. She felt rather as if Pritchard had thrown her to the wolves, but why?

She thanked the girl and proceeded to the den, wishing it was interrogation by Alec she was going to face.

Without knocking, she went straight in and announced baldly, 'I'm Mrs. Fletcher. You wanted to see me?'

'Ah, yes, Mrs Fletcher.' The man behind the desk rose and came round to offer her a chair. His face gave away nothing of his thoughts, neither irritation at having been told by Pritchard what to do, nor gratitude for her compliance, but he said, 'Thank you for coming. I'm Detective Inspector Boyle of the Wiltshire police, and this is Detective Sergeant Thomkin.'

'How do you do?' Daisy sat down. 'What exactly makes you think I'm the best person to help you get started?'

'Mr. Pritchard told me you're a straightforward sort of person, madam. I'd say his judgement in that is already borne out. He also said he believes you to be observant, clear-sighted and unbiased.'

Even as Daisy stored up these compliments to relay to Alec, she felt herself blushing as she made a couple of mental reservations: She was not so unbiased as to credit for a moment that Lucy or Julia could have anything to do with the explosion. 'That's a lot to live up to,' she said guardedly.

'We shan't hold his words against you, if he was – ah – exaggerating a little,' said Boyle with apparent solemnity.

'I should hope not! What is it you want to know?'

'I gather you and Lady Gerald have been here several days. Tell me about the people who were here when you arrived. Let's keep it simple: make it in order as you encountered them. I'll probably interrupt with questions.'

'Right-oh. The first person we met was Lord Rydal, the victim. He had fetched our suitcases from the station, as no one else was available.'

'He was a friend of yours?'

'Lucy – Lady Gerald – knew him slightly, just because they both move in the same circles of

209

society. I'd never met him before. I'd heard of him, but only because my brother was at school with him.'

'A friend of your brother's, then.'

'I don't think he ever was, but in any case, not for the past several years. Gervaise was killed in the War. I rather doubt Lord Rydal had any real friends. One way or another, he managed to insult practically everyone.'

'Including you, Mrs. Fletcher?'

Daisy frowned in thought. 'To tell the truth, I can't remember any specific incident. He was just so generally objectionable, there was no point in taking it personally. Half the time he didn't even realise he was upsetting people, perhaps didn't realise other people have feelings to be hurt. I think– I have children, you know. Do you, Inspector?' Boyle nodded, and she went on, 'I think little children have to be taught to consider the feelings of others, and perhaps Rhino never was. He went through life like a blind bull – or rhinoceros – in a china shop, never noticing the destruction he wreaked.'

Boyle nodded again, but gave no other sign that he understood what she had tried to explain. 'Rhino was his nickname?'

'Thick-skinned, and pots of money.'

'Who's his heir?'

'Good heavens, I haven't the foggiest! Do you suppose his heir could have followed him here and somehow found out he was going to–'

'I don't know enough yet to suppose anything. He made enemies of everyone in the house?'

'"Enemies" is a bit strong. Umm...' She

reflected on the past couple of days. 'I can't actually name anyone he wasn't rude to at some point,' she confessed. 'But people don't go about murdering people just because they were rude.'

'It's not unknown,' Boyle said dryly. 'Let's continue with your arrival. What induced Lord Rydal, not a personal friend and so generally disobliging, to fetch your and Lady Gerald's bags for you?'

Daisy hesitated. But if she didn't tell him, plenty of others would. 'Julia. Miss Beaufort. He believed himself madly in love with her.' No need to explain that Julia had more or less invented the errand to get rid of him for a while.

'Miss Beaufort told you Lord Rydal was in love with her?'

'Gosh, no. Julia isn't the sort to boast of something like that.'

'Boast?'

'Well, however appalling he is – was – there's no denying he was an earl and a very well off one. She would have been a rich countess.'

'So Miss Beaufort was eager to marry Lord Rydal?'

'On the contrary, she couldn't stick him at any price. It was her mother who thought he was a great catch.'

'Her mother.' Boyle consulted a list. 'Lady Beaufort was pressing Miss Beaufort to accept the suitor she hated, and lo and behold! The suitor is murdered.'

'Bosh! Nowadays girls don't let their mothers choose husbands for them. Besides, Lady Beaufort changed her mind. I heard her say so.'

'To her daughter?'

'Who else would she tell?' Daisy hoped he wouldn't notice the evasion, but his next question suggested he was well aware of it.

'Miss Beaufort is an old – let me rephrase that – a friend of yours of long standing.'

'She was at school with Lucy and me, but I hadn't seen her in years before we came here. Let's see, who did we meet next? It must have been Barker, the butler. A very superior sort of butler. And then Mr. Pritchard.'

'How long have you known *him?*'

'Neither of us had ever met him before. He invited us because he liked the idea of his grotto being in our book.'

'I can't say I've ever had much to do with house-parties,' the inspector said severely, 'but this seems to me a very odd one.'

'It is,' Daisy agreed. 'You have to remember that Lucy and I are here on business, and Sir Desmond, too, and our being here is the only reason Alec and Gerald and Lady Ottaline came.'

'Business?'

'Sir Desmond's on government business. Something to do with slum clearance, I believe, but you'll have to ask him.'

'And you and – uh – Lady Gerald? What's your business?'

'I told you, our book. Nothing to do with plumbing or gas or explosions. It's about follies and– Oh, gosh, I've just thought. Perhaps our publisher won't want to include the Appsworth grotto now it's in ruins and someone's been killed in it! I wonder if Lucy–'

'Mrs. Fletcher, could we please get back to *my* business?'

'Do you want to go back to the order in which I met people? Because Sir Desmond didn't come into it till much later.'

'He didn't?'

'No, he and Lady Ottaline–'

'Never mind! We'll get to them in their proper place. Let's see, you'd reached Mr. Pritchard, who you'd never met before.'

'That's right. He came out to the hall to greet us. He took us into the drawing room, where Lady Beaufort and Julia–'

'Half a mo. Didn't you tell me about them already?'

'Only because you asked about the baggage.' Daisy was beginning to feel as confused as Boyle sounded. 'This always happens when Alec wants everything in order from the beginning. It's all interconnected, but more like a web than a chain.'

'Always?'

'Always?'

'You said "This always happens..."'

Daisy felt the blood suffuse her cheeks. Twenty-eight years old and still blushing like a schoolgirl! It was downright humiliating. 'I've...' Assisted? Better not, Alec might deny it. 'I've been involved in a couple of his cases.'

Boyle's face went blanker than ever. 'No doubt that would explain why he...' He didn't voice the remainder of his thought, so Daisy was sure it must be uncomplimentary, but whether to Alec or herself she couldn't be sure. Which was probably just as well.

'I'll keep going with our arrival,' she said hurriedly. 'It was tea-time. Lady Beaufort and Julia – Miss Beaufort – were in the drawing room. So was Mrs. Howell. She's Mr. Pritchard's sister-in-law and she lives here, though they don't seem to get on very well together. Let's see, I think Mr. Howell had come home by then. He's her son, Mr. Pritchard's nephew, or rather his late wife's, if you want to be precise. He runs their factory. Fortyish, and a confirmed bachelor to all appearances, but I haven't talked much to either of the Howells. I think that's all– No, Mr. Armitage was there, too. And Lord Rydal came in after us.'

'Armitage? Who's this Armitage?'

'He's staying here, but for a while, not just visiting for a few days as we are.'

'For a while?'

'I don't know exactly how long he's been here or how long he intends to stay. You'll have to ask him, or Mr. Pritchard. I don't know much about him except that he's Canadian.' And madly in love with Julia, but let Boyle find that out for himself. 'Oh, and he's a historian. He was very helpful in giving me information for my article.' After a still unexplained initial reluctance.

'Article? I thought you and Lady Gerald were writing a book.'

'I'm writing and she's taking photographs for a book. I'm also writing an article.'

DI Boyle's inexpressive face actually contrived to brighten. 'Lady Gerald has taken photographs of the grotto?'

'Of the two outer caves, at least. I don't think

214

she took any of the bit that blew up. It wasn't very interesting. But they're not snapshots, they're plates, and she'll want to develop them herself.'

'I would remind you, Mrs. Fletcher, that this is a murder investigation.'

'You don't need to remind *me*. It's Lucy you'll have to convince that your investigation is more important than her art. Irreplaceable art, what's more. We need those pictures. Lucy–'

'Do I hear my name being taken in vain?' Lucy drawled from the doorway. 'Rumour reached us, darling, that you were all on your lonesome being interrogated. Julia thought we'd better come and make sure you're holding your own.' She sauntered into the room.

Her words implied that Lucy herself was not at all concerned about Daisy's ability to stand up to a policeman or two. As usual, she was cool, calm, and collected, unlike Julia, who followed her in.

But of course, whichever way you looked at it, Julia had a great deal more to worry about. Not that Lucy's calm was destined to last very long.

Inspector Boyle stood up. Daisy introduced him. 'Darling,' she continued, 'Mr. Boyle is sure your photos of the grotto are going to prove very useful to him.' She sat back to enjoy the fireworks.

'My photos?' Lucy sounded as if she couldn't believe her ears. *'My* photos? The ones I've spent the last three days getting absolutely perfect? You can't be serious!'

'Absolutely serious, Lady Gerald. All I have is a rough sketch plan. Your photographs may be vital in working out exactly what happened.'

'What happened is that some benefactor of humanity turned on the gas and let Rhino blow himself up. You don't need my plates to work that out. And you're not getting them.'

'Lady Gerald, you are obstructing the–'

'I've obstructed the police in the course of their duties before, and no doubt I'll do it again!'

'Well, now, what have we here?' Alec came in, looking much more himself, though either his dark hair had greyed a bit while Daisy wasn't watching or he still had chalk dust in it. 'Three little girls from school. I do beg your pardon, Miss Beaufort. We're not well enough acquainted for me to–'

'Really, Alec!' said Lucy in disgust. 'That is not at all helpful. This person wants me to hand my photography plates over for some incompetent nincompoop to ruin, after I–'

'I'll get a warrant if I have to, sir. They may–'

'Now just calm down, both of you. No, Lucy.' He held up his hand. 'Hear me out. Boyle, is there any reason Lady Gerald should not develop her own plates and provide you with prints?'

'I suppose not,' Boyle admitted grudgingly. 'But we don't have our own darkroom in Swindon. I'll have to make arrangements.'

'Saturday evening,' Daisy pointed out. 'You won't find a commercial photographer open till Monday.'

'It seems to me,' Lucy said, a waspish note in her voice, 'if I have to do it, it'll be quickest and easiest if I dash back to town and use my own darkroom. I don't know how Gerald's going to like leaving a couple of hours after he arrived, having spent the interim digging.'

'I haven't had a chance to talk to Lord Gerald yet,' the inspector said doggedly. 'I need him to stay, as a witness to finding the victim. Or victims.'

'I'm quite sure my husband will have nothing to add to what Detective *Chief* Inspector Fletcher can tell you.'

'Nonetheless, I need to hear his description. And if you were thinking of staying in London, I'll be needing you to come back as soon as the photos are ready. I'll send Detective Sergeant Thomkin with you,' he added with a reckless air. 'Leave your notes with me, sergeant.'

Thomkin looked alarmed – even though he was ignorant as yet of Lucy's driving habits.

Lucy was furious. 'For pity's sake, Inspector! You expect me to drive off into the night with that...' She glanced for the first time at Thomkin. '...With such a dashing young man? My husband would definitely not approve.'

Daisy and Alec exchanged a glance. Gerald might be a rugger Blue and a financial wizard, but he'd never had a determining influence on Lucy's actions.

The sergeant protested incoherently, whether at being sent to London with Lady Gerald or at her imputation of dashingness was impossible to disentangle.

'On the other hand,' said Lucy, amusement abruptly taking the place of annoyance, 'did you want prints of all the pictures, Inspector? Every single one?'

'Certainly. It's for me to decide which are important.'

Lucy heaved a deep, dramatic, and undoubtedly spurious sigh. 'If you insist, I suppose I have no choice. Come along, what's your name, no time to waste. You can carry the plates down to the car for me.'

'Yes, your ladyship. Thomkin, your ladyship.' He gave his superior a reproachful look and his notebook, then followed Lucy out.

Inspector Boyle turned to Julia. While he explained to her that he would take her statement later and she had no need to stay at present, Alec said to Daisy in a low voice, 'What the deuce is Lucy up to?'

Daisy had an inkling of what was in Lucy's mind, but she gave him a wide-eyed, misleadingly ingenuous look as spurious as Lucy's sigh. 'Up to, darling? What makes you think she's up to something?'

'I know Lucy,' said Alec grimly.

CHAPTER 23

'Now I have no one to take notes,' said Detective Inspector Boyle gloomily. 'I've got some men coming over from Devizes, but it'll take them a couple of hours to get here. Swindon can't spare anyone on a Saturday night, what with the railway works and all.'

'I'm very good at taking notes,' Daisy said at once. 'Aren't I, Alec?'

'I've known worse.'

'You write shorthand?'

'Yes,' she said firmly.

'If you don't mind that she's the only person who can read it.'

'Darling, must you be so damping?'

'It's only fair that Mr. Boyle should know what he's getting himself into, if he decides to get.'

'Am I to assume, sir, that Mrs. Fletcher has taken notes for you in the past? In a police investigation?'

'Often,' said Daisy.

'Occasionally. She has never to my knowledge suppressed information she has written down in the course of an interview.'

Daisy was about to protest against his 'to my knowledge', when Boyle, passing over that derogatory caveat, pounced on the rest.

'Are you saying Mrs. Fletcher is liable to suppress information otherwise acquired, sir?'

'I've been told so often that hearsay isn't evidence,' Daisy told Boyle, 'that I don't report it, or gossip, unless it's of vital importance.'

'And just who decides what's of vital importance?'

'Who decides what's hearsay?' Alec put in. 'You must admit, love, that you're not altogether certain of the definition.'

'Even the courts don't seem able to decide on that,' said Boyle. 'All right, Mrs. Fletcher, I'll accept your kind offer to take notes, but I'd appreciate it if you'd allow me or the chief inspector to determine what's allowable evidence and what's not. Come to that, even inadmissible evidence can lead us in the right direction. Now, where were we when we were interrupted?' He opened Thomkin's notebook, turned to the last written-on page, and stared at it blankly.

'May I?' Daisy asked, reaching for it. 'Perhaps I don't write the clearest shorthand in the world but I'm an expert at deciphering it. Besides, what he wrote is what I told you.'

Reluctantly Boyle handed the notebook over. 'You'd better read it out loud from the beginning. Mr. Fletcher missed it.'

Daisy had no difficulty reading the detective sergeant's shorthand. She found her description of residents and guests at Appsworth transformed into indigestible officialese, so she transformed it back, in the process glossing over certain aspects. After all, her worry about the publisher refusing to include the scene of a murder in the folly book was not relevant. Alec wouldn't want to hear her philosophising about Rhino's upbringing and the twins. And she had exaggerated Julia's dislike of Rhino, giving Boyle the false impression that it could have led to murder. No need to repeat his words to Alec, who would much prefer to draw his own conclusions. Reaching Lucy's interruption of proceedings, she rushed on before Boyle had a chance to question the thoroughness of her report. 'Actually, now I come to think of it, Armitage and Howell weren't at tea, I didn't meet them till just before dinner. That was when the Wandersleys arrived, too. I already told you about Sir Desmond Wandersley. He's from the Ministry of Health, here on business.'

'I don't suppose you happen to know his rank?' Alec asked.

Daisy pondered. 'Principal Deputy Secretary, I'm pretty sure. Unless it's Deputy Principal Secretary...'

'No such thing. Lower level of the upper tier,' Alec informed Boyle. 'It behoves us to tread with care. What's he like, Daisy?'

'Expert at presenting a façade to the world.'

'That's what it takes to rise in the bureaucracy.'

'Good at small talk, fund of entertaining anecdotes–'

'Also prerequisites,' Alec said cynically. 'You said he's here on business? What's that all about?'

'Well, I haven't been privy to their discussions–'

'You surprise me.'

She frowned at him. '–Which were held at the Pritchard Plumbing plant in Swindon. But I gather he's in charge of some sort of contract for plumbing supplies for slum clearance. I did wonder– But that's not even hearsay, just pure speculation.'

'What did you wonder, Mrs. Fletcher?' Boyle demanded.

'If you get her going on her wild theories,' Alec warned, 'we'll be here all night.'

'Likely we will anyway. Sir. Mrs. Fletcher?'

'Oh, it's just that in spite of the façade, I could tell he wasn't at all pleased to find out I'm a journalist, and I wondered whether there might be something fishy about the contract.'

'Payments under the table?'

'I've no idea. His reaction wasn't necessarily anything to do with plumbing. Some people have an aversion to journalists as others do to police-men. After I assured him I was neither an investigative reporter nor a gossip-column tattler, he was quite friendly.'

Alec asked, 'Can you pinpoint whether one or the other was more responsible for his change in attitude?'

Daisy tried to remember. 'No, not really. Though subsequent events have made me wonder–'

'I see what you mean, sir,' said Boyle. 'Mrs. Fletcher is much given to wondering.'

'Is this material, Daisy?'

'Absolutely. But the best way to explain will be to go back to Mr. Boyle's method of telling you about each person in turn as I met them.'

'Not,' Boyle muttered, 'that you have been doing anything of the sort.'

Treating this observation with the silent disdain it merited, Daisy continued, 'Lady Ottaline Wandersley came in with Sir Desmond. I'd never met her, but Julia and Lucy told me– No, that's definitely hearsay. Isn't it, darling?'

'I expect so,' Alec admitted with a sigh. 'If it seems necessary, we'll ask them what they told you.'

'Not that it wasn't pretty obvious. She's one of those women who...' Daisy hesitated, not wanting to sound catty. 'You know the sort. She must once have been truly beautiful and she can't accept the fact that she's growing older and is no longer irresistible to men. She dresses to the nines, and she's still attractive–'

'When not covered in chalk dust!'

'You weren't terribly attractive yourself in the same condition,' she retorted. 'The important thing is that Lady Ottaline was pleased to see

Rhino – Lord Rydal – and he wasn't at all pleased to see her.'

'What made you think that?' Boyle asked sharply.

'I was standing beside Rhino, having recently suffered what passed for a conversation with him. When Lady Ottaline came in, he came over all tense and wary and made no move to greet the Wandersleys, although as later became apparent he was acquainted with both of them. And it wasn't at all like Rhino to be put out by anyone or anything.'

'And her ladyship?'

'She looked like the cat that stole the cream. A sort of self-satisfied smirk.'

'Sounds to me as if we should be arresting Lord Rydal for the murder of Lady Ottaline,' Boyle complained.

Daisy decided against trying to describe, let alone explain, her subsequent observation of Rhino and Lady Ottaline's behaviour and attitude towards each other. It was all hearsay and guesswork. She didn't mind expounding her theories to Alec and being told they were pure speculation, but she was getting tired of Boyle's quibbling. She was just plain getting tired, come to that. The day seemed to have gone on forever.

'Mr. Carlin arrived with the Wandersleys,' she said. 'He's Sir Desmond's Private Secretary, capital *P* capital *S* as in civil service rank. He was talking at breakfast today about getting back to town this evening for a golf match tomorrow. He went to Swindon with Sir Desmond and Howell.

I gathered he didn't intend to come back to Appsworth Hall.'

Boyle consulted a couple of sheets of paper on the desk in front of him. 'No doubt that's why Carlin is on the butler's list but not Mr. Pritchard's. I assumed he must be a servant. We'll have to get hold of him.' The inspector jumped up and rang the bell. 'I hope Thomkin hasn't left yet.'

'I'm sure Lucy's still packing up her stuff.'

'Undoubtedly,' Alec agreed. 'Speaking of servants, Daisy, I don't suppose you know anything about this Gregg chap, Lord Rydal's chauffeur-valet or whatever he was?'

'I never saw him, to my knowledge, but I heard about him shortly after meeting Rhino. Not by name, though. He was furious with him because when Julia asked him to fetch our bags, mine and Lucy's, from the station, he said he had to remove a grease spot from his dinner jacket so he couldn't go.'

Boyle blinked. 'Have I got this straight, Mrs. Fletcher: Miss Beaufort asked the chauffeur Gregg to fetch–'

'No, no, she asked Rhino – Lord Rydal – and he wanted to send his servant, but Gregg said he had to clean the jacket – Rhino's, that is, of course – so he couldn't go. He was acting as valet as well as chauffeur. Rhino told us he – the servant – was a lazy good-for-nothing, or something similar, and should have done it the night before. Gregg apparently claimed he hadn't been able to see it by artificial light. But that's hearsay,' Daisy added hurriedly.

'There was already bad blood between them,

then,' said Boyle, 'before Lord Rydal gave him the sack. What do you reckon he was doing in the cave, Mr. Fletcher?'

'I can't believe he'd be stupid enough to set up the explosion and then stay around to watch. Nor can I believe he was up to any good.'

'He might have seen whoever did set it up,' Daisy suggested, 'and hoped to return to Rhino's good graces by warning him. Not that Rhino had any good graces. Nor that anyone in their senses would want the job back.'

'And the doctor's sedated both him and Lady Ottaline,' the inspector said, morose now, 'so we can't ask any questions.'

'Tomorrow. Neither's badly injured. Daisy, you don't happen to have any other ideas about what Gregg might have been up to?'

'It would be the wildest speculation,' Daisy said virtuously. A parlourmaid came in. Boyle told her to find his sergeant and say he was wanted double-quick.

'He's in the hall, sir, waiting for Lady Gerald.'

'Good. Send him in. Mrs. Fletcher, do you know this Carlin's Christian name? Anything else about him?'

'Only that he's a civil servant. Ministry of Health, like Sir Desmond.'

DS Thomkin came in. Boyle explained about Carlin's departure. 'You'd better try and bring him back with you,' he said. 'Find out what you can about his likely whereabouts from Wandersley before you leave and see if you can track him down while Lady Gerald is working on those photographs.'

'Yes, sir,' said the sergeant despondently.

'Here.' Alec handed him a bit of paper on which he had just written a name. 'Call the Yard and ask for this chap. Tell him to give you a hand, as a purely unofficial favour to me.'

'Yes, sir!' said Thomkin, looking a trifle more hopeful.

'All right, get on with it. Let's hear your wild speculation now, Mrs. Fletcher.'

'What— Oh, yes, about Rhino's servant. Well, Barker didn't mention it, but I bet Rhino refused to give Gregg a letter of reference. It wouldn't surprise me if Gregg followed him in hopes of doing a little blackmail, not for money but for a good recommendation.'

'Blackmail?' Boyle said in surprise. 'On what grounds?'

'Sorry!' said Alec. 'I thought someone would have told you by now. It seems to be common knowledge that Lord Rydal and Lady Ottaline had an assignation in the grotto.'

Boyle glared at Daisy. 'Somehow that vital detail failed to reach me. But "common knowledge" is hardly meat for blackmail.'

'It depends how common it is,' Daisy argued. 'I expect Rhino would have given a good deal to conceal his liaison from two people in particular. Or possibly three.'

'Who?'

'Well, Julia, obviously, since he adored her. Insofar as he was capable of adoration. And her mother, Lady Beaufort, who had been supporting his suit, but would more than likely change her tune if she found out he was consorting with his mistress while courting Julia. And Sir Desmond, of course. Except that I doubt he was still in ignorance, or, come to that, whether Rhino cared whether he knew.'

'When you say it was common knowledge, Daisy, what exactly do you mean? How common?'

'Umm. Actually, I just guessed. I put together the way they behaved, something I overheard–'

'What?'

'Isn't that hearsay?'

'Not if they were speaking of their own actions,' Alec said patiently.

'Oh, really? Lady Ottaline said they'd never manage to find privacy in the house, which was why... And then the door closed so I didn't hear why what. But when Lord Rydal missed coffee after lunch and then I saw Lady Ottaline sneaking off through the garden, I put two and two together. Lucy guessed, too, and the Beauforts' maid told Julia, so I presume most if not all of the household servants knew. Goodness only knows whom they told.'

Boyle pounced. 'Miss Beaufort told you she knew?'

'This afternoon.' Daisy attempted to sound as if she was clarifying her statement, though her intent was to obfuscate. She didn't know when Julia had found out, and she shouldn't have mentioned her in justifying the statement that the rendezvous was common knowledge. 'But once Lucy was aware that Lady Ottaline had been injured and Rhino was missing, she said it was obvious what they'd been up to.'

'The first thing is to talk to the servants,' Boyle proposed to Alec, 'see what they know, how they know it, and who they've told. They'll probably know more than most about people's movements, too.'

'A good place to start,' Alec agreed smoothly. 'If you want to get going on that, I'll just get the details from my wife as to exactly when and where she overheard Lord Rydal and Lady Ottaline.'

'Right you are, sir. I'll go and talk to them in the servants' hall. I'll take my own notes.' With a pointed look at Daisy's blank notebook, he departed.

'Oh dear,' said Daisy, 'I didn't take any notes after all. It would have seemed rather odd taking notes of my own interrogation.'

'Never mind notes. You may have pulled the wool over DI Boyle's eyes, though I wouldn't count on it, but you can't distract me so easily. When did the maid tell your friend Julia about that pretty pair making their assignation?'

'What does it matter? Julia had no reason to blow Rhino up. She just had to keep saying no.'

'Daisy, you know I can't let it go at that. I agree that there are others who would appear to have better motives, but Julia Beaufort is definitely on my list. Now tell me about your eavesdropping.'

'Eavesdropping! They knew I was there.'

Before she could explain, the door swung open. Mrs. Howell marched in. In a shrill voice, she announced, 'I know who did it!'

CHAPTER 24

As Alec sprang to his feet to offer Mrs. Howell his chair, Daisy scribbled on her pad: *Don't believe a word she says!* Certain that he'd move to his preferred position behind the desk, she tore off the leaf and slid it across the leather top.

He glanced at it, then at her with a frown, then continued seating Mrs. Howell with his best soothing manner.

Daisy had no idea what Mrs. Howell was going to say, whom she was going to accuse. But the woman was full of rancour and didn't seem to care about anyone except her son. Even there, it was a case of care *about*, not care *for*. Daisy had seen no signs of affection between them. If Mrs. Howell promoted Owen's interests, it was, to all appearances, only because they meshed with her own.

Besides, Lucy had said their hostess seemed to be developing some sort of religious mania. None of that had seemed relevant when Daisy was telling DI Boyle about the Howells, but if she was going to go round accusing people, her state of mind could not be ignored.

Alec sat down behind the desk. Reading the note without touching it, he leant forward. 'Please go on, Mrs. Howell.'

Since her dramatic entrance, Mrs. Howell hadn't said a word. She didn't seem to notice

Daisy sitting there with her notebook at the ready. She stared wild-eyed at Alec, her mouth opening and closing silently. Even if she happened to be telling the truth, she didn't at present look in the least like a credible witness.

'You say you know who blew up the grotto?' Alec prompted.

'An evil place! Full of pagan idols and popery! *He* built it and *he* destroyed it.'

'Mr. Pritchard?' His tone was so neutral as to express incredulity. 'Why should he destroy his own creation?'

'I told him.' She was triumphant. 'I convinced Brin of the wickedness, the shame of it.'

'How do you know he acted on his conviction?'

'I saw him.' Mrs. Howell looked away from Alec and started to fidget with her skirt. 'I saw him going to that place this morning, after breakfast. I didn't go down to breakfast and I happened to glance out of my bedroom window, and I saw him.'

'You're certain it was Mr. Pritchard?'

'Of course,' she asserted, gaining confidence. 'I've known him since my poor sister married him forty years ago. I couldn't possibly be mistaken.'

'What time did you see him?'

'I can't say for sure. I didn't think anything of it then. Why should I? He's obsessed with his horrible grotto! He's so eager to show it off, he lets complete strangers come and stay in the house if they express the slightest interest, without any regard for my convenience. He even lets that man live here, just because he wants someone to play hermit now and then. What does

Mr. Armitage want, poking about in dusty old papers that should have been cleared out years ago? Up to no good, if you ask me, and carrying on with that girl, into the bargain. But Brin won't hear a word against him.'

Alec responded to this tirade with a mild 'How long have you lived in Mr. Pritchard's house?'

'What does that have to do with anything? We're not living on his charity, I assure you! My husband left me plenty of money, and half the firm to Owen. Brin only invited us to live here so as to have someone to entertain his guests and so he can keep his thumb on Owen.'

'Oh?'

'He's supposed to have retired, but Owen can't do a thing without consulting his uncle. I don't know why Owen doesn't let him get on with it. My son could live like a gentleman if he sold off his half of the business. But no, all he cares about is Pritchard's Plumbing. He hasn't even got his own name on it! I should never have let him visit the plant when he was a boy. My husband never went near the place.'

'Could we get back to what you saw this morning, Mrs. Howell? Where exactly was Mr. Pritchard, and what was he doing?'

She blinked at Alec vaguely, as if she'd forgotten the purpose of this interview. Perhaps Lucy was right, Daisy thought, and she had developed a mania, though it seemed to be more concerned with her brother-in-law than religion. Why had she turned against him?

'He was walking along the path towards the grotto,' she said at last. 'Almost running. And he

231

kept looking behind him as if he was afraid of being seen. I knew he was up to something terrible. He's an evil man. You must arrest him at once and take him away.'

'I'm afraid I can't do that, you know, not simply on your word. Especially as he doesn't seem to have done anything dreadful while you were actually watching him.'

Mrs. Howell deflated. Rubbing her forehead, she complained, 'I have a frightful headache. I'd better go and lie down till dinnertime.'

'We'll talk again later, when you're feeling well enough.'

Alec went to open the door for her. Closing it behind her, he ran his hand through his hair. The crisp crop shed a dusting of chalk and became one shade nearer its usual dark hue. 'Whew!' he exclaimed, returning to the desk. 'What a virago. I hope you're going to explain what that was all about.'

'She seems to have gone completely dotty!'

'She's got it in for Pritchard all right. But at a guess there's method to her madness. When one gets a wild accusation like that, it's often an attempt to cover up guilt, either her own or her son's.'

'Pure speculation, darling, and I doubt it. Rhino was rude to her but no more so than to everyone else. She forgave him because of his title.'

'She seems to have a genuine hatred of that wretched grotto. Perhaps she wanted to blow it up and didn't consider that someone was bound to get hurt in the process.'

'It's possible, I suppose, but I don't believe

she's that dimwitted. In any case, it wouldn't surprise me if she hadn't the slightest idea how to do it, or even that turning on the gas could cause an explosion. *That* dim-witted she is.'

'What about protecting her son?'

'Owen Howell – well, I just can't imagine him blowing up perfectly good machinery, if that's the right word. Technical equipment. He got quite indignant over Rhino being careless with Lucy's camera stuff.'

'Indignant at Rhino?'

'Yes, but not violently. In general he's cool, calm, and collected. He rejoices in what you might call an orderly brain. In fact, he's one of the most rational people I've ever met. I can think of much more likely motives for Mrs. Howell to try to get Pritchard arrested.'

'Such as?'

'It boils down to simply getting rid of him. She may have enough money to be independent of him, but she likes being chatelaine of Appsworth House. I've heard him talk about letting women have their own way in the house, for the sake of peace, but in actual fact, as far as I can see, everything is run his way. He invites whomever he chooses, his favourite food is served – and his unfavourite not served–'

'What do you mean by that?'

'It's a fishy tale, darling, that's completely irrelevant. I'll tell you sometime. Suffice it to say, they don't get on at all well. He teases her and she carps at him– Oho, more fish! I'll have to tell Lucy and Julia.'

'Daisy!'

'Sorry. The important thing is that Owen inherits the house, I gather, as well as everything else, including Pritchard's interest in the company. He doesn't seem to be in any hurry, but obviously if Appsworth was his, his mother's position would be much enhanced. She could even consider herself safely ensconced for life, because he's not the marrying kind.'

'How on earth do you know?'

'For a start, he's forty and unmarried. And he appears to appreciate Julia's looks, but doesn't follow her about with his tongue hanging out, like Rhino and...' Bother! She didn't want to draw attention to Charles Armitage's passion for Julia.

'And?'

'And I've never seen him show the least sign of jealousy. He's far more interested in explaining the latest technological improvements in the safety of water heaters than in Julia being beautiful and in need of a wealthy husband.'

'The safety of water heaters? Was it a water heater that blew up out there?'

'Probably. But, if I've got this right, it couldn't have been a steam explosion because – let's see – because the gas can't be turned on before the water is. Or something of the sort.'

'I'm going to have to talk to Howell and Pritchard about the technical aspect of the explosion. Or rather, Boyle is. I suppose I'd better bring him up to date on Mrs. Howell's rant.'

'You don't believe her, do you?'

'Great Scott, no! Too many inconsistencies in her story, not to mention her manner. But all the

234

same, as you're well aware, I don't know nearly enough to cross Pritchard off the list.'

Daisy sighed. 'I like him. I can't believe he'd destroy his beloved grotto just to get rid of an irritating guest who was leaving soon anyway. But I know you and your precious list.'

'"You know my methods, Watson." Can you spare a sheet from your notebook, or shall I pinch some of Pritchard's paper?'

'He wouldn't mind, but if you feel it's inappropriate for a policeman to misappropriate his host's stationery, here you are.' She tore off a blank page and handed it over. 'What's it for?'

'Just a note for Boyle. I don't want to send a verbal message and have it published to the world before it reaches him. Ring for a servant, would you, love?'

The little maid Rita scurried in a very short time later, as flustered as ever.

'Have you been promoted to parlourmaid, Rita?' Daisy asked her.

'Oh no'm. That Mr. Boyle's asking Lily questions, and Mr. Barker said I was to come.' She scurried off again with Alec's note, but some time passed before Boyle appeared. While they waited, Alec asked Daisy what she had really been going to say when she'd stopped herself after comparing Lord Rydal's pursuit of Julia with Howell's lack of interest. She should have known he wouldn't miss her hesitation. She managed to fob him off with the fish story, which made him laugh, but she knew the reprieve was temporary.

Boyle arrived before he could press her. 'Sorry to have kept you waiting. The girl only just gave

235

me your note. She didn't want to interrupt. What's up?'

'The lady of the house has accused her brother-in-law of blowing up the grotto.'

'Wonderful!' the inspector said acidly. 'I can't possibly get a warrant at this time on a Saturday evening.'

'Not so fast. Wait till you've heard what she said. Daisy?'

Daisy read her notes aloud. She had written them recently enough to be able to decipher them without difficulty. Mrs. Howell's ranting didn't sound quite as mad in her own prosaic voice, but it was still pretty mad.

'Well now,' Boyle said doubtfully, 'that's not good enough for a warrant, agreed, but Mr Pritchard's going to have to account for himself. What was he doing trotting off through the gardens towards the grotto at that time in the morning?'

'I think it's pure fabrication,' said Daisy. 'He told me he had a few things to do in here before he gave me a tour of the house, and I bet he was right here the whole time.'

'Why should Mrs. Howell fabricate a story to incriminate her brother-in-law?'

'You'll have to explain, Daisy.'

'But it's all speculation, darling. With a bit of hearsay mixed in, I shouldn't be surprised.'

In spite of his naturally inexpressive features, Boyle's look spoke louder than words. 'If you recall, Mrs. Fletcher, I told you I want to hear *everything*.'

So Daisy repeated the arguments she had already given to Alec.

'Sounds reasonable,' Boyle conceded. 'All the same, sir, we'll have to ask him about it.'

'Of course. I didn't mean to suggest otherwise. However, I don't consider it urgent. But it's your case,' Alec apologised.

'Maybe we'd better change that, put it on a formal footing. In the morning I'll ring up my super and ask him to put it to the Chief Constable–'

'Great Scott, no! The more informal we can keep it, the happier I'll be. You may have to remind me now and then, though, Inspector, that I have no standing whatsoever in this case. I am merely a consultant.'

'Well, sir, if you insist. For the present at least. Suppose I was to want to consult you right this minute. What'd you say's the most urgent item on the agenda?'

'First, did you get anywhere with the servants? I'm sorry I interrupted you, but it seemed to me that, being in charge, you'd have had every right to be annoyed if I hadn't let you know immediately about Mrs. Howell's claim.'

'Even though you don't think it's important. I would've been. I found out what we wanted to know. The parlourmaid, Lily Inskip, she overheard Lord Rydal and Lady Ottaline last evening, arranging a rendyvoo. She was in the drawing room, seeing everything was put straight after Mrs. Howell went up to change for dinner, when those two came in from the grotto. That right, Mrs. Fletcher?'

'Yes, most of us went to the grotto after tea. Lady Beaufort hadn't seen it yet. Lady Ottaline

237

said she was getting cold and Pritchard suggested Lord Rydal should escort her back to the house. He didn't want to but Julia made some remark about being ungallant so he went. We were all glad to see the back of both of them.'

Boyle nodded. 'Miss Inskip, she says they looked like they'd been arguing. They didn't see her at first. As Lady Ottaline stepped in through the French window, she turned and said to him, "The grotto, at two tomorrow, if you know what's good for you. No one will be there then." His lordship muttered something the maid didn't hear. Then they saw her and shut up. Then – and this is the most interesting bit, to my mind – Sir Desmond came in. Miss Inskip had left the door to the hall open to make it easier to carry out ashtrays for cleaning, so she didn't hear him arrive and can't say if he heard what Lady Ottaline said.'

Alec nodded. 'Sir Desmond has by far the most obvious motive.'

'But he's a bigwig, and if he didn't do it, we don't want to have given him cause to bring a hornet's nest about our ears.'

'Very true. Did you find out who else knew about the planned meeting?'

'Miss Inskip went straight off to have a good gossip with the housekeeper and the cook, and one way or another all the indoor servants got to hear about it. The visitors' servants, too. Miss Willett told Lady Beaufort and Miss Beaufort when she went to dress them for dinner – not this afternoon, like you said, Mrs. Fletcher.'

'I didn't! I said Julia told us this afternoon that

Willett had told her. I didn't know when.'

'You gave me the impression—'

Alec intervened. 'Who else among the household and guests was told?'

'Most of 'em,' Boyle said morosely, 'one way or another. There's not a one I can say for sure didn't know.'

'You obviously didn't have much difficulty getting them to talk.'

'The butler, Barker, said right off he wasn't going to gab about anything he hadn't seen for himself, and for a moment I thought they were all going to go bolshie on me. But most of 'em were dying to talk, and the housekeeper said it was their duty to help the police, so after that it was plain sailing. Barker never did come round though. Said it wasn't his business to gossip about his employer's household or guests. Very high and mighty, is Barker,' he said with considerable resentment.

'A cross between Jeeves and the Admirable Crichton,' Daisy observed. 'Even Rhino, though he was forever moaning about the failings of servants in general and his own in particular, never complained about Barker. You'd almost think Barker had a hold on him, like Lady Ottaline.'

Boyle stared at her, mouth open, as if struck by a *coup de foudre*. 'What if Lord Rydal – him being a ladies' man – what if he once seduced Barker's daughter, or sweetheart, or even his wife? What if the butler did it?'

CHAPTER 25

'No,' said Daisy.

As though summoned by the monosyllable, Barker entered in his stately manner. He didn't look at all like a man who had just taken violent revenge on the noble ravisher of his beloved.

He addressed Alec. 'I beg your pardon for interrupting, sir, but Mr. Pritchard wishes to know whether you will be free to dine with the company.'

Alec turned to Boyle. 'What do you think?'

Boyle glanced at Daisy, then said firmly, 'Yes, you'd better.'

'Then I shall.'

'Thank you, sir. Dress will be informal.' The butler turned to Boyle. 'A tray will be brought to you here,' he said with severity and no 'sir'.

Bland and impassive, Boyle said. 'That'll do me nicely, thank you. All you servants working on those timetables I asked for, are you?'

'Insofar as it is compatible with preparations for dinner.' He bowed to Daisy and departed in good order.

'Snooty, bloody-minded s– If you'll excuse the expression, Mrs. Fletcher. What did you mean by "No"?'

'I can't believe the butler did it.'

'It's hard to see Barker as an explosive sort of chap,' Alec agreed, 'though I'm sure he'd do it very efficiently if he set his mind to it. But something less violent, poisoning for instance, would be more his line, I'd say.'

Daisy agreed. 'But it's not only that. My impression of Rhino is that it's dashing ladies of the smart set who appeal to him, not ruining innocent servants and shop girls. Lucy would know if there are any rumours to the contrary.'

'And Lucy's in London. Still, I wouldn't put Barker high on my list. You know, Inspector, while timetables are going to be useful, we're not going to get far until we have some idea at what o'clock the trap must have been set. If I remember correctly, a certain proportion of gas in the air is a necessary condition for an explosion.'

'How the deuce are we going to work that out? Wouldn't we need to know the volume of the room for a start? Well, it hasn't got a volume any longer.'

'No,' said Daisy, 'but I bet Mr. Pritchard knows, or could work it out. Look at that cabinet, darling. Aren't those deep, shallow drawers meant for plans and technical drawings? Blueprints? I can't see why he'd have stuff from Pritchard's Plumbing at home. It's far more likely to be the plans for the grotto.'

Boyle jumped up and went to open the top drawer. 'Yes! Appsworth Grotto it says. Good thinking, Mrs. Fletcher.'

Daisy preened. 'I have my uses on occasion,' she said modestly.

'I can't read 'em, can you, sir?'

'Not me. There's gas pressure to be considered, too. We'd better have Pritchard in and ask him to explain the whole thing.'

'Howell at the same time, d'you think? He must know a lot about gas, if not the grotto itself.'

'At the same time? What do you think, Daisy, if Pritchard tried to mislead us, would Howell back him?'

'How would I know? But no, I don't think so. He has too much respect for matters technical. He came back from Swindon, I take it?'

'Yes, he and Sir Desmond, while I was talking to the servants.'

'Well, I don't suppose Howell would outright contradict his uncle, but he'd probably argue.'

'That's my feeling,' Boyle agreed. 'These engineering types can't stand it if everything's not spot on.'

'Let's get them in here, then,' said Alec, 'and get that sorted out before we – you – start asking them questions that will upset them.'

'I'll ring for Barker.' Boyle reached for the bell.

'Don't bother,' said Daisy. 'If you can spare me, I'm off. It's no good asking me to take notes of what they say. Technical stuff sends me to sleep. I'll tell them you want to see them.'

'Thank you, Mrs. Fletcher. Don't tell them what we want them for, please. Would you mind writing up what notes you've already taken so that they're ... available when my men arrive?'

'Legible, you mean. Right-oh.'

Daisy went to the drawing room. There she found Pritchard and Howell, as well as Julia and Lady Beaufort, Charles Armitage, and Gerald. Pritchard and Howell had their heads together. When Daisy gave them the message, Howell said, his tone congratulatory, 'You were right, Uncle. Good job we've got it straight in our heads. Won't take half a moment to look up the numbers for them.'

'Now don't you go giving them the impression we can provide an exact answer,' Pritchard said as they headed for the door. 'There's too many variables. We don't know how many gas taps were–' The door cut him off.

So much for not telling them what they were to be asked, Daisy thought. No doubt Boyle would blame her, though he had seemed to be softening a little.

'Daisy, what the deuce is going on?' Gerald asked. 'Miss Beaufort says Lucy's dashed off back to town with a copper in tow, to develop some photos the police need. It's not like Lucy to go out of her way to help the police, not even Fletcher. What does she have up her sleeve?'

Daisy was in a quandary. It seemed only fair for Gerald to know what his wife was up to, but it wouldn't be fair to Lucy to spoil her surprise. She glanced at Julia and Armitage, who both looked amused, so they had presumably worked out what was going on.

'They want her pictures of the grotto,' she said at last, 'and she doesn't trust them not to spoil her plates. Neither Alec nor the inspector saw it before the explosion so they don't really have an idea of what it was like.' She turned to Lady Beaufort. 'How is Lady Ottaline?'

'Uncomfortable. Her back is considerably bruised and she has a headache from a knock on the head, but no concussion, the doctor says, and no broken bones. He's given her some powders. He says she should be up and about in a couple of days, though moving stiffly.'

'No! Don't tell me Dr. Tenby actually managed to utter so many consecutive words.'

'Far from it. The information was conveyed in a series of grunts. After living so long in France, I'm quite good at interpreting incomprehensible utterances.'

'Mother, your French is as good as mine.'

'More than one of the Dinard tradesmen spoke in grunts, you must admit, my pet, and French grunts at that. But I shouldn't be joking when poor Lord Rydal is lying dead and Lady Ottaline in great discomfort.'

'Is Sir Desmond with her?' Daisy wondered aloud.

'Yes. He's very much shocked at what happened in his absence. One must hope,' Lady Beaufort said doubtfully, 'that the disaster will bring them closer together.'

'Should've put a stop to her nonsense years ago,' Gerald muttered.

Lord Gerald Bincombe being almost as devoted to taciturnity as Dr. Tenby, Daisy hadn't considered him as a source of information. 'You know Sir Desmond, Gerald?' she asked.

'Only to nod to at the club.'

'But you've known about Lady Ottaline's ... activities for years?'

'M'father warned me to steer clear when I first went up to town,' he said uncomfortably.

'You're older than Gervaise, though younger than Alec, so she was already notorious before the War. Sir Desmond *must* have known she was apt to stray. The only question is, did he know specifically about Rhino?'

'Look here, Daisy, it's not the sort of thing a chap likes to talk about in the drawing room!' He glanced at Lady Beaufort.

'Let's go somewhere else, then.'

'Don't mind me,' said her ladyship robustly. 'I lived with the Army too long to pay any heed to what's fit to discuss in a drawing room. If there's someone else with a better motive for doing Rydal in than Charles Armitage, I want to know about it.'

Julia gaped at her. 'Mother!'

'I'm not blind.'

'But you don't want me to marry him, so why should you care—'

'I changed my mind when I discovered Lord Rydal's character. A woman is permitted to change her mind, I believe.'

'Why on earth didn't you tell me?'

'That's *my* business.'

'It may not remain your business,' Daisy warned. 'I don't know along what lines Boyle is thinking, but the police are liable to ferret out absolutely everything.'

'Let them try,' said Lady Beaufort. 'Now, Lord Gerald, did Sir Desmond know about his wife's ... connection with Lord Rydal, or did he not?'

'He didn't confide in me,' Gerald said stiffly, 'but it was common talk. I doubt he could fail to be aware of it.'

'Quite apart from her behaviour here,' Armi-

245

tage put in, tearing his bemused gaze from Julia's glowing face. They were now openly holding hands.

Daisy looked pointedly at the clasped hands. 'The police may ferret out everything, but there's no need to make it too easy for them.'

Armitage dropped Julia's hand as if it were a smoking gun.

Julia frowned. 'You think it's best to pretend we aren't ... um...'

'On second thought, no. They'll find out anyway and it'd just look fishy. At least, I'm not sure of Inspector Boyle's abilities, but Alec will find out.'

'Fletcher's in on the investigation?' Gerald asked.

'Sort of. He's caught between two stools. He doesn't really want to get involved, but he already is, having seen the explosion and found the body. Boyle's in the same position: He doesn't want Scotland Yard taking over his case, but having an expert on the scene and already mixed up in it, how can he avoid asking for help? So they're trying to keep their collaboration informal. The trouble is, Alec finds it frightfully difficult not to take charge.'

'Is it a good thing for us if he takes charge?' Julia asked.

'He won't let my opinions influence him,' Daisy said, 'if that's what you mean. But he'll get at the truth with the least disruption possible, and he'll rein in the inspector if he gets any wild ideas into his head. At least, he'll try,' she amended.

Lady Beaufort looked alarmed. 'Wild ideas?'

'Well, Boyle's already proposed applying for a warrant to arrest – a certain person, on very slim grounds. Alec dissuaded him, but there's no knowing what direction he'll go off in next.'

'What it boils down to,' Boyle grumbled, 'is that you can't give us an answer.'

'Not unless you find all the gas taps,' said Pritchard.

'Even then, we couldn't be precise, Uncle,' Howell objected, 'not with the ventilation being natural and its flow never measured.'

'Close enough for these gentlemen, I daresay.'

'What beats me is how *he* worked out how long it would take for the gas to build up to explosive proportions.'

Boyle pounced. *'He?'*

'The murderer,' said Howell patiently.

'You think it was a man?'

'Stands to reason, doesn't it? Ladies aren't really interested in the technical details. Mrs. Fletcher asked for a demonstration of the new safety features on the hot water geysers, but I could see, her attention soon wandered. None of the rest even expressed an interest.'

'Did any of the men?' Alec asked.

'Er, well, no.'

'So you two are the only ones with the necessary knowledge,' said Boyle, darting a significant look at Alec.

'Except that even we couldn't be precise,' Howell repeated, in the tone of one prepared to reiterate the point as often as necessary.

'It seems to me,' said Alec, 'that everything

points to someone who in fact had no expert knowledge. Someone who had heard of coal-gas explosions, but had no idea they only occur if the proportion of gas to air is between five and fifteen percent.'

'Roughly,' Howell insisted. 'It depends to some degree on the local distribution of the various components of the gas. Some are heavier than air, some lighter, so—'

'I think Mr. Fletcher has grasped that point, Owen.'

'In your discourse on the geyser, Mr. Howell, did you happen to mention that explosive fraction?'

'Certainly not. I was talking about the new safety feature that prevents a steam explosion. I'm not at all sure all my audience grasped the difference, but I didn't touch on gas explosions at all. They are much more difficult, if not impossible, to prevent, but considerably less likely to occur.'

'What happens if the concentration's too high and someone walks in?' Boyle asked.

'They smell the gas and walk out,' said Pritchard. 'In a hurry. Unless there's a spark or flame entering with them.'

'As was presumably the case with Rydal,' Alec put in.

'He always had a lit cigarette, or was in the process of lighting one. If there was too much gas to explode, there would almost certainly be a fire, which could well have killed Lord Rydal equally effectively.'

'*Almost* certainly,' Boyle groaned. 'You're right,

Mr. Fletcher, it looks as if he was killed by someone who had no idea what he was doing. And that means *she* is just as likely as *he*.'

CHAPTER 26

Even with the addition of Alec and Gerald, a diminished company sat down to dinner. Lucy had left for London and her studio; Carlin for London and his golf match; Lady Ottaline and Mrs. Howell had both taken bromides and stayed abed; and Rhino's absence made itself felt in a curious combination of lightened spirits and wariness.

Sir Desmond had come down at the last minute. He responded to queries about his wife's condition with his usual suave courtesy– 'resting as comfortably as can be expected' – but, not unnaturally, he looked harried.

Mr. Pritchard invited Lady Beaufort to take Mrs. Howell's place at the end of the table. With six men to only three women, seating was necessarily informal, though Daisy suspected Mrs. Howell had in any case been responsible for previous attempts at formality. Sir Desmond, of course, had a proper appreciation of hierarchy. He appropriated the place to Lady Beaufort's left, leaving that on her right to Gerald, but Gerald chose familiarity over precedence. He sat down next to Daisy, who had found herself on Pritchard's right, opposite Julia.

Lady Beaufort beckoned Alec to the empty chair beside her. Howell beat Charles Armitage to Julia's side – or perhaps Charles was being discreet. He took the one remaining seat, between Sir Desmond and Gerald.

Daisy was amazed at how much one could guess about people simply from where they chose to sit at an informal dinner.

As Barker and the parlourmaid started serving the leek and potato soup, Lady Beaufort said to Alec, 'Well, Mr. Fletcher, were you able to pin down the time to your satisfaction?'

'The time, Lady Beaufort?' Alec asked cautiously.

'The time the trap was set. The time someone was out in the grotto turning on the gas.'

'Not exactly.'

'Anything but exactly,' said Howell. 'There are just too many variables.'

'The best we could do,' Pritchard confirmed, 'was to place it somewhere between eight in the morning and noon.'

'Is that helpful to you, Mr. Fletcher?' Lady Beaufort enquired.

'Better than nothing.'

Armitage said, 'I assume you'll be asking us all to account for our time between eight and noon. It's a long period to account for.'

'Not really. It was just this morning, and unless you're an early riser–'

'Which I am not,' Lady Beaufort declared. 'I walked all the way to the grotto and back yesterday afternoon and again in the evening – all those steps! – and I was quite exhausted.'

'Exhausting,' Alec murmured, a trifle ironically. Daisy could tell he hadn't intended to ask any questions during dinner, but he wasn't displeased to have the subject raised.

Lady Beaufort gave him a shrewd look. 'I know you've been there all afternoon, and digging besides, but I'm an elderly lady.'

'Not at all!' Pritchard protested.

'Do go on, Lady Beaufort,' Alec suggested.

'I slept until nine o'clock and then I had breakfast in bed, so it must have been quite half past eleven before I came down. I hadn't been in the drawing room more than a minute or two when Mrs. Howell came in. We sat together until lunchtime. So there you are, time all accounted for. And I can assure you that had I risen early, I should not have ventured to the grotto without an escort, for any purpose.'

Pritchard sighed. 'I'm afraid it'll be a long time before I shall have the pleasure of escorting you there again. When I think of all the... But it's no use crying over spilt milk. Now let me see, what time did I get up?'

They all started discussing their movements and trying to work out times. Daisy hoped Alec was succeeding in keeping it all straight, because she soon found herself losing track.

Her mind wandered. No one seemed to be taking the exercise seriously, perhaps because no one was really mourning Rhino. Though she had disliked him, Daisy wondered sadly whether anyone, anywhere, would mourn Rhino. That brought her to his family, if any, and consideration of his family led to Boyle's question about

251

his heir.

Greed was a common motive for premeditated murder, perhaps the commonest, Daisy wasn't sure. It would be comforting to presume that the unknown heir to the earldom and pots of money had sneaked into the grounds of Appsworth Hall and turned on the gas. Unfortunately, she couldn't imagine how a stranger could be sufficiently familiar with the grotto, let alone have known about Rhino and Lady Ottaline's assignation.

If she wanted to cling to the money motive theory, only one among the assembled company could possibly be a long-lost heir: Charles Armitage. He would have had a double motive, greed and jealousy, and he obviously had some mysterious secret in his past, something he didn't want to talk about. But Daisy didn't want to believe he was a murderer. In fact, she refused to believe it.

Her unbelief did not dispose of his motive of jealousy – and a secret.

Lady Beaufort had a secret, too. Why did she refuse to discuss her reason for having delayed disclosure of her change of heart about Rhino's suitability as a son-in-law? The delay was a great pity. With Rhino no longer a rival, Charles would have had little cause for jealousy.

Of course the motive of jealousy applied equally to Sir Desmond, in fact even more so. Apparently unruffled, he was now tucking into roast pork with apple sauce and broad beans (no fish course!), having briefly mentioned his simple movements of the morning. He had risen from his bed – he could not name the hour, but no doubt his valet would know – and after breakfast had been driven into Swindon to the Pritchard plant. Howell and the missing Carlin could vouch for his presence there.

Carlin. He'd skedaddled in rather a hurry, but Daisy couldn't think of any reason for him to have murdered Rhino. The only insults flung his way had been general animadversions on the bureaucracy, nothing to take personally. He hadn't shown any particular interest in Julia, either. Probably he considered her to be an 'older woman,' Daisy decided gloomily, just as she and Lucy and Julia had pigeon-holed Lady Ottaline.

What had Lady Ottaline been doing this morning? She wasn't present to speak for herself. She hadn't come down to breakfast, either. That was hardly surprising. Women *d'un certain âge* (how much kinder the French phrase) often breakfasted in bed at country-house parties.

Daisy's attention was drawn back to present company as Julia said, 'Mr. Armitage wanted me to see Barbury Castle. He is a historian, after all.'

'I wasn't aware of that,' Alec said mildly. 'And I'm afraid I've never heard of Barbury Castle. Tell me about it.'

'It's an Iron Age...' She glanced at Charles and he nodded. '...An Iron Age fort. There are barrows, too. Those are ancient burial places. There's supposed to have been a battle nearby, as well, in five hundred and something A.D., between the Britons and the Saxons.'

'Who won?'

'I can't... Oh, the Saxons, I suppose. They drove the Britons out, to Cornwall and Wales. Do you remember, Daisy? The Angles, Saxons, and Jutes?'

'How could I forget? Lucy used to complain that the Angles belonged in geometry and the Jutes in geography. The exports of India or somewhere.'

'How far from here is Barbury Castle?'

Charles answered. 'It's a couple of miles as the crow flies, on the ordnance survey map. Farther walking, of course, and quite rough country in places. We went on beyond for a bit, too, hoping to get within sight of one of these white horses carved in the chalk – I expect you know about them.'

'I've seen the Pewsey White Horse. I didn't know there were others. Why didn't you get as far as this one?'

'Julia – Miss Beaufort was afraid we'd be late for lunch, so we turned back.'

'It was quarter to one when we got back, just time enough to tidy up before lunch.'

'Which direction is Barbury Castle from here?' Alec asked.

After a painful pause, Armitage said, 'More or less south.'

'Beyond the grotto.'

'Yes.'

'It sounds like an interesting place.' Pritchard seemed to have decided his guests had been interrogated sufficiently at his dinner table. 'I'd like to see it. You must take me there when the weather improves, Armitage.'

'Certainly, sir. You won't have to tramp as far as Miss Beaufort and I did. There's a lane goes quite close.'

Lady Beaufort, whose obvious anxiety had eased at Pritchard's words, turned to Alec and asked, 'Are you interested in history, Mr. Fletcher?'

'Yes, as a matter of fact. My degree is in history, but I specialised in the Georgian period, not the Ancient Britons.'

'Darling,' said Daisy, 'I've just had a brilliant idea. We should collaborate on a book about the early history of the police and call it *From Beadles to Bobbies.*'

Everyone laughed.

'A catchy title,' Armitage remarked. 'If you ever write it, I'll certainly recommend it to my students.'

'Students!' Lady Beaufort exclaimed. 'You're a teacher?'

'University lecturer, actually.'

'Why–?' She had been going to ask why she hadn't been informed, Daisy was sure. But that would imply she had a reason for expecting to be informed, and that in turn might lead the police to question the relationship between Julia and Charles. Though Alec's face gave nothing away, Daisy could have told her he had already drawn his own all too obvious conclusions. 'How interesting,' her ladyship said weakly instead.

'In Canada?' asked Gerald. He had been ploughing silently through the meal, no alibi being required of him. Now Barker and the maid, Inskip, were clearing the dishes in preparation for serving pudding, so momentarily Gerald had no excuse for failing to do his conversational duty.

The arrival of plum tart and a pitcher of thick cream put an end to his participation, but he had diverted the stream. Life in Canada, life in France, relations between France and Canada, relations between French Canadians and British Canadians – there was plenty to keep everyone going. Daisy would have liked to ask about the Royal Canadian Mounted Police, but in the circumstances, she decided, the less said about any kind of police the better.

All too soon they'd have to face once more the unpleasant demands of the murder investigation.

'Good grub,' said Boyle as Alec returned to Pritchard's den. He put a spoonful of plum tart in his mouth and chewed.

'You were right, I learnt quite a bit at dinner. They were actually keen for me to ask them where they were this morning.'

'All of them?' Boyle grunted sceptically.

'Some were keener than others. But I got stories from all of them, for what they're worth.'

'What are they worth, d'you think, then?'

'Some more than others. Let me write it all down – I couldn't very well at table – and we'll go over it.'

While the inspector finished his dinner, Alec made notes. They'd have to ask each person the same question all over again, but how they answered the second time was often more significant than the first. Omissions and additions, alterations, or repetitions in the same words, suggesting rehearsal, might all be clues to the truthfulness of the speaker.

Boyle heard him out, then said, 'I still haven't got a real grasp of who all these people are, or why they're at Appsworth Hall. Not that Mrs. Fletcher wasn't helpful, but I'd like to hear from Pritchard what they're doing here in his house. If you've no objection, sir, we'll have him back first.'

'Do you regard him as a suspect?'

Boyle frowned. 'Not on such information as I've got already. But, of course, there's no knowing what I'll – we'll dig up. Nor there's no knowing what'll set some people off, and Mrs. Fletcher did say Rydal insulted Pritchard, along with everyone else.'

CHAPTER 27

Boyle was about to summon Pritchard – or rather invite him to step into his own study – when the troops from Devizes arrived at last. They consisted of a detective sergeant, a detective constable, and two uniformed constables, all damp. The rain was coming down in torrents by now.

The inspector wanted to send one of the uniformed pair to relieve PC Endicott who was still out there on the hillside in the storm, guarding the site of the explosion. 'And the other to the grotto entrance, don't you think?' he asked Alec. 'You said you couldn't see for dust, but when that's settled, and in daylight, it ought to be searched, as well as the hole.'

Alec nodded, forbearing to point out in the presence of Boyle's subordinates that all the suspects had visited the cave in the past few days, so any evidence of their presence was unlikely to be meaningful.

The two men stood stolidly waiting for instructions. After a moment of thought, Boyle said gloomily, 'The only thing is, how the devil are they going to find their posts in the dark? One of the outdoor servants'll have to guide them.'

'Ask Barker,' Alec suggested.

'Mr. Barker's eating his supper, sir,' protested the maid who had shown the policemen into the room.

'Can't be helped,' said Boyle curtly. 'Take these fellows along, and tell Mr. Barker there'll be a detective following in a minute or two to collect the timetables you should all have made out. When he arrives, take my compliments to Mr. Pritchard and tell him we'd like to have a word with him in here.'

With a doubtful shake of her head, the girl took the constables away.

The junior detectives were eyeing Alec askance.

'This is Mr. Fletcher. He's a guest here. As he's ... connected with the police, he's lending a hand. Unofficially.' Boyle went on to explain to DS Gaskell that he wanted him to go over with the servants their statements about the household's movements that morning. He was to make sure they not only made sense but didn't contradict each other. 'And see what they can tell you about

258

the victim's chauffeur, the bloke that was caught in the collapse,' he added.

'Pity we can't talk to him yet,' Alec said as Gaskell departed.

'That doctor's a bit quick with the sedatives, if you ask me! It'll be interesting to see if the servants agree with what the nobs told you about what they were doing and when,' Boyle remarked to Alec. To the detective constable, he said, 'I hope your shorthand is up to scratch. I want a verbatim record of the interviews I'm going to be doing. Got plenty of pencils and an extra note-book?'

Alec thought regretfully of DC Piper, his usual notetaker, who was never caught without a supply of well sharpened pencils. He could only hope Gaskell got on half as well with servants as Tom Tring, the massive and superlatively competent detective sergeant who was his right arm.

Pritchard came in. He moved more slowly than earlier and looked tired, but he asked with unabated courtesy, 'What can I do for you now, gentlemen?'

'First,' said Boyle. 'I'm looking for a bit more information about all these people you've got together in your house. It's what you might call a mixed bunch, if you don't mind me saying so, and I don't properly understand how they fit together, so to speak, or what they're doing here.'

'I'm not surprised you're confused,' Pritchard said with a weary smile. 'I'm none so clear on the subject myself. But let's see if I can help. It all starts with my sister-in-law, I suppose.'

'Mrs. Howell. She's been living with you for a

long time?'

'Several years. Her husband, my partner, died soon after my wife and I moved to Appsworth Hall, and naturally Glenys invited her to stay while she decided what she was going to do next. Daffyd left his half of the business to Owen, his only son, but Winifred got their house and a good deal of money.'

'She told us she wasn't living on your charity.'

'Well, not from necessity. But after she sold the house for a pretty penny, she couldn't decide where she wanted to live so she stayed on. Then Glenys died – and Winifred stayed on.' He shrugged wearily. 'I like having Owen about the place, and his mother's a capable manager, so...'

Alec wondered how much the inestimable Barker had to do with Mrs. Howell's capable management.

Boyle finished Pritchard's incompleted sentence. 'So Mrs. Howell is what you might call a permanent resident? You're on good terms?'

'Good enough. Most of the time. The reason I've gone into all this is that she's responsible for the presence of some of my guests. Not that she'd invite anyone without consulting me.' His tone suggested a sudden doubt as to whether it was just a matter of time before his sister-in-law overstepped this particular boundary. 'Owen went up to London over this government contract business, meetings at the Ministry of Health and so on. Sir Desmond kindly invited him to dine at his house, and there he met Lady Ottaline, of course. Lady Beaufort and Miss Beaufort were also dinner guests. He wrote to Winifred about them. She was all agog to meet them–'

'Why was that, sir?'

'She's a bit of a... She fancied the notion of entertaining titled people. In the normal way, she has to make do with the vicar, the doctor, our solicitor, business associates, a few old biddies from the village – that sort of people. Of course I wouldn't have presumed to invite them to stay just because Owen had casually made their acquaintance. Then it turned out that Sir Desmond had to come down to take a look at the works. It seemed easiest to keep Winifred happy by saying we'd be delighted if he brought his wife. To tell the truth, I was surprised when she accepted. I suppose she just happened to be at a loose end this weekend.'

Boyle grunted.

Alec thought it more likely that Lady Ottaline had heard about Lord Rydal's pursuing Miss Beaufort to Appsworth. 'What about the Beauforts?' he asked.

'I'm not entirely clear about them, though I'm very glad they're here. Delightful guests. As is Mrs. Fletcher,' he added, with a nod to Alec, who noted with amusement the omission of Lucy. Lady Gerald Bincombe could be a prickly companion. 'I only wish Lord Rydal hadn't offered to drive them down. Once he was here, I felt I had to offer hospitality for the night – it was a foggy evening – and he seemed to assume he'd been invited to stay as long as they did.'

'Mrs. Howell didn't kick up a fuss about an unexpected guest?' Boyle asked, possibly with memories of Mrs. Boyle's feelings in like circumstances.

'What, with a genuine earl under her roof? Even if it's actually my roof... No, she was thrilled. So thrilled she put up with rudeness– Well, if the Czar of Russia treated his peasants and workers like that, I for one don't blame 'em for having a revolution. I can tell you, if I spoke to my factory hands that way, I'd have 'em out on strike within the hour.'

'Bad language?'

'No, not that. It was more as if he'd learnt by heart all the rules about acting the gentleman but didn't really grasp what it was all about. I can't explain properly. Maybe Mrs. Fletcher, being a writer, can describe what he was like. I'd've kicked him out – asked him to leave – a dozen times if it wasn't that Winifred wouldn't have it.'

'She didn't mind how he behaved?'

'Far as she was concerned, he was a lordship so whatever he did was all right by her, right up until it came to meeting his fancy woman in the grotto. That she wouldn't stand for. I'll say this for Winifred: She's a snob, but she was brought up Chapel, and she's never turned her back on it, no matter that all the nobs go to Church. She'll have the vicar to dinner, but that's as far as it goes.'

'Not...' Alec hesitated, trying to word his question tactfully, then decided there really wasn't a tactful way to put it. 'You wouldn't say there was a touch of religious mania?'

'Certainly not.' Inevitably Pritchard took affront. 'I'm Chapel myself.'

Boyle made no attempt at tact. 'Yet you put pagan statues in your grotto, and some Papist idol Mrs. Howell was carrying on about. An evil place, she called it.' He glanced for confirmation at Alec, who nodded.

'Evil?' Pritchard was startled and worried. 'She never liked it, but she's never said anything like that before. It does sound as if she's got some sort of bee in her bonnet. Sounds to me as if the explosion and Lord Rydal's death have been too much for her nerves. I wonder if I should call the doctor to her?'

'Couldn't hurt,' said Boyle, 'unless she takes it into her head that you're conspiring against her.'

'Conspiring?' Now he seemed bewildered.

'To get her out of the way. She made a serious accusation—'

'Against me? Surely she can't imagine I blew up my own grotto! If you knew the time and effort I put into restoring it – to say nothing of the money – and the fun I had, the fun I've had showing it off, too! All those years of perfecting and peddling plumbing – not that I regret a moment, plumbing's important, but the grotto was ... artistic. I don't suppose any real artist would think much of it, but it was my own creation. And Winifred claims I blew it up? She *must've* gone round the bend!'

'Unless she was trying to protect her son,' Boyle proposed, his face more than usually blank.

'No, that's going too far! I'd as soon believe I did it myself, walking in my sleep, as Owen. He helped me build it, and he'd no cause to want to murder Lord Rydal, neither. If that's what

Winifred thinks, she's even madder– But she wouldn't have told you that. You've made it up out of your own head.' He gave Alec a reproachful look. 'Heads.'

'We have to explore every possibility, Mr. Pritchard, especially when an allegation has been made.'

'Well, if Winifred's suddenly convinced herself the grotto's evil, and on top of that it was being used for immoral purposes, maybe she did it herself!'

'That's another possibility we have to explore.'

'Come to think of it, she never did like the hermit business. She never could see it was just a bit of fun. If it wasn't popery, she'd say, it was sacrilege. I never could persuade her it was either both or neither.'

'That's another thing I haven't quite got the hang of,' said Boyle. 'This hermit business. You hired the Canadian just to play hermit in your grotto?'

'Not exactly.' Pritchard showed a sudden unexpected touch of shiftiness. 'In the summer I hire someone from the village to play the part. You'd be surprised how many visitors we get. I don't usually bother before Easter, but when ... Armitage wrote to ask permission to take a look at the old documents in the muniments room, I told him he could come and stay and pay for his keep by dressing up as the hermit in the grotto if anyone happened to turn up to see it.'

'There's the curious coincidence of his name, too,' said Alec.

'What? Oh, yes, quite a coincidence, isn't it?'

'The name?' Boyle asked, genuinely blank this time.

Pritchard seemed disinclined to answer, so Alec explained, 'The name Armitage is derived from the word hermitage, I believe.'

No police detective could let such a fishy coincidence pass without question. 'I hope you asked him for references,' Boyle said.

'Certainly,' Pritchard recovered his composure. 'I'm a businessman, Inspector. He showed me his passport and a letter from his university. Perfectly satisfactory, I assure you. He's been here for several weeks, apart from occasional trips to London to look things up in the big libraries.'

'Could he have met Lord Rydal in London?'

'He wasn't interested in high society. "A great waste of time," he told me more than once. Frankly, I should've thought Rydal had much the same opinion of libraries. It doesn't seem likely they'd meet, but they might've run into each other somewhere.'

'Neither of them acknowledged having met before when Lord Rydal arrived here?'

'Not by a flicker of an eyebrow.'

'Was Lord Rydal ever insulting to Mr. Armitage?'

'What you have to understand,' Pritchard said patiently, 'is that he insulted everyone, though I must say Lady Gerald gave as good as she got. Except I never heard him being rude to Lady Beaufort. After all, he wanted to marry her daughter.'

'What about Miss Beaufort herself? Surely he

265

wasn't rude to her!'

'But he was. Very odd I thought it, when he was courting her.'

'Odd! I'd call it downright peculiar. Are you sure?'

'Yes. The young ladies were giggling about it.'

'Oh, then they were just joking about,' Boyle said large-mindedly. 'The nobs have their ways.'

'I don't think so.' Alec remembered what Daisy had said. He hadn't taken it very seriously at the time, but he was once again reminded that dismissing her theories was frequently a mistake. 'My wife told me Rydal simply didn't realise how offensive he was.'

Boyle nodded. 'Mrs. Fletcher said to me she thought he had never been taught to consider anyone else's feelings. I don't suppose you know anything about his childhood, Mr. Pritchard?'

'Not a thing.'

'If he acceded to the earldom at an early age,' said Alec, 'it could be that he was brought up by servants and perhaps dependent relatives, who were afraid to cross him.'

The inspector was scornful. 'Sounds like something one of those psycho-doctors would say. I can't see it makes any difference one way or the other. If someone goes around offending people, they're not going to worry about whether he's doing it on purpose or can't tell the difference.' He reached for Alec's notes on the dinner-table alibis. 'Let's see here. You claim you were alone in here for half an hour this morning.'

'That's right. I had some accounts to make up. I came straight here after breakfast and was here when Mrs. Fletcher and Lady Gerald came to fetch me to give them a tour of the house.'

'Mrs. Howell said she was alone in her bedroom all morning and saw you walking towards the grotto.'

Pritchard sighed. 'Then I don't know whether to hope she was hallucinating or making it up. Either way, it's a sad state of affairs.' He sat there with his hands on his knees, looking tired and worried. 'I don't know what I'm going to say to Owen.'

'I'd rather you didn't discuss this with anyone for the moment, sir.' Boyle glanced at Alec. 'Any more questions, sir?'

'Not for the moment. Thank you for your co-operation, Mr. Pritchard. I hope this will prove a momentary aberration on the part of your sister-in-law.'

The moment the door closed behind Pritchard, Boyle said, 'I don't think he did it, do you? But this Mrs. Howell's another kettle of fish. Sane or not, she had it in for both Mr. Pritchard and Lord Rydal, not to mention the grotto itself. Then there's this Armitage fellow. Something dodgy about him being here in the first place, if you ask me. All the way from Canada to look at some fusty old papers! Out walking with Miss Beaufort, he claims. Walking out, more like, I shouldn't wonder. After her money.'

'Miss Beaufort is an extraordinarily beautiful young woman,' Alec informed him, 'and I have a vague memory of my wife mentioning that she and her mother are far from well off.'

'Oh,' said Boyle, disconcerted. He rallied. 'At

any rate, Armitage wanting to marry her, him a professor – if he's telling the truth about that! – and her courted by a rich lord. Stands to reason he'd want to get his rival out of the way.'

'But Miss Beaufort also says they were walking the entire time. Why would she back his story if he'd destroyed her chance of an excellent marriage?'

'Because Lord Rydal insulted her. Strange, that. What do you reckon to this theory of Mrs. Fletcher's, sir?'

'About Lord Rydal's upbringing? I think she may well be right, and you may well be right that it doesn't make any difference to us. Except insofar as it's always useful to understand the victim.'

'I daresay.' Boyle sounded unconvinced. 'Seems to me it's more important to know he was rude to everyone than why. It gives us a lot of people with reason to dislike him, but the ones with the best motive *and* opportunity are Armitage, with or without Miss Beaufort as accessory; Mrs. Howell, assuming she's batty; and Lady Ottaline Wandersley, that he wanted to throw over for Miss Beaufort, as your good lady told us.'

The door opened, and Alec's 'good lady' appeared.

'Darling, I've been thinking,' she announced.

CHAPTER 28

Daisy shut the door and advanced into the room. She didn't recognise one of the three men who rose to their feet. He must be a new arrival.

Perhaps his presence explained why she didn't hear the groan with which Alec usually greeted any declaration of hers that she had been thinking. It was too much to hope he at last realised the value of her thoughts.

'Is this urgent, Daisy? We've got a lot of people to interview this evening.'

She sat down, and they followed suit. 'It might be urgent. I was thinking about Lady Ottaline. I assume she's near the top of your list of suspects?'

DI Boyle answered. 'She seems to have had a strong motive, though we've not got much to go on yet besides your word for it, Mrs. Fletcher. Same goes for opportunity. I'm waiting for DS Gaskell to bring me the servants' reports on that. He and DC Potter here arrived at long last from Devizes.'

Daisy smiled at the large young man. 'It's a good job you're here. You're the very person to guard Lady Ottaline.'

'What?' Alec and Boyle exclaimed together.

'The thing is, it's all very well – in a manner of speaking – if Lady Ottaline blew up Rhino. But supposing she didn't? Whoever did probably intended to blow her up, too. Isn't it quite likely they'd have another go? Possible, at least. There she is, alone and helpless under the influence of whatever powders Dr. Tenby gave her–'

'Daisy, do you know something you haven't told us?'

'No, of course not. At least, not consciously. I have a feeling there's something I've missed. Oh, and I heard Sir Desmond ask Barker to move him to a separate room, because he's a noisy sleeper – presumably he snores – and he doesn't want to wake his wife. They have separate rooms at home, I expect. He'll have to have Rhino's room. It's the only good room unoccupied. Either he doesn't realise, or he's not afraid of ghosts!'

'Daisy!'

'Well, it means she'll be alone all night. Unless you've found out enough to be sure she's safe, I really do think she ought to have a guard, just overnight.'

'You're right,' said Boyle, clearly pained to have to admit it. 'We can't risk it, and you're the only one we can spare, Potter. Off you go. Ask the butler which is her room. If there's a connecting bathroom with another door, make sure it's bolted from the inside.'

'But sir, I can't do that without going through the lady's room!'

'Use your initiative, man. Take her maid with you or something. And give me your notebook before you go. Mrs. Fletcher,' he went on sourly, 'I'm going to have to ask you to stay and take notes again, until Gaskell finishes with the servants. He shouldn't be much longer.'

Daisy sighed. Though Alec wouldn't be deceived, with luck Boyle would believe she was doing him a favour. 'Oh, all right. Devizes didn't send you enough men. I haven't brought my notebook, though. May I use DC Potter's?' Perhaps she'd have time to skim Potter's notes of the interview with Mr. Pritchard. She hoped his writing was easily legible.

'If you have no preference, Mr. Boyle,' said Alec, 'I like to clear what you might call the dead wood out of the way. That is, to question the least likely suspects first.'

Foiled! Daisy naturally was much more interested in what the most likely had to say for themselves.

Luckily, so was Boyle. 'That's a good idea, sir. It's getting late, and it'll speed things up no end if we split the load, though Lady Ottaline won't be available till the morning, I suppose. Do you want to stay in here? I'm sure the butler can find one of us another suitable room for interviews.'

For once outmanoeuvred, deliberately or inadvertently, Alec gave in gracefully. 'You stay. I take it you want Armitage first? I'll send him to you.'

'Thank you, sir.'

They both looked at Daisy, and then at each other. Daisy wasn't sure whether each wanted to shuffle her off on the other, or each hoped to retain her services. Whoever kept her would have better notes for the other to read later. She knew where she wanted to be.

'Mr. Boyle has more need of me, darling,' she said. 'You'll want a verbatim report of what the chief suspects say, won't you?'

'I'm just lending a hand,' he reminded her, 'not officially a part of this investigation. But yes, you'll be more useful here. I'll ask Armitage to bring his passport and letter of recommendation, shall I, Boyle?'

'Er ... yes. Yes, I'd better take a look at them. You really think that's not his real name?'

'I think we ought to have evidence to settle the question. Right-oh, I'm off. The one I really want to see is Lucy – Lady Gerald – whose view of things, I'm sure, is very different from Daisy's. In her absence, Lady Beaufort first, I think.'

'If you see my sergeant, tell him to buck up. When he comes, I won't have to trouble Mrs. Fletcher any longer. She can give you a hand.'

'Right-oh.' Alec went out.

Boyle looked glumly at Daisy, then suggested, 'You'd better read through Mr. Pritchard's interview, I suppose.'

DC Potter's shorthand was much better than Daisy's. It took her only a couple of minutes to read his notes. 'I see why you're suspicious of Charles Armitage,' she had to admit.

'It's odd about his name, but I'm sure there's an innocent explanation. Such as it really being his name. Coincidences do happen. I *would* like to know what drew his interest to the papers here at Appsworth Hall, though.'

'I hardly think that's relevant to the enquiry into the death of Lord Rydal.'

'You can't be sure. Alec always insists that any detail may turn out to be significant. And you yourself said you wanted to know absolutely everything I know, hearsay and all, so that you can decide for yourself if it's important.'

Armitage came in so quietly they didn't hear him until he said, 'Fletcher told me you wanted to see me?'

The inspector waved him to a seat and held out his hand. 'Your passport. Please.'

'I'm afraid I don't have it on me.'

'Didn't Mr. Fletcher tell you I want to see it?'

'Oh yes, but you see, I don't have it here. I keep a room in London, and I leave it there while I'm travelling. I don't need it. I've never been asked for it before.'

'I daresay. But you do need to keep your introduction from your university to hand, surely. That will do to be going on with.'

'It's upstairs, in my bedroom, yes,' Armitage acknowledged reluctantly. 'But I can't see how it's going to help you, Inspector. It doesn't have a photograph attached, eh, so there's no proof I'm the person referred to, assuming you suspect I'm not.'

Boyle leant forwards, his eagerness obvious. 'Are you admitting that you're here under false pretences? A con-man, is that it? Lord Rydal was onto you, so you had to put him away?'

Daisy was too horrified to remember she was supposed to be taking notes.

Armitage shook his head wearily. 'Nothing so dramatic. I told Mr. Pritchard it was bound to come out. I was willing to help him avoid embarrassment – myself, too, really, but not to the point of being arrested for murder.'

'What the deuce are you talking about? I warn

you, everything you say will be taken down and may be used in evidence in a court of law.'

Hastily Daisy started scribbling.

'I told you, I didn't kill Rydal. But you're obviously not going to believe me. I'd better fetch that letter.' He started to stand up.

'No! You just stay here under my eye if you please.' Boyle looked at Daisy, irritated. 'You're going to have to go and get it, Mrs. Fletcher. Mr. Armitage – or whoever you are – tell her where to find it.'

'In my chest of drawers.' Armitage grinned at Daisy. 'Top left, under my socks and ... other things, an ivory envelope with the university crest embossed on the flap.'

His underwear, no doubt, Daisy thought indignantly, but Boyle didn't seem to have drawn the inference. She could hardly inform him she objected to rummaging through Charles's pants and vests, especially in search of an incriminating letter she'd prefer not to find. Yet if she refused to go without giving a reason, he might use her unhelpfulness as an excuse to bar her from the investigation altogether.

On her way out of the room, she wondered momentarily whether she ought, for Julia's sake, to steel herself to the distasteful task and then to destroy the letter. However, its disappearance would probably cause Charles more trouble than whatever it revealed. She decided to ask Barker to send one of the staff. Then she reconsidered. The envelope must be unsealed, because Charles had made use of the letter. If the servant yielded to temptation and peeked, the entire household

274

would have the information in no time.

Daisy resigned herself to carrying out the job.

She had just reached the foot of the stairs when she heard footsteps behind her and turned. A man – to Daisy's practised eye obviously a policeman – was crossing the hall, carrying a wodge of scraps of paper, all sizes and shapes and of varying degrees of cleanliness.

'Hello, are you DS Gaskell?'

He looked a bit surprised by her glad greeting. 'Yes, madam?'

'I'm Mrs. Fletcher, DCI Fletcher's wife. Mr. Boyle's been wondering when you'd be finished with the servants' timetables.' True. 'He needs a letter from Mr. Armitage's chest-of-drawers.' True. 'Top left, in an ivory-coloured envelope with a crest on the back.' All perfectly true, if somewhat misleading. But Boyle would undoubtedly have sent the sergeant if he'd been available. 'Shall I take those to him?' She indicated the papers in Gaskell's hands.

He handed them over like a lamb. 'They're a bit confusing. That's what took me so long, working out what they were trying to say, and then checking the times and places to make sure they didn't contradict each other. Er... Can you tell me where this bloke's room is? So's I don't have to ask that snooty butler?'

Daisy gave him directions and watched him hurry up the stairs. So far so good. Now all she had to do was to present the *fait accompli* to Boyle in such a way that he wouldn't be annoyed with either her or Gaskell.

She riffled through the papers, but she couldn't

make head or tail of them at a glance and she didn't dare delay to study them. They couldn't help Armitage, in any case. His opportunity to turn on the gas in the grotto had already been established by his own admission.

In Pritchard's den, Charles Armitage was staring at the floor in gloomy silence, while Boyle read through the papers on the desk. Both looked up and started to rise as Daisy entered. She waved them down.

'I've brought the servants' timetables, Inspector.' She set them before him. 'I met DS Gaskell on his way with them. It seemed best that he should go for Mr. Armitage's letter. Being a police officer, I mean.'

Boyle grunted what might conceivably be approval, or possibly thanks, and started to sort out the heap of scraps: used envelopes; the backs of shopping lists, receipted bills, and notes for the milkman; and even a torn triangle of butcher's paper. Daisy, realising that her presence would be superfluous as soon as Gaskell arrived, found an inconspicuous seat against the wall, in an ill-lit corner, well to one side and slightly to the rear of the desk.

She gave Charles (if Charles was actually his name) an encouraging smile and he smiled back. Insofar as it was possible to judge his mood, he seemed more exasperated than worried. This, Daisy thought, was a good sign, suggesting that his deception had innocent roots.

Nothing to do with murder, at least. What secret could he and Pritchard share that would embarrass both? She was baffled.

276

CHAPTER 29

Alec ushered Lady Beaufort into the breakfast parlour, pointed out to him as a suitable location by the butler. He held a chair for her, and she sat down with a sigh. She was a handsome woman still, though a little inclined to embonpoint.

'My dear man, you are a lesson to me.'

Alec opened his mouth, closed it again, then said cautiously, 'I am?'

'A lesson already learnt,' she went on, confusing him still further, 'but too late, alas. I'm afraid I'm responsible for the shocking occurrences of today.'

Doubtless Boyle would have applied for an arrest warrant instantly. Alec merely blinked and was glad he'd ended up interviewing her on his own. He didn't for a moment suppose she was physically responsible for turning on the gas taps in the grotto.

'Would you please elucidate, Lady Beaufort? Explain,' he explained, when she looked uncertain.

'Of course. Where shall I start?'

'At the start of the events that led to the murder of Lord Rydal.'

'Oh dear, I suppose it all began in my girl-hood–'

'Perhaps not quite that far!' Alec said quickly.

'That's when I was taught to believe in the im-

277

portance of a girl marrying well, and *well* meant money and if possible a title. I don't know how much Daisy has told you about our circumstances?'

'Very little. Nothing, really, except that she and Lucy were at school with Miss Beaufort and you have been living in France.'

'My late husband was a younger son of a baronet, and everyone said he would do brilliantly in the Army, as indeed he did,' Lady Beaufort declaimed somewhat in the style of a Victorian melodrama. Alec suspected she was quite enjoying herself. 'He was made a general while still in his forties, and knighted.'

'Admirable,' Alec murmured,

'But the Beauforts, though aristocratic and all too numerous, were not wealthy. George had a little money of his own, but army life is expensive. When he was killed in the War...' She paused to dab her eyes with a lace-trimmed but substantial handkerchief. '...I found it had all been spent. Julia and I were left in straitened circumstances.'

'So after the War you went to live on the Continent.'

'Yes. And then I came into a small inheritance and decided to use it to make sure Julia never had to suffer such deprivation.'

'Hence Lord Rydal.'

'He was everything I'd been brought up to think was necessary in a husband. Rich, an earl, and he loved her madly into the bargain. He would do anything for her. Almost. I managed to overlook his faults for far too long.'

'I still don't quite understand how he and the

278

two of you ended up at Appsworth Hall.'

'I'm not surprised,' Lady Beaufort said frankly. 'I'm not at all sure Julia didn't outwit me. We met Mr. Howell at a dinner party at the Wandersleys'. Not that we knew them well. If I'd known then what I know now, we shouldn't have known them at all, I assure you!'

Accustomed to Daisy's sometimes convoluted sentences, Alec had no difficulty disentangling this. 'But you didn't expect to meet them here?'

'Not in the least. Julia seemed to get on well with Mr. Howell, so... Well, I suppose I had two possibilities in mind, besides the fact that I found London quite tiring. Endless shopping and parties and theatres... I expected a week in the country to be restful, to set me up to tackle the rest of the season. Little did I know!'

He brought her back to the subject: 'And your two possibilities?'

'Possibilities? Oh, either Julia would see the difference between a manufacturer and a nobleman and come to her senses, or else she'd captivate Mr. Howell and be rich if not titled. At the time, she had recently told me about making the acquaintance of a Canadian in some library or other. It's quite shocking the way young people fall into conversation these days without waiting to be properly introduced. How did you and Daisy meet?'

'She felt obliged to draw to my attention a murder which was about to be passed off as an accident.'

'No!' Lady Beaufort laughed. 'I don't suppose Lady Dalrymple– But I mustn't waste your time in idle gossip. Where were we?'

'Miss Beaufort met Armitage in a library.'

'Yes, well, she's always been what we used to call bookish.' She sighed. 'I daresay a professor will do very well for her. But at the time I didn't think so. In fact, I didn't even know he was anything so respectable as a professor. I seized what seemed to be an opportunity to get her out of town and away from him. I cajoled Mr. Howell into inviting us–'

'How?'

'As it has nothing to do with your investigation, Mr. Fletcher, I'm not prepared to reveal my methods. But I will say that I'm quite an expert cajoler when I put my mind to it. It's a skill necessary to the wife of a general.'

'I can imagine,' Alec said with a grin. 'And then you cajoled Rydal into driving you down?'

'That wasn't necessary. I didn't expect that it would be. He really doted on Julia, you know, a most determined pursuit. He offered his services as soon as he heard she was going to the country for a week, though not without some grumbling about the idiocy of leaving town at the height of the season. Julia never breathed a word about her Canadian being a temporary resident of Appsworth Hall, the sly thing!'

'When did you come to the conclusion that Armitage is preferable to Rydal?'

'In the grotto, yesterday afternoon. I'm not a great walker. Brin – Mr. Pritchard was keen for me to see it, and I gave in yesterday. Fortunately as it turns out. Not that I did decide in favour of Mr. Armitage, mind you. Merely against Lord

280

Rydal. His behaviour was outrageous.'

'And when did you inform your daughter of your changed opinion?'

'Good heavens, I can't remember. With all that's been happening, it's a wonder that I remember to bring my head with me!'

'Not immediately, though. Why was that?'

'It wasn't convenient just then. Other people were about. Besides, I was in no more hurry than the next person to admit I was wrong.'

It was reasonable. Still, she didn't quite meet Alec's eyes and he was sure she was not telling the truth. Not the whole truth, at least. Odd, but probably not significant, he decided. At this stage in the investigation he couldn't afford the time to stray down every enticing by-way. Later, too, he might have to try to pin her down as to exactly when she had told Julia of her change of heart. He'd wait and see what Julia had to say on the subject.

He wanted to see Julia next, but Boyle probably considered her a major suspect and therefore wanted to question her himself. With dismay, Alec recognised in himself a disposition to regard her as innocent simply because she was Daisy's friend.

Julia Beaufort had been out on the downs with Armitage. If he had gone to the grotto, she could hardly have failed to know. She might not have had the slightest idea what he was doing there at the time, but since the explosion she could no longer plead ignorance. If he was guilty, she was concealing evidence, and that made her an accessory after the fact.

She didn't have much of a motive for killing Rydal, but despite Daisy's glossing over the relationship, she had the best of motives for protecting the man she loved.

Not for the first time, Alec was going to have to perform a delicate balancing act, between leniency because of Julia's friendship with Daisy and undue harshness because he was afraid of being lenient. He reminded himself with gratitude that this was not his case.

Lady Beaufort was fidgeting under his blank gaze. 'Well?' she asked, a challenge in her voice. 'Are you always in a hurry to admit when you've made a mistake?'

Alec smiled and shook his head. 'It depends on the circumstances. In general, I don't claim to be any more eager than the rest of the world. But if I've arrested someone and discover I shouldn't have, the sooner it's put right the better for all concerned, including me.'

'Fair enough.'

He liked the lady. He could only hope he wouldn't have to assist in the arrest of her daughter.

He stood up. 'Thank you for your cooperation, Lady Beaufort. That will be all for the moment.'

'For the moment! Next time it will be the local inspector, I suppose. It's too much to expect that he, too, is a gentleman.'

'More to the point,' said Alec, absorbing the implied compliment without a blink, 'Inspector Boyle appears to be a competent officer.'

He escorted her back to the drawing room, thinly populated by Pritchard, Howell, Wandersley, and Bincombe, all with glasses in hand. Wandersley was standing with his back to the fire, apparently holding forth. The other three rose as Lady Beaufort entered. Pritchard and Bincombe in particular looked delighted to see her.

Pritchard came to meet them. 'Let me get you a liqueur, dear lady. Crème de menthe, as usual? And a whisky for you, Mr. Fletcher?'

Lady Beaufort sank into a chair. 'I think I'll take something a little stronger tonight, Mr. Pritchard. Brandy and soda would do nicely.'

What the hell, Alec thought. He was unofficial, after all. 'Yes, please. With plenty of soda. Mr. Howell, I've a couple of questions for you, if you please.'

'Or if I don't please?' But he spoke mildly, a comment, not a hostile protest. 'I was in Swindon most of the day. I doubt I have anything useful to tell you.'

'That's what we'll find out.' He took the glass Pritchard proffered. 'Thank you, sir.'

Howell was already at the door. As they walked towards the breakfast parlour, he said, 'You've saved yourself some work. Much longer stuck with Sir Desmond's funny stories about politicians and I'd have up and strangled him. You'd have had another murder on your hands.'

'On DI Boyle's hands, not mine. You'd have done his arrest statistics a bit of good. I take it Wandersley is better to do business with than to entertain, if that's the right word.'

'If only he wouldn't insist on being entertaining. In the circumstances, it's a bit much.' Entering the room ahead of Alec, he sat down at the table. Alec took a chair opposite him. He continued, 'As for business, I can't complain. He's going to recommend that we get the contract. Contracts, rather. It's for local governments to make the purchasing decisions, but with a recommendation from the ministry, most are not likely to want to spend the time and money to vet other companies.'

'Congratulations. What is it you would complain about otherwise?'

'Oh, just that he's wasted a good deal of my time. These bureaucrats keep very short working hours. It's incredible that they ever get anything done. I'm a businessman. If I made a habit of starting work at eleven o'clock, the firm would be bankrupt by now.'

'You didn't get going till eleven this morning?'

'Nearer quarter past. Wandersley came down late to breakfast for a start. We still could have left for Swindon at a reasonable hour if he wasn't such a – a hearty eater.'

'Pig?' Alec proposed with a grin.

'You said it, not me. I got tired of watching him stuff his face and left him in here.'

'Alone?'

'No, several other people were still here.'

'Do you recall who?'

'Let me see. My uncle had already gone. Mrs. Fletcher and Lady Gerald left with me. Lady Gerald said something about sorting out her unused photographic plates. She was going to take some interior pictures of the house for Mrs. Fletcher, I gathered. That would leave Miss Beaufort, Armitage, and the abominable Rhino.'

'Where did you go?'

'To Uncle Brin's den, to have a word with him about–'

'How long after he left this room was that?'

'Quarter of an hour. Perhaps twenty minutes.'

'And how long were you with him?'

'No more than five minutes, I'd say.'

The exact length of time didn't matter. Pritchard had had at most half an hour or so to get to the grotto, turn on the gas taps, and return to the house to be waiting in his den for Daisy and Lucy. That was the bare minimum necessary. If Owen Howell had spoken with him during that period, he was out of the picture.

Except that Alec was pretty sure Howell would lie for his uncle, especially in what he might consider a good cause. He'd do it well, too. Men of business, like policemen, were on the whole adept at hiding their thoughts and emotions.

'The *abominable* Rhino, you called him.'

Howell shrugged. 'I can't think of a better word for him. He was abominably rude to my mother. There was no point having it out with him, though. He just didn't seem to understand why people got upset with him. I put up with it, in the certain knowledge that he wouldn't be here forever. I'm a peaceable sort of chap. More important matters on my mind than squabbling with an aristocratic ass.'

'A very sensible attitude. But how did your mother feel about it?'

He hesitated. 'I'm afraid Mother was dazzled at first by having a living, breathing earl under her roof. Well, under Uncle Brin's roof, but she tends

285

to regard it as her own. All the same, I can't see how she can go on living here after what she's said about him.'

'He told you? Or she did?'

'He told me Mother went to the police – to you and the inspector both, was it? – and accused him of blowing up the grotto.'

'So you expect him to ask her to leave Appsworth Hall.' Alec felt for him. He had twice had to ask his mother to move out, because of clashes with both his first wife and Daisy.

'Uncle Brin? Good lord no! He wouldn't do a thing like that. I'm trying to work out what's best for all concerned. For a start, I think when she's well enough to travel, she must go away for a rest cure – Bournemouth, or Harrogate, Switzerland even.'

He didn't sound like someone with a guilty secret, whether his own or Pritchard's. He didn't seem very interested in Rydal's demise at all. Mrs. Howell's behaviour was monopolising his thoughts. That his mother herself might have been responsible for the explosion didn't appear to have crossed his mind.

'I'm afraid she won't be allowed to go abroad until Inspector Boyle has cleared up this case.'

'It's probably better if she stays in England, in any case. Less agitating than foreign travel ... and fewer Papists,' he added with a wry grin. 'How long–? No, that's a stupid question. I suppose you'll want to interview her tomorrow.'

'I'm sure Boyle has a few questions for her.'

'I don't want to teach the inspector his job, but you'd upset her less than he would. And get more answers from her.'

'I'll see what I can do, but it's his call. Just one more point: What did you do this morning after leaving Mr. Pritchard in his study?'

'I went to my room to check some figures, to save time when we got to the works. One of the maids came to tell me when Sir Desmond was ready to leave. That must have been about half past ten. By then I was fretting and fuming, I can tell you! Half the morning gone.'

'It often amazes me that the Empire survives, run by bureaucrats,' Alec agreed dryly. 'That will be all for now, thank you, Mr. Howell. Would you mind asking Sir Desmond to come and see me?'

'Running shy, are you?'

'I suspect he'll kick up less of a dust if the request comes through you, rather than directly from me.'

'We won't have any data for comparison, but all right, I'll do your dirty work for you!'

As with Lady Beaufort, Alec didn't think Howell was Rydal's murderer and he hoped not to see the man's nearest and dearest arrested. The hope was not as strong as in the lady's case, however. If Julia Beaufort was guilty of anything it was because she had fallen in love with a jealous young man, whereas Mrs. Howell had bitten the hand that fed her.

An enormous yawn caught Alec by surprise. He was very tired, he realised. He had got up early to finish reading and writing reports at the Yard, so as to be able to join Daisy for a couple of lazy days in the country. Instead he'd spent several hours digging in the rain, a level of physical exertion he wasn't accustomed to these days. Here he was enmeshed in a case that wasn't even his own, that could bring him no kudos yet might very well get him into trouble if his informal part in the investigation ever came to official ears.

For once he couldn't even blame it on Daisy. It was entirely his own fault.

Ah well, involved he was, so he'd better see that it came to a satisfactory conclusion. With a sigh, he extricated from a pocket the sheets of writing paper he'd filched from Pritchard's desk and scrawled a few details of his interviews with Lady Beaufort and Howell.

CHAPTER 30

DS Gaskell entered Pritchard's den with an ivory-coloured envelope held by one corner between finger and thumb, as if he expected it to be covered with useful fingerprints.

'Mrs. Fletcher said—'

'Yes, yes, put it down here.' Boyle gestured at a bare spot on the desktop, and then at the scatter of notes covering most of the rest. 'I hope you can explain all this muddle to me.'

'Yes, sir. Like I told Mrs. Fletcher, that's what took me so long, sorting it all out with them so's it makes sense.'

'Good. You can write it all out neatly for me later, but first, tell me what they had to say about whatsisname, Lord Rydal's chauffeur.'

'Gregg, sir. Not strictly speaking a chauffeur, more of a valet. His lordship preferred to drive himself, but required his manservant to be able–'

'All right, all right, I don't need to know the details. Not yet, at least. What were his relations with his employer?'

'For a start, he'd only been with him a couple of months and wasn't planning on staying, from what he told the others. The fellow before him wasn't there more than six months, neither. Gregg told them he never kept servants long. If you done something wrong and get sworn at, that's one thing, he said, and par for the job, but getting blasted all the time for what can't be helped is more than flesh and blood can stand.'

'Did anyone know he hadn't left Appsworth?'

Daisy stopped listening. She wasn't interested in the hapless Gregg. She didn't believe for a moment that he had anything to do with the explosion, apart from getting caught in it. No one could be so stupid as to set a trap of such magnitude and then hang about to see what happened. Whatever he had been up to, it wasn't turning on gas taps.

Nor did she believe Boyle was so stupid as to suspect Gregg of murder. The inspector was trying to rattle Charles Armitage, who so far was far too blasé about his fateful secret. The envelope lay there on the desk between them, an innocent rectangle of ivory paper, waiting to explode.

Or was it fateful? More likely, as he had claimed, merely embarrassing. Nonetheless, Daisy was dying to know what the contents would reveal.

289

Armitage took his tobacco pouch and pipe from his pocket and started to stuff the bowl. Getting a pipe going was a wonderful cover for nervousness – or irritation. Daisy thought he was more irritated than nervous as he tamped down the tobacco and took out matches.

He was striking the third when Julia marched into the room. Armitage leapt to his feet.

'What's going on?' she demanded militantly. 'Charles has been in here for hours.'

'Darling, it's quite all right. They're not giving me the "third degree."'

'What's the *third degree?*'

'Strong-arm methods the American police are known to use sometimes in interrogating suspects.'

'Strong-arm... You mean hitting?' Julia was appalled.

'Not the English police,' the inspector protested, scarlet with indignation.

'I should hope not! But you're not a suspect, Charles. You were with me the whole time this morning. I know you didn't go into the grotto.'

'*I* don't,' Boyle pointed out.

'You're saying I'm lying about it? Why should I tell a lie?'

Boyle looked significantly at Armitage, whose arm Julia was holding, and back at her. She wilted into the nearest chair.

'Perhaps you're not aware, miss, that it's a felony to conceal evidence from the police.'

'I haven't! We didn't go anywhere near the grotto entrance, just walked over the hills.'

'That's for you to know and me to find out.'

The inspector picked up the envelope and tapped with it on the desk, looking again at Armitage.

'Julia, you'd better go back to your mother and let Mr. Boyle get on with his finding out. He can't find out that I was responsible for the explosion, because I wasn't.'

'I'm staying,' Julia declared, no longer militant, but determined. Glancing from Boyle to DS Gaskell, she caught sight of Daisy. Her eyes widened.

Daisy frantically but fractionally shook her head. If Julia addressed her, she was sure to be sent out. It was touch and go for a moment whether Julia herself would be expelled, whether by the police or her beloved, but both subsided.

Julia watched, obviously puzzled, as Boyle untucked the flap of the envelope, pulled out the letter, and opened it. He started reading.

His jaw dropped and he said incredulously, *'Appsworth?'*

For a moment, Daisy felt as blank as Julia looked. Then she had to bite her lip, hard, to stop herself laughing aloud. *Appsworth!* Was Charles a long-lost son of the family?

'What do you mean, *Appsworth?*' Julia said crossly.

Boyle gestured at Armitage/Appsworth. 'Ask him.'

'It's my name,' Charles explained, rather flushed. 'That's why I'm interested in the old family papers. It's – or more accurately, it was – my family. Mr. Pritchard asked me not to use the name down here. He was afraid it would start all sorts of rumours flying, people saying there was something fishy about his buying the house and I

291

ought to have inherited it.'

'And is there something fishy?' Boyle enquired. 'Should the place be yours?'

'Good lord no! My great-grandfather was a fourth son. He emigrated to Canada and lost touch with the family. To tell you the truth, I think he started out as a bit of a ne'er-do-well, but he made good. My grandfather made a fortune in wheat, in Alberta. So we're a junior branch at best. I suspect the senior branches have died out, though I haven't finished tracking down the details. There have been a number of distractions.' He smiled at Julia, who was still looking somewhat bemused.

'So you may be the Appsworth heir,' the inspector persisted.

Daisy couldn't see why he was interested. After all, it was Rhino who had been blown up, not the usurping Pritchard, who might conceivably have been a target to Charles. But she wanted to know the whole story – and she didn't want to draw attention to herself – so she didn't interrupt.

'Good lord no! I'm not even an eldest son of an eldest son. If any of my immediate family were the heir, it would be my uncle, and since all my cousins are girls, my father after him, followed by my older brother. But the entail was broken long ago. My uncle may be able to call himself Lord Appsworth, but he has no rights in the estate whatsoever. It was left jointly to the two daughters of the then holder of the title, failing male heirs-of-the-body. When the younger died, the elder was perfectly at liberty to sell the place lock, stock, and barrel. She retired to a cottage in

Dorset, I believe.'

'We must look her up, darling,' said Julia, 'and make sure she's all right.'

'Yes, I'd intended to, before I go home. Before *we* go home.'

They gazed into each other's eyes.

Boyle broke up this picture of love's young dream with a loud cough. 'Yes, that's all very well, but it's got nothing to do with my investigation.'

'At least you know now that my presence at Appsworth Hall isn't a long-laid plan to do away with Lord Rydal.'

'That's as may be. I've got plenty more questions for you, Mr. Arm– Appsworth, so–'

'Inspector, as long as you're not about to arrest me immediately and need my right name to do so, would you mind continuing the fiction? The possibility of embarrassing Mr. Pritchard continues.'

'I suppose it doesn't make much odds,' Boyle grumbled. 'Gaskell, you're to write down Appsworth, though, whatever I say. In the meantime, I'll thank Miss Beaufort to take herself off until I send for her. I promise not to engage in any strong-arm tactics.'

At this point, an enormous yawn overcame Daisy. It drew the attention of both Julia and Charles, and Boyle turned his head to see what they were looking at.

'Mrs. Fletcher,' he said, his tone resigned. 'All right, I don't need you, either, now Gaskell's here to take notes. Perhaps Mr. Fletcher can avail himself of your services.'

'Right-oh.' Daisy was actually quite willing to leave now that she knew Charles's secret.

Julia was not. 'But I don't see why I shouldn't–'

'Come on, darling,' said Daisy. 'It's no good arguing with a copper in full cry. You'll get your turn, never fear.'

'But what am I going to tell Mother about who you really are, Charles?'

'Don't tell her anything until you've warned Pritchard that my alias is blown. See what he says, but I should think he'll want to keep quiet about it as long as possible – with your co-operation, Mrs. Fletcher? Inspector?'

Daisy nodded. 'Of course. Except Alec.'

'I was going to say,' Boyle said, 'except Mr. Fletcher. It's all the same to me. At present, at least. I can't see your name has anything to do with your committing murder.'

'Thank you,' Charles said ironically.

'Though it does show a talent for deceit.'

Julia wasn't going to let that pass. 'For Mr. Pritchard's sake!'

'Don't worry, Julia. Just think what a story we'll have to tell our grandchildren when we're old and grey.'

Daisy managed to get her friend out of the room without any further outbursts. 'Darling,' she said, 'you really must stop showing yourself so partisan. You make it less and less likely that Boyle will believe anything you say about Charles.'

'It's already too late. He thinks Charles turned on the gas when we went out, and I'm aiding and abetting him. After all, apart from Pritchard and Howell, Charles knows about the gas supply in the hermitage better than anyone.'

'Bosh! Anyone who's been in there knows about all the lights and the fire. I expect there'd have been enough gas to blow up without using the geyser, but anyway, we were all there when Pritchard was talking about it. Most of us. Let's see, who was actually there?'

'Charles and I,' Julia said gloomily. 'And Rhino.'

'Lady Ottaline and Sir Desmond. Carlin. Lucy and I. And Pritchard and Howell, of course, but the gas was no news to them. Mrs. Howell didn't come, nor your mother.'

'Nor the doctor and his wife. They came to dinner, remember? But I think they'd gone home by the time we got back to the house. It all seems so long ago. Whatever became of Carlin? Oh, Daisy, you don't think he's out there under the rubble?'

'Heavens no! Didn't you hear him at breakfast? He was engaged to play in a golf tournament tomorrow so he went back to town by train. Does – did Rhino play golf?'

'No. He called it a footling occupation for fools who had nothing better to do with their time. Why?'

'I was just thinking it was a bit fishy the way Carlin disappeared so promptly. Pritchard telephoned Sir Desmond in Swindon when we got Lady Ottaline back to the house, so the three men were still there, so Carlin must have known about the explosion before he caught his train. It's a bit cool, if you ask me, his just going off like that.'

'What's that got to do with Rhino and golf?'

'Well, suppose he and Rhino had quarrelled over a game sometime in the past. Men get frightfully worked up about it. Rhino might forget, but Carlin brooded about it and—'

'But Rhino didn't play.'

Daisy sighed. 'No. Pity.'

'All the same, I don't think the inspector should let Carlin off without being interrogated.'

'He told his sergeant to find him in London and bring him back, I hope Lucy took the Daimler or poor DS Thomkin will be stuck in the dickey all the way down. Always supposing he manages to find Carlin and persuade him to abandon his match.'

'It sounds like a tall order.'

'Alec gave him the name of an inspector at the Yard who'll help him. I just hope it doesn't get Alec into trouble.'

They had been standing talking just outside the drawing room. Now Julia said, 'Are you coming with me to warn Mr. Pritchard about Charles having to reveal his alias to the police?'

'Not me. I'll leave that to you. I'm just going to find out where Alec is, then I'll go and see if—'

'Madam!' It was the little housemaid, Rita. Twisting a corner of her apron in nervous fingers, she was obviously upset. 'Oh, if you please, madam!'

'What is it, Rita?' Daisy asked.

'Oh, madam! Mr. Barker said I got to tell you.'

Daisy envisioned her best evening frock ruined by over-enthusiastic application of the smoothing iron. She gave Julia a little push towards the drawing-room door, and taking the hint, her friend went in alone.

'What do you have to tell me?' she asked.

'Oh, madam!' Rita glanced wildly round the hall.

'Would you like to go somewhere private? How about the dining room?' Daisy led the way. 'Now sit down and spit it out. I won't eat you, you know.'

'Mr. Barker said you was the best one to tell. I'm sure I couldn't say a word to that inspector, but you'll know what to do, madam. Oh, madam, I never thought he meant it.' The girl flung her apron over her face and started crying.

'Who? Who meant what?'

'Mr. Gregg, madam.' Her voice was muffled by the cloth and interrupted by sobs and hiccups. 'His lordship's man, madam. And I'm sure I wish he'd never said a word to me!'

'Oh dear!' said Daisy and set about coaxing the story from the frightened maid.

CHAPTER 31

When Howell left him, Alec folded his arms on the table and laid his head on them for a moment's respite. Feeling his eyes inexorably closing, he changed his mind, stood up, and went to one of the windows. He parted the curtains and looked out at belting rain, illuminated by electric lamps at the front door, under the portico. The window faced the carriage sweep. The room was at the northeast corner of the house. Thinking back to his arrival with Gerald that afternoon – could it possibly have been this very day? – he reckoned the view from the other window must be across a narrower drive to the service entrance and a group of outbuildings, including garages, partly concealed by shrubbery.

At any rate, it was impossible for breakfasters in here to see anyone heading for the grotto.

Alec rested his forehead against a windowpane. The cold glass revived him a little and the sound of heavy footsteps approaching the door, which Howell had left ajar, completed the process. Given a villain to track down, he could stay awake all night.

Sir Desmond Wandersley was still an enigma to him. They had been introduced just before dinner and sat opposite each other at the dinner-table, on either side of Lady Beaufort. When everyone had started to discuss their whereabouts during the morning, Sir Desmond had said briefly that after breakfast he had gone into Swindon, to the Pritchard works. Apart from that, he had made little effort to converse, preoccupied, presumably, by his wife's accident. Yet Howell had said he produced an endless supply of funny stories later, in the drawing room. Curious. Still, Daisy described him as being an expert at presenting a façade to the world.

Alec waved him to a chair and sat down, saying, 'How is Lady Ottaline, Sir Desmond?'

'Sleeping soundly. She wasn't seriously injured, you know, just considerably shaken.'

He didn't sound at all concerned. Alec assumed he hadn't actually been to see how his wife was doing. He surely would have commented on the presence of DC Potter guarding her door.

When dealing with bureaucrats, it was safest to make sure all *t*'s were crossed and *i*'s dotted. 'You're aware that I'm a Scotland Yard CID officer, giving Inspector Boyle of Swindon a hand quite informally with preliminary questioning? I have no official standing in the investigation. If you prefer to speak to Mr. Boyle—'

'No, no, my dear fellow. I'm sure I can count on your tact, your understanding, as a man of the world, so to speak. A matter of some delicacy...' He hesitated. Though a pause of that sort was usually a sign of uncertainty, Sir Desmond's urbane manner never faltered. 'I'll let you decide whether it's worthy of being passed on to the inspector.'

Alec waited. When nothing further ensued, he prompted: 'Yes?'

'Do you know, I find this deuced difficult.' Yet he was still cool, calm, and collected.

'Perhaps we should start with your movements this morning. I couldn't take notes at dinner, obviously. Would you mind telling me again, for the record?' He smiled. 'We coppers like to have a solid foundation for further enquiries.'

'It's quite simple. I came down to breakfast – doubtless my valet will be able to tell you the precise time – and after breakfast I drove to Swindon, to the plumbing works. That is, my chauffeur drove me and Carlin, my Private Secretary. Howell took his own motor-car. I was at the factory, apart from a break for luncheon, until Pritchard telephoned to tell me Ottaline was hurt.'

'Thank you. Now, what about this delicate matter you want to talk to me about?'

'Dammit, man, it's not easy. If it weren't that—' Sir Desmond took off his gold-rimmed glasses and fixed Alec with eyes like blackcurrant wine-gums, dark and opaque but with a slight sheen. 'You realise that in my position, any breath of scandal can be fatal.'

'Sir Desmond, until I know what you have to tell me, I can't give you any assurances, except that the police do not disclose information unless it becomes necessary in the prosecution of a court case.'

'Which I'm terribly afraid... If only I knew what to do!'

'If you are aware of facts that could materially affect police enquiries, it is your duty as a citizen – and especially, surely, as a servant of the Crown – to pass them on.'

'My duty! Yes, it's my duty, however painful.' He shaded his eyes with one hand. 'I fancy you must already have heard certain ... rumours about my wife and Lord Rydal?'

'We have.'

'The inspector, too? I suppose I should have expected it. Ottaline was obsessed with the fellow, couldn't leave him alone. You didn't have the doubtful pleasure of meeting him, I gather, but your wife must have told you what an unpleasant specimen he was. I can only believe that Ottaline was ... unbalanced. It's dangerous to

300

thwart a woman in such a condition.'

'You didn't consider consulting a psychiatrist?'

'No. I didn't realise until recently to what extent her mind was affected. And I must admit, it was abhorrent to me to have her – and, I confess, myself – exposed to the talk that would surely have arisen. These things get about. I felt certain it would blow over in time, so I didn't kick up a fuss. Then I heard that he was pursuing a young lady with a view to marriage. She – I'm speaking of Miss Beaufort, of course – was badly off and not at all likely to refuse a rich peer. I assumed his ... connection with Ottaline would come to a natural end. A reasonable assumption, don't you agree?'

'Certainly.'

'When she said she'd like to come into the country with me, I was sure it was over. I didn't know Rydal was here, although, as I found out too late, she did. I could see right away that she still wanted him, and if she couldn't have him, she'd have her revenge. She's a vengeful, grudge-holding person. But I was thinking in terms of petty revenge, and I guessed wrongly that Miss Beaufort would be her target. If I'd had the slightest inkling of what she planned...'

Alec let the silence hang for a moment. Then he said impassively, 'You'd have warned Lord Rydal? Warned your host? Somehow prevented Lady Ottaline from blowing up the grotto? That is what you're telling me, isn't it? Your wife killed her lover.'

Momentarily, Sir Desmond slumped. Then he stiffened and stood up. He leant forwards with

301

both fists on the table. 'I've said enough. I have no proof. But I couldn't let you arrest someone who may perhaps be innocent because you hadn't considered all possibilities.'

'Oh? Whom do you think DI Boyle is about to arrest?'

'Why, the Canadian, of course. Lady Beaufort favoured Rydal, who was pestering the girl. Obviously Armitage was jealous. At one blow he rid himself of his rival and freed her from harassment. But I shan't try to teach you your job. Good night, Mr. Fletcher. No doubt I shall see you in the morning. I must warn you, however, that I must leave for London tomorrow, or early Monday without fail. Perhaps you will be so good as to point out to the inspector that the nation's business cannot wait on the convenience of the provincial police.'

'I'll let him know.' But a trifle more tactfully. Not that he could hold anyone against his will, government business or no government business. 'Good night, Sir Desmond.'

A slight scuffling sound out in the passage was muffled by Sir Desmond's heavy footsteps. Alec wouldn't have heard it had he not been listening for it. In the middle of the interview, he had seen the door handle turn and the door open an inch. He hadn't wanted to stop Sir Desmond in full flow, though he would have done so if he hadn't been all but certain the eavesdropper was Daisy.

Sir Desmond's weighty tread receded down the hall. A moment later Daisy came in.

'He didn't see me, the snake!'

'Snake?'

'All those nasty insinuations about Lady Otta-line, and he admitted he had no evidence what-soever. He's trying to get rid of her. Well, one can't help but sympathise a bit, but still... Darling, you don't believe him, do you?'

'There isn't anything to believe or disbelieve, since he didn't make any direct accusations. Snake, yes. I was thinking rat. You shouldn't have been listening.'

'I had to see you, and I didn't want to interrupt. Oh dear, more insinuations, I'm afraid, but without malice.'

'Daisy, what are you blithering about?'

In response, she stuck her head out of the door and called, 'Rita, come along now.'

Rita?

'Come on, he doesn't bite, I promise.' She ushered in a very young housemaid. 'Rita has something to tell you.'

'Oh, madam, cou'n't you tell for me?'

'Right-oh.' Nothing loath, Daisy sat down at the table. 'But he or the inspector is going to want to ask you some questions. You know, I told you they would. Alec, Rita is the third housemaid, so she does the senior and visiting staff bedrooms. That's how she came to chat with Gregg, Lord Rydal's manservant. And perhaps to flirt a little?' She gave the nervous girl an encouraging smile.

'We didn't do nuthen wrong!'

'Of course you didn't. I'm just telling him that so he understands how it came about that Gregg told you things he didn't tell anyone else.'

'I never thought he'd really go and do it,' the

maid said tearfully.

'Brace up. Perhaps he didn't. It's for the police–'

'Daisy!'

'Sorry, darling. This morning, when Rita went in to make Gregg's bed and dust around, as usual, he was in his room packing his belongings. He was in a "state," and he told her he'd been sacked.'

'For nuthen!' Indignation overcame fright. 'Just his lordship wanted to wear a tie Mr. Gregg'd left behind in Lunnon.'

Daisy continued. 'He said he'd put up with enough and he was going to get his own back. He told Rita about a neighbour of his aunt's who had tried to commit suicide with gas. She'd turned on the oven and put her head in, then grew uncomfortable and impatient and decided to have a last cup of tea. She struck a match to light the burner. The gas exploded and burnt off her eyebrows. Gregg decided it would be a good idea to burn off Rhino's eyebrows. I must say, I agree, only he did it rather too thoroughly. If he did it.'

'I never thought he would,' Rita wailed. 'I thought it were just talk.'

'You couldn't possibly have guessed,' Alec said soothingly. 'He knew about Lord Rydal and Lady Ottaline's plan to meet in the grotto, did he?'

'Oh yes, sir, everyone knew. Wicked, I call it.'

'Thank you for telling Mrs. Fletcher about Gregg's threat. Does anyone else know?'

'Just Mr. Barker, 'cause I didn't know what to do.'

'Good. Don't tell anyone else, there's a good girl.'

'What about that inspector, sir? Will I have to tell him?'

'I'll tell him. I expect he'll want to ask you some questions, as Mrs. Fletcher warned you. You can run along now. Remember, not a word to anyone else.'

'I'll keep mum, sir. Oh, madam, thank you ever so. I'd never 've done it without you.' Departing, the maid cast a dubious backward glance at Alec and added, 'Not but what he's not as scary as you might expect.'

Daisy managed to shut the door before she collapsed in laughter. 'Darling, what a comedown! The great Scotland Yard detective can't even scare a third housemaid!'

'I could and I would,' Alec said darkly. 'What do you think of her story?'

'I'm sure it's true. What it means is another matter. The fact that Gregg was on the spot when the place blew up suggests he wasn't expecting anything half so dramatic.'

'Which need mean no more than that he simply didn't know much about the properties of coal-gas.'

'What do you mean?'

Alec explained what Pritchard and Howell had said about the necessary concentration to cause an explosion. 'Now I come to think about it, whoever was responsible probably didn't realise how uncertain the outcome was. Even those two experts couldn't predict a specific result, taking into account how many taps were turned on for how long.'

'I don't believe Gregg did it. I can't imagine

305

him going to the grotto, turning on the gas, then waiting right there for long enough for enough gas to escape to cause an explosion, expected or unexpected. If you ask me – which I suppose you won't – he'd have hung about the house or garage or somewhere until half an hour or so before the assignation. When he got to the grotto, he would have opened the door at the back and smelt gas and promptly closed it again, thinking someone had got there before him.'

'And waited to watch Rhino get his come-uppance?'

'Yes. To be charitable, he may also have intended to warn off Lady Ottaline if she arrived first. He had no quarrel with her, did he?'

'Not as far as I know. But I know very little. If he really meant to release only a small amount of gas, as much as he expected to be enough to burn off Rhino's eyebrows, what made him think Rhino wouldn't smell the gas too soon for his purposes and depart in haste, or at least put out his cigarette? In fact, that seems to me a flaw in the scheme whoever did it, and whatever they hoped for the outcome to be. As far as I know, the door of the hermitage wasn't airtight. A certain amount of gas must have seeped under it.'

'Darling, if you'd seen the way Rhino smoked, you wouldn't wonder. I very much doubt whether he'd had any sense of smell for years.'

CHAPTER 32

'If I tell him, he's bound to complain that it's nothing but hearsay,' Daisy grumbled as she and Alec approached Pritchard's den. 'Why can't you?'

'Because from me it would be at third hand.'

'He'll want to talk to Rita himself, anyway.'

'Yes, but with luck not until tomorrow. You can explain better than I can that she's an extremely reluctant witness, and I doubt he'll have any desire to tackle her at this time of night.'

'Oh, all right.'

The door opened just as Daisy reached for the handle, startling her. Julia came storming out, startled in her turn as she nearly ran into Daisy.

'Oh, the beast!' she cried, tears in her eyes. 'He absolutely refuses to believe me!'

'It's his job to be sceptical, Miss Beaufort.'

'Call me Julia, for heaven's sake, or I'll think you don't believe me, either.'

'I don't.'

'Oh! Well, call me Julia anyway. But I'm telling the truth, and so is Charles.'

'If it's any comfort, I don't actually disbelieve you. I have to keep an open mind.'

'Boyle had Charles's ordnance survey map. He made me look at it and tell him exactly where we went, to see if I agreed with Charles, but I've never had to read one before and I had no idea.'

307

'You win!' Alec said out of the corner of his mouth to Daisy. 'I'll tell him.' He made a shooing motion.

Daisy took Julia's arm and urged her drawing-roomward. 'Come along, darling, you need a drink.'

'He obviously thinks Charles killed Rhino out of jealousy. I told him Charles had no reason to be jealous because I loathed Rhino and swore I'd never marry him, but he seemed to think Mother could stop me marrying Charles. Did you ever hear anything so Victorian? I wish Mother had decided sooner that she didn't approve of Rhino!'

'So do I,' said Daisy. 'And I can't help wondering why she didn't tell you right away.'

Julia wasn't listening. 'And he said – *soooo* sympathetically – it was quite natural that I'd lie for Charles because I loathed Rhino and was glad to be rid of him. He twists whatever you say to fit his beastly theories.'

They reached the drawing room. Pritchard and Lady Beaufort, on a sofa by the fireplace, were so deep in their conversation that they didn't notice Daisy and Julia's entrance. Charles, Howell, and Gerald sat in reasonable proximity to each other, but not quite in a group, all smoking, all looking slightly uncomfortable. Daisy guessed they had probably been exchanging occasional remarks, probably on the weather, for some time. All three jumped up when she and Julia appeared.

'Drinks?' Howell offered.

'Think I'll go and telephone Lucy's studio, make sure she's arrived safely,' Gerald muttered. 'All right, Howell?'

'Of course, but with the inspector in my uncle's den, you'll have to use the phone in the hall.'

'If Lucy's in the middle of some delicate process, she won't thank you,' Daisy warned.

'She won't answer,' Gerald responded.

Daisy forbore to point out that in that case he wouldn't know whether or not she had arrived safely.

By that time, Julia and Charles had retreated to a far corner of the room.

'Like a drink, Mrs. Fletcher?' Howell said.

'Yes, please.' Daisy almost asked for cocoa, but she didn't know how much longer this dreadful evening was going to last, so she could do with a bracer. 'Julia, too,' she added as they went over to the dresser-bar. 'A brandy and soda, I should think, for both of us. Just a drop of brandy and plenty of soda.'

'I'll give Armitage another whisky.' Howell gave Daisy her drink, poured a small brandy and a hefty shot of whisky into tumblers, and carrying a soda syphon, took them over to the couple.

How long ago Daisy had discussed with him the principle of the syphon! How simple life had seemed then, just a matter of keeping Lucy from insulting their host.

She went to sit in an easy chair on the opposite side of the fireplace from Pritchard and Lady Beaufort. Both looked up to smile at her.

'Got everything you need?' Pritchard asked.

'Yes, thanks.'

They returned immediately to their earnest, low-voiced conversation. Howell came and dropped with a sigh into the chair next to Daisy's. He, too, had a drink, but it was as pale as Daisy's, more something to do with his hands than anything else.

'What a day!' he said. 'I'm afraid you haven't had the pleasant visit my uncle hoped for.'

'I'm just glad it wasn't Lucy and I who brought the scourge upon you. Rhino being the scourge,' she hastened to explain.

'Good lord, we don't hold the Beauforts to blame. My mother was to some degree resposible. Believe me, Uncle Brin is quite capable of having sent him off with a flea in his ear if he wasn't so soft-hearted as to give in to Mother's wish to entertain a real live lord.' He hesitated, and Daisy was desperately trying to think of something kind to say about Mrs. Howell when he continued in a lowered voice, 'You were present when my mother ... at her outburst, weren't you.'

'Yes. I'm sorry. Having Rhino about the place must have been a great strain on her nerves.'

'She always did dislike the grotto. If you ask me, it was hearing of the use Lord Rydal and Lady Ottaline intended for it, even before the explosion, that sent her over the edge.'

'Some kind of nerve storm, I suppose.' Daisy wasn't very sure what a nerve storm was, but it seemed a tactful thing to say.

'She'll have to see a specialist,' Howell said sombrely. 'Don't you think a rest-cure would be the thing? By the time she gets back, I'll have set up a house for her in Swindon. She may complain at first, but in the end she'll be much happier there. She likes the idea of living in a mansion, but she really prefers town life.'

'I suppose it would be a bit difficult for her to stay on here after what she said about Mr. Pritchard. Will you go and live with her?'

'That would never do! As a matter of fact, I've been making plans to set up my own household for some time now, only I just didn't know how to break it to Mother that I'm going to get married.'

'Married?!' Daisy hoped she sounded more interested than astonished. After all, why shouldn't Owen Howell marry? He was well off, not bad looking, not too old; she had even seriously considered him as a husband for Julia.

'You may well be surprised. My fiancée is getting tired of keeping it secret from Mother.' He followed Daisy's glance at Pritchard. 'Uncle Brin knows. He's met Jeannie. He thinks I should have told Mother ages ago, but... Oh well, this situation is dreadful but it does make things easier for me in that respect!'

'Your uncle will miss your company.'

'I daresay Jeannie and I will be in and out. They like each other. But in any case, I hope Uncle won't be living here alone for long.' Howell gave a significant look at Pritchard and Lady Beaufort, still in animated conversation.

Once again, Daisy was astonished. 'Good heavens, you think...?' Was that why Mrs. Howell had taken against both of them, afraid for her position in the household? 'Well! I did notice right away that they seemed to get on very well together, but–'

'Nothing is settled,' he said hurriedly. 'You won't mention it?'

'Of course not. It would be a very good thing,

though, especially if Julia's going to be emigrating to Canada. As long,' she added with foreboding, 'as Boyle doesn't go and arrest both her and Charles.'

Alec found DI Boyle looking pleased with himself.

'I'd lay odds the Canadian did it,' he said, rubbing his hands together. 'I never heard a thinner story in my life, taking off tramping over the hills when there's rain on the way, just to see a bit of an old grass-grown bank. It's not even like this here Barbury Castle is a real castle, you know, with towers and battlements and such.' He started folding the ordnance survey map spread out on the desk.

'Armitage is a historian,' Alec reminded him.

'Armitage! Your good lady hasn't told you, then? His real name's Appsworth,' Boyle said triumphantly.

'Great Scott! Masquerading under an alias.'

'Well, not exactly. Pritchard knew all along, but no one else, not even Miss Beaufort. Or so they say. What I say is, it shows a talent for deception.'

'For what purpose?'

'So's not to cause a lot of rumours about a missing heir come to claim his inheritance. Or so he claims.' Boyle handed the half-folded map to DS Gaskell. 'Here, you deal with this damn thing.' He leant forwards over the desk and stabbed a finger at Alec. 'And when I ask the girl to show me on the map which way they went to get there, to confirm what Appsworth told me, she claims she can't read it.'

'Perhaps she can't. She has lived in France since the War, in rather restricted circumstances, I gather. Besides, some people just have difficulty relating a map to the actual landscape.' Alec's facility in that regard, together with his name, had led to his RFC nickname during the War: Arrow. In his single-seat spotter plane, a fabrication of canvas, balsa wood, and piano wire, he had almost always come back with information about exactly the target he had been sent to observe. But the very fact that his ability to home in on his target like an arrow had resulted in the nickname suggested that many pilots failed to do so.

'You don't believe she's protecting Appsworth?' Boyle snorted. 'Not that I'd blame her, mind, a young lady in love. But it's accessory after at least, if not before. I suppose you'll tell me next you don't believe he blew up Lord Rydal.'

'I have an open mind on the subject. I'm not half so convinced of his motive as you are. He seems to have come to an understanding with Miss Beaufort some time ago. Rydal was an irritant, not a threat. As an irritant, the man spread his net wide.'

'Yes, just about everyone here loathed his guts, servants and all—'

'Speaking of servants, I'd better pass on what one of the housemaids told my wife.'

'Your wife!' Boyle was outraged.

Alec decided to suppress the butler's role in sending Rita to Daisy. 'It happens,' he said apologetically. 'Witnesses see her as a more sympathetic listener than the police, yet they can be sure the information will reach me if necessary.'

'If Mrs. Fletcher considers it necessary,' the inspector growled.

'Yes. Unsatisfactory, I know, but I've learnt there's really nothing to be done about it, short of ignoring what she tells me. If she refuses to listen, the chances are they won't be coming to spill the beans to me themselves, or else they'll waste my time with completely irrelevant waffle.'

'All right, what did this maid have to say?'

Alec related Gregg's threat. The inspector came to the same conclusion as Daisy – though Alec didn't tell him so: The chauffeur might have stayed to see Rydal suffer, but was not likely to have set things in motion.

'He was hanging about the servants' quarters till after one o'clock,' he said. 'You haven't seen their evidence about times yet, have you. Here, see what you make of it all.' He passed Alec a handful of papers, but didn't give him a chance to study them. 'I don't think it was Gregg. You don't think it was Appsworth. Who does that leave us? Lady Ottaline and Mrs. Howell. Explosions – that's not a woman's crime, to my way of thinking. You mark my words, Appsworth is our man.'

'You've no proof, I take it.'

'Not a smidgen. Nor I don't see how I'm ever going to get any, not what you might call solid evidence.'

'What's your next move?'

'My next move? Not to say *move*, but you and me and Sergeant Gaskell here are going to make sure we've all of us got all the information, seeing

314

we've been working separately. Then Sergeant Gaskell is going to drive me home, and on the way we're going to have a bit of a think and a bit of a chat. I hope you'll have a think, too. I daresay you'll have a chat with your missus. I'd rather you didn't, but I can't stop you. Tomorrow I'm going to let them all stew in their own juice for a few hours. First thing in the morning, I'm coming back with every man I can muster and search the hole and what's left of the grotto.'

'I hope it'll have stopped raining by then. It's going to be a hell of a job even if it's not pouring. You're looking for the gas taps, are you?'

'If we can find 'em all and see how many were turned on, it might – might, mind you – narrow down the time.'

'Did you test the ones we found for dabs?'

'Not yet. As a matter of fact,' Boyle said sheepishly, 'Thomkin seems to have gone off with it in his pocket. How he can have failed to notice it...'

'I expect Lucy – Lady Gerald was rushing him.'

'Do you really think fingerprints would tell us anything? We know they were all in there at one time or another.'

'Except Mrs. Howell, I believe. Hers would be definitive. It seems to me unlikely that anyone other than Pritchard, Howell, or Appsworth would touch the taps in the ordinary way of things.'

'So Appsworth's wouldn't amount to proof.'

'If they were smudged?' Gaskell contributed his first mite. 'Meaning someone else touched them after he did.'

'Or he did it wearing gloves to mislead us,' the inspector pointed out. 'Let's wait and see what

315

we've got before we start speculating. I hope Lady Gerald gets a move on bringing back my only concrete clue, my sergeant, her photographs, and that young man who did a bunk.'

'Yes,' said Alec thoughtfully, 'I'd like a word with Carlin. I can't help feeling we're missing something somewhere.'

CHAPTER 33

Considering all that had happened at Appsworth Hall on Saturday, Sunday breakfast was amazingly normal. Daisy was surprised, however, that both Mrs. Howell and Lady Ottaline, both of whom usually breakfasted in their rooms, came down to join the rest, as did Lady Beaufort.

Mrs. Howell was very subdued and avoided meeting anyone's eyes. She was all in black, not – it transpired – in mourning for her deceased noble guest, but for Chapel. Her son and Pritchard wore black suits for the same reason.

'I'll go with Winifred and Owen,' Pritchard said to Lady Beaufort. He didn't seem to hold any grudge against his sister-in-law. 'Madison will be waiting to drive you down to the village to Church when you're ready.'

'Thank you.' She beamed at him. 'Daisy, you'll come with us, won't you?'

'Er, I think not, Lady Beaufort. I have to make a fair copy of some notes I took yesterday. Besides, I'd better be here when Lucy gets back, in case ... um ... in case she needs my help explaining her photographs to the inspector.' Not for the world would Daisy miss Boyle's reaction to a certain one among the photos.

Lady Beaufort seemed a little puzzled, and Alec gave Daisy a suspicious look. Julia and Charles, knowing just what she was referring to, exchanged a glance. Daisy smiled at them all sunnily and spread marmalade on another piece of toast.

Outside the sun was peeping through the last ragged remnants of the storm. A beautiful day for a walk, and Daisy was keen to inspect the damage to the grotto – not the bit that had caved in on Rhino, but the entrance. She decided that would be pushing Inspector Boyle too far. He was searching it this morning, she vaguely remembered Alec telling her when at last he came to bed last night. She had been half asleep.

What on earth did he hope to find there?

Her thoughts returned to the present as Julia said, 'I'm glad you've recovered so quickly, Lady Ottaline. You've really been in the wars the last couple of days.'

'I'm not an old crock yet!' Lady Ottaline snapped. Then she pulled herself together and said with a strained smile, 'Sorry. I'm nervy and I ache all over but the doctor said there's nothing very wrong and if I stay in bed too long I'll stiffen up like a board.'

'Did he really?' said Daisy. 'I wouldn't have thought he was capable of stringing so many words together.'

'He succeeded in conveying his meaning in two

or three brief phrases. I gather you and Miss Beaufort rescued me from my second mishap, Mrs. Fletcher.'

'Not really, did we, Julia? Charles carried you halfway. When he met us, he left you with us and went back to help Alec and Gerald. We were expecting servants to come along after us, you see. But you were getting awfully chilly, and we were just wondering whether we'd be able to carry you between us when Madison arrived. So he carried you till we met the gardeners, then he handed you over to one of the gardener's boys. Fred was his name, wasn't it, Julia?'

Julia laughed. 'No, that was what Madison called him, and the head gardener got shirty about the chauffeur giving his lads orders, remember? The one who actually carried you to the house, Lady Ottaline, was Billy.'

'I seem to have been passed round like a parcel. You'd better hand out a few hefty tips, Des.'

Sir Desmond grunted. He looked, if anything, less well than his wife, as if he had spent a sleepless night. It didn't seem to have affected his appetite, however, and what little he said was as suave as ever.

Neither he nor Lady Ottaline made any mention of church-going, but Charles said he would join the ladies. At once Gerald looked up from the heaped plateful he was methodically demolishing, and caught Alec's eye.

'I'll accompany you, if I may, Lady Beaufort,' Gerald said. 'It's been a while, I'm afraid. You won't mind guiding me through the Prayer Book. I bet I remember the hymns, though. Had them thoroughly drummed into us at school.'

Daisy guessed that Alec had asked him to keep an eye on any suspects who left Appsworth – which meant Charles was still on the list, alas. She wondered about the chapel-goers. She was pretty sure Pritchard and Howell were in the clear. Perhaps Alec had asked Pritchard to make sure Mrs. Howell didn't flit. He might not hold a grudge, but he had no cause to love his sister-in-law. In any case, her chances of getting far under her own steam appeared slight.

In fact, she was such a wishy-washy person, Daisy simply couldn't believe she had the gumption to blow up the blasphemous grotto, with or without the immoral Rhino and his mistress in it. Her outburst against Pritchard, if not a fit of madness, had been more spite than a deliberate attempt to implicate him.

People dispersed. Daisy felt she ought to have a go at the few notes she had made for Boyle, having given them as an excuse for skipping church. She had been too tired to tackle them last night. She took her notebook to the library, where she sat and stared at the hieroglyphics. Her mind was elsewhere. She had a familiar feeling she was missing something vital, some clue, some observed quirk of character or behaviour, that would change the picture entirely. The more she sought it, the more elusive it became.

Alec came in. 'I'm going over to the diggings, love, the place where the hillside collapsed, to see if Boyle's found anything. Want to come?'

'Seriously? Don't you think he'll throw a fit if I turn up?'

'He can't stop you going for a walk. He can keep you at a certain distance, and of course he doesn't have to tell you anything. Or if he makes you shake in your shoes, you could hide behind a tree–'

'Darling, honestly! I'm not *afraid* of the man. I just don't want to queer your pitch. But I'd like to come. I was thinking earlier that it's a beautiful day for a walk.'

'Let's go, then.'

They went out by the terrace. As they crossed the paving stones, Daisy's nagging sense that she was forgetting something returned.

'Your forehead's all wrinkled,' Alec said. 'Better hope the wind doesn't change. What is it?'

'That's the trouble, I don't know. I'm sure I do know something helpful, something important, but what it is...' She shrugged helplessly.

'You, too? It's far more likely to be valid in your case than mine, though. You've known these people longer than I have, and you were here yesterday morning.'

'Yes, but you know much more than I do about what they claim they were doing, and what they say about each other. I missed lots of it.'

'I told you pretty much everything last night.'

'I was half asleep, darling. Suppose you start again from the beginning now. Perhaps it will spark an idea in one or t'other of us.'

Alec sighed but obliged. In general, he was much more obliging in this investigation, which wasn't his own case, than when she 'meddled' in an affair for which he was responsible.

'That's the lot, I think,' he ended. 'Why don't

320

you give me your views of all the people involved and their relationships with Rydal? Come to think of it, I missed a lot of it the first time round. When you were telling Boyle, I was trying to wash the chalk out of my hair.'

'Right-oh. As long as you're not going to make a fuss if I go round in circles a bit. Relationships simply can't be described in a straight line.'

'Make it as straight as you can, Daisy. We'll be there in five minutes.'

They had started on the path to the grotto but taken a branch to the right well before reaching the bridge. It climbed more steeply than the other, without any steps to aid the ascent. Now they came to a drystone wall with a stile made of flat stones sticking out. Alec gave Daisy a hand over, but she managed to catch one stocking all the same.

'I'm going to start wearing trousers for country walks,' she said, regarding the ladder with disgust. 'I don't care who thinks they're improper.'

On the far side of the stile, the path was no more than a sheep-track across the short, wiry grass of the slope. No sheep were in sight. Doubtless they had made themselves scarce because of the thumps and shouts coming from the excavations, ahead and uphill.

Daisy talked faster and faster and increasingly breathlessly. They stopped for a couple of minutes before they reached the site so that she could finish the story of the night outing and mass ducking, which she hadn't got round to describing to Boyle.

Then they had to wait a couple more minutes

for Alec to recover his gravitas.

'It's all very well laughing,' Daisy said severely, 'but I wouldn't be surprised if Lady Ottaline was pushed, by either Rhino or Sir Desmond. Lucy's inclined to think that Rhino might have been pushed, by either Sir Desmond or Julia. Of course, by the time he went in they knew it wasn't really dangerous,' she added. 'Charles – unless it was Carlin – called up that the water wasn't very deep, just enough to break the fall.'

'No water in the stream-bed now,' said Alec.

'No. But darling, that makes me think–'

'Tell me later. I want to know whether Boyle's chaps have found those gas taps.' He set off over the last rise.

Daisy followed. In her view, her sudden insight made it virtually impossible that Charles had caused the explosion. If only she could be sanguine that Alec and the inspector would be equally convinced.

She caught up as Alec called down into the dell, 'Any luck, Inspector?'

Boyle yelled back. 'All but one tap, and the chauffeur's bowler.' He climbed the steep, tumbled slope towards them, leaving eight or ten men behind him at the bottom.

The hole in the ground wasn't very large or very deep. About as deep as the hermit's room had been high, Daisy supposed. 'Not so deep as a well, nor so wide as a church-door' – a cathedral door, anyway – but it had served to kill Rhino.

'How could anyone have known the roof wasn't too thick to fall?'

'If the blast had been contained,' Alec said, 'it would have been much stronger. That alone could well have done for Rydal. As for who could have foreseen the actual effects of the explosion, as far as I can make out most of it seems to have been sheer guesswork.'

'That's what I...' But Alec had turned away to give Boyle a hand over the rim of the crater.

'Morning, Mrs. Fletcher. All but one,' the inspector repeated to Alec. He was lightly dusted with white, but didn't look as if he'd played an intimate part in the digging. 'Two large, the fire-place and the water-heater, presumably, and two small, two of the three lights. They're all turned on, so the third light probably was, too. We'll have to consult Pritchard and Howell, but we can assume that narrows the time period we have to consider.'

'Good work! The hat's not going to help us much, as we know Gregg was there.'

'No, only if it'd been in the back room, which it wasn't.' He gestured. 'Over there it was, which I reckon to be the middle part, where you found him. We're not likely to find anything more. A proper mess it is. We can't turn over every lump of chalk or limestone or whatever the muck is, hoping it's just a coating on something of interest. The rain last night washed a lot of it off the brass taps and copper tubing and they shone in the sun, is the only reason we found them. Did you talk to Gregg, sir?'

'Yes. Sullen, but of course he can't deny having been there. He swears he just wanted to embarrass Rydal by bursting in on him and his

323

lady-friend. In any case, intending blackmail isn't a crime, and he didn't have a chance to commit it.'

'I can't see how anyone could have proposed to blackmail Rhino,' Daisy said, 'when what he was up to was known to everyone at Appsworth Hall and half the population of London.'

'That's a point, Mrs. Fletcher, though villains are often much stupider than you might expect.'

'It's hardly fair to call Gregg a villain,' Daisy protested. 'To all appearances he was a perfectly blameless manservant. I wouldn't blame him for talking about blowing off Rhino's eyebrows–'

'But the only way we'll prove he went further than talk is if his dabs are on the gas taps.' Boyle looked down at a figure who was toiling upwards, a canvas bag in one hand, and called, 'Got those safe, Gaskell?'

'Yes, sir,' the sergeant said hoarsely, and coughed to clear his throat. Clad in a bulky overall, he was caked with grey-white soil.

While they waited for him, Daisy made another attempt to share her revelation. 'Alec, you said no one could have been sure what would happen when Rhino walked into the hermitage with a lit cigarette. It was sheer guesswork.'

'Yes, but with all the taps turned on, it was liable to be pretty drastic. A fire if not an explosion.'

'But don't you see, it was just a guess that he would arrive before Lady Ottaline. Or rather, no one could know who would arrive first. She smoked quite a bit, too. It was odds on that she'd have a cigarette burning. That means – it *has* to mean – that the person responsible didn't care if she was blown up, instead, or as well.'

'That's what it was!' Alec exclaimed. 'I knew something was out of key.'

Boyle frowned. 'Unless she did it herself.'

'I wouldn't put it past her,' Daisy agreed, 'but don't you see, the important thing is that Charles Arm– Appsworth had absolutely no motive for doing away with her. If anything, he had cause for gratitude to her for taking Rhino away from Julia. It's inconceivable that he'd risk killing her by chance.'

'It does seem highly unlikely,' Alec agreed.

Boyle's frown deepened. 'What we don't know is whether they'd arranged it that way, that he'd arrive first to warm the place up, say. It wouldn't have been cosy. The servants were asked who knew about the meeting and when, not whether they knew or discussed the details of Rydal and Lady Ottaline's plans. Maybe Appsworth found out she was going to follow him later. Gaskell!' He turned to the sergeant as the latter reached the top, huffing and puffing.

'All safe and secure, sir,' he gasped, patting the canvas bag.

'Get everyone out of there and out of their overalls. There's no point going on mucking about here. We've got work to do back at the house.'

'You'd better hop it, Daisy,' said Alec, 'if you don't want to find yourself surrounded by large, dirty men undressing. You're right about Lady Ottaline. We should have thought of that. But Boyle is right, too. We've got some questions to ask.'

At least Alec hadn't already decided that Charles was guilty, Daisy thought mournfully as she made her way back down the hill, hitching up her skirt to scramble over the stile. Unfortunately, Boyle still seemed to be keen to arrest him. She hadn't much hope of being able to prove him innocent. If only he and Julia hadn't decided to go for a walk just then!

CHAPTER 34

Walking through the gardens, admiring the daffodils nodding in the sunshine, Daisy noticed that the grass round them had been recently mowed. Not today, Sunday, a day of rest; not yesterday afternoon, when it was raining and in any case all the gardeners were busy digging up Rhino; it must have been done yesterday morning.

Surely DI Boyle must have asked the gardeners whether they had seen anyone? Yet all Daisy had heard about was the information garnered in the servants' hall. She knew she had missed a fair bit of what was going on, partly just because she hadn't been present, partly because of the innate tendency of the police to keep things to themselves. But *had* Boyle questioned the gardeners?

He had arrived late on the scene and had been very busy all evening. With Alec involved informally, there was no clear line of command, no coordinating strategy (or did she mean tactics?).

The more Daisy thought about it, the more likely it seemed that the gardeners had been over-looked.

After a glance at her shoes, she went into the house by the side door. When she reached the hall, Barker was coming out of the drawing room. He looked irritable, though his face smoothed into his customary blandness the instant he caught sight of Daisy.

'What's the trouble?' she asked.

'Trouble, madam?'

'Come on, tell me. You never know, perhaps I can help. The household must be all at sixes and sevens, and I'm afraid it's going to get worse. Inspector Boyle's got another round of questions for the servants.'

The butler went so far as to utter a groan – not a loud one, but definitely a groan. 'I beg your pardon, madam. I must confess, I am a trifle put out. It's not what one is accustomed to. My im-mediate difficulty is – er – one of Mr. Pritchard's guests. He desires a drink before luncheon, very much before luncheon, and, to tell the truth, more than one drink. Yet being a gentleman, he refuses to help himself to his host's spirits. This is the second time he has summoned me from duties which are pressing.'

'Sir Desmond's intent on getting blotto?'

'Such would not be an inaccurate way of put-ting it, madam.'

'Well, I'm sorry if I led you to expect my assis-tance, but I'm not prepared to help him on his way. Barker, do you happen to know whether the coppers had a go at the gardeners last night?'

'I cannot say for certain, madam, since in normal times they come to the house only to bring garden stuff to the kitchens. However, I doubt it. I believe the man Boyle arrived after Mr. Simmons's assistant and the two boys went home to the village. Mr. Simmons himself has a cottage over near the greenhouses. I cannot speak for him.'

'Of course not, but you can direct me to the cottage, if you'd be so kind.'

Barker obliged. 'Will that be all, madam?'

'Yes, thanks. Barker, I don't want to appear to try to teach you your job, but if I were you, I'd fail to hear the bell next time Sir Desmond rings. Either he'll pour for himself, or he won't, which would on the whole be a good thing, don't you think? Is Lady Ottaline with him?'

'No, madam. I believe her ladyship is writing letters in her room. Goodness knows,' he added gloomily, 'what she's saying about Appsworth Hall.'

'Goodness only knows!' Daisy agreed.

The butler hurried off. Daisy turned towards the door by which she had come in, then changed her mind and headed for the front door. If Alec had been about, she would naturally have pointed out the necessity for questioning the gardeners. But he was unavailable, no doubt tramping down from the hill with Boyle and his crew. If she went out the back way, she might meet them heading for the servants' entrance. Boyle would not be happy, she told herself, to have it pointed out to him in front of his men that he'd overlooked several possibly vital witnesses.

She was doing him a favour, avoiding him.

The gardener's cottage was easy to find but hard to see, being overgrown by a huge wisteria already in full bloom on the south-facing wall. Daisy ducked under the drooping purple clusters, still dripping with rain, and knocked on the door. It was opened by a thin, spry, elderly woman enveloped in an apron as thoroughly as the wisteria enveloped her house, and equally flowery.

'Mrs. Simmons? I'm Mrs. Fletcher, a guest of Mr. Pritchard. I'm hoping for a word with your husband.'

'Simmons is out the back, madam, staking some of his blessed p'rennials, but I'll get him in in a trice. It's a labour of love with him, you see, all the same if he's working for the master or himself. Come in, do, madam, if you don't mind me getting on with the pudding for his dinner. It don't do to let it sit once you've beat in the eggs, that's what I say. Best to get it into a hot oven quick as–'

'I don't want to disturb you,' Daisy broke into the flow of words. 'Suppose I go round the side and find Mr. Simmons.'

'Well, you could,' Mrs. Simmons said doubtfully, 'but the path's overgrown something dreadful with them blessed flowers. Won't trim 'em till they finish blooming, he won't, and that won't be till–'

'That's all right. I'll manage. Thank you!'

No Sunday best for Simmons. He was wearing an ancient tweed jacket of indeterminate hue, with sagging pockets, and moleskin trousers tied at the knees with the same twine he was using to stake his plants. He looked round as Daisy pushed open a creaky gate.

His garden was crammed with colour. Spring bulbs – daffodils, narcissus, iris, hyacinths pink, white, blue, and yellow – vied with polyanthus and nodding columbines, violets and pot marigolds. Even the surrounding fences were starred with clematis. To an artistic eye, Daisy thought, it probably was a horrendous hodge-podge, but she didn't claim to have an artistic eye so she was allowed to enjoy it.

She introduced herself. 'I expect you know my husband is helping Detective Inspector Boyle with the investigation. I have a question for you.' The truth and nothing but the truth, if not exactly the whole truth. She took out her notebook to make herself look more official. 'Were you or any of your staff working in the gardens behind the house yesterday morning?'

'Yes, madam.'

'Who? All of you?'

'No, madam. Just young Billy, the lad you took to carry that ladyship to the house.' He sounded as if he still resented her endorsement of the chauffeur's illegitimate order to the gardener's boy.

'He mowed the grass round the daffodils?'

'Yes, madam. He's good with a scythe, and I told him I'd use it on his ears if any of the daffs got cut down.'

'Did he mention seeing anyone while he was working?'

'Not to me. He'd no business looking about

him, nor doing aught else but concentrate on his work.'

'Mr. Boyle's going to want to talk to him. Where is he to be found today?'

'I can't speak for what he may be up to on his day off, but he lives with his parents in the village.'

Daisy wrote down the address, thanked Simmons, and headed back to the house. Three factors made her decide against going in search of Billy. First and least important was Boyle's ire. He would already be annoyed with her, and a little extra annoyance wouldn't hurt either him or her. Second was that she didn't know how long a walk it was to the village. It hadn't seemed far when she and Lucy drove through it on the way to the Hall, but Lucy's speed made apparent distances deceptive.

The third difficulty was decisive. She remembered being unable to understand more than one word in three of Billy's Wiltshire dialect. A fat lot of use it would be to question him if his answers were incomprehensible to her. One of the local police would manage better.

By the time Daisy had finished with the police, receiving a little grudging gratitude along with the expected telling off, the Church-goers had returned. She joined them in the drawing room. Lady Beaufort was talking to Sir Desmond, who looked as if he wasn't hearing a word. Daisy wondered whether he had started helping himself from the bar when Barker quit answering the bell.

Gerald left Julia and Charles and came over as Daisy entered. 'Lucy sent a wire,' he told her. 'She's expecting to get here shortly after two. She says, "watchdog collared bureaucrat." Telegraphese! What's she talking about?'

'The inspector sent a sergeant with her, didn't you know? He's the watchdog. His original purpose was to stop her flitting to the Continent, but when Boyle heard about Carlin, he told whatsisname – DS Thomkin – to get hold of him and bring him back.'

'Carlin? That's Wandersley's secretary?'

'Yes. He left from Swindon to go and play in a golf tournament. As he must have heard what happened here before he caught the train, Boyle is understandably unhappy.'

Carlin. Daisy didn't imagine for a moment that he had blown up Rhino, but he had some connection with whatever it was she was trying to recall. Something he'd said? Something he had done?

'I hope Lucy's photos cheer him up,' Gerald interrupted her thoughts.

'I shouldn't think so. I don't see how they can help him much. One of them, if she really intends to show it to him, if it doesn't make him laugh – well, there'll be another explosion. I wonder if it worked. I can't wait to see.'

'Daisy, what are you talking about? It's not something he could arrest her for?'

'Blue? No, not at all. How could you think such a thing! Feelthy pictures are not at all Lucy's style.'

Gerald laughed. 'Oh, you know Lucy. Always

332

experimenting. I live in dread.'

The arrival of the Chapel party put an end to the topic. Pritchard and Howell started to dispense drinks. Sir Desmond perked up.

Barker came in. In his discreet butlerian undertone, he said something to Mrs. Howell that sent her scurrying out of the room, her lips pursed. A night's sedated sleep seemed to have calmed her *crise de nerfs*. At least she wasn't foaming at the mouth.

Barker next spoke to Pritchard, and then came over to Daisy. 'Mr. Fletcher desired me to inform you, madam, that he will be lunching with Boyle. I understand they have much to discuss.'

'Thank you, Barker. Bother!' she said to Julia as the butler bowed and turned away. 'I wonder what...? I suppose I'd better not go and try to find out now.'

'I wouldn't. But I'm a suspect, not an amateur detective.'

'Darling, I'm just trying to work out what really happened. I know you and Charles weren't involved, so the sooner we nail whoever did it, the better.'

Pritchard came over to see if they wanted their drinks topped up. 'Barker let you know your husband won't be eating with us?' he asked Daisy. 'I told him to give them the same as we're having, but he said they requested sandwiches.'

'Easier to eat at the desk,' Daisy explained.

Lady Ottaline came down last, alarmingly bright-eyed and bursting with energy.

'I hope I'm half as merry and gay when I'm as old as she is,' Julia whispered to Daisy. 'How does

333

she do it, after what she's been through?'

'Some kind of pills, I expect, or cocaine.'

'No, surely...'

'It wouldn't surprise me. Don't tell anyone I said so, even Charles.'

Mrs. Howell rushed back into the room, her face now a mask of tragedy. 'The police are pestering the servants again! Brin, how can you allow it? Right before lunchtime! I dread to think what the meal will be like.'

'Perhaps Alec's the lucky one,' said Daisy.

The soup was too salty. The beef was like boot-soles, the roast potatoes limp, the gravy lumpy, the carrots bullet-hard, the brussels sprouts grey mush. The Yorkshire pudding had gone flat and was burnt round the edges. Remembering Mrs. Simmons, Daisy was prepared to bet her pudding had turned out beautifully and wished she'd invited herself to the Simmonses' midday dinner. Mrs. Howell wrung her hands while everyone else tried to pretend the food was edible, though Lady Ottaline didn't eat a single morsel.

They were sitting pushing soggy jam roll round their plates when Lucy sauntered in.

'Hello, all,' she drawled. 'Do you mind if I abstract Daisy, Mrs. Howell? I need her support to face the massed constabulary.'

'Lady Gerald! Have you eaten? I'll have something–'

'We stopped for a bite on the way, thanks.'

'You're early, Lucy,' said Gerald.

She smiled. 'Darling, the time I told you was based on the fact that Sergeant Thomkin refused to let me drive back.'

Gerald was aghast. 'You let him drive my car?'

'No, I thought you'd prefer Carlin at the wheel. He treated your car with tender care, but poor Thomkin! He must have assumed a civil servant would drive sedately. Carlin's time wasn't much slower than mine.'

'Young Carlin?' Sir Desmond frowned. 'What the deuce is he doing back here? You brought him, Lady Gerald?'

'Depending on how you look at it, I brought him, he brought me, or the police brought both of us. He's talking to Alec and the Boyle man now.'

Sir Desmond looked confused, as well he might. Lucy's oracular explanation on top of his libations – he had done well by the wine with lunch – was enough to confuse anyone. 'Boyle – the inspector? I haven't spoken to him. Fletcher asked me a few questions.'

'Much more fun, darling,' said Lady Ottaline with a coy, girlish giggle.

'If you ask me,' Daisy whispered fiercely as Lucy tugged her from the room, 'it's a pity she didn't go up with Rhino.'

'Don't take any notice of the poor old thing, darling.'

'If she goes round saying that sort of thing, it could ruin Alec's career.'

'Bosh, no one pays her any attention.'

'Lucy, does she take drugs?'

'I should think so. Lots of people do. How else could she keep up such a killing pace? Come on, Boyle is panting for my pictures.'

'Did your experiment work?'

'*À merveille*. Wait till you see it. They're all pretty good. There are three I'd like to use for the book, if they go forward with it, and three or four that should do for your article.'

They reached the door of Pritchard's den. Daisy put her finger to her lips, Lucy nodded, and quietly they went in.

CHAPTER 35

To Daisy's disappointment, as she and Lucy entered the den, Boyle was saying, 'Thank you for your help, Mr. Carlin. Not that it helps much, but that's not your fault, I suppose.'

'I can't see why you had to drag me all the way back, make me miss the tournament, for that! My partner's furious.'

Daisy had missed hearing his evidence, but the sound of his voice brought back to her the last time she had heard it, at breakfast the day before. Surely he couldn't have told everything, or Boyle wouldn't have been so disappointed. Unless he had already heard from someone else? But in that case he should be glad of confirmation.

Daisy decided she'd better wait until Carlin left the room before she cast doubt on the completeness of his answers to Boyle's questions.

'I suppose I can leave now, after this totally unnecessary journey,' Carlin said sulkily.

'I'd prefer that you not leave Appsworth, sir,' the inspector said. 'And I'd be obliged if you'd stay just now and give us a hand. Good timing, ladies. Let's have a look at these photographs.'

DS Thomkin went to Pritchard's blueprint drawers and took out a large sheet printed with what turned out to be a ground-plan of the grotto's three caves. Boyle picked up a large manila envelope and opened it as the sergeant spread the plan on the desk.

'Here, let me,' said Lucy, reaching for the envelope. She took out a sheaf of photos. 'You said you wanted to see all of them, didn't you?'

'I did.'

Alec pulled his chair closer.

'These first few are of the front of the house,' Lucy spread them before Boyle, who pushed them aside with a grunt of irritation. 'All right, here's the stream.'

'Now dried up,' said Daisy.

The inspector contradicted her. 'Not any more it's not. There's a fair trickle in it. All that rain last night, it broke through again. The stream, that's another thing I want to talk to you about, Lady Gerald, but let's see the rest of the pictures first.'

Lucy laid out several shots of the grotto entrance from outside. Boyle glanced at them, but it was the interior he was interested in. He had Lucy, Daisy, and Carlin try to place the location of each photo, one by one, on the plan. They had a few disagreements.

'We'd better get Pritchard or Howell for this,' Alec suggested, 'or even Appsworth–'

'Appsworth?' said Lucy and Carlin together.

'Armitage,' Daisy enlightened them. 'It turns

out he's really Charles Appsworth.'

'Really!' Lucy was sceptical. 'The long lost heir, I suppose.'

'No, he's—'

'Please, ladies! Mrs. Fletcher, you can explain later. Lady Gerald, you haven't got people in these photos, except the ones of the entrance, where he's too small to identify.'

'Oh, that's Armit – Appsworth. For that sort of shot one wants a figure to show the scale. The others, well, I wasn't taking holiday snaps, you know.'

'So I– Strewth!' The inspector had reached the last of the grotto pictures.

Lucy's ghost had come out beautifully. The white statue of St. Vincent Ferrer, cowled, marble flame in hand, was distinct against a dim background. At his shoulder stood a doppelganger, a murky, blurred figure, but definitely another monk.

'Very nice, Lucy,' said Alec dryly.

'Do you think I can sell it to the Society for Psychical Research?'

'Probably. Who is it?'

'Appsworth again. Wouldn't you expect him to haunt his ancestral home?'

'Very good at play-acting, that young man,' Boyle growled.

'Not really, inspector.' Daisy was well aware of the natural distrust of the police for acting ability. 'Lucy told him exactly what to do, and with that robe and hood to hide inside, anyone could have done it. You'll have noticed that the statue is of a Catholic monk. He's the patron saint of plumbers. That's what got Mrs. Howell carrying on about Papism.'

'And the others are heathen idolatry.' He shuffled through the images of gods, goddesses, and half-clad nymphs. 'Thank you, Lady Gerald. Now, while I have the three of you here, what's this Mr. Fletcher tells me about people being pushed into the stream?'

'Pushed!' Carlin exclaimed, startled. 'Lady Ottaline fell in. She was wearing high-heeled shoes, completely inappropriate for the path. Mrs. Fletcher turned her ankle earlier in spite of wearing walking shoes.'

'Mr. Carlin was the first to jump in to rescue her,' Lucy said. 'Quite the hero.'

Carlin flushed at her mocking tone. 'Nothing heroic about it. The water was only four foot deep or so.'

'But you didn't know that,' said Daisy, 'and it was dark.'

'And you might have landed on top of her, for all you could see,' Lucy pointed out.

'I was careful to jump in upstream of where she fell,' he said indignantly.

'Charles – Mr. Appsworth – was ahead of us,' Daisy went on, 'already past the corner. He heard Lady Ottaline scream and ran back, and he was the second to jump.'

'A positive multitude of heroes. There stood Rhino on the brink, pretending to take off his coat, with Julia on one side of him and Wandersley on the other. Nothing will persuade me that *he* wasn't pushed.'

'Would you agree, Mrs. Fletcher?' Boyle asked.

339

'I'd agree that he wasn't at all keen to go in. He was so slow that Julia made some remark about his being too elderly for such exploits. He did take his coat off then, and next moment down he flew. He could have decided he'd better show willing after such a comment from the woman he loved.'

'Much more likely Sir Desmond pushed him,' Lucy insisted.

'You believe Lady Ottaline was also pushed?'

'For heaven's sake, Inspector, I don't know! Perhaps it was her shoes. But considering she was with her cuckolded husband and the lover who wanted to ditch her – well, perhaps one of them succeeded.'

'Succeeded?'

'Ditched her.' Lucy was so pleased with her pun that she actually asked Boyle's permission to go to the grotto. 'I brought some more plates and I'd like to get a couple of shots of it the way it is now. Not for any particular purpose, more for my records. For the history books.'

Boyle glanced at Alec, who shrugged.

'I suppose…' The inspector paused. 'Yes, why not? Don't go up there alone, though, please. Take someone with you in case of accidents.'

'Daisy?'

'Of course, darling, but not right now.'

'I'll go with you, Lady Gerald,' Carlin offered, nobly in view of her sarcastic comments on his heroism.

'Right-oh. I expect Gerald will, too. We'll wait for you, Daisy, if you're not too long.'

'Just a couple of minutes. Get my coat for me,

340

will you?'

Lucy and Carlin departed.

'What now, Daisy?' Alec asked.

'You have information for us, Mrs. Fletcher? About Carlin?'

'Yes. He may have told you already...'

'Never mind. At worst you can confirm his statement.'

Her pointing out of the overlooked gardeners seemed to have raised her in Boyle's estimation. 'Well, first, it's something he said at breakfast. Howell was complaining because Sir Desmond hadn't come down yet, thus delaying their business in Swindon. Carlin said something – I can't remember his exact words, I'm afraid – about it being no use trying to hurry him, because he always went for a stroll after breakfast for the sake of his digestion. If he missed it he got dyspepsia and became thoroughly disagreeable.'

Boyle perked up. 'Sir Desmond always took a walk after breakfast?' He exchanged a look with Alec.

'So Carlin claimed. Howell could confirm that he said so, I'm sure, because it annoyed him. Julia and Charles were there, too, I'm pretty sure, though whether they were listening is another matter.'

'Do you know whether Wandersley actually did go out for a walk?' Alec asked.

''Fraid not. Shortly after he came down at last, Lucy and I left. That was just after the second thing I thought I ought to make sure you know. Carlin was the butt of one of Rhino's sneering insults and departed in a huff.'

'Well, now, he didn't happen to mention that, either, Mrs. Fletcher.'

'In exchange, I hope you're going to tell me whether Billy saw anyone in the gardens.'

Alec smiled. 'He saw Julia and Appsworth making off over the hills, in the direction of the area of the later explosion. They didn't go anywhere near the grotto's entrance.'

'Thank heaven! Anyone else?'

Boyle regarded her for a moment, his face expressionless. Then he said, 'Billy saw someone going towards the grotto. He only caught a brief glimpse, between bushes or hedges or whatever, because he'd come to a tricky bit of mowing and had to watch his scythe. He didn't recognise the person.'

'Man or woman?'

'I've told you all I'm going to, Mrs. Fletcher, and probably more than I ought. You've been very helpful. Have you got any more questions, Mr. Fletcher?'

'Just one. Let me make sure I've got it straight who was in the breakfast room when you and Lucy left. Howell, Rydal, Wandersley – anyone else? Pritchard?'

'No, he went off earlier. Carlin left just ahead of us, and Howell was close behind him, I think. Julia and Charles were still there, if I remember correctly. Yes, they must have been, because Julia told Rhino he was appallingly vulgar. Can you believe it, he said she must be thinking of someone else and he started blethering about his quarterings!' Seeing Boyle looking blank, she explained, 'The bits of an escutcheon – a family's

342

coat of arms – that show which noble families they've married into. He said with pride that the Earls of Rydal hadn't married a commoner in centuries, which, come to think of it, was a sort of backhanded insult to Julia.'

'He insulted everybody,' said Boyle, 'but insults just rolled off his back.'

'Exactly. Small wonder he got blown up! I wonder if anyone will truly mourn him. What has he got in the way of family? Perhaps he's another person at home, kind to dogs, children, and his aged mother.'

This flight of fancy alarmed the inspector. 'He has an aged mother? We haven't done anything about informing next of kin. It's impossible to get hold of lawyers on a Sunday, even if we knew who his lawyer was.'

'I haven't the foggiest about his mother. I can't imagine him having anything so normal as parents or brothers and sisters, which may sound unkind but you didn't know him until he was dead. Mr. Pritchard probably doesn't run to a *Peerage*. Mrs. Howell might possibly pore over one in the solitude of her room. Lucy probably knows, though she'll never be as omniscient as her Great-aunt Eva.'

'I'll ask Lady Gerald later,' said Boyle impatiently. 'If you've no further revelations for us...'

'None that come immediately to mind. May I tell Miss Beaufort and Mr. Appsworth that Billy's saved their skins?'

The inspector shrugged. 'If you want. Don't tell anyone else, though, and tell them to keep quiet about it.'

'Right-oh.' Daisy blew a kiss at Alec and whisked out of the room.

In the drawing room, she found Lucy, Carlin, and Gerald only waiting for her arrival to go out. So were Julia and Charles, who had decided to join them for a breath of air. Lady Ottaline wanted to go, too.

'I'd have thought you'd had enough of that place,' Sir Desmond said, sounding bored. 'Not to mention that you ought to take it easy till you're fully recovered.'

'Do stop fussing, Des, I'm perfectly all right. I might get an inhibition about grottoes if I don't go. I can tell you, though, I shan't smoke in there.' Waving her cigarette holder, she said to the hovering butler, 'Barker, have my maid bring down my coat.'

'I suppose I'd better come with you,' her husband said, 'as your usual escort is – unavailable.'

Carlin, standing near Daisy, whispered to her, 'D'you think I ought to offer to take his place?'

'Absolutely not. You steer clear of that imbroglio.'

Looking relieved, he nodded. 'Besides, you'll need me as Mr. Fletcher isn't going with us. He's splendid, isn't he? Not at all like that inspector chappie. You know, I rather wish I'd gone into the police instead of the civil service, only the parents wouldn't have heard of it.'

Which would have sounded like an insult in the mouth of Rhino, Daisy thought, but from the baby bureaucrat was merely a wistful musing.

Pritchard now made up his mind that he must brace himself to see his ruined grotto for the first time. 'Better get it over with in company, don't you think, Owen?'

'I want to see it in ruins,' said Mrs. Howell malevolently. 'Owen, wait while I change my shoes.'

Lucy had waited for Daisy, but she wasn't about to wait for anyone else. She gathered her chosen companions together and shepherded them out through the French doors. Behind her, Daisy heard Lady Beaufort say placidly, 'No, I think not, my dear. I'll come and see it again when you have restored it – and installed a few seats along the path.'

CHAPTER 36

'I hope Mrs. Fletcher isn't going to come up with any more inspirations.' Boyle was thoroughly disgruntled. 'We're getting nowhere fast.'

'We're getting along nicely,' said Alec. 'We've eliminated Julia and Appsworth–'

'That may look like progress to you, sir, but to me it looks like we just lost our most likely suspects.'

'We have plenty left to work with, more than we had a few minutes ago. Look, man, if you think the Yard expects to clear up a murder case in twenty-four hours, I can assure you you're mistaken. You're getting along nicely. We have Wandersley and Carlin to replace the two that Billy cleared, and Mrs. Howell and Lady Ottaline are still in the picture. More's the pity. I'd rather have got rid of them.'

'Billy did think the person he saw was a big man, but he's on the scrawny side so anyone might look big to him. Anyway it could have been Rydal off to make preparations for his love-nest. Or if it was Sir Desmond, likely he was just going for his stroll, like he said. I just can't see a Principal Secretary going round bumping people off. And a "Sir," too.'

'Principal *Deputy* Secretary. Somewhat less exalted. Not that I think civil service rank has any correlation with murderous tendencies, or the reverse. He's spent his life repressing his feelings, in his marriage as well as his profession, apparently–'

'Oh, that psycho-stuff. I don't cotton to all that rubbish.'

'It has its points. As for his having been knighted, neither knighthood nor nobility ever was or ever will be a guarantee of virtue. The Wandersleys both have strong motives.'

'Carlin hasn't got much.' The inspector was determined to look on the gloomy side.

'Not for long premeditation. Unless there's something in their past dealings to be dug out.'

'Which we're not likely ever to dig out.'

'It shouldn't be very difficult. But let's cross that bridge if we come to it. Let's suppose a flare of temper when Rydal insulted Carlin. He leaves in a huff, as Daisy said, then he remembers Rydal's rendezvous and the talk of explosions in the grotto. He himself has already announced his intention to go up to town from Swindon with-

346

out returning to Appsworth... It might look like the ideal way to get his own back without risk of consequences. Probably without any idea beyond singeing Rydal's eyebrows.'

'Like the chauffeur,' DS Thomkin put in.

'I can see he might think it up,' said Boyle, 'but I'd expect him to cool off on the way to the grotto. Still, we'd better have another go at him after what Mrs. Fletcher told us.'

'Perhaps we ought to confirm Daisy's story first,' Alec said diplomatically. 'She said Appsworth and Julia were still at breakfast with Wandersley and Rydal when she and Lucy left.'

'Right, sir. Thomkin, go and get those two.'

Alec and Boyle barely had time to start discussing whether any of their suspects could have foreseen the dire consequences of turning on the gas, when Thomkin returned.

'They've gone to the grotto, sir,' he reported. 'They've *all* gone to the grotto, with Lady Gerald, like you said she could. All 'cepting Lady Beaufort.'

'Bloody hell!' swore Boyle. 'What the devil are they playing at?'

'I don't know,' Alec said grimly, 'but if Daisy's gone to the grotto with a bunch of dodgy characters against one of whom she's liable to have to give evidence, I'm going after her.'

Daisy stopped on the platform at the foot of the steps, facing the much diminished waterfall. Lucy went ahead up to the grotto, followed by Carlin bearing her impedimenta. She'd been muttering all the way about swarms of people getting in the

347

way of her photography.

'You can't really tell what it was like,' Daisy said to Gerald. 'The waterfall was very pretty, and marvellous at night, lit from behind. And that statue up there in the middle had a head. I wonder if it fell in the pool.'

She went to the edge and, hanging on to Gerald's arm, peered over. The once-charming pool was an expanse of mud with a trickle winding across it. Tethys's spattered face stared blindly up at her.

'Nasty business,' said Gerald.

'The explosion, or the collapse, must have shaken the whole hill. I hope Mr. Pritchard is able to restore the grotto. For the second time, poor man! But look, Gerald, I do believe the flow is increasing.'

'Possibly,' Gerald said cautiously.

'The stream must be gradually washing away the debris blocking it.' Hearing voices, Daisy looked back as Julia and Charles came round the bend.

'Of course you don't have to,' Julia was saying passionately. 'Who cares what anyone says. Let alone what they think.'

'You don't understand. It's not that, it's what I– Oh! Hello, you two.'

'What's wrong?' Having averted an arrest, Daisy wasn't going to put up with misunderstandings where she had been counting on a wedding.

'Nothing,' said Charles.

'Yes there is.' Julia was too upset to pretend.

'Julia, don't!'

'Charles was buried alive in a collapsing trench

during the War.'

'I know,' Gerald mumbled uncomfortably.

Julia turned to Daisy. 'When the grotto blew up, it reminded him, and now he thinks everyone will say he's a coward if he doesn't go back in.'

'Of course he's not,' Daisy said firmly.

'That's what I keep telling him.'

Gerald shook his head. 'It's not you he has to convince, Miss Beaufort. Not us. It's himself. If what it takes is going into the grotto, don't make it more difficult for him.'

Without another word, Charles started up the steps, his face set. Julia went after him.

'I suppose we might as well go, too,' said Daisy.

'Don't crowd him.'

'Oh. Right-oh.' She turned back to the waterfall, just in time to see it suddenly double in size with a whoosh. 'Look! The water *is* breaking through.'

The trickle in the mud became a rivulet. Daisy watched fascinated as new geographic features were carved in miniature before her eyes. Then she heard voices again.

'Here come the others. Let's get out of their way.'

Glancing up at the grotto she saw no sign of Charles lingering near the mouth. Lucy had probably roped him in to help. Being obliged to do something – anything – was usually the best antidote to an excess of emotion of any kind, in Daisy's experience.

She started up the steps, but Gerald stayed below, doubtless to avoid embarrassing Charles

349

after Julia's outburst (to be blamed on the French influence, perhaps?) about his weakness. Daisy thought Gerald had handled the situation with unexpected delicacy. He was usually such a taciturn chap that when he did open his mouth and reveal glimpse of his character, it quite often surprised her.

Halfway up she looked down. Gerald was pointing out the fallen head of the river goddess to Pritchard and Howell. Mrs. Howell stood with her back to the cliff, staring up at the headless torso with an expression of grim approval. She didn't appear to have any desire to inspect the destruction of the idols from a closer vantage point. Daisy wondered if it was wise of Pritchard to stand on the edge with his back to his sister-in-law. Then Lady Ottaline and her husband came round the corner, crossed between Mrs. Howell and the men, and approached the steps.

With the sound of the waterfall so much diminished, Daisy heard Lady Ottaline say sharply, 'Come along, Des. I'm the one who was battered. Twice. If I can manage the climb, so can you.'

Why she was so insistent on returning to the scene, Daisy couldn't imagine. Having no desire to speak to Lady Ottaline, Daisy hurried up the rest of the way and stepped into the grotto. She couldn't see much for a minute as her eyes adjusted to the dimness. Julia came to meet her. Further back, Charles and Carlin were apparently clearing a space for Lucy to set up her tripod.

'Daisy, I'm so sorry,' Julia said in a low voice. 'I shouldn't have blurted out ... what I did. Charles had just told me and I was so upset I wasn't thinking straight.'

'I know. You needn't be afraid I'll tell anyone else. Even Alec.'

'I gather Alec already knows, as Lord Gerald does. My poor Charles had to explain why he couldn't help them in here right after the explosion. I feel such a fool for embarrassing him and you– Oh, blast, here come the Wandersleys.' Julia took Daisy's arm and stepped backwards into the shadow of the headless Tethys.

Following, Daisy looked back. Lady Ottaline came into the grotto. As Sir Desmond reached the top step, she moved further in, out of his way and turned towards him. The moment he was clear of the railing, she gave him a vigorous shove.

For a moment he tottered on the edge. Then, with a shout of terror, he toppled over.

Julia screamed.

How deep was the mud? The question hammered in Daisy's mind. How deep? The depth might be the difference between life and death.

'Daisy, get away from the edge!' Charles yelled.

She hadn't realised she was approaching the edge, hadn't consciously wanted to see what had happened to Sir Desmond. Julia grabbed her and pulled her back as Charles and Carlin pounded past Lady Ottaline and down the steps.

Lady Ottaline was laughing, high-pitched, hysterical. Grabbing the end of the stair-rail, she hung on and leant forwards to look down.

'She pushed him!' Daisy cried.

'No, darling.' Lucy seemed to think Daisy was also hysterical. 'That was the other evening, and I said he pushed her into the stream, but I wasn't serious.'

Instantly Lady Ottaline stopped laughing. 'Not serious?' she hissed. 'He did push me. I felt his hand on my back, and then I was flying through the air.'

'It could have been Rhino who pushed you,' Lucy pointed out.

'He wouldn't! He loved me. That's why Des blew him up, the bastard. Not jealousy. Oh no, he didn't care about me. His reputation was all he cared about.' Lady Ottaline stared from one to another of the three facing her, and alarm flickered in her eyes. 'But you're wrong, I didn't push him over. How could I? A big, heavy man like Des! I'm not strong enough.'

'I saw it, too,' said Julia. 'You caught him off balance. If he's dead, you–' She broke off as a peculiar roaring noise came from behind them.

Daisy swung round just in time to see a surge of water burst through the rear wall. The gaping sea-serpent, already missing several teeth, cracked and crumbled. The renascent stream swooshed along its bed, flinging spray over the low wall, rushing towards the drop into the mud puddle, soon to be a pool once more.

A pool with people in it. Even as the realisation dawned, Daisy dropped to her knees and stretched out full length with her head and shoulders over the edge.

'Water coming!' she shouted, waving her arms.

'River's rising! Flood! Ring the alarum-bell! Blow, wind! Murder and treason!'

Somehow Charles and Carlin had already got down to the fallen man. Knee-deep in mud, they seemed to be trying to sit him up. Alive, then, Daisy thought thankfully. At her shout, they looked up, then redoubled their efforts. Gerald, lying flat on the platform – perhaps he'd lowered the other two? – called to them and they changed their tactics. They grabbed Sir Desmond under the armpits and started to drag him towards the side of the pool.

The waterfall arrived. As it hit, mud fountained upwards.

'She's getting away!' Lucy cried, releasing Daisy's ankle. Until she let go, Daisy hadn't noticed that Lucy and Julia were both hanging on to her. Julia let go, too, and they stood up.

Daisy rolled over and sat up. 'Who? Oh, Lady Ottaline!' The lady in question was stepping carefully but swiftly over Gerald's outstretched legs. Pritchard and Howell, kneeling on either side of Gerald, didn't notice her sneaking by behind them. Mrs. Howell stared at her but made no attempt to stop her. Why should she? She couldn't have seen what had happened up above.

Round the corner came Detective Inspector Boyle, followed by Alec and two hefty detective sergeants.

'Thank heaven,' said Daisy with a sigh, relaxing. 'They'll take care of everything.'

Julia gripped the railing, as Lady Ottaline had, and leant over for a better view of what was going on directly below. 'They've got Sir Desmond over to the rushes. It's shallower there, but the water's rising. I'm going down.'

'Phew, what's that foul smell?' Lucy demanded.

Daisy sniffed, and wished she hadn't. 'They must have stirred up the bottom mud.'

'It's disgusting. I hope Gerald stays out of it. I'm going to get on with the photos before I'm asphyxiated.' With the arrival of the police to take charge, the single-minded Lucy had lost interest in mere mayhem. 'Come and hold the flash for me, darling.'

Daisy hadn't lost interest, but she was in no hurry to report what she'd seen and heard to Inspector Boyle. Besides, a certain amount of mud was bound to be splashed about in the course of the rescue of the men in the pool, and though less fastidious than Lucy, Daisy had no desire to be on the receiving end.

'Right-oh, darling,' she said.

CHAPTER 37

'It's a damned awkward situation,' Alec said irritably, wrestling with his collar stud. He hated wearing his dinner jacket, and stiff shirts were anathema.

Mrs. Howell, having lost three of her more distinguished guests to death and the police, had chosen to show the flag with a decree that the rest were to dress for dinner. She would not reign at Appsworth Hall much longer, but for the moment Pritchard was still prepared to indulge her.

'Let me get those studs for you, darling,' Daisy offered.

He held his arms out to allow her access. 'I don't know why I let Boyle inveigle me into being his unofficial assistant.' At least for once he wasn't blaming Daisy for his entanglement. 'I must have been mad.'

'If Superintendent Crane gets to hear of it, you can always plead temporary insanity. Is that what Lady Ottaline's going to do, do you think?'

'Who knows? With your and Julia's evidence, she can't avoid a charge of assault and battery, but there was no grievous bodily harm, just an unbelievable amount of mud.'

'I'm glad you didn't have to go in to help. Charles and Carlin both still have a faint miasma floating round them.' She fastened the last stud and his arms closed round her.

'Mind my frock!' she yelped. 'And your shirt.' After a careful but thorough kiss, she resumed. 'Mmm, very glad you didn't land in the pool, darling. You're quite sure it was Sir Desmond who killed Rhino, I suppose? All you said at tea was that he'd been arrested.'

'Not everyone wants a review of the evidence with their scones and Welsh-cakes.'

'Freshly baked scones! I do think Barker is a marvel to keep the household running so smoothly with all the upsets the servants have been having.'

'No, we are not getting a butler.'

'I wouldn't dream of suggesting it, even if we

could lure Barker away, which I doubt. I don't think he'd approve of us, what with your irregular hours and the twins. Besides, Mrs. Dobson would be terribly hurt. Sir Desmond...?'

'For a start, your friend Billy–'

'My friend!'

'That's how Boyle refers to him: "Mrs. Fletcher's friend Billy." He saw a big man hurrying down through the gardens from the direction of the grotto. He had no notion of the time – he works till he's finished the job or the head gardener calls him for his dinner. Of course, Rydal himself could have gone up there for some reason. Billy wouldn't necessarily have observed anyone else going or coming later.'

'But Sir Desmond and Rhino were the only two noticeably large men. Until Gerald arrived.'

'Yes. Still, it's not proof. Wandersley could have been taking his daily stroll, as advertised. Howell confirms that Carlin told him about Wandersley's digestive difficulties. Julia and Appsworth agree that when they left the breakfast room, shortly after you and Lucy, only Wandersley and Rydal remained.'

'A combustible – not to say explosive – combination, especially as Rhino had just made that remark to Carlin about bone-lazy bureaucrats. I wonder if that's when the idea of actually blowing him up occurred to Sir Desmond.'

'It hardly matters, from a legal point of view. He can't very well claim there was no premeditation. Still, it's always awkward arresting a bigwig. I must say, Boyle handled it with suitable dignity and solemnity.'

356

'Good for Boyle. But you have no real proof, just circumstantial evidence.'

'Circumstantial evidence is perfectly valid in a court of law, though juries tend to prefer eye-witnesses, however unreliable, and fingerprints, however smudged.'

'He might get off. I have to admit to a certain sympathy.'

'For a murderer? And you the wife of a copper?'

'You didn't meet Rhino.'

'True. He seems to have made a present of motives to practically everyone. The manservant is clear on technical grounds, but unfortunately, we haven't been able to completely rule out the other two remaining suspects.'

'Lady Ottaline and Mrs. Howell. No dabs on the gas taps, I take it.'

'Nothing useful. He was probably wearing gloves, or else he gripped them by the edges. What we do have is a confession—'

'Well, what more can you want?'

'—Of sorts. Not to a sworn officer, unfortunately. Wandersley told Appsworth and Carlin, when they were extracting him from the mud, that he wished he'd bagged Lady Ottaline in the explosion, but he had failed to take into account her persistent unpunctuality.'

Daisy couldn't help laughing. 'She is practically always late.'

'But now he's shut up and won't say another word without his lawyer's advice,' Alec said gloomily.

'I suppose you couldn't find the torch.'

'Torch? What torch?'

'Darling, he must have had an electric torch. It was pitch-black in the back room, no natural light, and he could hardly use an open flame to find the taps when he was about to turn them on, could he?'

'Great Scott, Daisy! I must phone Boyle at once – no, he won't have reached Swindon yet. Why didn't you say something sooner?'

'Actually, it's only just dawned on me.'

'It should have dawned on me or Boyle. One gets so used to clicking a switch.'

'I was remembering getting Lady Ottaline back to the house after her ducking, because even soaked and freezing, she managed to delay us. Julia had a torch she'd taken from Charles's pocket. Barker put it on a shelf by the side door – back door, whatever you want to call it. The one in the passage next to the drawing room. I suppose it's kept there with the lamplighter's pole, for whoever goes out at night to light the lamps in the grotto–'

'I'll check there first.'

'And for daytime, an electric lantern behind a nymph at the back of the first cave. Rhino probably knew about that and counted on it, but I don't see how Sir Desmond could know about it. The only time he went was at night.'

'Oh hell!' Shrugging into his dinner jacket, tie untied, Alec dashed off.

Running down the stairs, he wondered what Boyle would say if Daisy's belated stroke of genius meant bringing all his men back to search the grotto, the area of the explosion, and the gardens for an electric torch. He would have to do it, on the slim chance of finding incontrovertible evidence – not only the torch but Wandersley's fingerprints on it.

Unless...

The dining room door stood ajar, and Alec heard a sound of movement within. He looked in to find, as expected, the butler straightening a fork here, giving a glass an extra polish there, making sure his domain was in perfect order for dinner.

'Barker, I need your help.'

'Sir? Your tie, sir. Allow me–'

'Devil take my tie. You keep a torch near a side door to the terrace, Mrs. Fletcher tells me?'

'Yes, sir. If you take the passage on your left as–'

'Show me. I may need a witness.'

'Certainly, sir. This way if you please.'

The passage was too narrow to be called a hall, too wide for a mere corridor, just wide enough not to be obstructed by one of those curious pieces of furniture, that combine a pair of umbrella stands, hat and coat pegs, a looking-glass, a small cupboard, and a shelf. One umbrella stand contained three umbrellas, the other a lamplighter's pole, but Alec had eyes only for the chromed-steel torch on the shelf.

'Here it is, sir.' Barker reached for it.

Alec gripped his wrist. 'Don't touch it!'

'Very good, sir.'

'May I?' He whipped from the butler's shoulder the snowy napkin with which the man had been buffing up silver and glasses. With the cloth enveloping his hand, Alec picked up the torch by the lens end and held it up to the none-too-bright electric light, turning it this way and that. 'Fingerprints!'

'Indeed, sir!' The butler looked quite put out. 'The third housemaid is required to polish it daily.'

'Thank heaven she didn't. I'd like a word with her.'

'So,' muttered Barker grimly, 'would I. In the circumstances, sir, perhaps you had better come to my pantry.'

Alec had dealt with enough butlers to appreciate the honour of this invitation. 'Thank you, that will do very well.'

Bearing the torch, he followed Barker through the green baize door.

The third housemaid was the child who had reported Gregg's threat against Rydal's eyebrows. Rita came in eyes wide with apprehension, summonses to the butler's sanctum being associated with reprimands too severe for the housekeeper to handle. Her eyes flew to the torch, displayed on the napkin on the table where Barker was wont to do his serious silver-polishing.

Alec got his question in before the butler's rebuke could frighten her out of her wits. 'Rita, when did you last polish this torch? It's the one from the hall stand by the back door.'

She addressed her reply to the butler anyway. 'Oh, Mr. Barker, I tried and tried but I just cou'n't get ever'thing done what wi' the p'lice an' all, the way they kep' coming back.'

After a pregnant pause, Barker said judicially, 'It has been a trying time for all of us. Be a good girl and answer Mr. Fletcher's question.'

'Oh, sir, I reckon it must 'a' bin yes'dy morning, like every day 'cepting today.'

'What time, do you know?'

Barker answered. 'The ground floor rooms are supposed to be finished before the master finishes his breakfast.'

Long before Wandersley finished his, Alec thought. There was something to be said for an old-fashioned household. It was still possible that Sir Desmond had used some other torch and thrown it into the bushes on his way back to the house, but who else had had need of a torch since early yesterday morning?

'And what I need now is a telephone,' said Alec.

Twenty minutes later he dashed back upstairs to find Daisy waiting for him. While she tied his tie and made sure he was in all respects respectable, he told her about finding the torch.

'Boyle's sending a sergeant to fetch it and to get statements from Barker and me. He's as convinced as I am that the fingerprints on it must be Wandersley's

'I hope that means we can go home tomorrow,' said Daisy as the dinner-gong rang through the house. 'Come on, we're going to be late. I'm dying to see the babies. I feel as if I've been away for weeks.'

Hurrying down the stairs, Alec said, 'Yes, everyone's free to go. You'll undoubtedly be called at Lady Ottaline's trial, but Boyle's promised to do his best to do without my appearing in person as a witness. He's not a bad chap, but I must say I'll be glad to shake the dust of this place off my feet.'

'And out of your hair.'

Alec grinned. 'And out of my hair.'

'I don't expect Mr. Pritchard will manage to have the grotto rebuilt before we come back.'

'Come back? I've no intention of ever returning to Appsworth Hall!'

'Darling, you can't possibly miss the triple wedding.'

'Great Scott, Daisy, what–?'

'I had a feeling you weren't really listening at tea-time. Julia and Charles, and Lady Beaufort and Pritchard–'

'What? So that was her secret!'

'Yes. She wouldn't tell Julia she'd given up on Rhino because then it would have looked very odd if she hadn't decided to return to town at once. I'd guess she needed time to make sure she and Pritchard were really thinking along the same lines.'

Alec grinned. 'To bring him up to scratch.'

Daisy gave him an old-fashioned look. 'To continue: and Howell and his ladylove. They're all going to tie the knots en masse, before Julia and Charles leave for Canada, and we've already been invited.'

'Great Scott!' Alec repeated. 'Church or Chapel?'

'I don't think that's been decided yet,' said Daisy, opening the drawing-room door as the last reverberations of the gong died away.

Pritchard stood up with a smile. 'We were just wondering–'

His sister-in-law interrupted him. 'Since Lady Ottaline isn't here to come down late for dinner,'

Mrs. Howell said acidly, 'I suppose I should have expected that someone else would follow her example. I'm sure I don't know what the aristocracy are coming to!'

The publishers hope that this book has given you enjoyable reading. Large Print Books are especially designed to be as easy to see and hold as possible. If you wish a complete list of our books please ask at your local library or write directly to:

Magna Large Print Books
Magna House, Long Preston,
Skipton, North Yorkshire.
BD23 4ND

This Large Print Book for the partially sighted, who cannot read normal print, is published under the auspices of

THE ULVERSCROFT FOUNDATION